SAVING THE BILLINAIRE

THE JUSTIN TRAINER SERIES
BOOK 2

JANE HARVEY-BERRICK

HARVEY
BERRICK
PUBLISHING

DEDICATION

To Justin, still inspiring.
Still nuts.

CONTENTS

PROLOGUE

Hope.

Small word. Big meaning.

When I started working for reclusive billionaire Devon Miguel Anderson, I had no idea what a screwed up son-of-a-bitch he was, but live and learn.

He has more money than just about anyone on the planet, except maybe Bill Gates and God, and I'm not sure about God. That doesn't mean he's happy though. As a matter of fact, Anderson is not a happy guy: just miserable in Armani suits.

I'm not his friend, I'm not his drinking buddy, but I am the guy who knows him better than just about anyone else, and that includes his shrink.

I'm a close protection officer: that's 'bodyguard' to you. And when the shit goes down—which it will—I'm the one who'll take a bullet for the billionaire. I really hope that doesn't happen, because I've kind of got a thing for living. Who knew?

But Anderson? He has a lot to learn.

So if you want to know why this fucked up dude in Tom Ford shoes gives me hope, well, read on.

Chapter One

PRETTY WOMAN

This has been one of the longest weeks of my life, and that includes the winter tour I did in Afghan, up to my balls in mud in a shit-hole of a town called Now Zad. A place that put the hell in Helmand Province.

The boss is in a vile mood. So what's new? It's a good thing the hanging of employees has been banned, otherwise several who breathed out of turn would be dangling from the yardarm right now.

Everyone is tiptoeing past his office, and I wouldn't be surprised to see some of them on their hands and knees to stay out of sight. We're all waiting for the dam to burst and everyone is praying they're not in the firing line when it happens. Do I care that I'm mixing my metaphors? Not this week. Although the boss hasn't actually fired anyone today—that I know of—it's come close.

And when I say 'fired', the only reason that's not literal is because Anderson doesn't believe in the right to bear arms. Luckily for him, I do. My Smith & Wesson M&P never leaves my side.

Tessa, the assistant to Anderson's assistant and a woman who's been making her mascara run on a daily basis since I met her, nearly got her marching orders when she dropped a cup of coffee on the boss's Bauhaus table, her hands were shaking so much. Although with Tessa, I can never tell if it's nerves around the boss or the fact that she's panting for him. He should have chosen her as his new submissive.

Huh, guess I should explain that.

The boss is into a load of kink: threesomes, foursomes, orgies, whips, canes, belts, voyeurism, sadism, masochism, and a ton of other 'isms' that I can't even spell. His weekend home in the Hamptons, the Farm, is a den of inick ... inikwit ... inquity ... vice. It's also the play pen for the well-connected and unashamed of Manhattan. I've seen politicians getting it on with judges while the wife masturbates in the corner; I've seen a state attorney (Democrat) jacking off while a lobbyist fucks him in the ass (Republican). The breaking down of political barriers—it's almost heartwarming.

Anderson is more of a mystery. I thought he was gay, then I thought he was bisexual, now he's playing it straight. So I'm not sure, and he's undecided.

Today, there are two reasons that the boss isn't his usual sunny, happy-go-fucky self. First, there's the threat of blackmail that will bring his orgy-shaped secrets to public knowledge. So far, his IT geek, Howard, has out-nerded the blackmailer and hacked his way through cyberspace ending the blackmailer's plans *for now*.

Howard is enjoying the "epic battle", his words, but with a potential three hundred million dollar price tag, the boss is putting a lot of faith in a man MENSA can't categorize.

But there is a second reason that the boss ain't a happy dude.

He's interested in a woman.

Yep, I'll have to say that twice just to make sure *I* believe it. *A female woman.*

This is new. I've never seen him date, his family have never seen him date: all he does is BDSM shit to people he knows from a distance. He's never wanted anything approaching a relationship.

Until now.

He's interested in a woman who is separate to all the nasty shit that goes down at the Farm. The object of his undying lust is a dark-haired, dark-eyed girl from the Bronx: Maria Alvarez. How this will play out is anyone's guess. The boss doesn't do waiting: that he's left it ten days before taking further action or heading to the Bronx to see the object of his obsession is the only surprise. Well, Ms. Alvarez, you're over twenty-one, so the choice is yours. Will a black-hearted billionaire make you an offer you can't refuse?

Have I ever been tempted by any of the offers I've gotten from the boss's fuck farm buddies? That would be a *HELL NO!* Besides, I have a thing with the very intriguing and delectable Mrs. Smith, whose name I'm working on changing to Trainer.

She's the boss's housekeeper at his Tribeca mausoleum mansion.

And she cooks.

I'm blessed.

But back to this long-ass day.

Both Tearful Tessa and the table survive, thanks to Ryan, PA extraordinaire, saving the day with a handful of paper towels for the table and a bottle of Valium for Tessa. The man deserves a medal, although I think this week has aged him. Maybe he needs a vacation. Tessa spent most of the day in the ladies' room crying, so she wasn't doing much assisting.

Pam is the boss's right-hand, the most senior exec, and a double-hard I'm-calling-the-shots-and-you're-gonna-like-it kind of woman. She rolls with the punches and Anderson is smart enough not to yell at her. She'd probably lay him out cold if he tried. One punch. Plus, she's the Yoda of the thousand-yard stare, and as a former Marine, I know what I'm talking about.

By Thursday, I'm not the only one at DMA Tower desperate for the weekend. When a senior exec screws up a deal in South Korea and the bellows can be heard all the way to Pyongyang.

Stability in a CEO is so important, doncha think?

Saturday morning and this weekend already sucks ass.

First, Rachel, the love of my life and woman who will one day be persuaded to change her surname to match mine, has gone to stay with her sister. I only met Allison that one time at Thanksgiving, and that was more than enough. She doesn't approve of me: divorced, a kid, no home of my own, ex-military with the temperament to match. I don't know what Rachel sees in me either, but when I look into her sister's eyes, I know exactly what's there—and it's not good.

And second, the boss has turned into a stalker.

Let me recap—and I'll put this in words that even I can understand:

- The boss interviews for an intern
- He meets aforementioned brown-eyed girl (cue Van Morrison)
- He doesn't give her the job and blows her off, but weeks later tracks her down on a Tuesday evening to a club in the Village where she does a (really bad) standup comedy routine
- He decides it's a good idea to go visit her at her part-time job with *Value Carpets & More* on a Saturday morning.

Like I said: *stalker.*

Or maybe Anderson has decided that he needs to buy new carpets. Maybe a nice Paisley for his meditation room; something that says 'dungeon, but homey'.

At 8:15AM, I drive Anderson to the dismal carpet warehouse, a flea on the backside of New York in a dead-end industrial estate at the edge of the Bronx. I thank God that I hated my hometown so much I joined the Marines, because otherwise I could have ended up working somewhere like this.

Anderson is edgy, anxious, and if I didn't know better, I'd say excited, maybe even nervous. *Nervous?*

Ms. Alvarez is hovering at the entrance to the store, waiting for the manager to open for the staff. Her face shuts down when she sees Anderson. Poor kid. Poor, poor kid. The boss isn't a bad guy, but this is wrong.

"Wait in the car, Trainer."

Yup, wasn't planning on watching this disaster movie.

But just in case the boss needs a witness, I crack the window an inch.

"Good morning, Ms. Alvarez."

"What are you doing here? First the club, now where I work!"

He blinks, surprised by her hostility.

"I don't want to interrupt you."

"I don't want to break my back hauling carpet swatches all day," she snips out, "but we don't always get what we want."

Anderson folds his hands across his chest.

"What do you want?"

"For real?"

"Yes, tell me what you want."

She stands up straight.

"Fine. I'll tell you. I want to get a job where I can use my degree in business and environmental science and earn enough money to get my family out of the shitty apartment we live in and move somewhere decent. I want to enjoy my work and spend my time meaningfully; I want to contribute to the world somehow. I want to conquer my fears, I want to travel the world. And..."

"That's quite a long list, now there's more?"

He glances at her and he's got that look: you see it on wildlife shows when the lion is about to pounce on the little baby zebra who got separated from the herd.

She thrusts her chin out.

"I want to make people laugh at the comedy club because I'm funny, not just pity-applause because my routine is pathetic."

"I didn't think it was pathetic, Ms. Alvarez. I actually found it rather incisive wit."

She smiles for the first time.

"You like my routine about going for a job interview with a famously reclusive billionaire?"

Anderson almost smiles.

"It had a certain ring of authenticity."

She laughs out loud.

"I like a guy who can take a joke." Then her cheeks flush as she realizes what she's said. "I don't mean you. Not that you're awful or anything..."

Her words trail off and I gotta tell you, I really feel for the boss. He's getting shot down big time.

He takes a step back.

"I'd like to offer you an internship with my company."

The girl gapes, then her jaw shuts with a click and she crosses her arms.

"Why?"

"Because having reviewed your résumé," he says slowly, "I believe you'd be a good fit for my company."

"And it's taken you this long to figure that out?"

Anderson doesn't reply.

"I'm not going to sleep with you," she says quickly.

Anderson's expression becomes glacial, and I see Ms. Alvarez inch away from him.

"That would be most inappropriate. I have no desire to ... sleep ... with you."

The boss is telling the truth. He'd like to fuck her, probably beat her or have her watch him beating himself, but sleeping wouldn't be part of the trifecta of delights.

"I'm sorry," she says. "It's just weird, you coming out to the club, then out here."

"I'm not like other employers," he says starkly.

I can definitely vouch for that.

"So ... if I say yes, I mean *if*, it would be just like a regular job? No funny stuff?"

Ms. Alvarez has balls.

Anderson leans toward her, his dark eyes glittering.

"Ms. Alvarez, if you come to work for me, I can guarantee that there will be nothing regular about it."

"Show me a contract and I'll think about it."

"You can read the contract in my home office now."

"Email it to me."

"No."

"Why not?"

"Confidentiality. My last offer, Ms. Alvarez. Take it or leave it."

She sucks her teeth, thinking about that. She's talking tough but her eyes are saying something else. She's wary, excited, nervous, and yeah, flattered. The GQ billionaire has followed her to the Bronx—of course she's flattered. She's also right to be wary.

"Fine, but I'm bringing someone with me."

"I beg your pardon?"

"Dude, I'm not getting into your car with you and the Rock, and going to your home without having someone with me!"

She's comparing me to a guy who's known for his limited facial expressions while pretending to act? I'm wounded.

"Come back when I finish work. Six o'clock. *My* last offer."

She turns her back to Anderson as the lights go on in the carpet warehouse and the door opens. She walks away without a second glance.

Anderson watches her, bemused, and as far as I can tell, impressed as hell.

She's nothing like the scared, mousy woman that he interviewed two months ago.

Nope.

The rest of the day is spent with the boss's attempts to ignore the seconds and minutes ticking by. We go for a longer run than usual, twice around Central Park and back to Wolf Point. I'm ready to kick my feet up and watch a ball game on TV, but the boss heads to his pool, swimming laps until his arms fall off.

Yep, the boss is suffering from a lil ole slice of sexual tension. I'm waiting for the slam of the door to his meditation room, but the mausoleum is silent as the grave.

The traffic report says it will take 34 minutes to drive the 14 miles to the Bronx, but at 1700 hours, the boss is wearing a hole in his Italian marble flooring as he paces up and down.

It's weird to see him in jeans and a leather jacket. Maybe he thinks that will help him fit in at Value Carpets. I don't know, can you get designer nylon? 'Cause that's what Ms. Alvarez's uniform is made from.

At least the Rover will fit in with the drug dealers' rides of choice.

The drive to the Bronx is tense, and when the lights go off in the warehouse at six, the boss is on his last nerve, although you wouldn't know it unless you were me.

The girl pokes her head out of the door and seems surprised to see us.

"I'll open the door for Ms. Alvarez," the boss says quietly.

I watch them in my rear view mirror. They're staring awkwardly at each other like a couple of teenagers on a first date. It's weird to see the boss acting this way.

"Good evening, Ms. Alvarez," he says.

She smiles and nods politely, "Mr. Anderson."

When she sees me watching her, she smiles warily, "Hi."

"That's Trainer, my driver."

Jeez, demoted to driver. I'll complain to my union.

"Hello, Mr. Trainer."

"Good evening, Ms. Alvarez. And it's just Trainer."

Another girl approaches, a short woman wearing a poncho and heavy glasses. *The 'Ugly Betty' look is still in. Who knew?*

"This is my friend Dolores Quinlan. She's coming with us."

"Ms. Quinlan."

I open the door for the second girl who's trying not to be impressed by the boss, the Rover, or yours truly.

I nearly pass out when the boss offers his hand to Ms. Alvarez as he helps her into the SUV. And I try really hard not to listen to their conversation but I can't help myself. I have *never* seen the boss hold a woman's hand—not even his sister or his mom. *What the fuck is going on? When did the world stop turning and why did nobody tell me?*

"How was work?" he asks.

"Dull."

"That wouldn't happen if you worked for me."

"I'd like to see that contract now."

"I told you—it's at my house."

She glances at her friend.

"I texted Auntie Vera with the car's license plates. We're good."

Anderson raises his eyebrows but doesn't comment.

The sass that was there this morning has been replaced by something else, making me feel like a third wheel, or possibly a fourth wheel, which makes no sense. Dolores looks equally uncomfortable and is staring out of the passenger window, ignoring her friend, me and the boss. I get the feeling that if I wasn't here, Anderson would jump on Ms. Alvarez right now. Or maybe the shy and not-so-retiring Ms. Alvarez would make the first move. Pigs are flying in formation and all bets are off.

I slide further down into my seat and act deaf and dumb for the rest of the drive. I'd close my eyes, too, if it wasn't for the fact that I'm driving. I can't get to Wolf Point quickly enough.

Finally, I cut through the Saturday night traffic and we're there. I open the door for Ms. Quinlan, and then for Ms. Alvarez. The boss slides out behind her, as if he can't bear to be more than touching distance away from her.

"Trainer," he nods at me curtly.

I nod and get back in the Rover.

Ms. Alvarez—you are on your own.

Chapter Two

MOMMIE DEAREST

I'm sitting with my feet up, an empty plate that once contained one of Rachel's microwave dinners next to me, and a Dr. Pepper in my hand. I don't drink, ever, unless the boss has given me the night off, which he hasn't, and only then, one beer or one glass of wine so that if I was called on to drive in an emergency, I'd be well under the limit and in full control of my faculties, what's left of them.

I'm only truly off the clock when I'm far, far away.

There's a tentative knock on my door in the employees wing and I glance up to see Dolores Quinlan standing there, looking even more awkward.

"Hey, man, sorry to bother you, but I can't stand another minute watching those two. I mean, are they going to get it on or what? It's gone from a job interview to a dating interview. I can't keep up. It's weird."

She has my sympathy. The boss is a study in weirdness.

"Ms. Quinlan."

"It's just Dolores. So, can I hang with you? Just for a few minutes. I guess this is your place, huh? I never knew anyone who had live-in help before, except Luisa Santos, and that was because her *abuela* was bed-bound. This is kind of cool."

I'm irritated by the intrusion but wave a hand and invite her in anyway.

"Thanks."

She sighs and plops down on the other end of the sofa.

"So it's just you and Devon living here?"

And it sounds weird to hear the boss's first name—only his family and 'close personal friend' Hannibal Lecter Landon use it.

"On weekends, yes. During the week, his housekeeper lives here."

And I wish she was here now.

"Oh, okay." Her eyes flick to the TV. "Who's playing?"

"Orioles versus Twins."

She leans back, eyeing my Dr. Pepper.

I guess I should be hos ... hos ... hospitable, that's the word, not hostile.

"You want one?"

Her face lights up. She's got a sweet expression when she smiles.

"Hell, yeah! All Devon had was champagne. Tastes like piss to me."

The sweet expression doesn't match her mouth. Much like myself, I'd say.

I bring two cans of Dr. Pepper and a family-size pack of chips, dumping them in a bowl on the coffee table.

Dolores grabs a handful and talks as she chews.

"So, what's the deal with Devon? Is he a straight up guy? He kind of creeps me out."

Hmm, how to answer that question? Oh wait, discretion.

"I can't talk about my employer, Dolores. I like being employed."

She glances at me and frowns.

"Maria is my best friend in the whole world and she's a really, really great person. She's good, you know? So if Devon and all his millions are going to fuck her up..."

She leaves the sentence hanging, then sighs.

"Although things were so intense in there, I don't think she'd listen to me anyway. I guess it'll be what it'll be. Can you at least tell me if the internship is for real?"

I turn to look at her.

"Anderson interviewed three people: Ms. Alvarez came over well. The internship is real. That's all I know."

She smiles briefly.

"Thanks, man. Hey, what's your name?"

"Trainer."

"Your first name?"

"Trainer is fine."

She frowns.

"Whatever. So, is that Scottish? You've probably guessed I'm Hispanic-Irish-American. What are you?"

I shrug.

"American-American."

We watch the game for another hour, working our way through another family-size pack of chips. The Orioles win. I was backing the Twins.

Dolores checks her watch.

"I'd better get going. If Maria isn't coming home now, I got an early shift and *Mama* worries when I use the subway."

"I'll drive you."

She blinks, surprised.

"Seriously?"

"Yep."

I text Anderson to let him know that his *other* guest wants to leave. The building is eerily silent as I walk Dolores to the garage until my phone beeps with a message: **Fine.**

Then Dolores' gets a message on her phone.

"Holy crap! She says she's staying the night. I thought this was supposed to be a damn job interview."

Her expression probably mirrors mine.

No, wait. I'm more shocked. She'll be *sleeping* here?

I keep my thoughts to myself: Dolores is worried enough already and in two minds whether or not she should leave.

"I don't know, Trainer. It doesn't feel right leaving her here. I know she's a big girl, but for an A-grade student, sometimes she's not so smart.

What can I tell her? *Anderson won't hurt your friend, unless she asks him nicely?*

Instead, I keep walking all the way to the boss's underground garage. Reluctantly, she follows me.

The traffic is lighter now, so we make it back to the Bronx in 27 minutes.

"Thanks for the ride, Trainer. See you around, I guess."

"Night, Dolores."

I watch her short, ponchoed figure disappear into her apartment building, waving briefly before she disappears.

Just before midnight, I cautiously step from the elevator. Nope, no one around. I really don't want to bump into the boss fucking in his office, or anywhere else for that matter. There are some things the hired help don't need to see.

I'd really like to head to bed, well, Rachel's bed even though she's not in it, but there's something I need to do first. If the boss is taking Ms. Alvarez to the Hamptons tonight, he'll be using the limo service that's on-call when he remembers that mere mortals such as myself do occasionally need to sleep.

In the small staff office, Sandy 'Bullshit' McCoy, the standby driver, is already here, dozing over *Soldier of Fortune*. Yeah, that would send me to sleep, too.

"Hey, Bull, how you doing, buddy?"

My voice makes him jump and he drops his magazine.

"Aw, shit, Trainer! What did you wake me for, man? I was dreaming about Britney Spears."

"You really need to get a life, Bull."

"Says you!"

It's a fair point.

"Has Anderson spoken to you?"

"Nah. Not a sound. So what's the sit-rep? Why am I on standby all night?"

"Need to know, Bull."

"You're full of shit, Trainer."

Another fair point.

"You're getting well paid."

In this business, we've all had mind-numbingly boring assignments. Waiting for the call that never comes has got to be one of the worst. I can sympathize with Bull, but he's being well paid for sleeping on the job.

It would probably be okay to stand him down if Anderson hasn't been in touch and Ms. Alvarez hasn't headed for the hills so far, but that's not my call. And the boss is paying.

"You need coffee or food or anything, Bull?"

"Naw, I helped myself while you were out. I'm good." He sighs. "Say, what do you make of Anderson's housekeeper, Rachel? I only met her that one time. Nice lady. She had a great rack. Or maybe you didn't notice, huh, Trainer! Losing your touch?"

He'll fucking see if I'm losing my touch if he speaks about Rachel like that again.

Even though I haven't said a word, he can see that he's put his size thirteen boots over the line and is tiptoeing on very fucking thin ice.

His eyes widen and he rears back.

"Whoa! Just saying, just saying, no need to lose it, Trainer!"

Wisely, Bull raises his hands in a gesture of peace. I hadn't realized mine were balled into fists.

"Sorry, man, I didn't know you had anything going with the lady. Just saying, that's all."

"Yeah, well try engaging your brain before you open your mouth next time, or you'll be talking without your teeth."

My natural good will to all men seems to have evaporated during this brief but irritating conversation with Bull. And now I'm kind of glad he's pulled a boring all-nighter. Serves the fucker right.

Duty done and honor served, I make one final sweep of the building.

Oh crap! It's not quite as quiet as it was. The unmistakable sounds of orgasmic womankind are emanating from the boss's living room.

Even though I've never known him to have a woman here before, I'm not *that* fucking curious. Ms. Alvarez is full of surprises.

And the asswad architect who left out the soundproofing needs the toe of my boot up his ass.

I head to the staff quarters on the double.

With the door firmly closed behind me, I relax slightly. There's a message on my phone from Rachel.

> Hey handsome! How's your weekend
> going? Don't forget the chicken sub in the
> refrigerator and I left you a coffee éclair in
> the white cardboard box. And if you're not
> Justin Trainer, what are you doing reading
> this message? Rx

It makes me smile, but really I'm too tired to eat.

I undress quickly, throwing my clothes on the floor in a way that would make Rachel frown, then I collapse into bed. The pillow on her side smells so good that I hug it to me and hope I dream sweet dreams.

I'm mildly confused when I wake up. The light is brighter than expected. *Fuck! It's 8AM!* I've slept right through. I must have forgotten to set the alarm. *Shit oh shit oh shit!* I immediately check my phone. I have to look twice to make sure there are no texts or missed calls from the boss. Nope. Nothing. Nada. Zilch. That's just plain weird. I can only conclude the boss had a *very* good night and didn't feel the need for a morning run.

As for me, I slept soundly, but I miss waking up to Rachel's sweet face. And frankly I miss wakeup sex. The bed is a lonely planet without her.

Despite my sound sleep, I feel surly. *Get a grip, Trainer—you do have a life without Rachel.* Yeah, I do, I'm just not sure if it's one that's worth having. I *hate* the weekends that she's away. And I haven't seen my daughter for nearly three weeks. She'll be forgetting what her old man looks like. Lilly will be eight next month—and that is pretty damn grown up these days.

So I'm rattling around in the staff quarters like a bad smell, and the boss is screwing an intern. *Who ever said the world was a fair place, you sad fucker?*

I shower and shave and chow my way through the chicken sub that Rachel left for me. It's something of a joke between us, the whole 'sub' thing. And seeing as Rachel has been good enough to leave it and isn't here to say otherwise, I have the coffee éclair for breakfast, too.

I dress quickly and check my piece. I know, it's a Sunday, the Lord's day, but not being armed isn't worth the risk.

Then, feeling properly dressed, I phone Sandy. I think I woke him up again because he's in a really foul mood. Like a generous host, I tell him to help himself to the coffee machine before he drives the limo back to Newark.

I can hear someone moving in the main kitchen and seeing as the boss only knows his way to the refrigerator and microwave, I figure it must be Ms. Alvarez.

It shocks the hell out of me when I see her because all she's wearing is a bath towel and a smile. And when I say 'all', believe me I know what I'm talking about due to 20:20 vision. I'm glad she hasn't seen me, I'd feel like a perv.

I slink out of the room with my eyes closed. I only hit the wall once.

Officially, I'm still on duty, but with nothing to do I sit in my office, check out the CCTV while surfing the internet for cool clothes for girls. *Thongs for eight year-olds?! You've got to be kidding me? What sort of sick, twisted fuckers are there out there?* Okay, I work for a sick, twisted fucker but that's really not what I meant. Shouldn't an eight year-old look like an eight year-old and not a Vegas hooker? Maybe I'll stick to books for Princess Lilly.

By 11:30AM, I'm bored witless and shitless and wondering if I should learn to play Candy Crush after all. The boss and Ms. Alvarez have disappeared back into his bedroom, and I've had to play *Foo Fighters* loud to block out the noise. Either he's really good or she's just easily pleased, but inside I'm begging them to keep it down.

And then a car I recognize drives into the private underground garage. *Fuck-a-loolah!* Anderson's parents.

Oh, this is going to be interesting.

Feeling slightly nauseous at the coming confrontation, I wait by the elevator. It would almost be worth getting fired for ignoring the Anderson seniors right now. What am I supposed to say: *Sorry, but the son you thought was gay, a virgin and celibate is actually having sex in his bedroom for the first time instead of at the Farm, you know, his vacation home, the one with the whips and chains. Oh, and it's with a girl. Would you mind coming back later when she's finished her orgasm?*

Rachel's missing all the fun.

The doors slide open and the Andersons exit the elevator. They're holding hands and smiling at each other. I know they've been married nearly 40 years, and I wonder what that's like—to still be in love with someone even though you've seen the best and worst of them over a lifetime of shared memories.

"Morning, Trainer," says big daddy.

"Mr. Anderson, Mrs. Anderson."

"How are you?" asks Mrs. A. "How's your little girl?"

"She's good, thank you, Mrs. Anderson."

She smiles and they sweep past me while I stand like a fool with a broom up my ass.

"Is our son around?"

"Um, he's in bed, ma'am. Would you like to leave a message?"

"In bed?" They stare at each other in consternation, then at me. "But it's nearly lunchtime."

Mrs. A. frowns and looks at her watch.

"Yes, ma'am. Would you like to leave a message and..."

"Madre de Dios! Is he sick?"

More than you know.

She starts heading for his bedroom. *Oh crap! She's about to walk in on a sight no mother should see. I'm pretty certain it'll be NC-17.*

"Mrs. Anderson, please!"

She pins me with a thousand yard stare that would terrify a platoon of Marines. *I really wish Rachel was here—this is definitely a woman-to-woman moment.*

"I want to see my son. Now."

I am so fucked!

"Ma'am, sir, he has company." *And this is my last hope for keeping my job.*

"What do you mean?"

Oh, for fuck's sake! What do you think I fucking mean, woman?!

"He has someone with him."

"Gloria, I think Trainer is trying to tell us that Devon has been entertaining overnight. In his bedroom."

"Oh!"

Thank fuck! She finally gets it.

"I see. Thank you, Trainer. I think ... I think I'll go and sit down for a moment, if you don't mind."

No, I'm fucking ecstatic. By all that's holy, will you just fucking leave!

But her shrill voice has alerted the boss to their arrival, and in double quick time he's on his way to the main room. I head back to my office and leave them to it.

I can hear the murmur of voices in the room beyond, but not the words. I'm beyond surprised when Ms. Alvarez's soft lilt joins them. To my certain knowledge, the boss has never introduced a woman to his parents before. I bet they're delighted to meet Ms. Alvarez. Shocked, but delighted.

Abruptly, I realize that his parents have finally taken the hint and are leaving. I jog out to the main room to escort them to the foyer.

"Ma'am, sir."

"Thank you, Trainer."

We walk to the elevator in silence. I'm not the chatty type. Mrs. A, on the other hand is stunned into conversation.

"Well, goodness, that was a surprise, Trainer. How long have Devon and Maria been seeing each other?"

I remain silent.

"That's none of our business, Glor," Mr. A. says gently, still smiling at the shock of finding out his fine young son is straight.

"I'm sorry, I shouldn't ask you things like that. It's just the surprise."

I bet.

"Well, good day, Trainer."

"Ma'am. Sir."

I feel the girl's eyes on me. I turn to look at her, "Ms. Alvarez."

"Hey, thanks for taking Dolores home. That was really nice of you."

Nice? Is this how low I've sunk?

She gives me a sweet, friendly smile as I turn to leave. I hope the boss takes care of her.

Crap, that sounds a bit too *Godfather*-ish. And I am talking about the King of Pain.

Anderson is already in business mode when I go back to my office, leaving Ms. Alvarez hovering uncertainly in the main room. She seems overwhelmed by her surroundings and a little unnerved by the boss. And I *really* hope he isn't planning on introducing her to the dubious delights of his meditation room, but I guess that's too much to ask for.

Rachel

I saw Justin briefly on Sunday evening, but now he's with Mr. Anderson in Detroit all week. It's also my birthday today. Forty-two. Justin wanted us to go out for dinner, but that's not happening now. He hid a card under my pillow and French chocolates in my underwear drawer. He can be so thoughtful, but asking him to speak his feelings out loud is hard for him. Instead, he shows me by his actions every day that he cares.

I have something for him, too. I'm going to give him my gift in person.

The house is so quiet and empty without him and without Mr. Anderson. It makes it easy for me to do my work, but I miss them both.

I know Justin pretends not to be fond of Mr. Anderson, but he is, of course. And really, Mr. Anderson is a sweet man, easy to like and a good employer. He's a loving son, an attentive brother, and a hard worker. I don't understand why he needs to have a meditation room and why he needs to ... do whatever it is that he does. Well, it's obvious because I've been cleaning the meditation room for over a year now. All those whips and canes and other accessories. I just don't understand the *why*.

I know Mr. Anderson has a temper, Justin has mentioned it often enough, but he has never, not once, lost his temper with me. He's always grateful for the work I do and eats everything I put in front of him. If all employers were like that, it would be very easy to do my job.

My sister, Allison, is very curious about him. But I've signed my NDA and she understands I can't talk about my work. She's a lot more vocal about Justin, unfortunately. She hasn't used the word again, but I know she thinks that I'm *convenient* for him. Thanksgiving was very uncomfortable, so I'm not surprised he didn't want to spend Christmas with my family. Justin is astute enough to see what Allison thinks of him, so he clammed up around her: not that he's the most talkative person on a good day. But I wish she could see him the way I do, warm and funny and loving. Allison thinks Justin is *dangerous*. I don't like to dwell on that.

Our kitchen looks like a bomb hit it after I've been away for the weekend. Justin really isn't the tidiest person. Especially for someone who's ex-military. It's a full-time job looking after him.

Thank goodness Mr. Anderson is methodical and tidy. It's a joy working for someone who's organized; it really makes my life much easier.

I can't help smiling when I see that Justin has worked his way through half the contents of the entire refrigerator. It's a good thing he exercises so much because I wouldn't want to be responsible for his waistline.

It really is a wonderful thing for a woman in her forties to make love with a man like Justin. He has a fabulous body at a time when most of my friends are bemoaning their husband's beer bellies, double chins and, well, lack of appetite, should I say. There isn't a spare inch of fat on Justin, that's for sure. And he's a wonderful, thoughtful lover. And talk about stamina! I certainly don't have any complaints in that department. I really am very lucky.

He's asked me to marry him again. I won't, of course. I don't think he's really serious. After all, he's nine years younger than me and one day he might meet a woman that he wants to have a family with, brothers and sisters for Lilly. I won't be the one to stop him from moving on when that happens.

But there's another reason that I haven't told him about: it's the job he does. I've lost one husband and I couldn't bear to lose a second. I know there are many other dangerous jobs out there, but I hate, *hate* that Justin wears a gun every day and works in close protection. I couldn't marry a man who wears a gun to work, I just couldn't. The idea makes me feel sick.

But at the same time, I want to move on with my life—but am I making the right choice? Am I risking my heart again?

Chapter Three

DAZED AND CONFUSED

Today we're at the Crowne Plaza in Detroit. Must be Monday.

The boss had two more dates with Ms. Alvarez last week, and on a week night, too. Which means Rachel was introduced to her. During that brief meeting, I saw the moment when two women decide, for whatever reason, that they're on the same side. I don't know if they have a secret handshake or a code word, but they were definitely all smiles with each other. Makes me nervous. Rachel said she *liked* her.

See? I'm sure that's a code word.

Or maybe I just need to get a life.

The boss is working on his laptop, fixing some last minute orders on a multi-million dollar deal, barking orders into his iPhone every few minutes, and I'm left twiddling my thumbs and wondering whether to shoot myself just to alleviate the boredom.

I try to have a conversation with Siri, but she doesn't laugh at my jokes. All I get is, "I'm sorry, could you say that again?" Jokes aren't funny if you have to tell them twice.

I know. It's sad.

In war, there are always some soldiers who snap: some shoot themselves in the foot or in the hand just to get sent back from the frontline. But I suspect if I shot off a toe or two, Anderson would just tell me to hop more quickly and watch where I was bleeding.

All because of a certain Ms. Alvarez.

I spend most of my time in the gym and read the daily security reports from Mason. Nothing new. Nothing interesting. *Fuck! I mustn't think like that. In this job, dull is good.*

The only bright point in the day is phoning Rachel.

"Hey, baby, miss me?"

"Of course, Justin. I always do. How has your day been?"

"Dull. You?"

"Oh, well, okay," her voice sounds distracted.

"What's wrong?"

"Nothing. I'm fine."

"You don't sound fine, you sound weird."

"Well, thank you, Justin! That's good to know."

"Come on, baby, I don't mean it like that. But something's wrong—why won't you tell me what it is?"

She doesn't reply directly.

"Has Mr. Anderson spoken to Ms. Alvarez?"

"Probably, I wouldn't know. Why?"

"Oh, I just wondered."

"Wondered what?"

She hesitates.

"It's just that this girl seems ... different. Not like the others from the Farm, from what you've told me. She's much younger, isn't she?"

"She's 24. What's this about, Rachel?"

"Nothing. I'm being silly. Tell me what you did today."

I recognize that tone. Whatever she isn't telling me will have to wait. But then the phone buzzes irritatingly.

"Can you wait, babe? I've got another call coming in on my cell."

I put her on hold and answer. It's the boss.

"Trainer, I won't need you again this evening. I won't be going out."

"Yes, sir."

The line goes dead and I return to Rachel.

"Is everything okay, Justin?"

"Yeah, that was the boss. He's turning in for the night. Which probably means he'll be pulling an all-nighter. I guess it's this big deal going down."

"Oh, poor Mr. Anderson! But it's odd, isn't it? For him to get so wound up? Usually he's so calm about his business."

"Rachel, honey, 'odd' has been one of my favorite words since I met him."

She laughs lightly.

"Very true. Call me tomorrow?"

"You know I will. Miss you, baby."

"Miss you, too."

"Enough to marry me?"

"Goodnight, Justin!"

Oh well, it was worth a try.

And now I feel even more fucking irritated. Anderson is working, doing the things that make him tick, and I'm stuck in a hotel miles away from the woman of my dreams. Some guys have all the luck. Looks like I'll need to spend some time in the hotel's gym again or I'll be going to bed with a serious hard-on. Talking to Rachel always has that effect on me.

So I've been lifting weights and now I'm running on the damn machine next to a trio of fat, sweaty executives, and keeping an eye on the boss at the same time via the GPS tracker on his phone. Not that I don't trust him, but *I don't trust him*. He's been acting weirder than usual since he hooked up with little Ms. Alvarez. Even I winced when I saw her the morning after they'd hooked up, walking like she'd just gotten off a rodeo bull. The memory makes me cringe.

Tuesday is equally dull and equally long. It seems the boss has no meetings, so we head out for a long run instead. In Manhattan, I think we've exhausted every possible route in every possible part of the island. At least this is new. And at least the weather is cool. I had one job in Florida where the guy I was guarding ran every day in 98% humidity. Fine for him, but I had my piece strapped to my side and had to cover up with a lightweight running jacket. I nearly fucking melted. It was like a summer in Afghan wearing full body armor.

By Wednesday, I'm so bored that I'm thinking about shooting Anderson. But then he quietly informs me that we're heading back to NYC and he's having dinner with Ms. Alvarez at *Le Bernadin*. Oh, and I can wait for him to drive him home after. *Yeah, you fuck. I'll wander the streets of Midtown like some friendless, sad dickwad.*

From the airport, I take the boss straight to the upscale French seafood restaurant. I could tell the boss that it's not the kind of place where Ms. Alvarez will feel comfortable, but it's none of my business.

Just before 8PM, I'm sitting quietly in the car, waiting for the boss's date to arrive. And I have to say she's a knock-out, wearing a figure-hugging dress and heels, and looking a lot less like a woman who works at Value Carpets. Her hair is styled in loose curls that reach almost to her waist. There's not a man on the street walking by that hasn't looked appreciatively at Ms. Alvarez, but for once the boss doesn't seem to notice. He's looking at Ms. Alvarez like she's the last oasis in the desert.

I sit and read the paper, sip my soda and eat a sandwich, then call Rachel.

"Hi, baby."

"Justin!"

I hear her yawn.

"Sorry, babe. Were you sleeping?"

"Not really, just dozing. I didn't want to miss your call. Are you on your way home?"

"Not yet. Don't wait up."

Just the sound of her voice soothes me. Already the muscles in my body are relaxing and I ease my aching body in the seat, leaning back against the leather headrest.

There's a soft puff of laughter over the phone.

"I've got this enormous bed and you're not here."

"You could try that old fashioned thing called sleeping, babe."

"Where's the fun in that? Anyway, I sleep better with you." Her voice softens with concern. "You must be exhausted, Justin."

"I'm okay. How was your day?"

"Fine. The new drapes for the guestrooms arrived. The rooms look more homey now—less like a hotel. Oh, and a large parcel arrived for you—it's the bicycle you ordered for Lilly's birthday."

"Great! Does it look okay?"

"It's very pink." She laughs lightly. "I'm sure she'll love it."

"Wanna come with me when I give it to her?"

There's a long pause.

"I'd love to see Lilly again, but I think giving her the bike should be a special daddy and daughter day. But another time, yes, definitely."

"You're pretty damn wonderful, you know that?"

"You're not so bad yourself."

She laughs softly and I hear her trying to stifle a yawn. It's time to let her go.

"You sound tired, baby. I'll see you tomorrow."

"Okay. I love you."

"Yeah."

"Night, Justin."

"Night."

The phone clicks and she's gone.

I'm just thinking about taking a nap in the time accelerator (and if you've ever been in the military you'll know that's what we call our bedroll when we're on a particularly boring tour), when the boss and Ms. Alvarez exit, heading to a taxi.

I guess his plans for the evening didn't pan out after all. Bet that doesn't happen too often. *Yeah, my heart is fucking breaking.*

I guess he doesn't like her taking taxis late at night. Or maybe because she just turned him down for sex.

Ding! Ding! Ding! We have a winner!

Thursday morning, I'm booted and suited, standing to attention outside the boss's office at DMA Tower because today is the day that the boss breaks in two new interns: Cooper Sinclair III, all-American, Ivy League, privileged, smart as fuck ... and Ms. Maria Conchita Alvarez, UVM and Value Carpets, the Bronx. Also smart as fuck.

I'm shocked.

The boss is in danger of mixing business and pleasure.

Pam strides into his office, looking pissed and doesn't even bother to slam the door.

"Devon, is this supposed to be a joke?"

She waves two personnel files at him.

"What seems to be amusing you, Pam?"

She snorts and tosses the files onto the table.

"Two interns: one male, white, Ivy league; one female, ethnic, UVM."

"Your point?"

"You've given me the woman to mentor, presumably since I'm female, Black and graduated from community college; but you're taking the married and straight white guy who went to a top school, same as you—have you any idea what sort of message this sends to the troops?"

The boss stares back coolly.

"Enlighten me."

"Oh take the stick out of your ass, Dev! You *know* how this looks!"

"How it looks is irrelevant. I'm simply following the HR department's guidelines."

"And how is that?" she snarls, baring her teeth.

"It wouldn't be appropriate for me to mentor Ms. Alvarez because I'm in a relationship with her."

Clang!

That's the sound of Pam's jaw hitting the floor.

"You. In a relationship. With a woman."

"Yes."

"Well, I ... congratulations, Devon. I hope you'll be very happy. I apologize for my assumption." Her stiff voice eases. "Yeah, I should have known you wouldn't pull that shit. Fine. I'll mentor Ms. Alvarez, but she won't get any special favors, not from me. I'll treat her the same way I would anyone."

"I wouldn't expect anything else," the boss says wryly.

Pam turns to leave, then frowns.

"So, you're not gay?"

There's a long pause and the boss takes his time answering.

"It would appear not."

Chapter Four

NINE-AND-A-HALF MINUTES

I used to love Saturdays. When I was a kid, it meant no school and going fishing with my buddies or tearing up the backwoods with our BMXs. When I was in high school, it meant sleeping in after a football game the night before, then going to my part-time job stacking shelves at Walmart. When I joined the Marines, Saturday meant free time after PT.

Now, I fucking hate weekends. Rachel still goes to Allison's three out of four Fridays. She enjoys spending time with the girls, baking, shopping and doing girly shit. I know she loves all that, so even though I miss the hell out of her, I never want to make her feel bad about going.

So shitty-ass end of the working week for me means lurking in the boss's Tribeca mansion and accompanying him on his morning run.

At least he hasn't reinstated the weekend orgies, not yet.

But this Friday night, the boss informs me that I'll be driving him and Ms. Alvarez out to the Farm in the morning.

So far, the boss hasn't brought in a new manager, and the couple who did the catering have temporarily taken on some of the management and housekeeping duties.

The drive out is so ordinary, it should be in an episode of *The Brady Bunch*. I don't know what the boss has told Ms. Alvarez about what she's going to see when they get there—not much, is my guess.

If she's smart, which she is, she'll run screaming. But as Dolores said, she's only book smart, which means she and the boss are pretty much on the same page when it comes to relationships, if that's what this is.

I glance in the rear view mirror. She looks happy, chatting about the journey, the scenery, how "awesome" Pam Russo is and how much she's enjoying interning at DMA Solutions.

The boss is quieter, but I swear he's smiled several times, and even let Ms. Alvarez hold his hand, or lean her head on his shoulder.

But as we approach, I can sense the tension in his body. Ms. Alvarez is too excited to notice.

"Oh em gee, Dev! This place is amazing! I'd live here all the time, it's so beautiful! Wow, *all* this is yours? I guess you really are rich," she says, almost wistful.

I pull up in front of the main doors and wait for instructions.

Anderson doesn't move and the girl frowns at him.

"What? We've come all this way and now we're just going to glare at the door? Dev?"

"There's something I need to tell you," he says, his voice cold.

She glances at me, wondering, perhaps, why he wants to have this conversation in front of the hired help. I have no idea either. Although it could be boundary issues: the boss doesn't have any.

"Okay," she says slowly. "What's up?"

"I used to host parties here on weekends, up until recently. I stopped when my estate manager was ... shot. He died."

"Oh God, Devon! That's so sad! What happened?" Then she stares at the doors. "Wait, did it happen here? Is that why you..."

"No, it wasn't here. It was at DMA Tower."

She gasps.

"I read about that! I remember. It was a couple of weeks after my awful interview. Police killed him when he tried to shoot you or something."

Anderson lowers his head, staring out the car window.

"Not exactly. Aston used to work here."

She wraps her arms around him, hugging him tightly. The boss looks slightly green—he knows that won't be her reaction when she hears the rest of the story.

"Aston was my estate manager but he also organized the parties here. Special parties."

She meets his eyes, unsure.

"Why do you say it like that? *Special parties*. What sort of parties are we talking about? Raves? Ragers? Jeez, keggers? Spit it out, Devon!"

"Social occasions where consenting adults enjoyed mutually fulfilling intercourse. Sexual intercourse."

Her mouth drops open.

"Are you freakin' kidding me? *Orgies?!*"

The boss winces, then opens the car door.

"Let me show you around. Then you'll have a better understanding."

At first I think she's not going to get out of the car, but when I hold the door open for her, she slides out reluctantly.

The boss tries to hold her hand as they walk into the house, but she pulls free and wraps her arms around herself protectively.

She walks from room to room taking in the top class display of dark kink: the whips, the canes, the floggers, the spreaders, the swing, the cage, the viewing platforms, the bed big enough for ten people, her expression moving from shocked to more shocked, to sad, and then grave.

Finally, the boss can't stand it any longer.

"Maria, say something. Please."

She takes a moment too long, and even I'm holding my breath.

"You have *parties* here? Sex parties?"

The boss swallows and nods.

"Consenting adults, that's all."

She raises her eyebrows.

"And do *you* consent, Devon? Do you ... *share* yourself with other people? With strangers?"

"They're not strangers. They're all vetted and..."

She gasps and covers her trembling lips.

"*Strangers*, Devon! Strangers to your emotions, to your heart!"

The boss is dumbfounded. Yep, he is the foundation of all that's dumb.

"I ... it's not..."

"Let me explain how ... sad ... or bad ... this makes me feel," she says slowly. "Whatever ... enjoyment or pleasure or ... experience ... you get from this, it will *never* be okay with me while you and I are in a relationship. I will *never* take part in whatever goes on here. And I am *not* okay with you ... taking part ... in anything like this if you and I are in a relationship."

She's speaking calmly, but only just.

"You haven't tried it," the boss says tightly. "You might like it. You might like it a lot."

She shakes her head, caught between anger and sorrow.

"You're a smart guy, Devon, so you have to know that this," and she waves her hand at the viewing platforms and the saltire cross with its leather restraints, "you know this isn't ... *usual*. I'm not going to use the word 'normal' because that's different for everyone. But, Dev, not everyone has a damn dungeon in their vacation home, ya know? This is *not* what most people do after they've walked the dog and washed their car on a weekend. You get what I'm saying?"

His expression remains stiff and unyielding. And I'd rather be back in Afghan that see the boss fuck up something with Maria.

"Only because it's new to *you*. Many people find the ... release offered here enjoyable, even beneficial. Sexual experimentation involving consensual adults isn't anything to find repellent."

He sounds like he's quoting that from memory, which is pretty fucking whacked.

She looks away.

"I really like what we have, what we're starting to have, but I'm telling you now: I will *never* be a willing participant in what goes on in this room, any of these rooms. And I'll tell you why: because *you are enough for me.*"

She stares at him long and hard as confusion fills the boss's face.

"The question is, Dev, am I enough for you?"

She sweeps past him, ignoring me completely, as she heads for the clean air and sunshine outside.

I stand in the shadows, watching but unseen as the boss stares after her, his face immobile.

Then he turns on his heel and strides back into the silence of the house. Left to my own devices, I follow the girl.

She's leaning against the car, her arms folded, staring at the tall trees that flank the driveway. She's not crying, but her expression is desolate when she glances up at me.

I open the backdoor of the car, and she slumps inside, hiding her face in her hands.

I wish for the thousandth time that Rachel was here.

"Is it as bad as I think it is?" she whispers.

Jeez, ask the easy question, why don't you?

"I'm not sure I know what you mean, Ms. Alvarez."

She sighs, perhaps not having expected a straight answer. I hope she might stop asking me, but she doesn't. Instead, she turns to face me, her chin jutting aggressively.

"The sex parties: are they as bad as ... as..." but she doesn't finish the sentence. Or can't.

"I'm Mr. Anderson's bodyguard, Ms. Alvarez. As long as I deem his attendance safe, it's none of my business."

Her lips set in an angry line.

"Yeah? You join in, is that it?"

"No, ma'am. I don't."

Her cheeks flush and she bites her lip.

"Sorry, Trainer. That was rude. I shouldn't have said that. I'm just having a hard time wrapping my head around all of this."

35

Yup been there, done that, got the handcuffs to match.

A loud crash from inside the house has me running toward the sound, my Smith & Wesson in my hand.

"Stay in the car!" I yell over my shoulder. "Lock the doors!"

I don't have time to see if she's listened to me as I race through the house. More loud thuds ring through the emptiness as I slink toward the room where the noise is coming from. Keeping my profile low, I glance inside, but Anderson is alone, his face contorted with rage and regret.

Then I shoulder my weapon and watch as the boss wrenches the equipment from the walls, throwing it all into the center of the room. The saltire is at the bottom of the pile, and I guess that's the loud crash I must have heard.

I turn quickly when I hear a sound behind me, but it's just the girl.

I should be pissed that she didn't do as she was told and stay in the car, but when she rushes up to the boss and throws her arms around him, I decide to make a strategic withdrawal.

As I leave, I hear the boss's voice, muffled and upset.

"Maria, I ... I'll try. I promise I'll try. I want to try ... this is new for me, too. Give me a chance."

I hope they can figure this out, but if they can't, it's none of my business. I take a walk around the perimeter, checking the security surveillance, making sure there's nothing out of place. Then I check all the rooms, avoiding the boss's private bedroom, and eventually, I go wait in the car. And wait. And wait. An hour later, they follow. I wonder what they've been doing all afternoon. No, really. I'll be blushing next.

"Trainer, we're driving back to Wolf Point. The Farm will have contractors in next week to remodel the whole house. Entirely."

See, I knew the boss wasn't completely dumb. Maybe now he can finally step away from the darkness that Frederick Landon has brought into this life.

What will the boss do now that he's said sayonara to kinky

shenanigans at the Farm? I hope it doesn't mean his meditation room will get more use.

On the drive back, the boss barely seems aware of his surroundings. He takes the girl's hand and kisses it sweetly, gently. I have *never* seen him like this. And then it hits me: *he's in love*.

Well, fuck me sideways.

Chapter Five

LOVE, ACTUALLY

The boss is completely oblivious to everyone and everything. It's a good thing I'm on the case, otherwise he'd probably walk into a tree or stroll across a freeway. If I didn't know better, I'd say he's floating on a sea of happiness with this dumbass grin plastered across his GQ face.

I know. We've all been there. Too fucked up by a woman to think straight, but I *never* thought I'd see Anderson mooning over a woman. What is it about this Alvarez kid? She's attractive, any fool can see that, but the boss has had a lot hotter, more beautiful women throw themselves at him. What's special about this one?

I wish I could say that it's none of my business, but if he's off his game, I need to be even more alert than usual.

At any rate, he's too wound up to work on Sunday evening after she's left, so I pull on my sweats and we head off around Lower Manhattan and the East Village, and put in the miles. And let's face it, two nights without Rachel, he isn't the only one who's feeling sexually frustrated.

All I want to do is have a beer and a burger. Fuck, I miss Rachel's cooking. She knows how to please a man. In so many ways.

I have to take a rain check on the beer because I'm officially still on duty, and at this moment in time, the boss's plans are changing from moment to moment. I doubt Ms. Alvarez is aware of it, but she's seriously fucking up my social life.

Sure enough, just after 7:30PM, and thirty minutes before Rachel is due back, the boss phones to say I'm needed.

I drive him to her apartment and she's waiting outside for him.

Anderson waves me away, so I head for a Burger King where I can keep an eye on him through the window, then treat myself to that burger I've been craving. As I sit in the Rover enjoying every bite, I wonder idly when was the last time the boss ate a good ole greasy burger. Not since I've known him, that's for sure. What the fuck is quinoa anyway?

The boss and Ms. Alvarez sit on the steps outside her apartment, deep in conversation.

Aw, hell. I could be here for a while.

To pass the time, I call Rachel.

"Hey, baby!"

"Justin!"

And just the way she says my name...

"What are you doing?"

"Not much. I just got back. I thought you'd be here. Are you with Mr. Anderson? What are you doing?"

"Lurking."

"Excuse me?"

"I have lurking down to a fine art, and I'd like to think I'm the shit at loitering. Don't even get me started on skulking."

She laughs.

"Be serious!"

"I'm outside Ms. Alvarez's apartment waiting for the boss to ... well, just waiting for the boss."

There's a brief pause.

"I see. Dare I ask how it went when he took her to the Farm?"

"You know, babe, I'd say he's got it bad. You should have seen him today. She told him that shit don't fly with her, and five minutes later he was tearing the place apart and calling in someone to remodel the whole Farm. They'll be having a fire sale on kinky shit."

"Oh my! Do you think this girl will really be different?" Rachel uses the words tentatively, searchingly, hopefully.

"Maybe. Oh, wait ... he's showing her the Rolex he bought for her. Wow, she looks really pissed!"

"Oh?"

"Actually she looks really fucking angry."

"Oh, Justin! You know what this means, don't you?!" Rachel splutters.

"She doesn't like Rolex?"

"No, silly! She doesn't like expensive gifts; she doesn't want him for his money! Oh, this is wonderful!"

I'm not so sure.

"Don't you like expensive gifts?"

I'm thinking of the Victoria's Secret underwear I bought her that I really haven't had as much fun from yet as I hope to.

"Justin, I love getting gifts from you. You also know that I don't like you wasting your money on me ... you're going all moody, I can tell. Stop it!"

"I like buying you presents. What's wrong with that? It's my money to waste... although I don't see it as wasting it..."

She sighs.

"What are they doing now?"

"Talking. Well, she's talking; he's looking kinda whipped ... um, I mean ... she still looks mad. Wait, she's kissing him on the cheek."

"Oh!" Rachel sighs. "That's so sweet! Oh, I like this girl. What are they doing now?"

"Um ... you really want a description? He looks like he's forgotten they're outside. Good thing there are no paps around."

"I'm sorry you have to wait. Have you had something to eat?"

"Yeah, I grabbed a burger."

"That's not very healthy!"

I roll my eyes.

"Tasted good."

"Hmm! Are you trying to make me mad?"

"Is it working?"

"*Yes!*"

"How mad are you, baby?"

"I'll show you when you get back."

I groan and she laughs.

"Goodnight, Justin!"

"Wait! What are you wearing?"

"Justin!"

"Come on, I'm curious."

"I'm wearing that lovely black underwear that you bought me from Victoria's Secret..." I groan inwardly "...and I'm wearing a white blouse and navy blue pencil skirt."

"Take off your clothes."

"Justin!"

"Do it for me, baby."

I hear the smile in her voice.

"Okay, Justin. I'm unzipping my skirt. I'm sliding it down my hips. It's on the floor. Now I'm picking it up and folding it and putting it on the chair, like you're supposed to do with your clothes!"

"Oh, baby, don't ruin the moment. Undo your shirt: one button at a time."

"Here's the first button, now the second, now the third; my bra is showing through. Now I'm undoing the cuffs; I'm sliding my blouse over my shoulders. Now I'm just in my bra and panties. I'm going to put the phone down so I can unhook my bra..."

Oh, fucking yeah! Suddenly there's a thud.

"Oh, sorry, I dropped the phone. Allison is on the other line. I was supposed to call her when I got in. I'll have to go."

"What? No!"

"Bye, Justin!"

Fucking Allison! I knew there was a reason I hated her. And I've got a rock solid erection. Sucking in a deep breath, I lean back in my seat and try to think cold thoughts. Oh, for fuck's sake!

You're probably wondering why I don't just jerk some knuckle babies as no one's looking and I'm parked away from streetlights.

I guess you could say the Marines cured me of that—jerking it on duty is frowned upon. And maybe because I was doing an overnighter in a defensive watch post, alone in my shallow fighting hole, my buddies relying on me to be vigilant. I started getting sleepy, with only hourly radio checks to keep me awake. Rubbing one out seemed like a good way to stay awake. Accidentally leaning on the 'talk' button while in the midst of Operation Stay Awake, meant that all other radios heard me slapping and panting. And because you can't receive transmissions while broadcasting, no one could tell me to stop. The C.O. wasn't happy, but it kept the other guys entertained and awake.

A couple of minutes later, I see the boss leaving. He leans down to kiss the girl, and when he turns to face me, he looks so fucking happy. Her expression is harder to read.

He climbs into the back seat and asks me to put on some music, so we ride back to the hotel listening to Satie's *Gymnopédie*. I didn't know jack-shit about classical music until I started working for Anderson, but some of it's really good. I wouldn't admit that to my old platoon buddies, but I've got a thing for Puccini. Which reminds me, I have to pick up the tickets for me and Rachel to go see *Madame Butterfly*. It's playing at the Met—the boss is letting us use his private box. The bastard can be generous. It wasn't like I even asked him. He came into my office and saw me looking at the flyer. Next thing I know, the manager is phoning *me* to ask which night is convenient for me and *Mrs. Trainer*. I really liked the sound of that. I guess it's the boss's little joke.

He does stuff like that—never says a word. I know he's filthy rich, so it's not the money, it's the fact that he *notices*. Part of me wonders if it's not just to keep me sweet because he doesn't want to have to go look for another sucker to live in his weird twilight world. But the side of me that's being trained by Rachel thinks it's because he's good. That's the word she uses about him: good.

And I gotta say, the long-haired general makes a lot of sense.

I slide into the sheets next to her and she sighs, folding herself into my body.

I could get used to this.

The next day seems to last a lifetime.

The boss is distracted at the first meeting of the day, and Pam stalks me across the room.

"What's wrong with Devon?" she hisses.

"He looks fine to me."

"He's *smiling*," she says in an accusing tone.

It's true.

Ms. Alvarez certainly seems to be having a beneficial effect on Anderson, although not on his business.

The suits at the meeting aren't entirely sure what to make of this and nor does Ryan. They all do the smart thing and ignore it.

I position myself behind him so I have a clear view of the door and prepare to be bored half to death. I also happen to have a clear view of his laptop and I can tell you he's not as entirely engrossed in NASDAQ as it appears. In fact, if I didn't know better, which I don't, I'd say he spends the entire meeting sending emails to little Ms. Alvarez. For fuck's sake, at this rate he'll end up selling DMA Solutions to Azerbaijan for a dollar.

By 9AM, he's bored again and winds up the meeting. Waving away the minions, he breezes off to his office, cutting off Pam's annoyed words.

It's a long day, and his Ms. Alvarez-induced high doesn't last.

When we finally arrive back at Wolf Point, Rachel is asleep on the sofa. I guess she got tired waiting for me. God, she looks so beautiful, so peaceful. And that's what she makes me feel: peaceful deep inside. *And also fucking horny.*

I lean down and stroke her cheek.

"Hey, baby."

Her eyes flutter open.

"You're back! Are you hungry? I've got some..."

But I don't let her finish. My mouth is on hers, learning the shape of her lips again, remembering, breathing her breath. She sighs deeply, and the sound cascades through me, heating every cell of my body.

I scoop her up into my arms and she laughs.

"Justin! Can we have a conversation first?"

I don't think so. I plan on doing all my talking with my body.

Kicking the bedroom door open, I throw her onto the bed. She's breathless, smiling up at me.

"Talking later then?"

I throw my jacket on the floor, kick off my shoes and sink down next to her.

Sometime later, Rachel collapses onto my chest, breathing hard. I stroke her hair, feeling the silky texture under my fingers, but more than that, feeling like I've come home.

She sits up slowly, a soft smile on her lips.

"Do you feel better now?"

I nod, running my hands slowly up and down her spine.

She reaches across and takes a sip of water from the glass on the bedside table then slides down next to me, snuggling into my shoulder.

"What did you want to talk to me about, baby?"

She squints up at me, one eye shut and a sleepy look on her face.

"Talking usually works better when both people are awake," she says, trying not to yawn.

"That a fact?"

She runs a finger across my left pec, circling the flat nipple. Crazy how much of a turn on that is.

"I was wondering, would it be okay ... I mean it's fine if it's not ... but I thought I'd make a birthday cake for Lilly. Something in pink?"

She looks up at me, her expression hopeful and anxious. It kills me that she still doubts herself. Doesn't she know how fucking amazing she is? How decent? How damn good?

My voice is hoarse when I answer.

"That would be ... awesome."

Chapter Six

CAROUSEL

Abigail Anderson is back in town.

I know this because the boss is holding his cell away from his ear taking a call. I actually saw him wince. So with Miss Anderson's not-so-dulcet tones echoing through the car and probably most of Europe, I gather that the boss has been strong-armed into picking her up from the airport early tomorrow morning. Better him than me.

The next day, the boss is up at the butt crack of dawn and heading to JFK to pick up his sister and drive out to their parents at Scarsdale. He's taken the Rover on the (probably correct) assumption that she'll have a helluva lot more luggage than she left with.

She's been in Italy with the rest of her college class, learning some fancy-schmancy way of cooking. Or maybe just learning to boil pasta. The only trip I ever took in school was Spring break my senior year when a bunch of us bought a couple of crates of beer and went camping for the weekend.

I'm so fucking glad that the boss hasn't asked me to drive today.

Even better, I get to sleep-in with the beautiful Ms. Smith. A rare and very welcome luxury after the last week.

"Hey, blue eyes!"

She smiles up at me.

"Hey, yourself."

Then she feels what's pressing into her thigh.

"Justin Trainer, I think you're pleased to see me!"

Yep, and that's enough conversation for now.

Hours later (hey, it's a guy thing) ... okay, okay ... sometime later we're both lying on our backs. Rachel is gasping for breath and I've got the biggest fucking grin on my face.

"I think I'll cancel my Spin class," she says at last, still panting.

"I don't know why you go to those classes when you've got me to keep you fit, baby."

She frowns and her expression becomes serious.

"Because I'm nearly nine years older than you, Justin. If I've got any hope of keeping up..."

Not that old chestnut. Nine years is nothing. I don't give a shit. Never have.

"Baby, to me you're perfect."

She sighs.

The woman really doesn't know how to take a compliment.

"I mean it. Why would I even look at another woman when I've got you?"

She shakes her head as if my question baffles her. But it's true: having been married to my ex, I know what I'm talking about. Rachel is the real deal, the one I want.

I don't care how many women throw themselves in my direction, either getting a cheap thrill out of fucking the hired help, the hard-man bodyguard, or sometimes to get closer to Anderson. I've seen it all, and those types do nothing for me. I have perfection at home. But convincing Rachel of that...

I wonder if her sister has something to do with it, whispering crap to her when I'm not there. Rachel always seems more distant after she's visited her family. I'm going to have to face that head on one day.

"By the way," she says, obviously changing the subject, "I wanted to ask you about Ms. Alvarez."

"What about her?"

"Well, what's your opinion of her?"

Why women are so intrigued by other women they don't even know is a complete mystery.

"She's got the boss jumping through hoops. The poor bastard doesn't know if he's coming or going."

She smiles.

"That certainly makes a change."

"Yeah. But seriously, he's a fucking nightmare at the moment. One minute I'm expecting violins to start playing and the next he's biting the head off of some poor sucker who breathed without permission."

"He's never shouted at me."

"He wouldn't fucking dare!"

Rachel laughs. She's always laughing at me. Somehow I don't seem to mind.

"So you think he really likes this girl?"

"Head over fucking heels, in my humble opinion."

"You wouldn't know 'humble' if you tripped over it!"

"I can be humble."

"Oh Justin, a luau in the Antarctic is more likely."

Whatever.

"Do you think she loves Mr. Anderson?"

That's the part I'm not sure about. She certainly likes him a lot, but sometimes there's a look in her eye that tells me she's torn up inside. Like I can't guess what makes her feel that way.

"Maybe, if he'd let her," I say at last.

"Oh, dear."

Rachel looks unhappy about it.

"She just seems so young, you know?"

"Does it matter?"

She looks at me like I've just parachuted in from Mars.

"Of course it matters! You know what he's like, what he does in the meditation room!"

Yeah, I know and I don't like it much either.

"Rachel, she's a grown woman. I think you're all born knowing how to lead a guy by his dick, because I'm telling you, she's the one who's in charge in this relationship. She phones him or emails him, and he drops everything and comes running. Hell, he doesn't even do that for his own family."

She looks slightly happier. Good, because I'm done talking about the boss. It's not like we don't have our own lives to live.

And with that thought in mind, I duck down under the sheets and show my woman a thing or two about things she doesn't necessarily need to go on missing.

The next weekend is weird. Saturday night, I have the whole of Wolf Point to myself. Rachel is at her sister's and the boss is with Ms. Alvarez.

I make a couple of calls and find out that some guys from my old platoon are in town, so we catch up over beer and burgers. It's good, talking about the old days and just chilling, but when I get back home, it feels weird being in the place by myself.

I sleep later than usual then take a long swim in the pool, a rare luxury.

I've only just shit, showered and shaved when the boss drives into the underground garage, having stayed the night with his girl—at a hotel, I assume, since she lives with her grandfather and three younger brothers. I make sure I'm standing to attention when he exits the elevator.

"Sir."

"Trainer, I'm expecting Ms. Alvarez at 1PM. I've given her the codes for the garage and elevator, but be on standby just in case she has any problems. This evening we'll be having dinner with my parents, so I'll want to leave at 7PM."

That's shocked my fucking socks off. Dinner at his parents? At least I won't have Miss Abigail Anderson asking me leading questions about whether or not the boss and I like Abba and have I seen the movie *Mama Mia*—her idea of a joke. As a matter of fact I have, on one of the thankfully rare evenings when Rachel won the toss on movie night. *What the fuck was James Bond doing singing out of tune?* That's what I couldn't figure out.

But before I drive them out to Scarsdale and watch his parents celebrate their son's heterosexuality, I have a shrewd idea of what they'll be doing for the intervening six hours. Poor kid: I hope she's fit.

Chapter Seven

LA CAGE AUX FOLLES

In the end, I can't stand the silence.

At 1.15PM, they disappear into the boss's bedroom and I wander around the staff quarters. I don't know what I'm expecting: maybe for Ms. Alvarez to run out screaming. In the end it's me who has to leave—the tension is more than flesh and blood can bear.

I wander over to 'Hail Mary', a scuzzy sports bar in the Village. Rachel hates me going into joints like this. For some reason, she thinks I'll end up in a brawl. I'm not being arrogant, well maybe a little, but anyone who starts a fight with me ain't gonna go the distance. Anyway, I'd have to consider that getting into a fight in the first place as a major fail. In this job, you've got to be able to tell which people are all mouth and which are the real danger. And I'm fucking good at my job.

I'd really like to just sit at the bar, watch a Yankees game and shoot the breeze with a cold beer in my hand. But I'm on duty tonight, so I stick to coffee.

There are probably a dozen coffee bars within two clicks of a camel's fart that serve better coffee than this place. In fact, the coffee is so bad I think a badger must have washed its ass in it. It's un-fucking-drinkable. Maybe they named the place 'Hail Mary' because they haven't got a prayer of staying in business.

It certainly doesn't improve my mood as I wonder what it would be like to work for a regular boss and have a regular life. The truth is, I know I'm not the kind of guy who'd be happy dragging his weary carcass to an office every day, nine-to-five. I think that's why Rachel's sister doesn't like me: she thinks I'm not capable of being a regular guy with a regular life, and therefore I'm no good for her sister. What pisses me off is that she could be right.

These days, Mason has got the intel on threats to Anderson so tightly sewn up, we're pretty much ahead of the game. But that doesn't mean it's time to be complacent. Just because the blackmailer has gone quiet doesn't mean that he's given up. And a guy who's a billionaire makes enemies—lots of them. But it's not just that: look at the way little Ms. Alvarez has screwed up all our lives. Not that she means to, but she's leading the boss around by his dick, and everyone who works for him has to line up and play follow-the-fucking-leader.

At least Rachel will be home tonight. Definitely something to look forward to.

Shortly after 1800 hours, I head back to Wolf Point to get the sit-rep (or *situation report* as I had to explain to Rachel). I've got time for a quick shower, and I'm standing to attention, well, sitting on my ass in an office easy-chair, checking out the CCTV. There's nothing to report.

I feel someone looking at me, and turn to see Anderson standing at the entrance to the office.

"Sir?"

"I'd like to leave in fifteen minutes, Trainer. It won't be a late night. Ms. Alvarez will need to be taken home after we've had dinner at my parents."

He pulls a face, and I don't know whether it's because dinner with his folks is on the menu or because Ms. Alvarez won't be staying the night.

He wanders away like he doesn't know what to do with himself without his new playmate, and I'm guessing that Ms. Alvarez's stamina isn't all that. Maybe she should just enlist in the Marines: it would be easier. The boss's version of hell-week is fucking from dawn to dusk, and hanging from the rafters with your tits out. I never saw that in the Marine Corps Manual, not even in the appendices.

When I hear Bruno Mars echoing out from the main room, I know he's in a good mood again. The guy changes his mood more often than Meg Ryan changes her face. The singer-songwriter combo is usually his music of choice when he's feeling mellow. Rachel likes Ed Sheerhan but I'm more of a *Rammstein* man, myself.

Rachel likes to dance—she says it's the only area where I disappoint. I know she's just joking, but that comment stings. So I'm sensitive, who knew?

It's a strange job being someone's personal protection, the things we see and hear—but then we have to pretend we're deaf, dumb and blind. At least the boss doesn't expect me to act like a half-wit, too. Some employers can't stand having people with brains.

At the appointed hour, I bring the Rover around front.

Before I can climb out to open the door for them, the boss saves me the trouble.

The girl is staring out the window but the boss whispers something to her that makes her turn, and then he picks up her hand and kisses it. It's real sweet.

He'll be watching Julia Roberts' movies next and that English dude with the floppy hair—the one who got busted for being blown by a hooker—does all those sappy romances. Rachel likes those sorts of movies, it's her one flaw. But hell, they make her horny, too, so I'm not going to complain.

With a minute to spare, I cruise into the driveway of Anderson Seniors. They've improved security since I first started working for the boss, but it's still an easy place to penetrate if you know what you're doing.

They head in, and I take the car around to the back—the usual routine. Even from that distance, I can hear Miss Abigail Anderson shrieking like a drunken sailor on payday. That woman is *loud*.

I head for the kitchen and speed-eat my way through chorizo and scallops. It's good, but not as good as Rachel's.

I think I've been pretty damn fast, although not nearly fast enough. I've got my back to the wall, but it's not looking good because...

"Hi, Trainer!" says Miss Abigail Anderson, in the gentle tones of a trucker from Tacoma.

She walks towards me and I make a rapid assessment of the possible exits. I don't rule out digging a tunnel through the kitchen floor. Her eyes are all big and sad, and then she lays her hand on my arm and I get ready to take evasive action.

"I'm *really* sorry," she says.

She's looking at me like my dog just died.

"I know this must be hard for you. I just hope you know that ... whatever happens ... we'll always be grateful for the way you look after my brother. I'm sure Devon really cares about you ... in his own way."

What the fuck?!

"I'll give you a moment..."

What the fuck?!

Then she pats me on the arm again and walks out, glancing back at me as if to check I'm not slitting my wrists. I'm left with my jaw on the floor.

What the fuck?!

Did she...? Did I...? Was that...? Is she...? *WHAT THE FUCK?! I am NOT the boss's fucking BOYFRIEND! NO FUCKING WAY!*

Then Martha, the Anderson's cook/housekeeper, enters the kitchen. She's got a face like a bulldog chewing on a wasp.

"You cannot be serious! He likes *her*! That mousey little thing? Devon deserves better than *her!*" She glances at me. "Sorry, Trainer. I know you really like him, too."

Okay, so I'm not the only one who isn't taking this well—and I've had enough of this shit!

"I AM NOT GAY! I'm not gay! Okay? I have a girlfriend! A woman! A woman friend! And we have sex! Lots of it! Great sex! Really great sex! Get it?! Straight as a fucking ruler."

Then her face goes all soft and sweet.

"It's okay. No one cares these days. Even in the military, or, you know ... ex-military."

Now, I'm not usually a quick-tempered person, I'm more of a sort of slow-burn kinda guy, but it's been a really trying fucking day.

I glare down at her.

"I'm not gay. I've never been gay. I'm not even very cheerful. I like women. Understand?"

She gets a gleam in her eye and a speculative look on her face. That's it: I'm outta here.

I storm back to the car, trying really fucking hard not to look like I'm having an aneurysm. I sit in the car silently fuming. I need some music to calm me down, but when I turn on the radio....

"Whaaaat?"

Seventies on Seven is playing an *ABBA* compilation. I flip to another station and catch *iHeart* playing 'Candle in the Wind'.

"I am not a friend of Dorothy!" I yell at the radio.

Yeah, you could say I'm just a touch irate.

I know what would soothe me, some serious Rachel-time.

Chapter Eight

FRIGHT NIGHT

The boss really isn't a laugh-a-minute kind of guy—and I get why. He's pretty fucked up, although maybe Ms. Alvarez is helping with that. But he's also got tens of thousands of people in half a dozen countries living off of what he pays them. If he screws up, that's a lot of people unemployed. Plus, he's a walking, talking, fucking target for all the whackos out there who hate him because of his wealth, his agri-business, his techno-business, his anti-gun stance— you name it, people want to off him for it. Which is where I come in. And whatever went on with him and Norman Bates when he was a kid, he's been pretty fucked up about women ever since. Maybe it's true that everybody gets a chance at redemption. The question is: will he be smart enough to take it?

All this worrying about the boss is giving me a headache. I'm really glad that Rachel will be waiting for me when I get back. She is the best cure.

It's quiet as I make my way silently through the house. I wasn't trained in covert ops for nothing. Who knew it would come in so handy for being close protection for a twisted fucker like Anderson. Some weekends at the Farm, I needed a pair of blinkers to walk through the place. I *really* didn't need to see the boss fucking in the main room, in the kitchen, and once *in the swimming pool!* Bastard! Images like that get burned into a man's brain.

I turn off the lights as I go, but the place is never really dark, not with the city's glow painting the night sky with a neon halo.

Rachel's bedroom door is slightly ajar. Officially, we still have separate rooms, but mine hardly ever gets slept in. Sometimes I crash there if I've got a really early start and I don't want to wake her. I hate those nights—the bed is just too damn empty.

I take off my jacket and tie and drop them on the sofa, then push open her door. She's asleep on her side, one arm reaching out to the space where I really want to be. Her shoulder is bare, pale in the dim light. God, she's beautiful. Her hair is spread out across the pillow like strands of silver. I am one lucky bastard.

I'm moving as quietly as possible, but when I tug my shirt over my head, her eyes open and she blinks sleepily.

"Sorry, baby. I was trying not to wake you."

"I don't mind. Mmm, you've taken your shirt off. Do you need some help with your pants?"

"I need anything you can give me, baby."

She smiles like a sphinx and sits up. I can't help my eyes following the sheet as it falls to her waist. She's naked and just so fucking fabulous.

She reaches out and tucks her fingers into my waistband, tugging me towards her.

"I think you're pleased to see me."

I can't reply because she's running her hand over the fucking enormous bulge that's just made lift-off in my pants.

She unzips me real slow—it's such a turn on. And she's staring up at me the whole time. God, she's so .... she grips me—hard.

And I can't wait anymore. I pull off my pants and step out of them.

"Did you just drop your pants on the floor?"

"What? Yeah, so?"

"What have I told you about leaving your clothes on the floor?"

She looks really pissed. "You think I'm here just to pick up after you?" she says angrily.

"Of course not!"

She grabs the waistband of my boxer briefs and yanks them down. It's only just not painful.

"You've been bad, Justin. You need to be punished ... and you need to be restrained."

What?

And she pulls out a pair of pink, fluffy handcuffs from underneath her pillow.

I break out into a cold sweat. Since when was Rachel into this kinky shit? *She's been working here too long!*

"Um, Rachel ... I really don't..."

"Hush now, Justin. This isn't going to hurt ... much. Happy anniversary, darling."

She throws me onto the bed and straddles me.

"Aaaagh!"

"Justin! Justin! What's the matter?"

I wake up in a cold sweat, reality rushing through me, and I realize I'm thrashing around in the bed as Rachel sits up and turns on her sidelight.

I screw up my eyes against the brightness and let my breathing return to something like normal.

"Justin, what on earth is the matter?"

Her voice is filled with concern.

Christ! I just dreamed about Rachel and handcuffs and ... fuck me!

"Did you have a nightmare?"

Was it a nightmare? Mmm, maybe not. But, Rachel with handcuffs?

"Noooo, not exactly."

"Then what?"

She runs her soft fingers over my chest as I sit up and lean back against the headboard. And suddenly I really don't want to admit to her what I was dreaming about. *Fucking Anderson! It's his fault, the twisted fucker!*

"Tell me, darling," she says, her voice edged with worry. "You sounded like you were having a nightmare."

"No, just ... I'm fine. Sorry I woke you, baby."

"But..."

"It was a good dream ... surprising. Babe, you don't happen to have a pair of pink fluffy handcuffs under your pillow, do you?"

She starts laughing.

"No! What makes you ask that? Oh, is that what you were dreaming about?"

I eye her carefully. She doesn't seem upset.

"Maybe."

"Well, I'm sorry to disappoint you, but no, I don't."

"You could never disappoint me, baby."

Her smile fades.

"But you do get nightmares, don't you?"

I stare at her, surprised and uneasy. I didn't know that she'd ever heard me. I'd thought I was mostly over that part. I am, I think.

"I was probably having a nightmare about Anderson's meditation room."

Not a smile. Nothing. Instead, she watches me gravely.

"Why do you do that? Why do you always have to make a joke about it?"

Because it's better than being weak.

"I'm okay. You don't have to worry about me."

She sighs and looks away.

"I knew you'd say that, but I do worry."

"Rachel, seriously, I'm fine. Better than fine, I'm great."

She looks at me doubtfully.

"Last week ... well, you were shouting out something that sounded like 'Adam' or maybe 'Aiden'. I just wondered..."

The hair on the back of my neck stands up and I can't hold back a shudder. I never talk about Aiden King. Never.

I kick off the sheets and stalk into the bathroom, running cold water and splashing my face. As I stare in the mirror, the memories flood back. I've tried not to think about that day. The docs say that's why it haunts my nights.

I switch off the bathroom light and go back to the bedroom. Rachel is sitting up with her arms wrapped around her knees protectively. She's worried, and I know I've hurt her.

"I'm sorry," I say softly, pulling her into my arms.

Her body is rigid, but eventually she lets me hold her.

"I'm not fragile, Justin. You don't have to protect me. I'm stronger than I look."

"I know that ... it's not ... I've seen some bad shit. Hell, I've done some bad shit. I don't talk about it because I don't want you to have it in your head."

"Maybe I could help?"

"You can't."

My words are harsh, too harsh, and I hear her take a sharp breath.

"Shit, I don't mean it like that. It's because I can't un-see the things I've seen; I can't forget, although God knows I try to. You're the best thing that's even happened to me. *You* make it better."

There's a heavy silence before Rachel pulls away so she can look me in the eye. In the moonlit room, her irises are black and shadows shroud her face.

"I was married to Brian for ten years. He was a fire fighter for all of that time. I do understand the toll it takes, mentally and physically. When he was ... killed, there were times when I wish I'd died, too. It changed me. And I understand that what you've seen has changed you, as well. But you don't have to hide it from me, Justin. I don't want you to laugh and joke when you're hurting inside."

I refuse to unlock all the dark that lives inside me. And I definitely won't let it taint Rachel.

She rolls onto her side, facing away from me.

We lie in silence, the distance between us increasing. I'm a boat that's lost its moorings and every second I'm slipping further into the vast, empty ocean. I'm afraid of losing her.

"Aiden King was my buddy from Boot Camp."

Rachel stops breathing, her body too still.

"He died in an IED attack. Iraq. I was with him, sitting next to him. There was smoke everywhere and my ears were ringing. I couldn't hear anything. I think I was shouting, I don't know. And when the smoke cleared ... I was soaked in Aiden's blood. I tried to hold him together, but he was ... in pieces ... I couldn't and..."

I can't talk about this. I can't.

In the darkness, Rachel takes my hand and links her warm fingers with mine. She's my lifeline, and I know she won't let go.

It's Monday morning but I have the luxury of sleeping in. Once I knew that Ms. Alvarez had changed her mind and didn't need to be driven home last night, I guessed the boss wouldn't be going for an early morning run.

I was hoping to work on some more diversionary tactics with Rachel, but she swatted my wandering hands away and bribed me with the promise of bacon and pancakes ... if I'm 'good'.

Why, Ms. Smith! I'm always good with you around.

Rachel interrupts my pleasant daydreams by bringing me breakfast in bed. I can't help grinning at her.

Neither of us makes reference to the conversation we had last night. Thank Christ we don't need to. And yet somehow, I feel lighter.

"You are an accomplished woman, Ms. Smith."

Maybe it's kind of dumb, but I don't want to call her 'Mrs.' anymore. I know she's noticed, but she hasn't said anything.

"Why, thank you, Mr. Trainer. An unexpected but very welcome compliment."

"And you sure can cook, woman!"

"Is that the beginning and end of my talents?"

"Aw, no, baby. You're great in the sack, too."

I grin up at her, knowing that she wants to be mad at me, but is also fighting a smile.

"By the way," she says, changing the subject, "I just bumped into Ms. Alvarez."

"Oh?"

I'm surprised they're up already.

"I think I embarrassed her."

"Yeah, she and the boss fuck like it's about to be rationed."

"Hmm, well, it seems to be catching."

I reach up to grab her, but she dodges out of the way.

"You are not getting maple syrup on the sheets again!" she says sternly.

"You sure?"

"Well, not on a work day. Even though Mr. Anderson isn't going into the office until after lunch."

"I have a few ideas about how we can spend the morning until then."

And this time she's not quick enough. I'm *really* looking forward to getting her all sticky.

Chapter Nine

THE FAST AND THE FURIOUS

Today, I'm helping Rachel with the grocery shopping. Having four adults in the house has severely depleted reserves.

Rachel is waiting at the main entrance as I drive up. Damn, she looks *hot*. There's something so incredibly sexy about that crisp white blouse and slim-fitting pencil skirt: all that passion, all those amazing curves, hidden by a severe uniform. Maybe it's just me.

Nope, not just me. Frank, the doorman at the apartment building next door, has too many fucking eyeballs on her. *Back off, asshole! She's taken.*

I jump out and give Frank a warning stare. He steps back. *Yeah, message received and understood, pencil neck!*

I help Rachel into the Rover, and she raises an eyebrow, an amused expression on her face which I decide not to notice.

"Where to, ma'am?"

"I'll start at Brooklyn Fare. It's been lovely having Ms. Alvarez to stay, she's such a sweetheart, but we seem to have got through a lot more food than usual."

"Probably because they spend all their time fu— ... um ... screw — ... They need the energy."

"I could say the same about you," she says challengingly.

"I'm addicted, baby. You make me hungry ... and not just for food."

"Concentrate on driving, Justin!"

"Yes, ma'am," I grin at her.

She shakes her head, but she's smiling.

"Well," she says, amused, "at least with Ms. Alvarez away, Mr. Anderson will be back to his normal routine for a few days."

Yep, Ms. Alvarez is heading to Cancun with Dolores and a bunch of her friends for a bachelorette weekend and the boss isn't happy about it. And even if he was, normalcy and the boss aren't two concepts that I'd usually expect to find in one sentence. Besides, I'm guessing Rachel is wrong.

"Rachel, it's going to be early morning runs, working out in the gym at all hours, kicking the shit out of Enrico, and yelling at Tessa until she pukes. Better head for the storm cellar because Hurricane Anderson is back."

"Oh, dear."

Yeah.

"Poor Tessa."

There's a pause.

"Do you think that Ms. Alvarez is *the one*?"

I shrug. Before I met Rachel, a phrase like that would have me checking to see if my dick had dropped off and I'd grown a vagina, but now I understand that 'the one' is as real as a man walking on the moon.

"Maybe. But I expect the boss will manage to fuck it up."

"What do you mean? He really seems to like her. Why would he mess it up?"

It's a good question, but kinda hard to answer. Despite scaring the crap out of Tessa and most of his employees, he takes their well-being seriously. He offers first rate medical and dental, and given the fact that he hardly ever has a day off himself, his time off for vacation is more generous than most companies.

None of which can be applied to Ms. Alvarez's case.

"Because he's never had a girlfriend before. Because he doesn't know how to deal with it when she stands up to him. Because he's not used to putting someone else's feelings before his own. When I first met her, I thought she was this quiet, gentle little kid—but she's her own woman and she won't take any of his shit."

"That's good, isn't it?"

"Yeah, who wants a woman who does exactly as they're told all the time?"

Rachel lifts her eyebrows, and out of the corner of my eye I see her holding back a smile.

"I just mean that even though part of him likes that she stands up to him, he's got no coping mechanism for it except..."

I hesitate to finish the sentence, but I don't need to.

"Yes, I see what you mean," says Rachel, sounding serious. "I really hope you're wrong."

So do I.

I find a parking spot near the market and escort Rachel to the deli while she runs her eyes over what looks like a very long list.

"Justin, why don't you go get a coffee? This is going to take a while. Give me half an hour?"

"Sure, baby."

I head off to a nearby coffee shop, grateful for the chance to spend some quality time reading the sports section of the *New York Times,* and checking out the form of the New York Jets recent signings.

I've been here about twenty minutes when there's a loud commotion at the cash register. I shove my chair back, my hand reaching towards my shoulder holster, my automatic reaction to unexpected sound. But it's completely unwarranted, and I feel pretty dumb when I see two elderly ladies looking shocked and upset, their tea and muffins scattered over the counter, the change purse of the older one strewn across the floor.

I ease my hand away from my holster and take a calming breath.

Yeah, I can see the headlines: security officer in granny-gate massacre.

Luckily, no one has noticed my Smith & Wesson and the server is more concerned with clearing up the spillages.

I bend down and start picking up the dimes and quarters.

"Oh, thank you, young man! Thank you! I don't know what happened! I'm all fingers and thumbs. How clumsy of me."

"That's okay, ma'am. Happy to help."

About five bucks worth of change has gone flying across the café but I think I've gotten all of it.

"Oh, and you're such a polite young man, too!"

Never a truer word.

Meanwhile, the waitress has replaced the tea and muffins and dumped the tray on a vacant table. The old ladies are still chirruping their distress and I really want to shake the sour-faced pit-bull of a server.

I pour the heap of coins onto the table.

"There's your change, ma'am. You look after that."

"Oh, thank you so much, young man. Please, let us buy you a coffee for your trouble—we interrupted you."

"That's okay, ma'am. I'd about finished anyway. Just happy to help."

I shrug off their thanks as I check my watch. Time to go collect Rachel.

I can see them waving through the coffee shop window as I saunter out, and the one who dropped the change purse blows me a kiss.

Yep, still got it.

Rachel is finishing at the checkout when I catch up with her. I load the bags into the shopping cart and wheel it out to the Rover.

"What are you looking so pleased about?" she says.

I hadn't realized that I was smiling. I wondered why my face felt weird.

"A woman offered to buy me coffee. I guess she thought I was hot."

"Well, I can't argue with that. Should I be jealous?"

"No, baby. She wasn't my type."

We drive home listening to songs from *Wicked*. What is it about women and show-tunes? I don't get it.

I just have time to help Rachel get all the shopping bags to the staff kitchen when my iPhone buzzes.

"Gotta go, baby. The boss needs a ride."

"Oh, I'd better hurry and get dinner started."

She turns to go. *Oh no, baby, not yet.* I sweep her into my arms and kiss her hard. Her lip gloss tastes of strawberries.

"Justin! What has gotten into you this week?"

She pulls away breathless.

"I think it's the other way around, baby!"

She swats my ass and I make a strategic retreat.

She can't keep her hands off me.

I pull up in front of DMA Tower and text the boss to let him know that I'm here. I lean on the hood of the Rover, and the lobby security guard comes out to shoot the breeze.

"Hey, Walt. Anything to report?"

"Naw, Mr. Trainer."

"The boss fire anyone today?"

Walt snorts.

"Tessa nearly got canned. Heidi told me she's been crying in the ladies' room most of the day. Again."

I roll my eyes.

"What did she do this time?"

"The *New York Times* called to confirm a rumor that's going around. They'd heard that the boss was dating."

"And?"

"Apparently she said, 'I can't confirm whether or not Mr. Anderson is dating Ms. Alvarez'."

I shake my head. Tessa really is as dumb as wood.

"I can't believe she fell for that old trick. Ryan must be going crazy."

Walt grins.

"Yep, he's been fielding calls ever since. Mr. Anderson was pretty heated up about it. So is it true? The boss has finally gotten himself a girlfriend? I always thought he was the wrong way up the turnpike."

"No comment, Walt. No comment."

We see the boss cannoning through the lobby, employees diving out of his way as the tornado in Armani cuts through the herd. He really takes the phrase 'looking pissed' to a whole new dimension. So what's new? Walt straightens up and opens the car door. Anderson scowls at him before muttering a quiet 'thank you'. He gets in without speaking, tension heating the air around us until it crackles. It's going to be a long, long evening.

As I head out into the traffic, I can see in the rear view mirror that the boss is glancing at his cell every few seconds. It doesn't take a genius to figure out who he's waiting to hear from.

Finally, he gets a message and his whole body relaxes. Irritatingly, I find that I relax at the same time. I'm going to have to put a note on my calendar, *Get a fucking life*.

All the way back to Wolf Point, he's tapping messages into his cell phone, but he looks happy enough. Maybe she really will miss him while she vacations with her friends. I'm almost surprised he hasn't put surveillance in place, but then again, he already tracks her every movement via the new iPhone he gave her. It's compulsive: definitely stalkerish. If she knew half the time he spent worrying about her, she'd probably head for the hills. Or be flattered. Nope, I'm voting for the hills, or maybe one of those underground bunkers that end-timers build. Anderson on the prowl or a zombie apocalypse? Hey, zombies in suits! They could make a movie about that.

But Ms. Alvarez doesn't know. She really hasn't a clue that she's become the center of the boss's world.

He heads for his study, saying that he'll eat after he's been for a run. Which means after *we've* been for a run. Not that I mind. At least I get to stay fit in this job.

We pound our way around a six-mile circuit and it's the same thing all over again: running to calm his brain, running to escape his thoughts, running to escape his compulsion to control. He'll never run fast enough. I almost feel sorry for him. If I had any breath left.

Rachel serves him up a damn fine sea bass fillet with rice and salad when we get back. I know it's damn fine because we're having the same meal. But the boss eats alone.

"How is he?"

I frown at Rachel. *Can't we have* one *meal where we* don't *talk about him?*

"His normal fucked up self."

"Justin!"

I shrug. It's true, we both know it.

"Perhaps you should go talk to him."

"And say what? He's my boss, not my buddy. And the only person he wants to talk to has flown three-and-a-half thousand miles to get away from him."

"I thought it was a bachelorette party?"

"Sure, but she also told him he was intense."

"Oh, Justin! Sometimes you men are so literal!"

What? She's lumping me in with him*? I don't fucking think so!*

"I'm sure she'll miss him. Poor Mr. Anderson."

"Poor, he ain't."

"You know what I mean."

Whatever.

My iPhone buzzes.

"Trainer, I won't need you again tonight, but I'll be running at 5AM tomorrow."

Great.

I toss the phone aside and persuade Rachel that clearing up isn't nearly as interesting as what I have in mind. She's a woman of weak will. I fucking love that about her.

I fall asleep with her curled in my arms. But not for long enough. At some point in the night, I'm vaguely aware that the boss is prowling the premises and I hear the door to the meditation room slam shut. He hasn't been in there since he started dating Ms. Alvarez. I know for a fact that since the Farm fiasco, he hasn't shared any more of his secrets with her. She has no idea that his spare dungeon is next to his home office.

As I crawl out of bed at 4:45AM, I'm seriously thinking of

contacting Ms. Alvarez and begging her to come back early. Maybe if I paid her...

One good thing about running at this time, it breaks the routine. I get nervous if the boss runs at the same time for several days. It makes him an easy target. We vary the route but even so ... and with Tessa's foot-swallowing trick, the paparazzi will be out in force. Probably more on Saturday than right now. Although I don't see any of those lazy fuckers getting up before dawn.

He seems in a much better mood on the way to the office, so I can only assume Ms. Alvarez has deigned to send him an email, although he looks preoccupied, not his usual bastard self.

The day drags. The only entertainment is watching Tessa try to avoid Ryan's icy stare and get back in his good graces. It seems unlikely—not this side of the century. I wouldn't want to mess with Ryan. I reckon he could kneecap a guy from a thousand yards just by throwing him a harsh look. Which is how he's managed to keep a job as Anderson's P.A. for so long. The effete gay thing is just an act with him: you could freeze ice cubes on his ass when he's pissed. Trouble is, he'd like it. Ryan is my kind of gay. I mean guy.

The boss insists on another long run at lunchtime. It makes me laugh my ass off in a strong-silent-type sort of way when I see half the female employees hanging around in the lobby just to see the boss returning all sweaty. Dream on, ladies; it ain't never gonna happen. There's even one there his grandmother's age. Don't these women have any shame lusting after a guy of thirty? Nope. None. Zilch. Nada. Zip. Dumb question.

Shortly after lunch, Pam comes over to my office and knocks on the door.

"You got a minute, Trainer?"

"Sure, Pam. What do you need?"

She comes in and closes the door. *Hmm.* She wants privacy, and I'm assuming it's not for my dazzling good looks.

"What's up with Devon? He's been on a rampage through the building for the last half an hour. I'm surprised the place isn't on lockdown. Howard has threatened to quit and nothing usually bothers him. Tessa is crying, although that's nothing new, and Joyce in PR has had to order in Krispy Kreme for the whole floor to avoid a mass walkout. I need to know what's going on. I don't think it's anything to do with business, but if it is..."

"Pam, you know I can't talk to you about the boss."

"Don't give me that bullshit, Trainer. I've known him for nearly nine years and I've *never* seen him like this. I need to know what the problem is."

She's right. She needs to know, but I really don't want to be the snitch. I take a deep breath.

"You signed off Ms. Alvarez's vacation request."

"For a long weekend! Not a month in Maui! Really? This is what's gotten Devon bent out of shape?"

"Yup."

"Oh. Well, first love and all that. Okay, nothing for me to worry about. At least, I don't think so." She frowns as she walks away. "Well, well, well, Devon in love. This should be interesting."

Yeah, and the Chinese have a curse: May you live in interesting times.

Chapter Ten

HAPPY FAMILIES

My little girl is going to be eight years-old tomorrow. I can't believe so much time has passed since I held her in my arms for the first time.

As always, my ex is making it difficult for me to see Lilly. I know she's having a party, and I know that having her friends over is more important than seeing her old man, but I want to be there.

Carla isn't happy, but what's new?

"It's ridiculous! She won't have time to talk to you, she'll be with her friends. You'll be asking her to choose between them and you and that's not fair, especially on her birthday!"

"Jeez, I'm not asking her to *choose* because I'll be right there, *just like you*. I'm not saying I'll make her leave the party, I just want to be there."

In the end, I tune out and let her rant on. I'm going to be there whatever she says.

"You can't just come into *my* home whenever you feel like it, Justin!"

I bite back the retort that I pay for the damn place, because I know that's what she wants. Her favorite trick is to escalate any argument so I end up acting like a prick. I figured that out years ago, but sometimes it's hard to stay silent.

Before I hang up on her, I toss out a grenade, "And I'm bringing a cake."

As she hisses and spits, I end the call with a smile on my face.

Rachel has been working on the most amazing cake for days now. It's in two layers, like a wedding cake, but in different shades of pink, with white and silver decorations. It looks a bit like Elsa's ice castle. And yeah, it bothers me that I can recognize it.

Rachel helped me wrap the bike, too, adding a large pink and white ribbon with a ridiculously enormous bow. All this pink—feels like it sucks the testosterone out of a man.

I pull Rachel to me tightly, so fucking thankful that I took a job with a weird, fucked up, billionaire from New York.

The next day, I head out after prepping my stand-in for the boss's driving duties. He's got two meetings across town and a fundraiser tonight, but Mason has hired a guy that did stand-in last year when the very whacked out former fuck-buddy of the boss was on the loose. Even thinking about Van Sant brings back very fucking bad memories.

John Evans is former 101st Airborne, tough, handy and good at his job. He reminds me of me.

I've been thinking for a while that the boss is going to need more protection than one man can offer, especially if he and Ms. Alvarez become ... whatever they become. Because I know for a fact that the boss will put her safety before his own—and one man can't watch two people.

"Evans, how you doing?"

"Good, T. You? Any red flags for Anderson this week?"

See? Right to the point.

"Nope. Mason has the latest intel. It should be cool."

He flicks me an ironic salute and gets to work.

Feeling like I can leave Anderson in safe hands, I ignore Evans' raised eyebrows as I carry Lilly's bike down to the Rover.

The cake is next, and by now Evans is full out laughing at me.

I mutter something about 'Chicken Man' which is a derogatory name for his old Army division because their badge is a bald eagle, but he's grinning like an asshole so I load the cake into the car and give him the bird with both hands.

The drive up to rural Connecticut goes smoothly, but when I arrive at the house, parking isn't easy because the driveway and road is full of minivans and family hatchbacks. Once I open the car door, I can hear the party in full swing.

Ariana Grande rises above the shrill voices of two dozen kids and their parents. Despite the cool weather, I'd guess that most of them are in the backyard.

I wrestle the wrapped bike out of the trunk, swearing when I rip the paper in two places. Ah hell, it's gonna get ripped off anyway. So I lean it against the garage door and go back for the cake. I have to hold it carefully or Rachel warned it would slide right off the base and I'm not going to let that happen to a work of art.

I knock on the door with some difficulty but I guess no one can hear me over the ruckus, so I walk around to the backyard.

Several little girls see the cake and start squealing which draws Lilly's attention. She's been standing in the center of them like the Queen Bee, but when she sees me her eyes light up and she runs toward me.

I have to raise the cake above her head and hug her with one arm while she jumps up and down excitedly. It's touch and go whether the cake will make it, but eventually two of the mothers come over and take it off my hands.

I can see Carla watching me, her lips twisting with distaste as she walks over, her face as friendly as a bulldog chewing on a wasp..

"You always have to make an entrance, don't you!" she hisses.

"I brought a cake," I say reasonably, then ignore her, picking up Lilly and hugging her tightly while she pats my short hair.

"It's like fur, Daddy," she giggles.

I woof like a dog and she shrieks. Her little friends do the same and my ears start ringing.

I put her down and turn around to see that Carla has taken charge of the cake. She's set it on a low table and hasn't noticed that some of the younger kids are digging into it with their bare hands. One of the mothers looks horrified and Carla suddenly realizes what's happening and yells at the kids, but the damage is done and the fairytale castle is ruined.

A hot flare of anger rushes through me. Carla's face flushes and she hastily carries the cake into the kitchen, promising to cut it up for everyone. It feels like she did it deliberately, but I know she wouldn't want to hurt our daughter like that.

Lilly looks distraught and I only just manage to avert tears by showing her the bike.

Soon, pink and silver paper is scattered over the grass and the large bow has been tied around a tree.

"I love it, Daddy!" she yells. "It's so cool! Pink is my favorite color!"

"Yeah?" I pretend to be surprised. "I thought it was brown."

She wrinkles her nose.

"Or maybe khaki."

"You're being silly, Daddy," she says accurately, and I laugh with her.

Carla comes and stands next to me as Lilly wobbles around the yard on her new bike, the wheels bumping over the uneven turf.

"That's an expensive bike," she says, her voice critical, as always.

I don't bother to tell her that the GPS tracker that I attached to it bumped up the price by a hundred and fifty dollars.

"You can't buy her love," she sniffs.

I eye the mountain of presents and torn wrapping paper that had been piled up before I arrived.

"I know that. Do you?"

Her cheeks redden with resentment, and I can see we're heading for another argument. I need to back down.

"You're a good mom, Carla."

Her eyes widen and she stares at me, clearly surprised. Then her gaze narrow and she turns on her heel and leaves me standing.

I discreetly test that the tracker is working. I thought about giving Lilly a piece of jewelry with a tracking device so she'd always have it on her. But the only thing a school would allow a kid her age to wear is a Cross, and I know Carla wouldn't believe that it was just something I liked. She knows that me and God haven't talked in a while. Not since Aiden died.

Carla says that Lilly is getting her ears pierced soon. My baby is growing up fast and I'm not sure how I feel about that, but at least I can put in an order for some *very* special earrings with GPS tracking.

I take a can of Pepsi and go sit with the only other guy who's at the party.

He seems at home with the mothers and it turns out that his wife is a pediatrician who earns more than he could as a high school Math teacher, so he's being daddy daycare while she goes out to work. He seems cool with it.

I wonder what it would be like to have Lilly live with me 24/7. The old familiar tug of guilt pulls at my gut.

I stay for a couple of hours, storing up precious memories of my daughter's birthday, eat some amazing cake, and head home trying to think up a good enough lie to tell Rachel about why I don't have a photo of Lilly with the princess cake.

Chapter Eleven

BRIDESMAIDS

The boss is going to a wedding in the Bronx as Ms. Alvarez's date, which means that *I'm* going, too. And since the boss's girlfriend doesn't want anyone to know that he's like, rich, and that I'm, like, the bodyguard, Rachel is coming with me.

And yeah, like, she really did say it like that.

There's nothing about this that I like.

Double-dating with the boss? That wasn't on my to-do list in this lifetime.

And I have no idea how she's explaining away two extra plus-ones to the bride and groom.

"Don't be so grumpy, Justin. It'll be fun!"

I glare at Rachel as she smirks back.

"First, it's work, and that's never fun. Second, it's a wedding. I fucking hate weddings. All those smiles from people who are thinking, *Nice dress for a 1980s Madonna video* or *More work for the divorce lawyers*. Third, it's work; fourth, the temperature is in the high eighties and I'm wearing a vest and coat..."

"Just like most days, and very handsome you look, too."

"Fifth, it's work; and sixth, it's the Bronx and I don't speak the language."

Rachel laughs out loud, then steps toward me to straighten my tie. It doesn't need straightening but she does it anyway, and it takes the edge off my irritation.

Pissed off at the inevitable, I check my weapon in my holster, knowing that I won't be able to take my jacket off all day. I hope the Grand Slam Banquet Hall has air conditioning.

I also see the look on Rachel's face; she hates me being armed. I wonder if that's part of the reason holding her back from agreeing to marry me. I hope that's not it, because security is my job; carrying a concealed weapon is my job. There's nothing else I'm good at.

I put that thought on hold for another day.

We're just heading to the garage so I can bring the car around front when Ms. Alvarez comes racing down the stairs, definitely not dressed for her friend's wedding and still wearing cut-off shorts and a tank-top, her phone and purse clutched in her hands.

Did zombies in suits invade Manhattan? Did the Yankees win against the Mets? Has she finally realized what a freaky fucker the boss is?

"Rachel! It's a disaster! What am I going to do?"

She hurls herself at Rachel, almost knocking the breath out of her, and looks like she's about to cry.

"Ms. Alvarez! Maria! What's wrong?"

"My cousin Yolanda just called because Jacinta got sick from eating bad shrimp and she's puking everywhere and now she says that Silvia asked Leticia but she's six months pregnant so they've asked me, and I can't say no but Devon is supposed to be coming with me to meet everyone and now it's all a mess!"

I think my ears are bleeding but Rachel takes it in her stride and summarizes the almost incoherent rant.

"The bridesmaid got sick and can't go to the wedding, so the bride wants you to go in her place? Is that right?"

"Yes! But how can I be bridesmaid when Devon is so ... so..."

"When Devon is so what?"

He stalks down the stairs in a tux, adjusting his diamond cufflinks. Flashy bastard.

"When Devon is so what?" he repeats sharply.

Ms. Alvarez spins around and stares at him.

"You're doing it now!"

"What am I doing?"

The boss looks genuinely confused as well as pissed.

"Being all boss-like and intimidating! These are my *friends!* My *family!* And there's *no time!*"

Poor kid. She's about to introduce the Prince of Darkness to her extended family and now she knows she'll have to leave him to his own devices if she does bridesmaid duties. I don't know what she's afraid of? A hellmouth opening up under the banquet hall and disrupting the 'Once upon a Fairytale' themed wedding?

I can't help thinking that would be a relief for everyone.

Rachel grabs Maria's flailing hands and talks calmly.

"It'll be fine. We'll go to the hotel where the bride's staying, you can change into the bridesmaid's dress, and we'll follow you to the wedding. Mr. Anderson will be fine with us. Justin will look after him."

Ms. Alvarez looks relieved then confused.

"That sounds ... wait, who's Justin?"

Rachel raises her eyebrows and looks at me as Ms. Alvarez's gaze flickers between us uncertainly.

"Your name is Justin? I didn't know you had a first name, Trainer. I mean, obviously everyone has a first name, except maybe Eminem or Coolio, but I thought yours would be something like Vlad or Dolph or Kurt, so *Justin* just sounds really ... really ... I'm sorry I called you The Rock but you just..."

The boss steps in, stemming her flurry of words.

"We should leave now."

"Oh God, yes! We should leave right now! I'm panicking, aren't I?"

The boss gives the faintest smile and my teeth ache from the strain of seeing it.

"Yes, but it's going to be fine."

It's not fine.

Ms. Alvarez's bridesmaid's dress makes her look like a giant cupcake. All she needs is a couple of cherries on top of the frosting of hairspray. Her false eyelashes look like two spiders stuck on her eyes, and the pound of makeup is a better disguise than a Freddy Krueger mask.

Rachel elbows me in the ribs when I whisper that. Even the boss looks like he's concentrating on breathing instead of laughing. Ms. Alvarez looks flushed, her cheeks red with embarrassment and humiliation as she precedes the enormous ass of the bride down the aisle. It's possible that the bride has a great ass—just not in that dress.

The groom is sweating bullets. Maybe he's wondering about his wife-to-be's ass, as well.

Rachel is sitting between me and the boss, while I'm on the end of a butt-breaking wooden pew toward the back of the church. At least from here I can keep an eye on who's arriving and who's packing heat, which is at least three guys among the guests. On the plus side, I'd say they have no idea who the boss is and I'd like to keep it that way. That's one advantage of him not doing interviews or being pap-friendly, although he's definitely better known since Aston Van Sant made headlines by getting killed in the boss's lobby.

I did some recon at the church yesterday, so I know that there's a fire exit behind where the priest puts his robes on, and another door that's kept locked—I checked. There's room for 226 people sitting, although intel states that there are 196 guests on the list.

My mind is on the job, but the boss has his eyes fixed on Ms. Alvarez. He looks like he's deep in thought but whatever he's thinking, doesn't make him smile.

When the priest gets to the blessing, I'm half expecting

lightning to strike the boss or the Holy water to boil, but nah, it's just a set or words.

I don't know why I'm disappointed.

At the end of the wedding Mass, we all shuffle outside into the scorching sun. Ms. Alvarez has wedding duties but finally, photographs and brides' train arranged, she corrals three teenage boys with the help of an elderly man in a worn-looking suit, and drags them over to meet us.

"Devon, this my *abuelo* Javier Alvarez, and these are my brothers, Joachim, Francisco and Juan. Everyone, this is my boyfriend, and, um, friends from work, Rachel and Tr— Justin."

The boss shakes the old man's hand, his expression grave, then shakes hands silently with the boys.

They look wary, as if his silence among all the noise and laughter is abnormal. They wouldn't be wrong.

Rachel saves the day by charming the old man and asking the boys questions about themselves.

I find out that the eldest, Joe, boxes, and I do the boss a solid when I tell the kid that Anderson boxes with Enrico Basqiat, former Light Heavyweight National Amateur Champion, and also from the Bronx.

From that moment on, the boss removes the silver-plated stick from his ass and manages to mimic a human being. Ms. Alvarez beams in relief.

Then in a chaotic display of color and noise, car horns blaring in the afternoon sunshine, we head in convoy to the Grand Slam Banquet Hall.

"Sir, if you could wait in the car with Ms. Smith while I check the place out."

I phrase it as a suggestion because I'm as polite as shit, but it's really an order.

Anderson leans back in the seat and nods.

When I walk inside, my jaw falls open and I have to close my mouth quickly with a loud click. The decoration is ... something else. I can't help thinking that Lilly would love the explosion of pink ribbon and glitter, but she's eight. A Disney castle in cardboard stands at one end of the room with a pair of pink velvet and gold thrones in front of it.

My lips twitch when I think how much the boss is going to love this. Not.

But I've located the fire exit as well as a secondary exit through the kitchen. The threat level is minimal since the buffet looks more dangerous than any of the guests. It's a heart attack on pink linen: *empanadas*, *taquitos*, grilled marinated skirt steak, *tamales*, *quesadillas*, as well as *ceviche*, *guacamole*, *taco* salad, and the *tres leches* cake that I know from experience is so sweet, your teeth melt, along with *cajeta* Mexican caramel sauce. I can't wait to get stuck in.

When I return to the Rover, the boss opens the door and slides out, then holds his hand to help Rachel. My blood boils at that simple gesture because it's *my* fucking job!

Rachel rests her hand on my arm when she sees the look on my face, and Anderson raises an eyebrow.

"Trainer, for the purposes of this function, I think you should use my first name."

When Hell freezes over, fucker!

"Yes, sir," I snap back.

His eyes flash with annoyance, but he doesn't challenge me and walks into the building ahead of us.

Rachel grabs my arm, holding me back.

"What was that all about?"

"Anderson putting his hands on you."

"Justin, really!"

But I can see the quiet smile that she can't quite hide.

We enter the room and I see the boss's eyes widen at the blast of noise and color inside.

"Oh my!" Rachel says with her usual understatement.

"I thought we could have this for our wedding," I say casually, handing her a glass of pink Prosecco.

She blinks rapidly, uncertain whether or not I'm joking.

I lead the boss to our table and wedge him in the corner to

protect him from the avaricious eyes of the guests and other bridesmaids. A large-breasted woman in a shiny blue dress marches up to us, ignoring Rachel. Luckily, I don't have to effect evasive manoeuvers because Ms. Alvarez spots her first.

"Yo, Rosita. That's my boyfriend." Then pointing at me and Rachel, "And that's *her* boyfriend."

"Chill, Maria! I was only gonna ask them to dance, not mess with yous."

"Yeah, right. That's what you said about my high school prom date and two weeks later you were shacked up with him."

The woman leaves in a huff.

"Huh, she thinks who she is!"

Devon takes Ms. Alvarez's hand and kisses it sweetly.

"It would be my honor to dance with *you*."

He leads her to the dance floor, and Ms. Alvarez's grandfather nods with approval.

Rachel smiles, then stands.

"Come on, handsome. Your turn to impress me."

"I have to keep an eye on the boss."

"Great! You'll have the best view from the dance floor."

I don't think Rachel is taking my surveillance duties seriously, but I follow her all the same. I'll always follow her.

Ms. Alvarez and the boss are lost in their little cocoon, occasionally interrupted by her friends, all curious as hell to meet her boyfriend. The boss is grave and formal with them all, intimidating the shit out of them, but I can see that they're impressed, too.

Rachel tugs on my sleeve, drawing my attention back to her.

"Relax, Sarge. No insurgents here tonight."

Her words have the opposite effect of the one she wanted, and I stiffen immediately. Fuck, the power of words to bring back bad memories.

"Oh, Justin, I'm so sorry! That was thoughtless of me!"

I force myself to relax and run a finger down her cheek.

"It's fine, baby. So, I thought I'd book this place for our wedding. Whaddya say?"

She raises her eyebrows then smiles, her baby blues glinting with humor.

"Well, the setting certainly suits you."

I nearly swallow my tongue but then checkmate her.

"If it'll make you say yes, baby, you can have any wedding you want."

Her eyes cloud over and she looks away.

"Can we discuss this another time, please, Justin?"

I'm disappointed, but I try to hide it.

"Sure, baby. Whatever you want."

I thought weddings made chicks want to get married. It seems to be having the opposite effect on Rachel. Maybe all the pink is making her nauseous.

When the song ends, we go back to sit at our assigned table and the old man joins us. It seems that interviewing the boss for the position of his precious granddaughter's boyfriend is the first item on the agenda.

"So, Devon, Maria tells me that you're a businessman."

"*Abuelo!*" Maria hisses. "You promised you wouldn't do this!"

The boss takes her hand.

"It's fine, Maria. Of course your grandfather wants to know about me. Yes, I have my own businesses, DMA Solutions. We're involved in several new technologies: solar energy, wind power, wave power, alternative power sources, and GM farming. I'm also investing in several traditional areas to diversify, including ship building, and I've invested in carbon neutral construction of homes and office buildings."

I can see that Maria's grandfather is taken aback, but trying to sound unimpressed.

"That's good business sense. How many men do you have working for you?"

"Men *and* women," Maria says quickly and with a hint of annoyance.

The old man waves his hand dismissively.

"Of course, *nieta*, let the man speak."

"DMA Solutions has in the region of 30,000 employees."

The old man was about to take a sip of the Prosecco but ends up choking on the bubbles, and Maria leaps to her feet, as if prepared to perform the Heimlich Manoeuver.

"I'm fine! I'm fine!" he coughs and wheezes.

The boss looks on with a concerned expression, although he seems more worried about Maria's reaction than her grandfather choking in front of him.

Eventually, the old man wipes his eyes and glares at Maria.

"You did not tell me that Devon was such an important man!"

Maria rolls her eyes.

"Because I knew you'd overreact." And then more quietly. "I'm not dating him for his money, *Abuelo*. Did you know that his mother, Gloria, is from the Bronx? Like me."

The old man stares at her thoughtfully, then turns to me.

"And your role is?"

"Security advisor," I say smoothly.

"Ah."

There's a short silence as he gazes at me with calculating eyes, then the boss speaks.

"I have been fortunate in my business dealings and have been able to develop my interest in green technologies, but I have learned that without someone to share my life with, I have been poor indeed. Your granddaughter is very important to me, Mr. Alvarez."

Maria's smile goes from tentative to beaming, and Rachel clutches my hand, tears glistening in her eyes.

Jeez, the flood of estrogen is almost more than male flesh and blood can stand.

The old man inclines his head in acknowledgement."

"I'm pleased to hear that. She's a good girl. Her family is very protective of her since her illness, as you can imagine."

The blood trains from Maria's face, leaving her a sickly yellow color.

"*Abuelo! You promised!*"

The old man looks guilty and then annoyed.

"Maria! You have not told this young man something so important. He should know!"

"Yes, but it wasn't your job to tell him!"

She gets up from the table abruptly, shaking off the boss's hand.

Rachel stands up quickly.

"I'll go," and she hurries after Maria.

There's an uncomfortable pause as Anderson's dark eyes fix on the old man as a dull flush rises in his wrinkled cheeks.

"I ... I thought she would have told you."

"It appears not," says the boss icily.

At that moment Joachim wanders over.

"Are you talking about when Maria had leukemia?"

I see the boss grip the edge of the table.

"Leukemia?"

He gives the boss a penetrating look, and for a moment I think he won't continue, but then he does.

"Yeah, it was seven years ago, when she was a senior in High School. She was in the hospital on and off for over a year, but she's okay now." He gives a warm smile. "She says nothing is stopping her anymore—she wants to do everything. Did you see her at the comedy club yet? I've seen her practice her routine at home—she's terrible!"

He gives a happy grin, obviously proud of his sister.

And it all clicks into place. When Maria had her first interview with Anderson, she said that she *didn't want to be scared anymore.*

That's why she does things that challenge her. That's why the crazy kid wants to go skydiving. Although dating the Prince of Pain probably has the same risk to adrenaline ratio.

Twenty minutes later, Maria returns, her eyes a little puffy from crying, but she has a determined look on her face.

"I assume *Abuelo* has told you that I was sick?"

"Maria, it doesn't matter..." the boss begins.

"Yes, it does matter. I'll tell you everything. I was going to anyway ... I just didn't want it to change how you look at me."

"It won't."

"It will, it always does. I've seen people get that pitying look on their faces. I just ... I didn't want to see that on yours."

"Maria..."

"Let me finish. Seven years ago, I started feeling tired all the time. Mom took me to my doctor for a blood test, and they found that my white blood cells were ... abnormal. I had Acute Myeloid Leukemia. I seemed to go into remission after the first induction, the first round of chemo, but then it came back and I had to go through it all again. It was ... hard ... on my whole family. And then my parents were killed by a drunk driver when they were walking home from church one night." She wipes her eyes. "They'd been to pray that I wouldn't get sick again. After ... well, I had more chemo and I've been in remission for over three years now."

And she turns to look at the boss, her eyes glistening with tears.

"But Dev, it means that in all likelihood, I'm infertile. The chances of me having a child are slim to non-existent and I know how important family is to you, I know that."

The boss doesn't say anything, but Rachel grasps Maria's hand, and they share a look. My heart lurches painfully. Is that what Rachel wants, too? Does she want to have children? Would I want to be a father again?

It's scary as hell, but the honest answer is yes: if the kid was with Rachel, I'd definitely want that.

The boss still hasn't moved.

"Devon, say something, please!"

Maria sounds desperate. Finally, he speaks.

"I know I'm not the easiest man to be with, Maria. But you have accepted me in every possible way. Why do you think this would change anything? You know how I feel about you. This changes nothing."

And that's when Rachel pulls at my sleeve, leading me away.

I watch from a distance, because that's my job. The boss has arm around Ms. Alvarez and they're talking quietly.

I look down at Rachel. She doesn't speak but leans her head on my chest as we sway slowly to a rhythm that has nothing to do with the music playing over the speakers.

Throughout the evening, the rest of Maria's friends and family, cousins, uncles, aunts, , second cousins, great aunts and a great uncle, come to meet the boss. They don't know who he is exactly, but they sense he's not one of them. And still, he draws them to him. His icy politeness ought to drive them away, but it's that pesky charisma of his—he charms them all.

Bastard.

But at least the boss has survived his first wedding in the Bronx. And I can't help thinking that if little Ms. Alvarez manages to put up with his jaded heart, there might be another wedding.

Or it could be his funeral.

I'm known for my optimism.

Chapter Twelve

GAMES PEOPLE PLAY

The days of early summer have long gone, turning into one scorching hot July day after another. Time passes in relative peace and Rachel has started to spend most of her weekends at Wolf Point with me. Finally.

The boss and Ms. Alvarez are still acting like a couple of teenagers, texting each other day and night. But that's kind of apt when I think about the boss. He's never been on dates before, never taken a girl home. Nope, no homecoming dance or prom for Anderson. He's lived his life isolated from anything real. Why? I'm not sure, although I have several theories.

Ms. Alvarez banned him from stalking her at work. I happen to know this because Anderson was cursing blue and green when she told him. He argued that he's the boss so he can make the rules. She yelled back that she had a life and was trying to have a career and he had to let her do it on her own terms and own talent. He sulked for 72 hours but gave in eventually. He does that a lot around Ms. Alvarez—the sulking followed by the giving in.

So most days they don't see each other at DMA Tower. Rachel says they talk every night that Ms. Alvarez doesn't spend at the house, as well as all of those texts.

He wants her to move in. She's resisting because she says her grandfather is too old to take on the responsibility of three teenage boys by himself.

It hardly seems worth the argument, seeing as Maria has been spending so much time at Wolf Point, she may as well change the address on her driver's license right away.

He hasn't mentioned marrying her, but Rachel says it's inevitable. I'm still undecided, but when the boss makes a pit stop at the Cartier franchise in Saks, I think she might be right.

The sales area has pink marble floors and gilt wall sconces. Kind of reminds me of a high class whorehouse that I saw in Bangkok once when I was guarding a client.

I nod at the security guard as a professional courtesy. He's checking to see if I'm carrying. Pu-leeze: this is a custom-made suit —if you can tell I'm packing, I'd have to shoot my tailor.

I can also see what he's thinking: *You only look after one guy—I have a whole store full of expensive jewelry.*

Maybe he'd like to try being personal security for billions of dollars' worth of a walking, talking, fucking Mount Vesuvius.

Anderson glances at the engagement rings but ends up picking out a classy diamond bracelet. I'd bet my year's salary that it's not for his mother or sister.

I stare around at the stunning displays of watches, rings, earrings, cufflinks, pendants, chains and necklaces. For the briefest of moments I feel regret that there's nothing in here that I could afford to buy for Rachel. This store is for the seriously wealthy. But would I want all the shit that goes with it? No. I can walk away from this game at any time: Anderson can't.

But I would like to take her away somewhere warm and sunny and expensive. She deserves the best that life has to offer. Which isn't me. But thankfully she has low standards.

And she's great with Lilly. I couldn't be serious about any woman who didn't love my kid. I'm very serious about Rachel.

They've met three times now, well, twice more since Christmas Eve. That seems like a lifetime ago. The first official date was a trip to the zoo, and last month we took her to a pizza parlor and then played mini golf.

I'd like to have a family summer vacation for the three of us, but the boss might have to make a last-minute trip to Taiwan, so I can't give Carla a firm date. She thinks I'm being difficult just for the hell of it.

I'm pretty certain that she's seeing someone. She's not admitting it, of course. Not that I care who she sees, except that if it's a guy who's going to be around Lilly, I want to check him the fuck out.

Rachel said that Lilly is already talking about cute boys in her class—she's only just eight, for fuck's sake! If I have anything to do with it, she'll have no dates until she's graduated college. In fact, I'm seriously thinking about staking out her first boyfriend in the front yard as a warning to the others.

I'm guessing Maria's grandfather would feel the same if he knew Anderson's secrets.

And the boss's past is about to catch up with him one Thursday evening after dinner.

I get to have a lot more dinners at home with Rachel now that the boss's schedule is so different. I should thank Ms. Alvarez for that one day.

I'm vegging out on the sofa with Rachel, my eyes closed as she runs her fingers through my hair, something that she knows renders me comatose, when my phone beeps, informing me that someone has entered the building using the boss's private entrance code which was just changed.

"What's wrong, Justin?"

"Not sure. A visitor. Back in a minute."

I don't have time to retrieve my Smith & Wesson from my wall safe and that pisses me off. It's a timely reminder that I should be prepared 24/7. I'm getting soft, which means I'm getting careless. I've been in this job too damn long. The thought shakes me up.

When I reach the entrance, Frederick Landon has already

exited the elevator and is strolling through the living room, a well-dressed reptile.

"Well, well, well. If it isn't the bodyguard," he laughs mirthlessly. "Forgive me for not remembering your name, but Devon casts a wide shadow. Do you like being in it all the time?"

I don't reply because if I react, then it's given him what he wants. Maybe the boss will tell me to throw this basking shark out on his bony ass. Guess I'll find out.

"Mr. Anderson and Ms. Alvarez are in the TV room. I'll let him know you're here."

"Who? Oh, another Spic. Evidently it runs in the family."

His lips turn white as he presses them together, and I gather that the news isn't welcome. It interests me because it means that the boss hasn't updated Landon on his activities. That gives me a warm glow.

Landon probably smirks into one of those big ole mirrors hoping an inanimate object will tell him that he's the fairest of them all. Yeah, and I'm auditioning for *America's Next Top Model* wearing a Stars and Stripes Speedo.

I'll drag the bastard out of here by his fucking cravat if he so much as lays a finger on Ms. Alvarez.

Landon starts toward the TV room when I block his route.

"If you'll wait here, sir, I'll let Mr. Anderson know you're wishing to speak with him."

"No need," he sneers, trying to step past me. "I've seen Devon *in flagrante delicto* more times than you've shot your pistol."

He smirks at his joke, but I just give him the blank stare that I reserve for men I'm not allowed to punch.

"Wait here."

He huffs with frustration but has no choice.

I phone the boss who is definitely *not* happy to hear the news that his old friend has dropped in.

I decide to lurk in case I'm required for the very serious pleasure of applying the toe of my boot to Landon's bony ass as I kick him out.

The boss stalks into the living room looking stressed, glancing at me as I stare back impassively. Nevertheless, my expression says, *Over to you.*

"Frederick? Why didn't you tell me you were going to drop by?"

"Maybe I wasn't aware that an old friend needed an invitation," he replies tightly.

The boss is trying not to appear flustered but I see the muscles in his jaw jump as he clamps his teeth together.

Shaking my head, I start to leave the room, but bump into Ms. Alvarez.

She looks worried, and I don't know whether it's the sight of me smiling, or the thought of Gomez Addams lurking in the living room with Uncle Fester.

"Who is it, Trainer?"

"A Mr. Landon—I'm told he's a friend of Mr. Anderson's father."

She gives a small 'oh' of recognition, then a determined expression sweeps over her face and she marches into the living room.

I hesitate for half a second, then follow her.

"I have *company*, Frederick."

At least the boss sounds pissed, but Landon waves a hand dismissively.

"The little girl, I know. The muscle informed me."

Harsh words *and* sarcasm? Aw, does that mean we can't be friends? Thank fuck for that.

"The muscle has a name—Justin Trainer—and I'm not a little girl: I'm 24 and my name is Maria Alvarez."

Landon turns with a sneer on his face.

"How delightful. You must forgive me, my dear. I forget that you young people like to sound older, but believe me, that all changes once you hit forty. Well, I'm Frederick Landon, an *old friend* of Devon's father—and a very close friend of Devon, of course."

He extends his hand and Ms. Alvarez shakes it, turning red when Landon not very discreetly wipes his fingers with a handkerchief afterwards.

The boss stands between them uncertainly. *Why the hell isn't he kicking him out?*

There's a long, ominous pause, and the girl from the Bronx shows that she has better manners than either of these Hamptons inhabitants.

"Would you like a drink, Mr. Landon?" Ms. Alvarez says at last, breaking the heavy silence.

"How sweet of you to offer me a drink in Devon's home. But I suppose that's your service skills coming to the fore."

Ms. Alvarez flushes but remains cool.

"Yes, I did some waitressing when I was in college—you meet all sorts doing a job like that. It certainly teaches tolerance."

Anderson's watching them like a tennis match, or possibly one of those slo-mo car crashes that you see on TV.

Landon arranges himself on one corner of the sofa, crossing his legs while ensuring that the sharp creases in his five-thousand dollar suit aren't wrinkled.

"Devon knows what I like."

And I don't think he just means how to fix a dry martini.

And then I realize what this scene reminds me of: the time Carla met my old girlfriend from high school. Meagan was a nice girl and she ended up marrying one of the lumber men in our old town. But Carla acted like Landon is now—a hissing, snarling, scratching alley cat. It wasn't pretty, 'cause Meagan wasn't a pushover either.

Since the boss decides to pour Landon a glass of wine, I decide to leave them to it. If eviction is required later, he can beep me.

I head back to the staff wing, vaguely depressed. When the hell is the boss going to get rid of Landon?

"Who was it, Justin?"

"Frederick Landon."

"Ugh, that awful man. Why is *he* here?"

"I have no idea, but it looked like the first act of Gunfight at the OK Corral out there. Except the boss was pouring him wine and

Landon was spitting out the bullets. Ms. Alvarez was deciding which kneecap to aim for."

Rachel shakes her head sadly. I know how she feels.

I don't know what time Landon leaves, but it was late.

The next morning, the boss is surly and morose; Ms. Alvarez is almost mute, staring out of the car window as I drive them to work.

"I guess I'll see you," she says quietly.

"Fine," snaps the boss.

I open the door for her and she raises sad eyes to mine.

"Thanks, Trainer. Say bye to Rachel for me."

"I will, Ms. Alvarez. Enjoy your weekend."

She gives me a weak smile as the boss scowls. I know she has plans to spend some time with her brothers, time that doesn't include the boss.

Who'd have thought the former bootneck was giving the billionaire socialite tips on good manners? He's such an asshole.

The boss seems to relax slightly as we head home after work that evening. He pulls out his cell, and I'm really hoping he's not going to call Ms. Alvarez. I hate to blush and drive.

"Frederick ... yes. What? No ... are you free for dinner tonight? Eight? Good. I'll pick you up ... French. Okay."

I groan inwardly. How fucking dumb can you get? His girlfriend is busy for one weekend and the first thing he does is arrange to hook up with De Sade's second cousin. I really hope Ms. Alvarez doesn't find out about this because if she does, she'll kick the boss's sorry ass out of the state—in a quiet, non-violent sort of way. And, frankly, he'll fucking deserve it.

I admit I may not be one of those 'New Men' that Rachel tells me she's read about in magazines—Neanderthal seems to be one of her favorite adjectives when it comes to me, I have no fucking idea why—but even I'm not dumb enough to do what the boss is doing. And I have a horrible feeling he'll just go ahead and tell Ms. Alvarez that he's seeing Satan's chief cheerleader, because when it comes to reading women's feelings, the boss is still at the starting gate. Sure, he can make them come like the Orient Express, but he still doesn't know fuck-all about women.

I drop him at the entrance to Wolf Point then go park the Rover.

Rachel is in the staff kitchen and something smells really good —and it's not the baked salmon dinner.

I wrap my arms around her and kiss the back of her neck.

"Justin! I'm cooking!"

"So am I, baby. Warming up nicely."

She laughs and pulls free.

"How was your day?"

I shrug.

"Pam wanted to know why the boss was acting so weird again."

"What did you tell her?"

"She was freaking out that it was something to do with the business end of things. I told her that his girlfriend was busy this weekend, and let her work out the rest for herself."

She leans against me, and I enjoy the warmth of her body against mine.

"It's just you and me tonight, baby. The boss is going out."

"Oh! There was nothing on the calendar?"

"He's going out for dinner. With that Landon motherf— creep."

"*That man!*"

She folds her arms and looks pissed.

Yup. Pretty much the same reaction I had.

"I don't know what he sees in that *person*. Well, I hope Ms. Alvarez doesn't find out."

"Baby, he'll probably just tell her."

She gapes at me.

"Surely not!" She stops and purses her lips as I watch her curiously. "Oh, honestly! Sometimes I wonder about Mr. Anderson!"

"You, me, and half the western hemisphere, baby."

I run my hand up her thigh, tugging her skirt so that it's resting next to the top of her thigh highs.

"Got the whole evening to ourselves, baby."

She smiles and runs her hands over my hips giving my ass a good squeeze. I flex into her so she can feel my growing interest.

And I don't care that I'm so hungry my stomach thinks my throat has been cut, and I don't care that the boss is still in the building. I sweep Rachel over my shoulder and sprint to the bedroom with every intention of showing her who is on top in this relationship.

Or maybe we can take turns.

Chapter Thirteen

ENDGAME

The boss has dinner with Landon—it doesn't make him happy. What a shocker. Maybe I should go into the shrink business but I reckon anyone with any sense could tell him that Landon messes with his mind. This Stockholm Syndrome shit has a lot to answer for. And if it really is just a case of the boss meeting up with a guy, someone he later went on to have a sexual relationship with, riddle me this: Landon is supposed to have taught the boss to play piano —his whole family talks about what an amazing pianist Anderson is; he has a very fucking expensive Steinway Grand Piano in his living room, *and he never plays it.*

Rachel dusts that damn great slab of mahogany and ivory twice a week: he *never* touches it; never even looks at it, as far as I can tell.

That to me says it's a huge chunk of grief and guilt tied like a millstone around his neck while he tries to swim the Hudson River. *So why keep it?* But he won't get rid of it—or Landon.

The boss makes no sense—least of all to himself.

But the weekend finally winds to its weary end and Ms. Alvarez has reasserted visiting rights. But there's a tension in the air that wasn't here before, and she smiles less than she used to.

It's none of my business, but it pisses me off all the same.

I sleep badly, so lurk in the CCTV room instead when my tossing and turning is stopping Rachel from getting a solid seven hours.

At least Anderson has canceled the morning run.

At 6AM, I take a shower. When I look in the mirror, I realize that I'm beginning to resemble an extra in one of those damn zombie movies: bloodshot eyes—*check*; drawn, haggard face—*check*; rabid snarl—*check*; snazzy charcoal suit—oh, wait, that's just me.

I head into the main room and really wish I hadn't.

Ms. Alvarez is standing there, looking like she wants to audition for the same zombie movie. It's obvious that she's been crying. Questions wash over me in a red tide of anger. *Has the boss hurt her? Invited her to an orgy? Taken her to his fucking meditation room? That fucker! That lousy fucker!*

"Did you know?" she says, her voice strangled. "Did you know?"

I wish she'd be more specific.

"About his *meditation room?*"

Oh.

She spits out the words, then her rage fades suddenly and she just sounds tired.

"Of course you know. You live here, you've lived with him for months, years, maybe. Of course you know."

She slumps onto the sofa, her hands covering her face.

"I don't know how to do this. I don't know what to say to him, how I can make it better. Everyone says that when you meet a guy you want to change him, but people never really change. I didn't want to change Devon! I liked him just the way he was! I mean, I thought I did. But ... God, is there more? The sex parties at the Farm and now that ... that terrible room? Am I going to keep finding out that there's more, or worse? Something even darker? Because I don't know if I'm strong enough. I don't think I can do this."

She stares up at me, her eyes glassy with tears as she looks for answers she won't want to hear.

"Ms. Alvarez, this is a conversation for you to have with Mr. Anderson. But ... if it helps ... he *has* changed since he met you. For the better, ma'am."

She blinks back tears, surprise and confusion battling in her expression.

"Thank you, Trainer. Thank you, I ... well, thank you."

The boss walks into the room, his face defeated, his icy control gone.

"Maria, please..."

She holds up her hands like a traffic cop.

"Dev, no. I need to think about this. I don't understand why you do ... that. I think you need help and I don't think I can be the one to help you. I wish I could, but..."

"Maria, you do help," he says quietly, and I know he's telling the truth.

She shakes her head.

"You are not my only responsibility, Devon. I have three younger brothers—two of them are still at high school. *They* need me. *Abuelo* needs me. You're a grown man—you have to figure this out for yourself."

"I'm trying, Maria, I am. I ... I see a therapist."

"Oh ... a psychiatrist?"

"A sex therapist."

"A *sex* therapist? But ... you're not ... you don't ... you always ... oh my God, were you ... *abused?*"

She reaches out to touch his cheek, and I have to look away. It's too personal, but there's no way I can exit the room without drawing attention to myself.

He doesn't reply but she can see the answer in his eyes.

"Oh, Devon! Oh my God!"

She wraps him in her arms and he lets her, holding her gently as if the weight of his arms might be too much.

"I'm glad you're seeing someone, Dev. Does it help?"

He nods.

"Yes, but the meditation room helps, too."

She stiffens and steps backward, his arms falling away from her.

"Really? Beating yourself bloody is *helping?* I think ... I think, Dev, that you've got a long way to go yet. And I don't think that I can..."

"Maria, please. I am getting better. Just ... give me a chance. I'm trying."

"I'm not saying this is goodbye," she whispers, her voice soft with tears. "I'm saying I need *time*. Will you give me time, Devon?"

He nods stiffly, fighting to keep his emotions in check.

She stares at his face, looking for something, but I don't know what.

"Okay," she says, her shoulders slumping. "I'll see you."

The cost of this gilded cage was too high.

But the look on the boss's face shakes me: he's desperate.

I wonder how I'd feel if Rachel ever spoke to me like that. The thought chills my blood.

The world is a cold and lonely place without your soulmate, and without Maria, the boss's world is in danger of spinning into darkness. I know what that's like because I've been there.

And not for the first time, I pity him.

"At least let Trainer take you home."

I've never heard the boss beg before. I don't think *God* has heard the boss beg before.

"I'll bring the car around to the front door, Ms. Alvarez."

I can't bear the tension in the room. And Ms. Alvarez needs a ride.

She glances toward me without meeting my eyes and nods quickly. Then she walks out. She doesn't look back, so she doesn't see the bleakness in Anderson. I look away.

As Ms. Alvarez exits the elevator, I can tell that she's only just holding it together. I open the car door for her and she slides in, blank and wordless.

I head out into the traffic and she's trying hard not to cry, but tears are running down her face.

For only the fourth time in my life, I want to kill someone. The first time was when my bastard of a father hit my mom and I tried to rip his head off; I was fourteen. The second time was in Iraq. Then earlier this year when I saw Rachel tied up, with Van Sant holding a gun to her head. But the fourth time is right now: I want to hurt Anderson as badly as this girl is hurting.

How many more people are going to be broken on his rack? How many more like Aston? How many more like Maria? How many times will Rachel be put in danger because of his fucked up lifestyle. No. It stops here. It stops now, at least for me.

When I get back, I'm giving my notice—and for Rachel, too. I won't have her exposed to this fucked-upness anymore. I know I don't speak for her, but the need to keep her safe is my number one priority—screw job security.

As I help Ms. Alvarez out of the car, she can't meet my eyes. She just shakes her head when I ask if she'd like me to see her up. I watch her struggle to get her key out of her purse, her eyes blurred with tears. Through the small pane of glass in her front door, I see her gripping the doorframe to hold herself up.

"Goodbye, Ms. Alvarez," I say softly.

I need to get back in control, give my notice, pack up my shit—and get the fuck out.

But when the elevator doors open, I don't do any of those things. Anderson is sitting on the floor, his head in his hands. He looks up when he hears me—and I see a broken man.

Maybe it was his own stupidity ... maybe it was his own fucked up, twisted fault. But suddenly all I see is a broken man, a drowning man, a good man who made a mistake. A man who finally found love—and threw it away because he didn't understand what he held before he crushed it.

"I've taken Ms. Alvarez home, sir."

He stares at me like he doesn't understand the words, then nods very slowly.

"Thank you, Trainer."

He looks down, almost puzzled, as if he can't understand why he's on the floor.

I don't reach out my hand to help him up. I watch as he stumbles, off balance. I watch as he straightens slowly, and I watch as he walks away, his hands jammed into his pockets, his head hanging down. But I don't hand in my notice either.

I watch and I listen.

It's as if I can hear the sound of his heart splintering.

Chapter Fourteen

THE WELL OF LONELINESS

I feel so fucking useless.

Give me a target, give me something I can aim at, give me an armed insurgent with a Texas-sized death wish, *give me something tangible that I can wrap my hands around and choke the living fuck out of* —*give me SOMETHING I CAN DO.*

Allison is sick, so Rachel has taken some vacation and gone to look after her sister and nieces. I'm stuck with the Leonard Cohen of Lower Manhattan.

I want to be with Rachel but she insisted I stay with the boss. She says it's my job, and it is, but she's my *life*. It kills me that she won't let me be with her. I'm respecting her wishes—that shit is hard—when everything inside is telling me to be with her even when she visits with her sister.

The boss has disappeared into a black pit of despair. He showers and eats, impersonating a human being, then vanishes into his lair.

He's as coldly efficient as ever, dealing with Pam's calls and Howard's emails, but I see the storm raging inside.

I can't help him, and I'm not sure I would if I could. He's

dragging everyone else into his darkening world, and that is un-fucking-acceptable.

Instead, I go to my home office and work through the usual protocols: check CCTV *again*; check the alarms on entrances and exits *again*; check Mason's daily status report *again*. Nothing to raise my pulse, let alone provide a distraction.

Then on Saturday morning, before our run, Anderson comes to my office, lurking at my door like the Grim Reaper's long lost cousin.

"Trainer, I'm going to be doing some ... redecorating."

"Yes, sir?"

"I know it's not in your job description..."

If he's talking interior design, we're in trouble.

"But ... I'd appreciate your help."

Holy shit! The boss is asking me for a favor! Those pigs musta grown feathers over night.

"Sir?"

"I've decided to make some changes. My meditation room..."

He takes a deep breath and I can see how hard this is for him, to let go of this *thing*, this *process*, whatever it is, however it works, it gives him some sort of balance.

But there are other ways to find balance.

"Sir, when I was based in Okinawa, we were encouraged to meet and greet the locals. One of the brass, one of the officers arranged for us to visit a Buddhist monastery for a *meditation* lesson."

I know I've got his attention, so I continue.

"This old monk said he was going to train us to meditate the way he'd been trained by his master as a young man before the War. Hell, he was so old, he could have meant the First World War. So we all went to the meditation room, took off our shoes and socks, thinking it was damn funny, and knelt on tatami mats in complete silence. Then this old monk came up and thwacked us on the back with his bamboo cane to help us focus our minds, that's what he said. And if we moved, he'd do it again. Fucking stung, too, he wasn't taking it easy on us. I'm not sure how it was supposed to help me meditate because all I could think of for the next 20 minutes was how much he'd better not hit me again."

Anderson is frowning, but I also see understanding dawn in his eyes.

"So make it into a Buddhist-style meditation room: tatami mats on the floor, images of mountains on the wall, calming, peaceful." I shrug. "It's worked for those monks for a couple of thousand years —no reason it shouldn't work in Manhattan."

He stands upright and nods his head.

"Thank you, Trainer."

For the rest of the morning, we rip down all those depressing fucking religious messages that reinforce to the boss how fucked up he is, and toss all his whips, belts, floggers and canes. I haul them to the garage and put them in the trunk of the Rover to take to the dump, thus preserving what's left of Anderson's reputation.

Then I order two gallons of white paint and two roller brushes, and the boss and I work side by side, transforming the meditation room into a clean, white cube. No bad memories here.

He doesn't thank me but he doesn't need to. I'd do the same for any guy in my platoon, whether I liked him or not.

Then Anderson orders some tatami mats, and a well-known artist to render the mountains of Hakone onto the wall of his meditation room, with Fuji-san glowing under a red sunset. Apparently it's after the style of Hokusai, but whatever, it looks great.

If the boss still beats himself with a bamboo cane, I hope like fuck it's for the right reasons. Whatever those are.

By Monday, he seems to have reached some equilibrium, but Ms. Alvarez hasn't come back.

And it turns out that our weekend of *Fixer Upper* was the calm before the next storm. There have been so many storms in Manhattan that I'm thinking of relocating to Tornado Alley— Kansas is nice this time of year.

Howard is waiting for the boss in his office, his eyes gleaming with excitement, yesterday's dinner on his t-shirt.

"Boss man! Saruman is hunting the Ring! Price went up to three-hundred-and-fifty Benjamins!"

It takes me a second to realize that he's talking about the blackmailer; Anderson is quicker.

"Can you isolate his IP address?"

"Nah, man, he's bouncing it all over using a satellite relay."

Excuse me while I say, huh?

"But now he's out of his cave, the game is on."

"Did he release another video?"

Howard's smile dissolves.

"Um yeah, but I nuked it before anyone saw it."

"Good work, Howard. Anything else you need?"

"Nah, I'm pulling down some extra juice from the power company, but it'll just look like a power surge."

"You got a name for us, Howard?"

"Other than Saruman?"

"It might come in handy."

"Well, I don't know which ID he'll be living under these days, but he was born Neil Brown. He also goes by Oscar Black, Rufus Lovell and Maryann Summers."

"Okaaaay."

Howard shrugs.

"Dude has issues."

"And where can we find him?"

Howard frowns.

"He'll flip out if he's cornered, and then he'll swarm the boss's home videos all over the internet. If he even suspects that you're within two clicks of him, the guy will implode."

"We need to have eyes on him, Howard, but we won't move without your Bat signal."

Howard rubs his eyebrow with his middle finger. Either he's flipping me off, or just really, really distracted.

"He has an apartment in Princeton, a house in the hills behind the Hollywood sign, and he owns a condo on Cayman Brac."

And here I was thinking that crime doesn't pay.

He wanders out of the office, hitching his pants up and shuffling his feet. Hard to believe that a brain the size of Jupiter is hidden under that home haircut.

"Sir, we need to alert Mason's retrieval team. This guy is a computer geek but he's not working alone. Van Sant or someone connected with the Farm sold or gave those videos to a third party."

Anderson rubs his forehead.

"Fine. Update Mason, but no action until we hear back from Howard."

"Sir."

"And ... we need to increase security at Wolf Point. And Maria, Ms. Alvarez..."

"Yes, sir. John Evans is available full time."

"Good."

Mason has been running down some leads on Neil/Oscar/Rufus/Maryann, but there's still no solid news. With nothing else to go on, all I can do is increase security. Mason has briefed Evans who is now on stand-by 24/7.

One of the staff bedrooms in Wolf Point has been set up so Evans can be available. Rachel is working from Allison's to organize additional hours from the cleaning crew she uses, as well as a guy named Craig, a chef to provide breakfast and an evening meal. He's a nice enough guy, but it's thrown off the dynamics, and the staff wing no longer feels like my home. At least he's only there four nights a week.

Right now, Evans isn't here either, but renting a room in the apartment building opposite Ms. Alvarez.

The whole house feels different. It's Maria—her absence has left a big hole. I realize that I've gotten used to having her around. When she's here, there's always happy, salsa music; the sound of laughter. She's so full of life.

A pulse of anger surges through me as I think how he broke her.

Sex games, BDSM, contracts, subs—it's all shits and giggles until someone gets hurt.

But Maria isn't the only one suffering. As long as I've known Anderson, I've never seen him like this. He had three coping mechanisms for dealing with bad days: fucking at the Farm, hitting the gym and making Basqiat earn his money by getting the crap beaten out of him in the boxing ring, or beating the crap out of himself in the meditation room. Kind of ironic, when you think about it.

Right now, he's stopped the orgies at the Farm, redecorated the meditation room, and Basquiat isn't around because he's commentating on a big throw-down in Vegas.

It makes me nervous. My job is based on predicting the unpredictable. No easy thing around the boss, but I've recognized certain patterns, certain likely responses to situations. But this is a new situation and I have *no clue* how he's going to respond.

I decide to stroll by his home office and make sure he's not speed-dialing rent-a-sub.

His head is bent and he's leaning forward on his desk, ignoring the fucking spectacular view. I used to think he got off on seeing all the little people running around in their small lives below. But I realized long ago that I was wrong about that. He likes it on the top floor *because* he's further away from all that seething humanity: he can see it, but it can't touch him and he remains invisible in his eerie fucking eyrie.

And I feel so bad for her and bad for him, too. Hell, I'm so damn miserable I feel bad for myself and seriously consider ransacking Rachel's CD collection of show tunes to cheer myself up.

I'm not that desperate—not yet.

I watch for a few more moments, noting his total absorption, and reverse out of the study.

Someone who didn't know how that fucked up brain of his works might think he looks peaceful. I know that mad fucker better than anyone, and I can guarantee that his brain is whirling around like an ice-skater on acid. The only thing that's missing is the tutu.

What would I do in his situation? What would I do if Rachel decided to walk out? The thought chills me because she promised she'd call every night from her sister's, but so far she's only sent texts. Even I know that when your woman doesn't want to speak to you, things aren't looking so rosy in the garden. I'll put it down to the fact that she's rushed off her feet looking after Allison and the girls, but I don't like it. I really don't fucking like it.

Given the current Code Yellow situation, it would have been difficult to leave, but I really fucking want to. My ex is mad at me as well because I had to cancel plans with Lilly—or my 'long lost daughter' as she put it.

Makes me feel like a shit father.

I need a distraction, so I wander back to my office and surf the internet for suitable high schools for Lilly. Yeah, I know she's only just eight, but it's never too early to put her name down for a good one. At least I can feel like I'm doing something even if I can't be with her.

And then a stray thought finds its way into the empty cavity that used to be called my brain: if I put Lilly in a good school, the *best* sort of school—it'll be because Anderson is paying for it. I haven't been a complete dope. I've saved up a considerable chunk in the year that I've worked for the generous fucker, but if I left his employment, that would all end. And my savings wouldn't cover ten years of school plus college fees. Not if I plan on keeping eating as one of my favorite hobbies.

It's a sour thought: would I even want to stay with Anderson for —fuck—fourteen or fifteen more years? No freakin' way—with the emphasis on 'freak'. What else would I do? I can fix the rocker box of a leaky Triumph bike or JB weld a primer cover, but neither of those skills is going to pay for my daughter's college education. So the obvious choice is to stay in private security—unless I want to re-enlist and get my ass shot off in Syria or some other sandbox shithole.

Which leads me to another thorny problem: Rachel. I don't mean that Rachel is a problem, hell no! Rachel is Santa Claus, the Easter Bunny and a Dream Girl all rolled into one, and totally fuckable, just for the record (I may have mentioned that before), but she really isn't keen on the whole he-wears-a-gun-to-work scenario. I have my suspicions that her continued refusal to marry me has something to do with that. *Or maybe she's just not that into you, Trainer.*

Then a more sobering thought occurs: maybe I'm just good enough to keep Rachel's bed warm, but not good enough to marry.

Fuck! This is getting me nowhere—the boss's fucked-upness is contagious and I'm in danger of growing a vagina.

I decide to call Lilly.

"Hey, Princess!"

"Hi, Daddy! Are you coming to see me? Because I'm going out now. Miranda is having a birthday party and it's going to be totally cool! We're going to eat pizza and do each other's hair. Do you want to come? Oh, but you haven't got any hair!"

She giggles, and my heart sighs.

"Still packing a full head of hair, baby girl!"

"Yes, but it's too short, Daddy. I can't braid it or anything."

"No, baby. You'll have to braid Mommy's hair."

"I can braid Steve's hair—it's long."

I grip the phone tighter.

"Who's Steve?"

"He's Mommy's friend and he ... oh, Mommy says I have to go now. Bye, Daddy!"

"Bye, Princ..."

Then Carla takes over.

"What are you doing, Justin?"

"Talking to my daughter. Trying to."

"Why were you pumping her for information about Steve? It's none of your damn business who I see!"

I'm so furious that I'm grinding my teeth. Thank fuck Anderson pays for dental.

"I'm not pumping her for information. She mentioned his name —that's all. I don't see why I shouldn't know if some limp-dicked fucker is hanging around *my* daughter!"

Okay, so staying calm isn't working.

"Don't swear, Justin."

That's not the fucking point!

"Who's 'Steve'?"

"A friend."

"What sort of 'friend'?"

"Bye, Justin."

"What? No!"

But she cuts me off.

At least I have something to do now: find out who the fuck this Steve character is.

Feeling a rise in my blood pressure after that conversation with the bitch (Best in Show, seven years running), I wander over to the boss's study. I'm about to knock when I hear his phone ring. I wish I could say it was Ms. Alvarez calling, but it's not her ringtone.

He must have it on speakerphone because I can hear the caller as well as Anderson's replies.

"What do you want now, Frederick?"

The scary-assed Uncle Fester. The theme from 'Jaws' should be his ring-tone.

"Don't be petulant, Devon. I just phoned to see how you are." *Pause.* "Well? Did you find your little girlfriend as adorable as ever?"

"Fuck off."

"Oh, has something happened to your Manhattan Garden of Eden?"

Yeah, the damn snake in the Tree of Knowledge.

"Nothing."

"Don't go into acting. Honestly, Devon, I know you better than you know yourself. Let me get the Farm running again. I'm sure..."

"I don't want that."

"Of course you do."

There's a long pause, and I hope the boss is man enough to say it out loud.

"I want Maria."

His answer definitely doesn't please Charles Manson.

"Don't be childish. She's made it quite clear where her loyalties lie. Look, I'll come over and we can talk all this through. I'll..."

"No. I don't want you to come over, and I don't want to talk it through with you. I've made my decision."

"Devon, you're being unreasonable. Let's talk about this."

"Don't come over, Freddie."

He ends the call abruptly and I hear a thud as he drops his cell back on his desk. Then he sits with his head in his hands and he's so still.

Eventually, he sits up and I start to breathe again.

I give a quiet knock on the door.

"Yes," he says softly. Not his usual snarl. *He's off his game big time.*

"Are you planning on going out tonight, sir?"

"No. And I don't want any visitors. No one. Not even my family. Especially not them."

"Sir."

I sit in my office and watch the sun set slowly in the west. The boss is still in his study. He hasn't taken any calls, he hasn't made any calls, he hasn't drunk anything except whisky.

He just sits in his study.

Chapter Fifteen

THE CAT WHO WALKS ALONE

I don't sleep well. The bed is too big without Rachel. I miss her hair on my pillow. She smells like honey, sweet and strong. I miss the moment her eyes open when the first thing she does is smile at me. I miss the way she stretches her body around mine and we have slow, gentle wakeup sex. I miss the way she makes me laugh with just an expression, a raised eyebrow, a quirk of her lips. I miss the way she pours that fucking beautiful body into a sexy, pencil skirt and white shirt. I miss her food. I miss her jokes—even when they're at my expense. I miss the ways she fills the space in my days.

And I have morning wood the size of a giant redwood tree and no one at hand to help me sort it out. Sometimes life really sucks.

Then, of course, next door I have the King of Pain whose laugh-a-minute, breezy view of life has me reaching for the razor blades.

I decide to forego a shower and shave in case the boss is up for a run. But when I see him, I'd say he hasn't moved *all night*. He's still sitting at his desk, staring vacantly at his laptop. The screen is dark.

"Sir?"

He glances up. His eyes look black in the gray of dawn, and his expression makes me shiver. The lights are on, but there's nobody home.

"Are you going running this morning, sir?"

"Morning?" He looks bemused, then stares out of the window as if he can't believe the sun has decided to rise again. He looks down at his wristwatch.

"It's 5:30AM, sir."

"No. I won't be running today. Or going to the office. Thank you, Trainer."

Thank you? He never thanks me! Fuck! He must be ill.

I notice that the bottle of whisky is empty at the same time he goes to stand, leaning heavily on his desk, then he plunges forward. I catch him just before he head-butts the oak.

I carry him to his bedroom and lay him down on the bed in the recovery position. He is going to have a motherfucker of a hangover when he wakes up.

I fill a glass of water and leave it by his bed with some Ibuprofen.

I wonder if I should call one of those services that gives vitamins and saline through an IV to help cure the hangover, or maybe his parents, but think better of it. He said he didn't want to see his family. Can't say I blame him: they're like the Waltons on Ecstasy—there's so much love going around.

I head back to the staff quarters to take that postponed shower and to find something for breakfast. Craig doesn't work weekends, on the boss's say so.

I'm no great cook, but living with New York's answer to Paula Deen, I've picked up a few tips. I wonder if I should make something for the boss, but decide it would be way too cozy cooking for the fucker. He'd probably throw it up if I did.

By lunchtime, I've updated all the security reports and spoken to Mason. There's no news on the blackmailer or any accomplices, although he's still at large, and there's still no movement from the pit of despair.

I decide to take him a cup of coffee. I make damn fine coffee, though I say it myself.

So I carry a cup to his room.

He looks up, bleary-eyed and blinks.

"Coffee," I say, stating the blindingly obvious.

Yeah, I'm shocked too, boss. Just sharing the love.

He stares at me, then closes his eyes again.

So, with abso-fucking-lutely nothing on the agenda for the day, I run through the same old checks. But there's zero of interest on the CCTV, not even car sex by that guy in the condo next door who acts like a buck private with a forty-eight hour pass and his girlfriend's best friend.

Pity. 'Cause there's fuck-all on cable.

I decide to call Mason again.

"I need some intel on Frederick Landon."

There's a long pause.

"Anderson won't like it."

I don't respond and he sighs.

"When Anderson first retained my services, he specifically told me that searches into Landon weren't needed and definitely not wanted. This is a good contract for my company, J.T. I don't want to piss off the client."

I know I'm putting him in a difficult position, but my gut doesn't like the creep and my gut is rarely wrong.

"Something doesn't add up. He has connections to Anderson going way back, but also to the Farm; he keeps tabs on the boss, and I don't trust him as far as I could throw his bony ass."

There's a long pause before he gives in.

"What am I looking for?"

"Financial. Could be personal. Dig deep."

"On it. Anything else?"

"Nope."

I'm left contemplating the idea that I've just committed career suicide.

My cell rings, saving me from the appalling idea of spending another evening of sheer monotony with my own merry thoughts.

It's the light of my life.

"Hey, Rachel! I've been trying to call you."

"I know. I'm sorry. I've been so busy."

"Are you coming home soon?"

She sighs and I feel like every drop of blood in my body has just turned to dust.

"I'm not sure ... when."

And I live again. I can live with *when*, but not *if*.

"Allison is still sick but on the road to recovery; the girls are much better now. They're back to normal almost."

"Are you okay, baby?"

I hear the smile in her voice.

"I'm fine. One of us has to stay vertical. At least Bill hasn't caught it. How are Mr. Anderson and Maria?"

Oh, fuck.

"Justin?"

How the hell am I going to handle this one?

"Has something happened? Are they alright?"

"I think so."

Yeah, that's a reasonably truthful response. Or possibly an outright lie. It probably depends on your point of view.

"What happened?"

He showed her his dungeon; she bawled him out then cried enough tears to sink The Mighty Mo and then she left.

"I guess they had some kind of fight."

"Oh. Well, that doesn't sound too bad. They're always fighting. I think it's one of the things that he loves about her—that she stands up to him."

"Hmm."

"What do you mean 'hmm'? What aren't you telling me, Justin?"

Why is that woman so damned perceptive?

"She was crying. A lot. She didn't look so good."

"Well, I'm sure she'll be back."

"I'm not."

"Not what?"

"Sure she'll be back."

"Why do you say that?"

I sigh. Truth or dare? I go for truth.

"Because when she left, she told him that she needed time. That's usually code for 'leave me alone or I'll call the cops'."

"Oh no! Oh, Justin, no! Poor Mr. Anderson! How is he?"

Fucked up.

"He hasn't said much."

"He never does. What's he doing? Has he eaten?"

"No."

"He hasn't eaten at all?"

"Nope."

Not unless he licked the plates clean and put them back in the cupboard after drinking a bottle of whisky that cost more than my last car.

There's a long pause while I listen to her breathing.

"I'm coming home."

"What?"

"I'll leave first thing in the morning. I'll see you tomorrow. Bill said he could look after Allison and the girls."

"I ... okay. See you later."

She hangs up.

Fuck. She'll come home earlier than she'd planned *for him.*

Jealousy as strong as acid burns in my throat. Irrational, unreasonable, but I can't help it. I know she's just being Rachel ... the caregiver ... but it really, seriously pisses me off.

I think about heading to the gym to work off some of my irritation, but as I walk past the boss's home office I glance in. He's up and awake, looking like hell, the empty cup next to him, but *still* trying to work. I'd give a pint of blood just to hear him listening to some wrist-slitting music. But no, he sits there.

At least he drank the damn coffee.

With Rachel's voice in my head, I make him a PBJ sandwich and leave it on his desk. He doesn't look up.

I sleep badly and wake up early, wondering how soon Rachel will be home.

I check on the boss but the office is empty and the sandwich I made him hasn't been touched. *Who the hell doesn't like PBJ?*

I discreetly check the gym and watch him running on the treadmill for a while before he slows to a walk then heads to his private wing.

At 8:15AM, my face creases into something my mom used to call a smile: Rachel is back.

The elevator doors slide open. She's wearing jeans that hug her delicious ass and a t-shirt that makes me want to rip it off her.

"How is he?"

What? Fuck! She wants to know about *him*.

"He's just finished in the gym."

"Has he eaten?"

"Nope."

"You didn't make him anything?"

"I made him a coffee and..."

"For goodness sake, Justin!"

She bustles off, leaving me wanting to punch something. I didn't get a hug, a kiss, not even a fucking smile.

I go back to my office, too angry to breathe straight.

Twenty minutes later, the mouth-watering aroma of Rachel's blueberry pancakes wafts through the building. She walks past my office carrying a tray with a stack of pancakes and syrup. *Past my office.*

I can't hear the words, but she's talking to him like he's a small child, or a wounded animal. Well, I guess he's kind of both. Me, I'm just pissed. And hungry.

I wander into our apartment and wait for her to return. When she does, she doesn't meet my gaze.

Shit! This doesn't look good.

"Rachel ... is everything okay?"

She takes a deep breath. I think about running.

"No. Not really. Mr. Anderson looks terrible ... he barely seemed to know where he was. Have you called his parents?"

Now I know she's deliberately avoiding my *real* question. She knows I'd never call the boss's folks unless it looked like he was dying. Which he isn't.

"Rachel, I asked if *you're* okay?"

"Justin?"

"Yes, baby?"

"Will you hold me?"

And the world stops turning while I hold my precious girl.

The boss is up, washed, shaved and dressed to kick some corporate ass. But he hasn't slept and he's hardly spoken.

As we exit the elevator of DMA Tower at 6AM, having vetoed the morning run again, the only other people in the building are the security team.

Rachel is going to be pissed that we both left without having breakfast, but I couldn't bring myself to wake her. She didn't sleep well either.

The security officer on the thirtieth floor of DMA Tower gives me a discreet nod.

He's a good guy, knows his job. I've made sure that everyone here is the best of the best. No one sleeps on the night shift. Apart from anything else, they never know when Anderson is going to be prowling the corridors like an Armani-clad Hound of the Baskervilles.

I head for my office while the boss sits at his desk and waits for the world to fall at his feet. Despite this, I know for a fact that there's only one conquest he cares about today.

Tessa arrives at 7:50AM and heads to the ladies room and spends fifteen minutes fixing her face. Same ritual every stinking day. I don't need fifteen minutes to be as suave and good-looking as I already am. But nature is rarely fair.

Tessa trots to her desk at 8:05AM breathless. She's late again, and Ryan gives her a look that would freeze a solar flare.

At 8:30AM, I organize a quick catch-up with all security officers as they change from night- to day-shift. I remind them that everyone must display a valid security badge and I want spot-checks on those, as well. I reiterate my instructions to the security team that no fucker—other than the boss—is to get into his office, or even onto his floor. I'll tattoo it on their fucking foreheads if I have to. And then give them mirrors.

All visitors, even if it's the President, have to be vetted. Every visitor is to have their photo taken which is then checked against the FBI's facial recognition software. Everyone goes through the scanner. No exceptions.

The rest of the morning passes quietly until Pam comes to figure out what's up with Anderson.

"Come on, Trainer. Spill. Pleeeease don't tell me he's *still* got woman trouble!"

"You'd know more about that than me, Pam."

She growls something unprintable that rhymes with Lamar Hunt and stalks back to her office.

I'm sure glad she's batting for the other team: it would be terrifying having her on the loose in New York. No man would feel safe. How does her girlfriend Sheila put up with her? I mean, she's kinda nice. Nothing like old copper-drawers.

Yup, I do enjoy a bit of verbal sparring with Ms. Russo.

Next up for the Trainer treatment is Ryan. He's also noticed a change of demeanor in the boss. For a start, Tessa isn't the usual quivering wreck.

"I got a call from PR because *they* got a call from a newspaper about Devon dating. 'Fess up, Trainer. What's going on?"

Why do all these people come to me? I just live with the guy—it's not like I'm having his babies.

"It's all under control, Ryan. Nothing for you to worry about."

"Yeah, and a flying pig just shit on your shoes, Trainer. What's going on?"

He's such a nice, sweet-tempered guy.

It's a good thing I don't approve of gambling, liquor or strong language, because my poker face would bankrupt me going up against the queen of mean.

"The ongoing security situation."

"Bullshit! He looks like his best friend just died—except he hasn't got any friends. So, I'm wondering, does this have something to do with the new intern, Maria Alvarez?"

Well, it's the boss's fault that Ryan is getting so close to the truth: he didn't hire any dumb employees, that's for sure.

"You know he ordered flowers. Two dozen white Lily of the Valley. Dictated a message and everything. Melanie from the florists phoned me to check it wasn't a hoax and that it was really him. I guess he was apologizing for something, right? Guys like him only send flowers when they've done something they're sorry for."

I stare back, and his eyes widen.

"You're shitting me! She dumped him? *She* dumped *him?!*"

Ryan doesn't just *leap* to conclusions, he fucking triple salchows to them.

"I didn't say that."

"Wow! She dumped him! I bet that's never happened before. Apart from the fact that I always thought he was a-sexual, possibly gay. Wow!"

"I didn't say..."

But he's already out the door.

I hold my head in my hands, then decide that as it's going to be a long-ass day, I should find out what *Game of Thrones* is about after all.

Howard passes by just as I put my feet on the desk and look up HBO's website, but it's not my day for an introspective wallow.

"Hey, T!"

Howard wanders into my office. He could be looking for the meaning of life, or possibly the way to his desk. It's hard to tell.

"Halo-carbon based agents are thirty-eight per cent more effective than our standard foam and water combo."

He's got my attention.

"Tell me more."

I spend an interesting and informative half hour having the benefits of Halon explained to me. It's a relief to have a normal conversation. I decide it's worth the $4,200,000 cost to install at all

Anderson's commercial properties across the U.S. The boss will need to approve it, but I'm pretty certain he'll like what he hears.

"Go ahead and prep a report for the boss. It looks like a sound investment."

"Will do, Mr. T. By the way, what's up with the boss? He hasn't yelled at me even once today."

Nope. The boss didn't hire any turkeys.

"Princess Daenerys is hot," he says, casually. "She sounds like purple."

"She *sounds* like purple?"

He shrugs.

"I'm a synesthete."

"Is that some weird fanboy thing? You scare me sometimes."

"It means I experience sound as color."

I never know where the hell Howard gets half this stuff.

"What's up with Warpath? He looks like Luke Skywalker when he found out that Darth Vader was his father."

"Can't tell you, Howard."

"I know, T." He stares at the ceiling. "I kinda liked it when he was, you know, connected."

This guy has a PhD in talking riddles. I decide to play along.

"What do you mean 'connected'?"

"Well," he says, seriously, "the boss operates in the top quantile of mathematical reasoning and logic: abstractions, numbers and critical thinking. Fluid intelligence, ya know."

"Bear with me, Howard, when I say, huh?"

He continues staring at the ceiling, like the answer to life, the universe and everything is stenciled onto the fire-resistant tiles.

"It's the capacity to understand the underlying principles of some kind of causal system. I mean, the boss is a legitimate genius, and speaking as a fellow genius, I know what I'm talking about. But seeing him with Mrs. Anderson, it made me feel like if *he* could have a normal life, then there was hope for the rest of us."

I stare at Howard, slightly shocked that he's speaking in whole sentences.

"Seriously, MENSA doesn't have a category for people like us. No one does."

He shrugs and I know he's not trying to be funny, he means it.

"The boss is off the chart smart, but he's a dumbass, too. Like Raymond the Rain Man, you know what I'm saying, T? And it's no fun being the one who never makes connections with other people." He sighs. "Later, T. Look out for the Sith."

I have no idea what the hell just happened. Did I fall asleep? Slip through the cracks into an alternate reality? Or did Howard just tell me that the boss gives him hope?

Two episodes later, Daenerys has been married to Khal Drogo and I'm so confused, I think my brain has been shit out through my ass. My eyes are burning and gave up trying to work two hours ago.

Then Rachel calls.

"Justin! The *meditation room!* Oh my goodness! This is wonderful!"

"Yeah, baby. Learning has taken place."

I don't bother to tell her I helped the boss paint the walls—she'll have us going to spin classes together.

But I have to agree. Things are looking up.

I was wrong.

I feel like I'm living in Groundhog Day. Rachel is worried, the boss is showing Hugo Wolf the real meaning of insanity, putting the misery in *Misericordia*, and in between that and screaming through his nightmares, *I'm* about ready to start foaming at the mouth.

But for the first time in several days, the boss wants to go for a run. Rachel thinks that's a good sign—that, and the fact that he seems to be eating normally again. I'm not so sure: what if he runs under a truck? What if I push him under one? I think that could affect my end-of-year bonus.

He spent yesterday evening pacing up and down the main room at Wolf Point. I saw him check his phone a dozen times. I got the impression that he was hoping, *expecting* even, that Ms. Alvarez would call him.

I know he hasn't been into the whole 'girlfriend' thing that long —and I'm not counting the orgies—but if he really thinks sending some flowers is going to bring her running back after telling her that masochism is his favorite hobby after fucking, he's got a lot to learn. But I reckon that's *exactly* what he thought. And he doesn't understand why it hasn't worked. *Join the club, Romeo.*

Chapter Sixteen

MISS CONGENIALITY

"You're going to have to talk to him, Justin."

Rachel's lips are moving and sound is coming out but it makes no sense. I had been looking forward to good old fashioned eggs and bacon with a quiet coffee for breakfast, but now I sense that we'll be having *a conversation*.

"Talk to who about what?"

Rachel shakes her head and looks at me as if I've forgotten how to tie my shoelaces or zip my fly. I look down: nope, everything's in place.

"About Ms. Alvarez!"

Now I'm really confused. That one brain cell is feeling pretty lonely up there. At least, that's how Rachel is making me feel.

Then the light dawns. *Holy fuck!*

"Let me get this right, Rachel. You want *me* to talk to *the boss* about *Ms. Alvarez?!*"

She nods.

"And then after he fires me and kicks my sweet ass through the door, then what?"

She rolls her eyes.

"And what would I say to him anyway? Hey, bud, you know if

you want girls to like you, it's not a good idea to do kinky shit that includes orgies, whips and canes, *after* fucking them till they can't cross their legs."

"Justin!"

"Well, come on! First, it's none of my business; second, it's none of *your* business; and third, what makes you think he'd listen to me anyway?"

I think I might have gone too far because she gets a look on her face that would scare my old platoon sergeant into shitting his shorts.

"Well, first," she says, all sarcastic, like she's ticking it off on her fingers, "it *is* your business because you're the closest thing he's got to a friend; second, it *is* my business because I've worked for him for over a year, I *like* him and believe he's a good man; and third, actually, I can't think of a third reason, but you really should talk to him."

"First," I say, smirking back at her, "the only person he listens to is Ms. Alvarez and sometimes his mother; second, he's having lunch with his mom today; and third, his mom scares me."

"Aw, Justin, honey. Are you trying to tell me that a big, badass ex-Marine is scared of a lil ole mom from the Bronx?"

"Yup."

She sighs.

"Look, babe, I know you mean well and that you want to fix this for the boss, but you've got to accept that you can't. You can't fix him and you can't fix Ms. Alvarez. He's sent her flowers—she hasn't responded. You know how stubborn women ... um ... *some* women can be."

I grind to a halt, aware that I'm just opening my mouth to change feet.

Rachel raises an eyebrow, but she doesn't leave me wriggling on the hook.

"So he's seeing his mom?"

"Yep."

"Well, I'm relieved to hear that. At least he's talking to

someone. I half expected that *dreadful* man to be around fixing him up with a new *friend*."

"He tried."

"No! Really? When was that? What happened?"

"Landon phoned on Saturday. The boss was on speakerphone so I heard it all. He sounded like he was pleased that Maria had done a runner. Couldn't wait to set up the boss with a new fix at the Farm."

I really don't want to dwell on that image. That cold-hearted troll gives me the shivers.

"Ugh! I *can't bear* that man! He's just so ... ugh!"

Words fail her, which is really saying something. I happen to know Rachel was a straight-A student.

We're interrupted when the boss taps on our door. I hope he didn't overhear that conversation. But he looks so deep in thought, I'm not sure he'd notice a grizzly bear dancing the polka on Broadway. Then again, polkas are a bit cheerful for the boss.

We head out across town on our run. The boss's pace is slower than usual and his gait isn't as loose as it should be. He's obviously not into the exercise because generally he gets pretty competitive with me, but today he's some other place, and from the expression on his face, I'm guessing it's not somewhere happy.

Part of me wonders if maybe another woman or man—another orgy—*would* help him get over Maria Alvarez. But then again, does anyone ever get over their first love? Sure, we move on because we have to, because life forces us to carry on; but most of us get abused by love while we're still in our teens and we're young enough to believe that life will be a bed of roses now we've got enough manure to do a good job. But the boss is thirty-one—and I'm pretty fucking certain that he's never been in love before. That's from a year of too close observation, along with the Cadillac-size hints that Abigail Anderson dropped.

Ms. Alvarez certainly wasn't his first fuck, but she was his first love.

We make it back to Wolf Point with only minimal damage (the boss ran into the path of a bread van: it was parked at the time).

Then time to get suited, booted and beautiful, take three meetings with different members of the management team, a Skype call from Taiwan and possibly recalibrate NASDAQ before a visit to mommy at *Le Bernier*.

They're in there a fucking long time. I've watched penicillin grow at a faster speed. I trawl through every magazine in the bar. Who knew 'Horse and Hound' was such a racy read?

When the boss comes out he looks calm. I don't know what his mom said to him, but the woman is a witchdoctor. I'm definitely going to her when working for Anderson turns me into a complete fucking basket case. In fact, I could do with a session right now. I wonder how much she charges and whether it's included in my medical coverage?

At DMA Tower, my ass is barely in my office chair when I get a call from Mason.

"Anything new on Landon?"

"Oh yeah."

He draws out the word like it's going to bite him.

"And?"

"I'm still digging. Nothing concrete, just some rumors that his financing isn't as squeaky clean as it seems."

"In what way?"

"Let's just say that not all his seed money came from Anderson."

Interesting.

"Who then?"

"I'm looking into ties with Consolidated Iron, a shipbuilding company on the West Coast and possible mob ties."

"Dirty money."

Mason pauses.

"Couldn't say, but since Anderson is looking to expand into shipping, possibly partnering with that company in Taiwan he's been sniffing around..."

Light dawns...

"It would put him into direct competition with Landon's other backer."

"Yup."

"Shit."

"Yup."

"And Anderson has no idea?"

"Unlikely, not impossible," and I can hear the frustration in Mason's voice.

"Fuck's sake. He has a real blind spot when it comes to that shithead."

"Yup. I'll leave it to you to tell Anderson."

"Gee, thanks, Mason. All the best jobs."

"Kiss my ass, Trainer."

"I'd rather chew off a badger's scrotum."

I'm really not looking forward to giving the boss all this good news: the poor bastard is on a fucking Titanic of misery—and I just can't face being the one to tell him that there are icebergs ahead.

The next evening, I'm ready to kick back and relax for the evening, when Gomez Addams gets a surprise visitor.

Well, I'm surprised—I have no idea how Anderson feels ... shocked to the tips of his shiny shoes.

On the CCTV, I can see Maria's grandfather standing at the front door, leaning on a walking cane, a very serious expression on his face. But then again at his age, life is a serious business since you've already lived more of it than you've got left.

I text the boss with a heads up before I jog down to the front door.

"Mr. Alvarez, good to see you again, sir."

"Ah, Justin, *bueno*. How are you and Rachel?"

"We're good. Please, come on in. Mr. Anderson is waiting for you."

He gives a tired smile and hobbles inside.

"So he's not really your friend? You call him mister?"

"Ms. Alvarez thought for the purposes of her cousin's wedding that it would be best to keep things casual. How is she?"

He sighs, shaking his head.

"She is sad. I don't know what happened, she won't tell me. So I've come to ask Devon."

Ooh, this isn't going to go well, especially if the boss tells him the truth.

Just then, the man of the moment walks into the lobby.

"Mr. Alvarez, this is a welcome surprise."

"Is it?" the old man asks sincerely. "Hmm, we'll see."

The boss isn't fazed at all. Attempts at a hostile takeover are second nature to him; pushy relatives, also a breeze.

"May I offer you some refreshments while we talk?"

"Do you got beer in a place like this?"

Mr. Alvarez asks, staring at the enormous lobby area and the elevator doors on one side.

The boss inclines his head to one side.

"I believe I do."

That's my cue to leave.

I head back to the lower floor and find Rachel waiting in the kitchen.

"Is everything okay?" she asks.

I shrug.

"They're having a beer together."

"Perhaps I should offer Mr. Alvarez something to eat?"

"Leave them to it, babe. If Gomez wants something, he'll tell us."

"I thought Mr. Alvarez's name was Javier?"

"It is."

"Oh? *Oh!*" and she gives a quiet laugh. "Is that what you call Mr. Anderson behind his back?"

"Meh, it's kind of like the Inuit with words for snow: I have a lot of names for the boss."

She shakes her head.

"I won't ask."

We settle back on the sofa together, and I wait for further

instructions. I can't completely relax because I can make an educated guess that the boss will want me to drive Maria's grandpa back to the Bronx.

Sure enough, an hour later, the Bat signal goes up.

"Gotta go, baby."

"I'll warm the bed for you," she says with a smile.

God, she's the perfect woman.

Both the boss and Mr. Alvarez are smiling, sorta, and shaking hands. They look as though they've come to an agreement. And with my newfound understanding of womenfolk, I'm gonna say that Maria will be pissed that they've agreed it without her. But I just work here.

I bring the car around front, and the boss helps Mr. Alvarez into the back seat—the Rover is pretty high up.

We haven't even left the block before the old man starts with his questions.

"So, how long you worked for Devon?"

"A little over a year."

"Do you like working for him?"

Now there's a question I'm not going to answer with full disclosure.

"It's interesting."

"You didn't answer the question, young man."

"With all due respect, sir, I don't answer questions about my employer. Ever."

He seems to think about that, but he doesn't give up.

"My granddaughter tells me that you have a child, Mr. Trainer, a daughter. Is that right?"

"Yes, sir."

"Then you know. You know what a great gift it is, and a great responsibility, too."

I stay silent, because I have a very good idea where this conversation is heading.

"If your daughter were Maria's age, would you allow her to marry Devon?"

Not even if the planet was doomed and the boss had the last shuttle to Mars.

"Mr. Alvarez, I like Maria, but I still can't talk about my employer."

He's silent for several minutes.

"A man who inspires such loyalty must have a good heart."

Or a great lawyer who spits out NDAs like confetti at a Greek wedding. But I let the old guy think that.

Whatever helps him sleep at night.

Rachel

I was so worried about Mr. Anderson. He looked terrible, so sad all the time. And he hasn't been sleeping. Three times, I've started to call Ms. Alvarez but I don't know what I'd say to her. Justin is right: it's really not my business—except that it is.

I've worked for this man for over a year and I really do care about him. Justin does, too, of course, except he won't admit it. He pretends that he stays for the pay or for me, but he's fond of Mr. Anderson, too.

We're only his employees, but he treats us with respect and consideration. He trusts us with his secrets and he's never lied to us: he's always been completely frank about his unhappy predilections.

I was so pleased when he met Maria—we both were, and Justin absolutely adores her. She's so sweet and cheerful. She's like sunshine wrapped up in a person. If I'd ever had children, she's the kind of girl I'd want for a daughter. And it was obvious to anyone who saw them together that she was head over heels in love with Mr. Anderson, and he with her. I can't tell you what a joy it was to see him so happy.

It was a shock when we found out about Maria's battle with leukemia—it made me respect her even more. She's strong and smart and loving—she's perfect for Mr. Anderson. And I'd say that having her grandfather visit tonight, he must think the same and is trying to find a way to bring them back together. I hope I'm right, I really do.

I suspect Justin knows more than he tells me, whether or not that's to protect me or Mr. Anderson, I'm not sure. He said once something about the way Mr. Anderson's nightmares reminded him of being in Iraq. He clammed up after that, but I guessed it has to do with what he's seen over there and losing his friend.

I think we all agree that the best therapy for Mr. Anderson has definitely been Maria. She brought joy into his life when he never seemed to think he deserved any.

I'm still not comfortable being back at Wolf Point. I *hate* being in the mansion by myself. I haven't told Justin, but when John Evans is busy, I've started asking Frank the doorman from the building next door to see me inside—just to make sure there's nobody lurking. Frank is taking his escort duties very seriously, probably a little *too* seriously, if I'm honest. But I can put up with his clumsy flirtation a lot more than seeing a man with a gun pointed at me again.

I keep remembering Aston Van Sant staring at me with those empty eyes.

I really should focus on my work—that's Justin's recipe for getting through the rough times.

I wonder if Mr. Anderson will want to go over the menus for the next few days as a distraction. Probably not. I'll just choose some of his favorites.

But he's got a temper, as well. That I can attest to, having heard him on the telephone a time or two, although he's never shouted at me. And I hope he never does. If nothing else, Justin would make him regret it.

The thought makes me smile.

When my husband died, I didn't think I'd ever find love again. I certainly didn't think I'd find it with a younger man. I am a very lucky woman. I know the last few months have been hard for Justin: he feels so guilty that Mr. Van Sant got into the house.

It's been difficult, but I need to let him know that I don't blame him—that I still love him.

My time away looking after Allison and the girls clarified something for me: I don't want to lose Justin. I still think he'd be better off with a younger woman, but while he's interested in me, for as long as he's interested in me, I'm going to enjoy every moment of our time together.

And I've got something in mind.

The phone rings, shaking me out of my increasingly erotic reverie.

"Justin, is everything okay?"

"Everything is good. The old guy looked mostly happy when I drove him home. I'm on my way back now."

"Oh, that sounds positive! Do you think he's trying to help, with Mr. Anderson and Maria?"

"Yeah, I'd say that's the plan. Guess we'll find out..."

"But?"

"The boss said that he wants me to drive him to supper tomorrow evening."

"Oh, so he won't want me to cook."

"Nope. But that's not the good bit."

"Justin, you really do like to draw things out!"

I hear his deep laugh over the phone and I adore it. *Who knew such a grim-faced stoical man would love to laugh as much as Justin does.*

"You're the only woman who draws things out of me, baby."

He also loves to talk dirty.

"Maria's granddad persuaded him to surprise her, then take her out for dinner."

"Oh my goodness! I love Maria's grandfather! It's just what they both need. That's wonderful news!"

"Yep, it's a start. And I'd like to start something with you!"

I laugh lightly.

"Yes, well, I've been thinking about that. But you're free for the rest of the night?"

"I wasn't thinking of charging you, baby!"

"Very funny, Justin. Just hurry home."

And I have the biggest smile on my face.

Trainer

It's Tuesday evening and I'm thinking dinner a deux with Ms. Smith, when the boss throws a wrench into the finely-tuned engine that is my life, and summons me into his lair a.ka. his office at DMA Tower.

"I need you to drive me tonight, Trainer."

Has he decided to take Mr. Alvarez's advice at last?

"Yes, sir. Where to?"

There's a pause as he glances up from his laptop.

"Comedy Cellar, Macdougal Street, eight o'clock."

"Yes, sir."

"Oh, and Trainer?"

"Yes, sir."

"Dress casual."

"Sir."

I keep spare clothes at the office, but it's mostly shirts and gym clothes. Pure luck that I have jeans and a pair of cowboy boots with me.

I don't like dressing down around the boss—it blurs the lines.

Well, well, well—looks like the boss got tired of giving Ms. Alvarez 'space'.

At twenty-hundred hours, I'm waiting at the front of DMA Tower. The boss strolls out wearing jeans and a black t-shirt, which is pretty much what I'm wearing. Shit, we look like we're on a date. Awkward.

At least I'm wearing a coat that covers the Smith & Wesson.

The club looks exactly the same as last time: dark, dingy, with gaudy lights. The boss leads us to a table at the side but near the front. I position myself so I can see the whole room, especially who's coming and going; but the boss has his eyes fixed on the stage.

Finally, after an hour of listening to a bunch of wanna-be comics, some good, some bad, some ugly, Ms. Alvarez tiptoes onto the stage and blinks out at the people giving her a polite applause.

"Hi! Thanks for coming!"

She's about to continue when the boss stands up and calls out to her.

"Do you know any good jokes about billionaires?"

Her eyes widen and her mouth drops open. People turn to stare, uncertain whether or not this is part of her act.

Then she pops her hip and smirks at him.

"Dude, you from Scarsdale?"

That gets a laugh, and a ghost of a smile passes the boss's lips.

"Yeah, I know one," and she takes a deep breath. "A woman from the Bronx was driving down Bruckner in a bright yellow Volkswagen Beetle, when she pulls up next to a billionaire in a Range Rover at a stop sign. Their windows are open and she yells at the billionaire, 'Hey, you in the suit, you got a telephone in there?' The billionaire nods politely, 'cause that's what those dudes do, right? 'Yes, of course,' he says, looking down at this hot chica in her pimp mobile. 'I got one too, see?' says the chick from the Bronx. 'Hey, I gotta axe you ... you got a fax machine?' The dude looks puzzled. 'Why, actually, yes, I do.' The chica laughs and yells, 'I do too! See? It's right here!' The light is just about to turn green and the girl says, 'So, do you got a double bed in back there?' The billionaire looks surprised but eager, maybe 'cause she's a hot mamacita, you know what I'm saying? 'No!' he says. 'Do you?' The chica smiles at him. 'Yep, got my double bed right in back here,' then screeches past him when the light turns green. Well, the billionaire is pretty competitive 'cause he didn't get to be a billionaire without wanting to one-up everyone, and he's definitely not going to be one-upped by a chick from the Bronx, so he goes to a customizing shop and orders them to put a double bed in back of his Rover. About two weeks later, the job is finally done. Real nice mattress, matching linens, throw pillows, fluffy handcuffs..."

The audience laughs and the boss can't help shaking his head in amusement.

"So, the billionaire drives all over from Riverdale to Parkchester looking for the hot chick. Finally, he finds her car parked alongside the road, so the billionaire pulls his Rover up next to it. The windows on the Beetle are all fogged up ... oh yeah! You feel me? The billionaire doesn't know whether to be excited or pissed and he's kinda hoping that the hot chick will invite him to join in..."

I glance over at the boss, but his eyes are fixed on Maria.

"So the dude taps on the foggy window of the Volkswagen, and the chica opens it a crack and peeks out. The billionaire says, 'Hey, remember me?' The Bronx chick is annoyed. 'Yeah, yeah, I remember you. Wass up?' The dude winks at her 'cause he thinks she's gonna be impressed. 'Check this out, I got a double bed installed in my Rover.' The Bronx girl yells, 'YOU GOT ME OUT OF THE SHOWER TO TELL ME THAT!'"

I clap along with the rest of the audience and the boss raises his glass of beer to her. Ms. Alvarez is glowing and happy, and damn if that doesn't make me feel all warm inside.

I head to the bar to give them some privacy. The boss done good.

Thank fuck.

Chapter Seventeen

THE INVISIBLE MAN

I wake up with a smile on my face. Hell, my whole body is smiling from the inside out. And in recognition of my good mood, I poke Rachel in the back with an erection that makes the Empire State Building look like a toothpick.

"Justin," she says with her eyes still closed, "I'd have been quite happy with 'Good morning' as a wake-up call. Breakfast in bed is also traditional."

I wrap my arms around her waist and pull her into my chest.

"No coffee?" she asks breathlessly. "No breakfast in bed? Justin!"

Oh no, baby, I'm going to make a meal of you.

Although I say it myself, it's a very good start to the day ... and I didn't have to wait till my birthday for a blowjob.

When I get back from the morning run, my woman is singing to herself as she makes breakfast. Damn, I'm a lucky man.

And even though the boss has more money than the Federal Reserve and more snappy suits than an alligator in Savile Row, I'm not sure I'd call him 'lucky'. But, if he plays his cards right, and manages not to fuck up again, he might just get lucky tonight.

The poor sucker has to get through a ten-hour work day first— and so do I.

The drive to DMA Tower is uneventful, and despite the increased vigilance, there's still no sign of the blackmailer making a move. But in case Anderson is being watched, I've changed the route of our morning run every day, avoiding all the usual places; and Ryan is guarding the boss's calendar and appointments more closely than Monica Lewinsky guards her dry-cleaning.

Other than that, it's business as usual and he's working on a deal to buy a shipyard in Taiwan that's going to put the 'sick' in Min Keh-sik, and make the Boston Tea Party look like a Sunday school outing.

And here's the thing: I've seen the boss blow off multi-million dollar deals because some instinct told him to walk; I've seen him lose more on stock market fluctuations than most people make in ten lifetimes, but I've never seen him this jittery.

It's 19:30 hours and we're on our way to collect Maria from her home. Even though half the people in DMA Tower know they're dating or maybe-dating or sorta-dating, she insisted that they don't meet at work.

As I drive through the increasingly heavy traffic, I can see him in the rear view mirror.

Saying that the present atmosphere is tense is like saying the Titanic had a small leak.

I thought last night had sorted out a few of their issues, but when I pull up outside her building and suddenly we're at DEFCON 1—nuclear war is imminent. The sleazoid neighbor in dayglow orange sweatpants is escorting Maria to the car. The boss swears so badly my ears nearly melt.

Yeah, a nice intimate chat with the woman he loves—coming right up.

I step out of the car to open the door for Ms. Alvarez, and the hip hop dude's cold eyes lock onto mine. He's trying to work out if he's seen me before, and then he realizes I'm here for Ms. Alvarez. He checks out the Rover then grimaces like he's just chowed down on cardboard.

Suck it up, dickless.

I wait for Ms. Alvarez to acknowledge me, but her eyes are wide as she stares into the car. I wonder what the fuck she's seen and half turn, my hand moving towards my gun. The boss is glaring at her—fucking glaring at her.

Can't he see that the poor kid is crazy about him or does he need Spock to do a Vulcan mind-meld?

I want to slam my head into the steering wheel and inhale the airbag when he snarls, "Who is that?"

For fuck's sake! He even managed to screw up 'hello'!

Nope, I want to slam *his* head into the steering wheel until he sees stars, then kick his damn ass all the way to Boise and back.

But Maria's response makes me smile, in a completely face-non-moving sort of way.

She laughs. At him.

Does he take the hint? Does he sweep her into his arms? That would be too poetic for Mr. I'm-a-moron-with-a-broomstick-up-my-Ivy-League-educated-ass.

I stare at the sky, wishing that he'd take his foot out of his mouth before he swallows it.

"Who was that?"

Nope. A two-foot case of indigestion.

I start the engine and try to ignore the replay of the Bay of Pigs in the backseat.

If he keeps pissing on his own parade, he'll need a damn canoe to paddle out of here.

"That was my neighbor. He was just being friendly so you can stop glaring at me now."

Anderson, get a clue: you're in the last chance saloon and your horse just died of loneliness in the one-horse town that you call a life.

"I'm sorry, Maria. Forgive me."

Begging is good. Women love it when you beg.

"How have you been?"

"Since I saw you at work today?"

"Since you decided you needed some space."

She looks at her hands then manages to speak. Her voice is so quiet I can barely hear her.

"It's been ... hard."

"I know," he says softly. "I miss you."

I feel like fucking cheering and throwing tickertape. I'm so damn happy that he's managed to express an emotion that is real for once.

Then he holds her hand.

Hallelujah!

She hesitates. Jesus—I'm holding my fucking breath and I'm the damn driver. If we crash now, Rachel would have my ass. Well, she's had it several times already, but that's a bedtime story that's definitely NC-17.

"Maria, we need to talk."

No! I'm screaming in my head! KISS HER! KISS HIM! In a totally heterosexual way, of course.

Christ, if he doesn't kiss her soon, I'm going to give him Rachel's copy of *Ninety Days of Genevieve* and tell him to read the chapter entitled 'The Stallion'.

"Later," she whispers. "We'll talk later."

Finally, finally he remembers that he was asking her out for dinner. And he almost smiles when she says yes.

Who knew he could behave like a human being?

When I get to the restaurant, things are looking good for the boss, but he's not out of the woods yet. He's still got plenty of time to fuck it up.

Every time the boss meets someone, he has to think about what they want from him, how they're planning to use him. That's another reason why Maria means so much to him: she damn well dislikes that he's so wealthy. I don't know what her thinking is, because in other ways she's really smart, but she loves him for himself. Now if the poor bastard could get his head around that, he might actually have that slice of happiness he's reaching for.

I open the door for Ms. Alvarez and she slides out.

"It's good to see you, Trainer. How's Rachel?"

She's just so damn sweet—at least she knows what she's getting herself into this time. She's stronger than she looks—I just hope she's strong enough to take all his crazy shit.

"She's well, thank you, Ms. Alvarez. And it's good to see you again, too."

"Sorry I didn't get to talk to you last night."

"Not a problem, ma'am."

Yeah, I'm smooth. Watch, learn, and take notes, Anderson.

The boss is eyeballing me, but I ain't sayin' shit, no sir. He knows there's no point in asking me. Silent as the grave, me.

"Ten-thirty?" he says grittily.

Sheesh, just because I'm smoother than butter on hot toast and he's an asshole with cheekbones.

"Yes, sir." *You prick.*

I watch them as the boss leads Ms. Alvarez into the building for the 18th floor restaurant, Top of the Standard. I hope they don't have a table near the window because Ms. Alvarez is scared of heights.

They're holding hands and the heat that's coming off them is enough to solve New York's power shortages. That'll be one helluva elevator ride.

The scene is intimate, private.

Over the last year I've had to interrupt quite a few of the boss's 'intimate moments', although usually at the Farm, and I really fucking wish I hadn't. The worst was this one time when a suicidal employee was threatening to throw himself off the roof of DMA Tower and refused to talk to anyone but Anderson himself.

On that occasion, I had to knock on the door of his *rec room* at the Farm while he was engaged in something involving a lot of ropes and some poor bitch was suspended from the ceiling on a swing while another guy watched and ... yeah, you get the picture.

Damn room is soundproofed—I had to walk in ... and then had to look between my fingers. Not that I'm the sensitive kind, but *that* definitely isn't in my job description. And because we were in a hurry to leave, I had to help him get her down. I still get motion sickness thinking about it.

And all through that, Anderson was just irritated that he'd had his coitus interrupted.

But this is different. I feel like a fucking creepy voyeur because he and Maria are having a moment, and all they're doing is holding each other and kissing sweetly.

I walk away.

When I find a place to park, I stroll to the nearest McDonald's and avail myself of the facilities. I'm lovin' it.

Two hours later, my cell rings and I hear the boss's dulcet tones. "We're ready."

Now I've got the location of this rooftop restaurant in the GPS, I'm thinking intimate dinner à deux with the delectable Ms. Smith, with a view across the city. Anyway, I'm still working on the whole concept of Rachel being Mrs. Trainer, but I'm a patient man. And if a job's worth doing, it's worth doing well. And I do love doing Ms. Smith.

My cell lights up with a message from Anderson. What now?

Apparently, he needs some private time with Ms. Alvarez, I get the picture. I've got to be the invisible man again: deaf, dumb and blind, but somehow able to steer the SUV with three of my five senses out of use.

That's a warm and fuzzy feeling.

Rachel

I know that Justin won't be home for at least another hour, but even so I'm listening out for the sound of the elevator, his footsteps in the hall.

I miss Justin more each day. I should be worried, but I'm not.

As for Mr. Anderson, I was so glad when he found a normal girlfriend and he was different. He was happy. He introduced her to his family for a start and I have hopes for more, much more. I really want tonight to work out for both of them. It would be awful if he went back to that cold, emotionless, stunted way of life.

And, ugh, that awful Mr. Landon. I do *not* understand why Mr.

Anderson is friends with him. He really is unpleasant and I know that he was involved in recruiting Mr. Anderson's *friends* at the Farm. Do you know what he named his chain of cigar bars? Saint-Mars. Sounds pretty, doesn't it? But if you happened to look up what it means, you'd know that Bénigne d'Auvergne de Saint-Mars was a French prison governor in the late 17th century—best known as the keeper of the Man in the Iron Mask. Oh, yes, Mr. Landon has got a sense of humor: a very twisted, unpleasant sense of humor. Horrible, vile man.

If Mr. Anderson went back to his old ways, I don't think I could take it—I don't think Justin could either. He's terribly fond of Maria and has little tolerance for those sex parties. I'm ashamed to say that at first I was worried that he'd been tempted, but he said that he never was—thank God—and I believe him.

Maria brought Mr. Anderson to life and when she asked for space ... well, it was awful. Just terrible to see him so broken. But ... take a deep breath ... she's giving him a second chance. Justin was as pleased as I was when he heard that they were going to dinner. He pretended not to be, of course.

I understand his reasons for wanting to stay as detached and unemotional as possible when it comes to Mr. Anderson. Justin says that people working in close protection need to maintain some distance to keep their edge. He says that getting too close to the client could affect his professional judgment. Well, that ship has sailed, in my opinion. He can pretend all he wants that this is just another job, but I know better. He uses humor as a way of deflecting the truth from what he's really thinking.

But when he's with me, in bed, I see the real Justin: he's stripped bare, and I don't just mean of clothes, although that by itself is a delicious image. What I mean is—he doesn't hide who he is deep down. I love the way he gives me all of himself. I know he keeps work things hidden from me, things that he thinks will upset me, but he never hides himself, who he is.

And he still wants to marry me. I'm sure he thinks that one day he'll just wear me down and I'll give in, but we have things to

145

resolve between us: our age difference, does he want more children, because that could be an issue, and the gun he wears to work. Sometimes when I see it, I get flashbacks from being held hostage. That's not as often now, so maybe I'm dealing better these days. Perhaps we're getting closer. Or maybe nothing else is important but being with the man I love.

Finally, I hear the sounds I've been longing to hear.

I look up from the sofa and across the room, Justin is smiling at me.

"Hey, baby."

He looks tired. Well, that's hardly surprising; he's had a long day and he was up early as usual.

"Are you hungry? Can I get you something to eat?"

"I wouldn't mind a beer. Maybe a sandwich?"

I can't help smiling: 'maybe' means 'yes, but I don't want to look like I'm taking advantage'.

"I guess it's a good thing I made this chicken salad sandwich for you then, isn't it?"

"God, I love you! I'm a damn lucky man."

"Yes, you are and don't you forget it. But tell me how it went with Mr. Anderson and Ms. Alvarez?"

He smiles.

"Well, it was touch and go. If there was anyone who was more likely to screw it up than the boss ... but she's going to give him another chance."

I can't help sighing with relief.

"Thank goodness for that!"

He frowns.

"Justin, what aren't you telling me?"

"Nothing, well, something. It's just that the boss has bought the building next door."

"What does that have to do with Ms. Alvarez?"

"He's planning on moving her brothers and grandfather there."

Rachel's mouth drops open.

"When did he talk to her about this?"

"I'm not sure that he has, but Pam asked me about the realtor he was using and was the boss planning to expand Wolf Point since it had all happened suddenly today. But as he also asked Ryan to look into school districts for Junior High and High Schools, I put two and two together."

Rachel grimaces.

"He's planning this big move for her family and he hasn't even *discussed* this with her?"

"Probably not. But I'm guessing he discussed it with her grandfather when he visited—but who knows?"

"Oh dear! He can be a little..."

"Hell, yes he can. I don't want to be around when she tells him that—I might have to stop her from throwing things at him, and I know how much you hate washing blood out of my shirts."

"How very magnanimous of you."

"Oh, baby! I love it when you use big words. It makes me horny."

Hmm, I'll have to add that to the list of things that makes Justin horny. It's quite a long list.

"Do you like camping?"

I'm confused by the sudden change of topic.

"Sleeping in a tent?"

Justin raises a tired smile.

"Yeah, that's usually what it means."

"Uh, well, I haven't done that in a while, not unless you include sleeping in a tent in Allison and Bill's backyard with the girls for a night. Why do you ask?"

"I thought it might be kinda fun: you, me and Lilly. Go for a long weekend sometime? Maybe the weekend after Labor Day? What do you think?"

I hate sleeping on the floor, I hate not having a flushing toilet nearby, and I hate having to line up for a shower. But he's asking me to spend time with him and Lilly. I don't have to think about my reply.

"That sounds wonderful."

Chapter Eighteen

A WOMAN OF SUBSTANCE

I can't sleep. Rachel is lying beside me looking so damn beautiful that I want to reach out and touch her just to make sure she's real. But I don't want to wake her so I just stay on my side, staring at her.

Eventually, I decide to go make myself coffee even though it's still an hour before dawn. I check the CCTV room on the way, making sure everything is okay.

I'm getting as OCD as the boss. I'll be counting the number of times I say 'fuck' soon. His fucked-upness must be rubbing off on me. *One.* Next thing you know I'll be firing champagne fucking corks from my ass. *Two.* Okay, I don't actually have proof that the boss has done that, but I saw his recreation rooms at the Farm. They're featured regularly in my nightmares, along with the Olympic female wrestling team and a set of anal plugs (extra large). That's a fucking horror story waiting to happen. *Three.* And if I start thinking that listening to music from *La Traviata* is going to cheer me up, I'll know it's time to volunteer for that frontal lobotomy after all. I wonder if the boss's medical insurance will cover it?

The truth is, I've got all that shit running through my head. All the boss's horror stories from his fucked up life. *Four. FUCK! FUCK! FUCK! Five. Six. Seven.* I'd guessed at most of it—it's hard not to when the evidence is all over his body and I've heard those screams in the night too many times. I have a damn good idea what happened between the boss and Landon, and I can't understand how no one knew, why his parents didn't see it. It's so fucking *wrong! Eight.* If anyone touched Lilly like that, I'd kill them. I'd hunt them down and tear their fucking eyeballs out—and I'd enjoy it. *Nine. FUCK! Enough with the fucking counting or I'll have to take my socks off! Ten.* Oh, wait ... *eleven.*

I can't say this dark shit to Rachel, she'd totally freak out. She already thinks I'm a few bricks shy of a load. Maybe that's why she won't marry me. And, what's really scary, maybe this is why I can work for the boss: I know what it's like to have experienced horror. Show me a man or woman who's done tours in the Middle East that doesn't have that look. But you lock that shit away from normal people. You keep it in a box in a dark corner of your mind and you lose the goddamn key.

I used to think that the old me died over there ... until I met Rachel. You don't ever get over what you saw: you can get on with your life, but you don't ever get over it.

Why won't she see that the job I do is different from the person that I am? So, I carry a gun to work. Hell, this is America. It's in the constitution—the 'right to bear arms'. But if it's going to come between us, I might have to rethink my career path. After all, who lies on their death bed wishing they'd spent more time at the office?

Ms. Alvarez is taking on a challenge with Anderson.

Still studying The CCTV footage an hour later, it reveals nothing new. *Not a fucking thing.* I feel like I've pulled my brain out through my nostrils and reinserted through my eyeballs. It's like watching re-runs of *Dora the Explorer* with Lilly. I think the Ancient Egyptians used to do something like that—the weird brain shit, not *Dora the Explorer.* No wonder it took them so long to invent the wheel.

I'm pondering on the weirdness that is my life when I hear a noise behind me and spin around, reaching for a gun I'm not wearing. *Fuck!* My heart rate is going fast enough to make a speed-freak dizzy.

"Anything to report, Trainer?"

I'm going to put a bell around his neck if he's going to start creeping around like that.

"No, sir."

"Five minutes."

"Yes, sir."

See that? Not a word wasted. That's what I call guy talk.

I had no idea I'd ended up working through the night. Oh well, a cozy three hours sleep. That's enough to survive on.

I head back to my bedroom and pull on sweats and sneakers.

You know one of the things I love about Rachel? She irons my sweatpants. I know it's dumb and pointless and completely unnecessary, but she says laundry smells better when it's been ironed. I love that Rachel cares enough to do it for me. I think I love it *because* it's pointless: it's my gal looking after me. Not like my ex. Her idea of looking after me was making sure that my best friend's bed stayed warm while I was in Afghan.

Soon, I'm pounding the streets of New York, hyper-aware that my Smith & Wesson is playing a tune on my ribs. I know the boss doesn't approve, not that I give a shit, but I know that Rachel hates it, too. And that I *do* care about. But asking me to leave it behind, especially while the blackmailer is on the loose, would be like saying that Miley Cyrus is shy and retiring or asking me to take on Abigail Anderson without body armor.

Oh hell.

My sunny personality takes a dive when I remember I'll be seeing Abigail the Diva on Saturday—with fireworks. I wonder if the Andersons have a foxhole in the garden.

Just bury me now.

But then it's the boss who steps out into left field.

"Trainer, you'll be driving Miss Alvarez and myself to the Bronx Zoo today."

I will? I mean, *I am?*

Maybe the boss wants to feed some politicians to the lions, or maybe it's climate-change denialists this week.

And then a memory sparks inside me...

Or maybe he wants to do something nice for Ms. Alvarez.

"Dress casual," he says.

Jeez, don't make it sound like a date, boss!

"Yes, sir."

At 7.30AM, I park outside Ms. Alvarez's apartment a.

A few minutes later, the boss escorts Ms. Alvarez down the steps from her building. She's busy smiling and talking a hundred miles.

"Dev! Where are we going? What am I going to tell Pam?"

"I've told her you're with me. That's all she needs to know."

Ms. Alvarez laughs happily.

"Dev, is this spontaneous fun?"

"Possibly," he replies, his face unmoving.

"I love it! Hi, Trainer! Do you know where we're going?"

"Good morning, Ms. Alvarez. I'm not at liberty to disclose the destination."

"Pah! You guys! Strong silent types, huh?" and she laughs again.

I wonder if she'll be laughing when she realizes what the boss has in store, bearing in mind that facing your fears isn't always a laugh a minute.

As we head toward the Bronx River Parkway, she starts to look confused.

"Seriously, Dev, where are we going?"

There's a short pause before I take the turn to the zoo, and the boss nods at the sign.

"The zoo! That's fantastic! I haven't been there since I was a little k— Wait! What are we doing at the zoo? It's way too early—it doesn't even open until ten." She pauses as realization dawns. "Dev, you didn't, did you?"

The boss smiles and Ms. Alvarez covers her face with her hands.

"Oh my God! You totally did, didn't you? I don't know about

this ... I mean, I *do* want to do the zipline and the Treetop Adventure, but I have to psych myself up for it! I need to prepare! I have to..."

He takes her hands in his, holding them firmly.

"You can do this, Maria. You can do anything, remember? When you told me I could give up the Farm if I wanted to? Remember what I said?"

She glares at him.

"You said you couldn't."

A ghost of a smile crosses the boss's face.

"But I was wrong and you were right. You. Not me. So I know that you *can* do this, Maria."

She closes her eyes and takes a deep breath.

"I can't believe you were listening to me ramble on about ziplines and skydiving at my interview," she mumbles. "Oh God! We're not going skydiving as well, are we?"

"Maybe another time," smiles the boss.

"*Dios mio!* Because I think facing one mind-numbing fear in a day is enough."

I park the Rover and open the door for the boss and Ms. Alvarez, then lead them through the security entrance.

What? You thought the billionaire was going to get in line with everyone else? Nope. The boss has reserved the Treetop Adventure before opening hours for three people—and that includes yours truly.

Maria is given her helmet, which the boss enjoys making sure is strapped to the right degree of comfort. I go first on the climbing ropes, checking everything is in full working order. I'm not expecting problems, but I have to be ready for them.

There are seven different courses for visitors, ranging from beginner to expert. I'm really wanting to do the expert one because it reminds me of oh-so-happy days at Boot Camp, but I think that would be too much for Ms. Alvarez, although I have no doubt that the boss would be up for it.

He chooses a course of mid-ability difficulty, where we swing from ropes and navigate our way through the trees. The zoo's rangers are on hand to help, as well.

Maria is doing it all with grim determination. I don't think she's looked down once, but when we get to the rope bridge, her skin looks gray and clammy.

"I don't think I can do this," she whispers, her lips white and trembling.

"Sure you can," says the boss, sounding disturbingly like a cheerleader. "You can do anything."

"Not this," she says, her whole body shaking.

The rope bridge sways gently as Ms. Alvarez holds on with a Klingon death grip.

"Yes, you, Maria Conchita Alvarez! Don't tell me a tough chick from the Bronx can't hack a little vertigo."

"Fuck off, Anderson," she hisses, and the boss tries not to laugh.

She closes her eyes, takes two tentative steps on the rope bridge, muttering under her breath the whole time.

"Oh, yeah. Sure, Maria. You can talk the talk at in interview, or at the Comedy Club. Oh yeah, *there*, you're a mouthy chick from da Bronx. *I'm facing my fears.* What pyschobabble bullshit is this? You're dating a freakin' billionaire. Can't you get him to build you a bridge that doesn't wobble with every step? Holy shit, I nearly fell! Ugh, this is so stupid. And I told him I want to go skydiving. *Madre de Dios*, I'm going to die before I've paid back my student loans. *Abuelo* will be so mad at me."

Then she turns to the boss.

"You know what, *Devon*? If I die doing this, I'm coming back to haunt your ass!"

He gives her a devilish smile.

"I look forward to you haunting my ass, along with a number of other ideas I'd like to try out."

She blushes bright red and I cringe, hanging back as much as possible so I don't have to hear anymore.

"It's okay to be scared," the petite blonde Ranger who's

escorting us says to me. "Catch up with your friends when you feel ready."

Fuck, never a break when you need one.

We finally get to the zipline platform and Ms. Alvarez's knees are knocking together.

"You're gonna love this," the Ranger says brightly. "I'll strap you in for an epic ride across the Bronx River. You'll love it! They say it's a once in a lifetime rush, but I promise you'll want to do it again."

I glance at the boss's face and see the tightness around his eyes, and I realize that he's facing his fears, too. Not about the height, but about letting Maria jump off the platform when all he wants to do is keep her safe in his arms 24/7. Letting her live her life is him facing his biggest fear.

"Just 400 feet. My colleague, Jonathan, is on the other side ready to catch you. Okay?"

Ms. Alvarez nods, her eyes tightly closed. Then without another word, she steps off the ledge, a scream tearing from her lungs.

"Oh wow, I forgot to tell her it picks up speed in the middle," says the blonde Ranger.

The boss steps off the platform, rushing after Ms. Alvarez.

Chapter Nineteen

THE LONG WEEKEND

When I was a kid, my neighbor had this dog. It was always in the backyard, never in the house and desperate for attention, but it used to bark at everyone who went near it. Anderson kinda reminds me of that dog.

I've definitely seen a different side to him since Maria Alvarez came into the picture. And it scares the fuck out of him. Despite being a rich bastard, he doesn't really care that much about the money. Sure, he likes to have nice things, and I have to say he has A+ taste in cars, (even though I rarely get to drive the DB9), but all that pales into insignificance next to Maria. He's finally found something—someone—that is more valuable, that he really cares about losing. I can tell that he'd like to order Maria to stay at Wolf Point and never set foot out of the door. Hell, he'd bubble wrap her and chain her to the bed if he could, and not in a kinky way.

But that's not going to happen because Maria is determined to live her own life. I really admire her for that. She's just a kid, but she's been through a lot and she knows what she wants, and she doesn't want to live in a 24-carat gold cage. Pam also says that she's got a real smart head on her shoulders and will be an asset to the business.

She's already an asset in the boss's life: two pluses for the price of one.

It's official: the boss is in love.

We have a word for that in the military: SUSFU—*Situation unchanged, still fucked up.*

It was a different story on the night of the big reunion. And, by the way, the boss and Ms. Alvarez still haven't had any make-up sex, which I totally don't get because that's the best thing about having an argument. I love arguing with Rachel because when we make up, all bets are off, and there's that thing she does with her ... well ... yeah.

So, back to the boss.

He didn't know if the woman of his dreams was going to stay an apparition, or whether she'd swallow her better judgment and let Mr. Control-Freak-with-unmentionable-tendencies back into her life.

He was so tense, I wished I had my helmet ready for the moment he snapped. It was like driving a one-handed bomb disposal expert to neutralize an IED ... except this bomb was in the backseat, twitching.

And while I'm thinking about it, why do limeys—sorry, Brits, as we're standing shoulder-to-shoulder—why do Brits call their bomb disposal guys ATOs? I mean, come on! Ammunition Technical Officer? Sounds like some desk jockey who hands out the rounds of ammo, not the guy with balls the size of watermelons who takes the lonely walk to neutralize a bomb?

Yeah, I'm going off track again. It was thinking about that R-rated make-up sex with Rachel. Puts a man off his game. And once I pulled a muscle in my ... yeah, moving on.

So, I'm driving the boss and wondering if I should have his doctor on speed-dial. I'm thinking that if the boss's anxiety levels stay this high, his blood pressure will be joining the mile-high club and he'll be chewing on his $400 manicure. I'm a New Man, I know about these things.

Well, that evening, the boss's story had a happy ending. It was hard to believe that the man I'd driven out, Mr. Ticking-time-bomb, was the same one who sat with his sleeping woman in his arms during the ride back. He looked like he'd found a small slice of heaven. Yeah, I get that.

Now, if I could just figure out where Landon is.

I still haven't brought up what I know about Landon with the boss. That's not like me, but it's not dissimilar to taking a step into a minefield: I know there are IEDs everywhere, I just don't know which step is going to end with me being blown to pieces.

The following evening, I have the pleasure of driving the boss to pick up Ms. Alvarez from her apartment for a second date.

He's in there for all of two minutes before rushing back to the car, holding Maria's hand as she hurries to keep up.

She's got a look on her face like she's trying not to laugh at him. I love that look. *Shit! What's with all this 'love' crap?* I'm turning into a fucking cheerleader.

For once my sense of sarcasm is safely in control. He's happy, she's happy: if there was any more joy going around, the world would spin off its axis.

The boss barely acknowledges my presence as if he's forgotten I'm here: his eyeballs are only for Ms. Alvarez. And suddenly I'm really hoping he remembers that this car doesn't drive itself because watching my boss get it on with Miss Cute-and-Flirty is not my idea of fun. Call me old fashioned.

"Is there something you'd like to do this evening?" he says.

Did I just have an auditory hallucination? He asked her what *she* wanted to do? Stop the fucking press.

Like I can't guess. Like *she* can't guess. Hell, it's so fucking obvious he wants to work through the Karma Sutra starting from page one to the end, (and including all the appendices), that he may as well have me drive them to the nearest pay-by-the-hour motel.

But then she shocks my socks off.

"I want to go salsa dancing."

Hark, the sound of tumbleweed rolling across the back seat of the Rover.

"Salsa?"

"Yep, that's what I want."

To give the boss his due, he only blinks twice before he agrees. "Really?"

"You said you wanted to go dancing, Maria. The choice is yours. Just tell Trainer where to go."

Salsa Con Fuego isn't quite the dive I was expecting, but Ms. Alvarez bypasses the restaurant and leads us to another room where Latin music is blasting out.

I exchange a glance with the boss, and he pulls her toward the bar to buy drinks before I go check out the room.

I don't like it. There are too many people and too many cozy alcoves where anyone could be hiding. The only reason I'm not yanking the boss out is that no one could predict his presence here. On the other hand, if someone was tailing us ... no, I'm sure not, I would have noticed. And I sweep the SUV for tracking devices twice a day, other than my own, of course.

We should be okay here for a couple of hours, even if the music is as loud as a Taliban RPG barrage.

I find a table in the back that's fairly private and text the boss. He makes his way to the table and hands me a bottle of water. *Gee, that just warms my heart.* Then Ms. Alvarez winks at me and drags Anderson onto the packed dance floor.

He's not bad, definitely got some moves, but I can see that he's having trouble relaxing. I don't know if it's the number of people pressing around him or the fact that he's so far out of his comfort zone, he's practically orbiting Mars.

I get asked to dance three times—twice by a couple of hot Latinas who definitely look like they could give a guy a good time, and once by a skinny kid in spray-on jeans who hasn't yet had his gaydar tuned. *Kudos for asking, kid, but I'm not your type.*

The evening hasn't been the clusterfuck it could have been, but when the club closes, I'm half expecting things go downhill PDQ.

"Are you coming back to Wolf Point?" the boss asks, although it sounds more like an order.

You know, what's great about women like Ms. Alvarez and

Rachel? They're real good at letting us guys think we're the ones in charge. I know that Rachel calls the shots, and she knows that I know that she knows that she calls the shots, but she'll let me have that guy-pride thing and pretend I'm in charge. She's thoughtful like that. Ms. Alvarez is the same. Maybe that's why I like her.

But she lobs it right over his head.

"Maybe I already have plans."

Fifteen-love to Ms. Alvarez.

I begin to relax as the boss manages to have what passes for a normal conversation for him, until he says,

"Your neighbor wants you naked, Maria."

Yep, that's my boss, who really only opens his mouth to change feet.

Next thing I know, he's threatening to kick the creepy fucker's ass until she gets some better neighbors. I have no problem with that, but it means he's given away the closely guarded secret that's he's bought the condo next door to Wolf Point for her family. A secret he was trying to keep from Ms. Alvarez until he'd, you know, asked her if she'd like that.

Double fault.

"That's not likely in the foreseeable, is it?!"

"It could be..."

There's a long pause while Maria puts it all together.

"Devon, what did you do now?"

"I've bought the apartment building next door to Wolf Point. Your family can come and live there when you move in with me. It'll be much safer than where they are now."

The boss speaks confidently, but I sink lower in my seat.

Because Maria is pissed. Really pissed.

"Whaaaat?"

Dogs in Scarsdale probably heard that screech.

"You're making a decision just like that? About my life? About my brothers? About *Abuelo*? And when the hell did I agree to move in with you, because I'm drawing a blank. You've bought the whole damn building? Why the hell would you do that, Devon? What's wrong with you?"

I could write her a list.

"But I thought..."

"Did you, Dev? Did you *think?!* Because it sure the hell doesn't sound like it to me!"

Thirty-love to Ms. Alvarez.

The boss is getting hammered. I'm thinking of having commemorative t-shirts printed.

"Trainer," she yells, "I've changed my mind! Take me home!"

"Maria! Just ... just give it a chance! It's a great condo. The boys would love it there, and the public schools in the area are great or there are some private school options if they prefer. Joachim could attend whatever college in Manhattan he wanted, I'll help him with tuition."

Her eyes bulge and swivel at the same time, which is somewhat disturbing.

"Devon, just stop! For God's sake!" She takes a calming breath. "I know you mean well, I know that. But you can't just barge into all our lives like that. The boys go to good schools, ones where all their friends are. And Joachim is doing well at community college— it's giving him the stability he needs. And *Abuelo*, he's lived in the Bronx his whole life. He's 87, Dev, starting over in Manhattan without any of his old buddies, he'd *hate* it."

He grabs her hands.

"Maria, just ... just take a look. Your grandfather isn't getting any younger. I've seen how he struggles to climb the stairs to your apartment. You said yourself the elevators only works 10% of the time. We could adapt the condo for any future disabilities. He could have a driver to take him to the Bronx to see his friends every day. We can make this work, I know we can. Please, just ... will you just take a look? Your grandfather loved it."

Three...

Two...

One...

"Are you freakin' kidding me right now?!" she screeches. "You already talked to *Abuelo*? Who the hell do you think you are?!"

Good question.

I pull up outside Wolf Point act like the Pinball Wizard. *Retro pop culture reference.*

"Wait here, Trainer," says the boss.

Yup, already worked that out. You hired me for my brains, not my snappy suits, bossman.

She storms out of the car and starts off down the street, before she swings around to jab him in the chest with her fingers.

He tries to talk her down—*double fault.*

"It's wrong, Devon! You're wrong. It's so wrong I can't even believe you don't know it's wrong. What's wrong with you?"

Forty-love to Ms. Alvarez.

"I don't think I'm wrong."

"That's because you're a jerk!"

Game, set and match to Ms. Alvarez.

It could go either way. Inside, I'm *begging* Ms. Alvarez to put the poor bastard out of his misery—mostly because I have a couple of scenes planned out with Miss Moneypenny, one of which may involve fun with food, and I do not want Beethoven's *Pathétique* playing in the background if that dumb jerk fucks up again, no matter how apt a musical segue it is for the boss.

I can't help thinking that Ms. Alvarez needs a vacation named after her because of everything she's had to put up with. Well, the boss is rich: he should be able to swing that. Maybe a *That's love ... and it sucks* day. I can imagine the Hallmark cards now.

Eventually she agrees to go inside, and my torture—and his—is ended, at least temporarily.

Wait ... maybe ... could be ... yep ... thinking it is ... the boss is happy.

Doesn't it just make you feel warm all over?

I park quickly and hurry upstairs because I have every intention of making Rachel feel warm all over with the least amount of time between me exiting the vehicle and entering, well, the apartment, for starters.

"Justin!"

Rachel's voice is strained and immediately my hand reaches for the Smith & Wesson.

"Carla just left a message: Lilly isn't well. I was just about to call you."

"What? What's happened? Why the fuck didn't she call my cell?"

"I don't know, but yelling at me isn't going to help. Nor will yelling at her. She thinks Lilly has some sort of severe gastroenteritis. They've taken her to the emergency room."

I feel like every drop of blood has drained out of my body. *Not Lilly. Not my Princess.*

I pull out my cell and call my ex.

"Carla, how is she?"

"Justin, finally! We don't know yet. A doctor is checking her. I'll have to call you back."

And the fucking bitch hangs up on me, leaving me staring at a useless hunk of plastic.

"I'm going over there."

"Justin," Rachel lays a cool hand on my arm, "just give it ten minutes. Wait until the doctor has seen her."

I know she's right, but it feels wrong, standing here as useless as a sundeck on a submarine.

Ten minutes are up and she hasn't called back. I try her cell, but it's turned off.

"That's it. I'm heading over."

Rachel bites her lip, but doesn't try to stop me. I text the boss to tell him I have an emergency, and arrange for Evans to do the security sweeps. Just as I'm heading out, my cell rings.

"She's fine. She's okay. The doctor says it's just stomach flu."

I hear the tremor in Carla's voice and remember, for the briefest moment, that I cared about her once.

"Thank, Christ. I'm coming over."

"Don't be ridiculous, Justin," she snaps, reminding me why we got divorced. "It's late and I'm taking her home. I was just letting you know."

"I'm her father, for fuck's sake!"

"Don't swear at me, Justin, and stop trying to bully me."

"FUCK!" I yell into the phone as she cuts me off *again*.

Rachel wraps her arms around me, and with her touch, I feel like I can breathe.

I leave early the next morning and spend a couple of hours with Lilly. I can tell that Carla wants to kick me the hell out, but she doesn't because our daughter is happy to see me. I guess that makes her a good mom. Not sure what it makes me.

Saturday morning, and my woman is going away. It's only for one night, but it feels like someone cut off my right arm.

"Justin, put me down! I'm only going to be gone till Sunday evening!"

"Too long," I murmur into her warm, soft, deliciously-scented neck as I hug the shit out of her.

She gives a light laugh and tugs my hair.

"This is getting long! I thought you told me that if you could hold onto your sideburns, your buzzcut was in need of a trim. You'd better shape up, Marine!"

"It's because you're leading me astray, woman."

Damn, I love it when she's a bad influence.

"You don't seem to have any difficulty being led, Justin."

"Not true! I'm trying to make an honest woman of you, but you don't want to give up living in sin."

She stills, and I regret my words because now they've broken the mood.

"You know what I think about that, Justin. I don't want to discuss it again."

"Okay, but can we discuss some more sin when you get back?"

And that makes her smile.

"I'll think about it."

Oh yeah, me, too.

With the mansion empty and with no distractions, I can focus on keeping the boss safe. I check all the entrances and exits *again*, but still nothing.

I'm almost relieved when Mason calls me with an update. But not for long.

"We've got a problem, Trainer. Ms. Alvarez has a stalker. Evans spotted a tail on her twice this week. We ran the guy's facials but nothing so far."

"What the fuck?"

"Yes, a confirmed sighting yesterday."

"And you're telling me this *now?* What happened?"

"Evans spotted the tail in the morning and again at lunch time when Ms. Alvarez went to the deli. He didn't see him following her home. But twice in one day—I don't like it."

Neither do I, and the boss is going to do a St. Helen's.

"I'll add a twice-daily sweep of the Alvarez apartment to the security schedule. I'll make a personal inspection this afternoon."

"Who the fuck is doing this, Mason? Is it the blackmailer?"

"I wish I knew."

I put the phone down, and the first thing I do is check my Smith & Wesson because *nothing* is going to happen to Ms. Alvarez and the boss: *not on my fucking watch.*

I sweep the building *again*, and wait by the elevator when I see that the boss and Maria have arrived in the underground garage.

The boss gets straight to the point.

"Has Mason been in touch?

"Yes, sir."

"And?"

"It's taken care of."

"Good. And how is your daughter?"

See, this is why I put up with all the boss's fucked up shit: he's remembered that Lilly was sick. Gotta rate that twisted bastard.

"She's fine now, thank you, sir."

"That's good."

Ms. Alvarez smiles at me.

"How old is she?"

"She's eight. She lives with the B— her mother."

I follow the boss to his home office for my orders.

"We're having dinner with my parents tonight, Trainer. Leaving at seven."

"Bearing in mind the development of a possible stalker, would you consider postponing..."

"No."

"In that case, sir, I'd like to recommend that we keep a 24/7 guard at Wolf Point for now. Sir."

He rubs his forehead.

"Fine. Have Mason arrange it. But low profile."

Yeah, I can do that: the cool cat who walks alone.

"My sister will be pleased to see you tonight, Trainer," he says, blandly, as if it's an afterthought.

And I can't help groaning. I need a run-in with Abigail Anderson as much as Colonel Custer needs more Indians.

Chapter Twenty

GROUNDHOG DAY

Evans introduces me to Reynolds and Banner. I know Mason won't send me any greenhorns. Reynolds seems like a solid guy. Doesn't have much of a sense of humor though. He reminds me of me. But less charming. I'm a hard act to follow.

It'll be strange not having the staff area to ourselves anymore, me and Rachel. It's a development that I don't like. At all. But right now, I need the backup for a big ole fundraiser at Anderson's parents' tonight.

"Anything to report from Scarsdale?"

Evans frowns.

"Apart from the fact it's wide open? There's access from the golf course; the perimeter isn't viable—a ten year old could get over their boundary wall. I don't like it."

Then Banner speaks up.

"Any chance Anderson will cancel?"

"Why the fuck didn't I think of that? Oh wait, I did. And then I nearly got my ass fired for suggesting it. Anything *useful* you want to tell me?"

He has the sense to look pretty fucking embarrassed. I can see Evans trying to hide a smile.

Okay, so maybe I'm being an asshole, but I think I've got every reason. Like I really need another challenge.

"Got any *good* news?" I mutter, trying to calm down.

"Mason's arranged for a team to watch the perimeter: best I can say, boss."

Yeah, now he's trying to brown-nose me by calling me 'boss'. The only person I want calling me 'boss' is Rachel—and that ain't never gonna happen. On the other hand, she called me 'God' the other night. I guess that's a promotion.

Reynolds looks over his shoulder.

"Heads up, officer on deck," he mutters.

Anderson shakes hands and Reynolds discreetly sizes up the boss. Either it's Anderson's *interesting* reputation, or he's admiring the cut of his Savile Row shirt. Never underestimate your close protection squad.

"They've been out to your parents' house to do a sweep, and Mason has eyes on the perimeter. It's as good as it's going to get."

I shrug, sending him a loud and fucking clear message.

He frowns, but doesn't say anything.

"Banner will be up front with me in the Range Rover," I continue. "Evans will be in the escort car, and Reynolds will be at Wolf Point."

The boss looks irritated and I know it's not with me, but this fucked-up situation.

Banner, Evans and Reynolds are kicking back in my living room—that is, the staff living room.

"Everything cool with Anderson?" asks Lance.

"As cool as it gets for him. He doesn't want any fuck-ups tonight. I told him there wouldn't be any—don't you assholes make a liar out of me."

"You've got a really sweet deal here, T," says Evans thoughtfully. "Nice place, nice cushy number with Anderson."

I really didn't think I'd ever hear the words 'cushy' and 'Anderson' in the same sentence. I might have to rethink Evans' level of intelligence. Did he send his brain for dry-cleaning?

"But do you ever miss being a Bootneck?"

"You mean sharing living space with twenty guys and eating MREs three times a day in 120-degree heat? Not so much."

"Huh, you say so? What's it like working for this Anderson guy?" asks Reynolds. "You like this close protection work?"

I know he's only recently punched out from Navy SEALs.

"It's a different level of intensity. You're totally in some stranger's life, but you're not part of it either. It can get a bit crazy keeping everything separate. But Anderson isn't a publicity hound like some of the assholes I've worked for. He sees his family and his girl, and he works. That's it."

Okay, so I might have been economical with the truth, but it's no one's fucking business. I mean, the boss's fucking is no one's business.

"So how much of a problem is this stalker?" asks Evans.

"We don't know that he's after Ms. Alvarez—Anderson could still be the target," I remind him.

A couple of hours later, we all change into our fade-into-the-background good suits, and do a comms check while we're waiting in the foyer.

"Everyone know what they're doing?"

They all nod, and Anderson strides over, looking tense.

"Trainer?"

"We're good to go, sir."

And I realize I've only got part of their attention when Reynolds does a goldfish impersonation and Evans looks as if he's about to drool.

So fucking uncool.

I turn around and see Maria walking towards us. She looks stunning. I always thought she was a cute kid, but right now she looks beautiful. I feel proud of her. Maybe it'll feel like this when I see Lilly go to her prom. Not that I'll allow any creepy kid getting their paws on her. I read that teenage boys think about sex every fifteen seconds—or maybe that was Anderson, I can't remember. Either way, I'll be escorting Lilly to her prom. And I'll be armed.

"Maria, you look breathtaking."

I feel like fucking cheering. The boss has managed to compliment his girl without making an ass of himself. It's a Kodak moment, in a non-visual, auditory sort of way.

While Anderson and Maria enjoy a glass of champagne, I send the others to check the underground garage. I'm not expecting any issues on home turf, but you can never be careful enough.

When we arrive at Scarsdale, Banner jumps out to open Ms. Alvarez's door, then discreetly escorts the happy couple while I park the car.

Showtime.

I've just about finished doing a sweep of the house when the hairs on the back of my neck stand up. I whip around and try to frame words, but nothing comes out. It's like the nightmarish scene in 'Ghostbusters' where they conjure up the source of their own destruction just by thinking about it. But it's not a 100ft Marshmallow Man stalking me ... it's much, much worse.

Abigail Anderson.

"Hello, Trainer," she says. "I was hoping I'd see you ... by yourself. Mom says that she doesn't think you're gay? I really hope she's right."

I break out into a cold sweat and my pulse rate goes through the roof.

Where the fuck is backup?

"My date has been such a disappointment. But now you're here! It must be fate."

I try to speak, but my mouth has inconveniently frozen into the shape of a scream. Munch could have used me as his model.

The horror. The horror.

"Mom always says you shouldn't send a boy to do a man's work. I so agree, don't you, Justin?"

I wonder if I can make it to the door before...

"Will you dance with me, Justin? I'm sure my brother wouldn't mind. Just one little dance?"

Over my dead body—which looks like it could well be the case.

She takes a step closer, and I measure the distance to the window. If I don't stop to open it, I should be able to make it through into the garden.

But then there's a figure in the doorway, and relief floods through me.

"All clear on the second floor, T. Oh, sorry ... should I come back later?"

Lance Banner is staring at me, a puzzled expression on his face.

"Your nickname is 'T'? Oh, wow, is that like code? That's so cute! Who's your friend, Justin? Hi, my name's Abigail. It's really nice to meet one of Justin's *special friends* at last."

"Um ... good evening. The name's Banner, ma'am."

"Oh, it's so great to meet you, Banner. Is your first name, like, Bruce? Because that would be way cool. Or, it could be Justin's special nickname for you. That would be so funny!"

"It's Lance Banner, ma'am."

Don't engage the enemy! Retreat! Retreat!

"Hey, you've got those earpieces like real secret service agents! Who are you talking to, Justin? Are there more of you? More of your *friends*? Can I try?"

She reaches up to touch my earpiece and I make a tactical retreat.

"We're working, Miss Anderson," I say, severely.

She giggles. Christ she's annoying.

"You're so cute when you get all serious, Justin."

Banner is looking nervous.

If she wasn't my employer's sister I might consider drawing my gun, but the way my luck's going she'd probably catch the bullet in her teeth.

When she giggles again, I cringe.

"He's so cute! Is he your *special* friend?"

Banner's eyes look like they're on swivels, as his gaze toggles between us.

"I'm sorry, ma'am," I say, tightly, "I really have to go now."

She pouts.

"You're no fun, T," and she stalks off, looking for fresh prey.

I run my hand across my forehead, wiping off the sweat.

Across the room, Banner is tugging at his tie.

"Getting mighty warm in here, T," he says, nervously.

You've got that right.

Banner pats his chest and I know he's wishing he had a Kevlar vest. Although garlic and a Crucifix would probably work better.

At least I get to use my stealth and evasion training in the Marines to keep out of her sight for the rest of the evening.

The following day, the boss is back from lunch at *Le Bernier* with Ms. Alvarez. I've been watching their approach on the computer. Well, watching the positioning of his phone's GPS. Evans is on driving duty today.

"Banner, heads up. The boss is back."

Huh, alliteration. Damn, I'm The Man!

"Okay, T. I'll go cover the garage."

It's been good having Lance here over the last few days: he knows what he's doing and I know he's got my back. Although it's been weird having him and Evans sharing my office when they're on duty—and one of those bastards has eaten *all* the cookies that Rachel baked for me—but it made me realize something: Wolf Point is my home. I've gotten so used to thinking of this as a job, I hadn't even noticed the change. Or maybe it's not so much Wolf Point as the fact Rachel is here. Rachel is my home.

On the other hand, maybe it's just all the damn joy that Anderson has been radiating since Ms. Alvarez came back into his life. Now he knows what he'd be missing if she left again. And if Rachel left ... I really don't want to fucking think about that.

At least no one can get into Wolf Point unless Anderson invites them, and that isn't going to happen.

I head for the elevator and stand by, ready to meet Anderson and Ms. Alvarez. The doors slide open and I'm treated to the really private spectacle of them kissing as if the end of the world has just been announced.

I step back, out of their eye-line.

I still can't get used to seeing the boss lose control like that. I've seen him radiating red-hot fury to the point where Howard considered wearing fireproof pants to meetings, but there was always something calculated about it, like he knew *exactly* what effect this had on his employees. And he didn't do it very often—he didn't need to. His icy-cold anger was even more terrifying; that shark-like ability to hone in on anyone's weakness. Not me, of course.

The only other time Anderson lets any emotion show is when he's asleep. No man can out-run those demons.

"Good afternoon, Trainer."

"Ms. Alvarez, Mr. Anderson."

She beams at me.

"It's really great to see you. You look well."

I see the boss's fingers tighten on her with a death grip. He looks as if he'd like to rip my arms off and use them to beat me over the head. It's a pretty mild reaction for him, especially where Ms. Alvarez is concerned.

"If you've finished. I'd like a debriefing," he spits out.

Yeah, very fucking smooth. Not.

"I'll be with you shortly," snarls Anderson.

What he really means is 'you're so fucking fired'.

I'm almost surprised he doesn't piss on the walls to mark his territory. Maybe that will come later. But if he tries to piss on my shoes, I'm outta here.

I go wait in the office. Banner is still patrolling and I can see him on the CCTV cameras. He's checking out the cars belonging to other residents in the street.

Anderson strides into the office, still looking pissed.

I fold my arms across my chest and wait for his tirade. But it doesn't come. Instead he stares at me appraisingly.

"Report, Trainer," he says, almost mildly.

Did they fuck already?

Maybe his bedroom is like 'Brigadoon' and I've been standing here for a hundred years.

"All the locks and access codes have been reprogrammed using Howard's new algorithm; we've completed a search of the house, garage and staff areas of Wolf Point; I personally checked Ms. Alvarez's apartment and CCTV of the surrounding streets. We've found nothing, sir. No sign of the stalker. I also spoke to Ms. Alvarez's grandfather and apprised him of the situation. He's promised to be vigilant." *Although I'm not sure what help an octogenarian could be.* "No one will be getting in here or at Ms. Alvarez's apartment unless someone lets them in."

He nods, looking distracted.

"I've retained Banner's services 24/7 on a week-by-week basis with Evans, and Reynolds on-call via Mason."

"Has Mrs. Smith returned from her sister's?"

"Yes, sir, but she's out at the moment. Banner's checking the other residents' vehicles in the street. Sir, it's definitely a weak spot."

I shrug. *And unless you bubble wrap your girl, that's as good as it gets.*

He runs his hands through his hair and I know he's still worried. *Yup, join the club.*

"Thank you, Trainer."

And he walks out.

What? Is that it? No rampant jealousy? No yelling until my ears melt? The boss is getting *soft.*

I kinda miss the old days.

I go back to studying the surveillance cameras. Banner is using the under-vehicle search mirror. I'm not saying the stalker is capable of planting a car bomb, but I'm not taking the chance either.

But this frustrating day just gets very fucking perfect, and here's why...

I was still checking surveillance footage when Rachel got back from grocery shopping.

"Justin, haven't you eaten yet?"

"No, baby. Thought I'd wait for you. And I've been going over the CCTV tapes with Lance."

"Well, you should both eat. Where is he?"

"Finishing up in the garage. He'll be here soon."

"I take it Mr. Anderson and Ms. Alvarez are back. How did she enjoy the party?"

"Yeah, she looked amazing."

"Oh, did she?"

And there it was: a note of jealousy.

I have never, *ever* given Rachel the slightest reason to feel jealous. I haven't hidden anything from her: she knows I went kind of crazy when Carla and I first separated. Got drunk a lot. Slept with a lot of women—some of them I didn't even know their names. I didn't want to pretend with her. But she also knows I haven't looked at another woman since I met her.

"You like Maria, don't you?" she says, quietly. "Well, I'm not surprised. She's very pretty and sweet ... and young..."

But I couldn't listen to anymore.

"Rachel, don't. Yes, I like Maria. But not *that* way. I think of her in the same way I think of Lilly. I just want her to be safe, and I want the boss to not fuck it up with her. But you're my woman, babe. Hell, I'd make you Mrs. Trainer in a shot or faster. You know that. There's no one else I want, Rachel. I love you, for fuck's sake."

Yeah, I know. I'm smooth.

"I ... I'll think about it, Justin."

I wondered if I needed wax clearing from my ears because I thought she just said...

"You will?"

She laughs.

"Yes, just thinking though, okay?"

"Very okay, baby."

Just as the evening seems to descend into a pleasant and unusual tranquility, I see the shark-eyed king incubus drive into the garage.

Banner gives me the heads up.

"T, a Mr. Landon wants to see Mr. Anderson. He doesn't have an appointment."

I can hear the snake's voice in the background *and he's pissed that his fingerprint access has been removed.*

I'd love to tell him to crawl back to his cave and boil up some more bats' eyes, but that's the boss's call.

"I'll key him in, Lance. Send him up."

The boss is really not going to like this.

He's got his arms wrapped around Ms. Alvarez and they look happy.

I feel like such a fucking creep. I clear my throat, and the boss's head snaps up. Now he looks pissed. Great, shoot the messenger. But hell, I'd look pissed if I got interrupted like that. It's the price he pays for being rich, for needing someone like me.

"Yes?"

"Mr. Landon is on his way up, sir."

"What?"

All I can do is shrug. *Your shit, boss. Over to you.*

"Well, this should be entertaining," he mutters.

Ms. Alvarez looks *really* pissed. The boss is right: it's going to be a real showstopper.

I wait at the elevator as the doors open with a soft hiss.

"Good evening, Trainer."

"This way, Mr. Landon."

"Always so formal, Trainer."

Yeah, because I'd rather French kiss a bullfrog than spend time with you, cunt.

"I'm sure Devon feels reassured having you here to reprogram his access codes. Is there anything else you can do?"

I don't reply to his needling, but I really enjoy, *really fucking enjoy* seeing the shock on the reptile's face when he sees Ms. Alvarez staring back at him defiantly.

That's my girl!

I leave them to it, because no matter how much I care for her, I'm not her father. But if I was, I'd be fucking proud of her.

The Landon bastard stays for less than ten minutes before I have the extreme pleasure of escorting him out. Via the elevator. Although, kicking his skinny carcass off the balcony would be more rewarding. He's probably going home to stir his cauldron and stare in his magic mirror. I hope the fucker cracks.

Landon is furious and doesn't care that he's sharing that carefully guarded information with me.

"He's making a serious mistake choosing that little whore over me!"

I don't respond but enjoy slamming the door on his bony ass.

When the boss walks into his office, he looks tired and pissed. And yet, he just doesn't get that the Landon troll preys on his negative feelings. He always looks irritated when he's seen him. For a smart guy, he can be pretty fucking dumb.

But I've seen a change in him. Whether he knows it or not, he has less patience for Landon. And the Beast senses it, which is why he's clinging on with every shiny talon he has. I wish Mason had found more evidence on him, one way or another. But I can't wait any longer.

"Sir..."

"What is it?"

"There's something I need to talk to you about, sir."

He looks like he wants to say no, but he sighs and waits.

"Well?"

"Mr. Landon's business is partially financed by Consolidated Iron. Do I need to worry about industrial espionage?"

I've blindsided him. Emotions shimmer across his face: shock, rage, disbelief, until he locks them down and his poker face is welded into place.

"How do you know this?"

"A source, sir."

"Who is this source?"

"I'm not at liberty to say, sir."

I'm waiting for the whole 'I sign your checks so I own your ass' speech. I've heard it from employers when they don't get their own way.

But Anderson only looks frustrated.

"How good is your source?"

"The best, sir."

"I see."

"I know that you're in talks with the Taiwanese, sir. Do I need to worry about Mr. Landon?"

I can tell that he wants to say no, but he doesn't.

"I'll look into it."

That's all he says, but it's enough.

As the boss turns to his laptop, I decide I've stared at as many monitors as I can stand. I pull my tie free and go find Rachel.

"Has *that person* gone?" she asks tightly.

"Yeah, got back on his broomstick and disappeared in a cloud of sulfur."

Her whole body relaxes and she smiles.

"Coq au vin?"

Fuck, I love it when she talks French.

At some point in the night, I feel Rachel moving restlessly next to me. She turns over and sees that I'm watching her.

"It's *that man*. He always upsets everyone when he comes here."

I pull her into my arms and kiss her hair.

"Don't worry about it, baby. I don't think it'll be for much longer."

She turns and stares up at me, her fingers tracing over the scruff on my cheek.

"What makes you say that?"

I can't tell her about the intel Mason gave me, but I don't need to.

"Because sooner or later the boss will have to choose: Landon or Maria. And he'll choose Maria."

"I hope you're right, Justin. I really do."

I'm not worried because I know that deep down the boss has already chosen. He just doesn't know it yet. I've chosen Rachel, and I really fucking hope she knows it.

The next day, I hear the boss tell Maria that Lucifer is "in the past". I feel like fucking cheering, but that would be unprofessional. And really uncool. And Banner would have a coronary.

I drop off the happy couple at DMA Tower, then do all the usual checks and read Mason's overnight intel report.

You think being a billionaire is all peaches and cream and fundraisers? The population of the US is 320 million. We've got 540 billionaires. I worked out the math once: that's one billionaire for every 592,000 of us drones. That's a lot of people to envy or hate on you.

Yeah, you'd better watch your back.

Or pay a guy like me to watch it for you.

There are hearts breaking wide open all over DMA Tower as the word spreads that the boss is officially off the market since he was seen arriving hand in hand with Ms. Alvarez this morning. A lot of the women—and a few of the men—are devastated to hear that he has a real-life girlfriend. And not just an imaginary friend named Harvey.

Pam told me that we'd need a grief counselor. I think she was joking, but I'm not sure. Tessa hasn't been seen since the word went out. 'Allergies' is the official reason.

At 6PM, I'm outside with the Rover. Banner has already left to collect some clean clothes from his own apartment and check his mail. He'll be living at Wolf Point for the next few weeks with me and Rachel, and Evans, occasionally. I've already warned him off Rachel, in a completely professional way. *"Put an eyeball out of place and I'll fucking use it for a pool ball."* You know, a reasonable, measured approach like the professional I am.

The boss is grinning like a fool. And so is Ms. Alvarez. Damn, it's good to see. Makes me want to do my happy dance—which looks a lot like me standing still. But it's the thought that counts.

Maybe there is hope yet for the twisted bastard.

Funny word 'hope'. It's so small and insignificant-looking, but it's not. Hope keeps a man alive. And I'm speaking from experience.

Chapter Twenty-One

INDECENT PROPOSAL

"Hey, babe."

I'm so happy to see Rachel after another long-ass day.

"Well, that's quite a welcome," she smiles as I finally let her go, her cheeks pink.

I head for the refrigerator and hunt down a beer. I'm definitely feeling like self-medicating after the day I've had. The blackmailer posted another video which Howard managed to erase after three views, and it's wearing me down. I don't know what to do to keep my client safe. That's really hard to admit—hard to admit that I've failed.

"Bad day?" she asks gently.

Another one.

I blow out a long breath.

"The blackmailer struck again; Ms. Alvarez has a stalker that I can't find; I don't trust that Landon is out of the picture. I can't do this. I can't keep him or Maria safe. I can't keep *you* safe. I'm going to resign. I'll tell Anderson in the morning."

Her beautiful face crumples.

"Justin, no!"

"I have to, baby. I took my eye off the ball. You could have been hurt." *Or worse.* "I'm supposed to be fucking security. How secure have you been? How secure has Anderson been? I fucked up. I just want to know ... will you come with me? Fuck, I hate to ask, baby, but you're my life. I can't live without you."

"Oh, Justin! Please don't do this to yourself! You're a *good* man, a *strong* man, and Mr. Anderson will *never* find anyone as loyal as you. But you're human. You're not a damn machine and you're only one man. You simply *can't* be everywhere twenty-four hours a day. You did everything you could. Mr. Anderson knows that and I know that. You *can't* leave now—he needs you. More than ever. *I* need you."

I shake my head. Her words are meant to soothe me, but she doesn't understand. *I don't fuck up.*

"I have to, Rachel. I'm too close. I don't know, maybe I need a fucking change away from all this craziness."

She holds her hand to my cheek and my head sinks into her warm, soft neck.

"Justin Triton Trainer! Don't you dare give up on me now!"

And she slaps me on the chest—hard.

Fuck! That hurt!

I step back and rub my eyes tiredly.

"I'm not giving up on *you,* babe. You're the one good thing I've got going for me. But I can't do *this* anymore."

I wave my hand around, indicating the house, Anderson, all of *this.*

"You're not a quitter."

"For fuck's sake, Rachel! You're not hearing me! *I can't fucking do this anymore!*"

"Stop being such a drama queen!"

Did she just call me...?

"What?"

"Justin, during the time you've worked for Mr. Anderson, has one word leaked out about his unusual lifestyle to the Press? Don't bother to reply, because we both know the answer is 'no'. A large part of that is thanks to you and Howard. Mr. Anderson *chose* his lifestyle, which is extremely risky given his public presence and standing in the business world. You have moved heaven and earth to protect him. But it was Mr. Anderson who brought Aston Van Sant into his life and into his home; it was Mr. Anderson who wished to keep security unobtrusive; and throughout all this, throughout what you call this 'craziness', the one constant that he has had, the one constant that he has relied on, is you. You, Justin. Not me, not his therapist, not his family, and certainly not that Landon person—it's been you. If you leave now, you'll be letting him down and you'll be letting yourself down."

"Rachel..."

"For goodness sake shut up and listen to me for once, you wonderful, annoying, irritating, stupid, stupid man!"

Oh, fucking ouch!

"I'm stupid twice over?"

"That's a conservative estimate. Look, I'm sure if you talk it over with Mr. Anderson he'll be appalled at the idea of you leaving. He'll never agree to it."

"He'll have no fucking choice!"

"Oh, honestly! You're not perfect, you never were."

"Rachel..."

"And if you agree to wait and talk to Mr. Anderson ... then I'll agree to marry you."

Wow, that was weird. I could have sworn she just said she'd marry me. Have I got earwax? It's like hearing bad vocabulary that's as bad as, like, whatever.

"Wait, what did you just say?"

"I love you, Justin, and I want to spend the rest of my life with you."

I stare at her, utterly mute. *Yeah, I know. I fell out of the stupid tree and hit every branch on the way down. Then I climbed back up and did it again—just to be thorough.*

Please, please let me have heard right. God, I love this woman so much. I want her badly: today, tomorrow, forever.

"Why now?" I stammer out the question, but I need to know.

"I've asked you a thousand times to marry me and you've always said no."

She smiles at me softly, her deep blue eyes glowing with love.

"Tonight you needed me to say yes. Why, are you having second thoughts?"

"Fuck no!"

"You're so eloquent, Justin."

"Yeah, I know, baby."

And then I kiss her. *I'm not completely stupid.*

Her lips are warm and soft. She's like a freakin' drug to me. However much she gives me, I want more. Just as I feel that my swollen, happy heart will burst through my ribcage, she pulls back, breathless, and rests her head on my chest.

"I'll do anything, *anything* to make you happy, baby."

"I know that, Justin. That's why I said yes. Right now I want you go and check on Maria and Mr. Anderson."

"Okay, I'll ... *What? You want me to ... what?* I'm not going out there! It's like asking me to go see what that lil bitty bit of smoke on Mount Vesuvius is all about! The boss will be in hyperdrive by now. No fucking way!"

"Justin! The *very first thing I ask you to do...*"

Ah, hell. I know where that sentence is going. It's my own fucking fault for loving a clever woman.

"Fine. Fine! I'll go look. But if I come back with my ass kicked through my front teeth, *you're* paying for the dentist."

"Mr. Anderson covers our dental, so you have nothing to worry about. Now go see if they're okay."

I slouch towards the main room, my brain still on fire with the knowledge that Rachel has finally, *finally* accepted my proposal, that one day soon, she'll really be *mine.*

And then I hear yelling.

"I'm not going anywhere, Devon!"

Ms. Alvarez is screaming at the boss. I think he likes it because he's not screaming back. Weird.

"Why don't you understand that?"

Well, they haven't killed each other, they haven't hit each other
—not even in a freaky, kinky way. They don't need me so I'll just
skulk back into the shadows.

"There is one thing you could do for me," he whispers.

*The dance of the seven veils in a leather thong? Chinese water torture on
an intimate part of his body?*

"What?" she snarls at him.

She's going to regret asking that.

"Be my wife."

WHAT

THE

FUCK?!

*That fucking bastard! That's MY fucking line! And how come the
fucking world stopped turning and I'm the last to get the memo?*

I stomp back to the staff quarters seriously pissed off.

"Well?" says Rachel, her hands on her hips, looking all cute and
bossy.

"They're okay," I say sullenly.

"You're sure?"

"Yup."

"Well, what were they doing? Justin? What happened? Tell me?
I *know* there's something you're not telling me."

"The boss asked Ms. Alvarez to marry him."

She takes a deep breath and a huge smile breaks across her face.
"He did?"

"Yeah, he was on his knees."

"Oh, that's so romantic!"

"Yeah, whatever."

Rachel skewers me with a look.

"What's the matter? Why are you so annoyed?"

I know going in that this will sound pathetic...

"You finally get around to saying yes, which made me think the
world was about to end, and then the boss goes and fucking
copies me."

Rachel starts to giggle.

"I can think of worse role models, Justin, but I don't remember you getting down on your knees."

I raise an eyebrow.

"You sure about that, baby?"

She blushes.

"Not to ask me to marry you."

That is true.

"Are you sulking, Justin?"

Maybe.

"Are you pouting, Justin?"

It has been known.

"Do you want me to kiss it better?"

Has the dog got a boner?

Chapter Twenty-Two

LITTLE MISS SUNSHINE

The boss is smiling. *That's gonna hurt.*

I've just come back from dropping Maria at work. Jeff Gordon has nothing on me as I cut through the morning rush-hour traffic and slide to a halt outside DMA Tower.

Maria looked wide-eyed. Well, she always looks like that; I don't think it was my driving, she's not that much of a *girl*. I didn't even do a handbrake turn, not a donut in sight. I put it down to the fact that she didn't get much sleep last night.

I heard the boss prowling around in the early hours, but I figured Maria could handle it. She's been handling a lot lately. I hope it's not too much for her. But she's a helluva lot tougher than she looks. Like Rachel. *My* Rachel.

I can't believe she finally said yes! Wow, married. Again. Forever, this time. I can't wait to tell Lilly. Shit, I suppose I'll have to tell Carla.

My good mood fades when I remember I have to hand in my resignation this morning, despite Rachel trying to persuade me otherwise. I know it's the right thing to do. It's the *only* thing to do. I never thought I'd say it, but I'm going to miss working here.

I'm momentarily distracted by the thought that it's weird

Anderson isn't going to work on a week day. It makes me feel like I'm cutting school again. At least I'm suited and booted; the boss is loafing around in old jeans. Weird, Part Deux. But he's in his office, so I take a deep breath and knock on the door.

He looks up.

"Trainer?"

"Sir, about Van Sant..."

"Aston? Yes?"

I take a step inside.

"He should never have got in. It shouldn't have happened. I apologize and..." *here goes,* "I wish to offer my resignation. Forthwith." *I may be a pussy, but I can still do big words.*

He stares at me, then rubs his face tiredly.

"Take a seat, Trainer," he says, waving his hand at the spare chair.

"I'd rather stand, sir."

He frowns.

"Fine. I'm not accepting your resignation." He pauses. "Was there anything else?"

My jaw is hanging so far open, the boss can probably see my tonsils.

"Sir?" I croak, but in a manly way.

"I don't accept your resignation. The blackmailer is a situation I created. I don't blame you for what happened. It was..." he shrugs, "inevitable."

"But ... your safety has been compromised, and now Ms. Alvarez is ... and then there was Van Sant..."

A look of repressed horror skitters across his face and he faces his laptop again.

"That happened months ago, Trainer. Why are you bringing this up now?"

Good question. So I give him an honest answer, if a partial one.

"It's ... hard to let go."

He turns to look at me, understanding on his face.

"Aston was not a well man, Trainer. I'd known that for a long time. I should have ... done more. I do not hold you responsible for what happened here. I value your services, I hope that you will continue your employment here. Ms. Alvarez—Maria—she feels ... comfortable ... with you on duty."

I breathe deeply. Now Van Sant is no longer a threat, I can feel a micron of sympathy for him. He looked so broken.

And I know how easy it is for that thin veneer of self to be fractured. I've seen it happen. None of us know how far we can be pushed, how much can be taken from us, before we snap—the elastic shield that protects the core of a person. I've been through some shit I *never* want to see again or think about, but that doesn't mean I know how close I came to losing my mind. How far could I be pushed? Do I know? Does Anderson? Do any of us?

I told Maria once that Anderson was a good man. Why do I still think that after everything I've seen and heard? Easy. Psychology 101: because I've seen the face of evil—and it's not Anderson.

"Will you stay, Trainer?"

"Yes, sir."

"Good. Anything else?"

"No, sir."

And his gaze flicks back to his computer screen.

Over and fucking out.

I walk away dazed and confused.

Rachel is waiting for me.

"Well? What is it, Justin?"

"He wouldn't accept my resignation..." I mumble, scratching the back of my head with my thumb.

Rachel smiles.

"Of course he wouldn't."

"But..."

"He values you, Justin. Like I do. Well, not exactly like I do," she smiles. "At least I hope not!"

"But..."

"So, whatever you say, you're staying."

"Is anyone going to let me finish a senten..."

"No, I'm not, Future Husband."

She kisses me, effectively putting an end to my arguments, the verbal ones anyway. The mental ones continue to torture me.

I think about her words throughout the day. Why would Anderson want me to stay after I've fucked up? I wonder briefly if it's because I know so much about him and all his dirty little secrets. But that's not it. Anderson would hand me my balls on a plate before he let that happen, but what worries me more is that Rachel would help him. No, the only answer that I can come up with is that Anderson blames himself more than he blames me. He said it in his office: he was the one who let Van Sant into his life. *But I should have kept him out.*

I shake my head hard enough to rearrange my brain cells. Hell, if I don't stop this self-flagellation, it'll be *me* screaming about my demons in the middle of the night.

Been there, done that, ain't going back.

And I start to breathe easier.

I head to DMA Tower to pick up Maria and call Mason for an update on the way. There's not much to report. But I don't believe for a second that the blackmailer has given up: I can smell it, like a sixth sense. Or maybe that's one of the five.

Anderson is also proceeding with his purchase of the next door apartment building. Frank, the doorman who has a thing for Rachel, gets to keep his job and has added driving duties to his questionable expertise. Just so long as he keeps his hairy eyeballs to himself.

Maria's brothers love the fact that it has a swimming pool in the basement and its own private cinema. The old man admitted that the steps at their old apartment were getting too much for him and he was worried about drugs being sold semi-openly in the streets. But I'd say he's putting a brave face on it for Maria's sake—the guy has 'Bronx' running through his veins.

But the building next door will definitely be safer. Apart from anything else, it'll be secured with a state-of-the-art security system. Nah, probably just retinal scanning. The Ancient Etruscans used the intestines of animals to predict the future. I reckon Anderson might go for that. And I can guarantee it'll be the only condo in New York with that level of protection.

While I'm waiting, I head to my office to catch up on some paperwork.

Rachel texts me, and her message makes me smile. Either that or my face just got a cramp. I still can't believe she's going to marry me. I don't need anything big or fancy: read the book, saw the movie, never again. My ex was dressed in enough white lace to make curtains for a retirement village, and her relatives drank themselves into a blind stupor. The after-dinner speeches turned into an after-dinner free-for-all.

Marines 3: Bitch's relatives 0.

And then I wonder if Rachel would like a big wedding. I don't think so, but women and weddings are a strange and mysterious alchemy. Shit, I'll probably have to be nice to Rachel's sister.

Howard stumbles into my office—literally falls on his ass—and lies there, blinking up at my ceiling, interrupting my musings on whether or not there's a word that describes homicide of a sister-in-law.

"Huh, that plaster looks kind of Bosonic. Cool."

"Laying down on the job again, Howard?"

He sits up and blinks as if he's surprised to see me sitting at my desk in my office on a work day.

"Hey, Mr. T. Nice suit."

"Something you wanted to tell me, Howard?"

"Oh sure. The Halon suppression system has been installed. We'll be coordinating an isolated test over the weekend. Mr. Mason has vetted the technical team and there haven't been any alerts. I'll need access limited for the other dudes—halo-carbons are 38% denser than air—unauthorized personnel could be accidentally asphyxiated. That would be a bummer."

"Yes, it would. I'll see to it, Howard."

"Thanks, Mr. T."

"Make it so."

He blinks again, smiles, and gives me a Vulcan salute.

I think I made his day.

Maria calls me to say that she's leaving at six.

Since she came into the boss's life, we've all been leaving the office a helluva lot earlier. I could get used to that.

Traffic is light and we arrive at Wolf Point a couple of minutes before 6:15PM. The light is soft and still bright, and nearby cafés are filling up with people stopping for a coffee or a beer on their way home. The season for sitting outdoors is short in New York, so we make the most of it. Okay, damn it, I admit it. I'm so fucking happy I think I just heard birds singing and butterflies frolicking.

What the hell is happening to me?

When the boss sees Maria, he's smiling so much he could be auditioning for a toothpaste commercial. I need sunglasses.

Chapter Twenty-Three

NEAR DARK

The next day, Anderson informs me that Maria is going with him to see his sex therapist after work. I don't know if that's brave or plumbing the depths of sanity. Then a third option occurs to me: she's cracked under the strain of dating Anderson. I guess it'll work out. The boss knows that anyone who dates him has to be half-baked.

In fact, working for Anderson should come with a health warning.

Amazingly, Maria doesn't seem to be bothered by it. Maybe she's gotten enough practice dealing with weirdo fuckers by dating Anderson.

Next time I get to spend the weekend with Lilly, I'll show her some moves, in case any elementary kids give her grief. Can't start preparing for that shit too soon, in my opinion. Is eight too young to start taking her to the gun range? Her mom will hate it, and knowing Princess Lilly, she'll probably shoot the shit out of her Barbie dolls with a BB gun if she's anything like her old man. Not that I have Barbie dolls. I'm more a GI Joe kinda guy. Was. *Was* a GI Joe kinda guy. When I was a kid.

So, moving on...

I've got the evening off with nothing to do but remind Rachel why she's agreed to marry me. And all the things I plan to do to her. Decisions, decisions.

"Hi honey, I'm home," I call out, pulling off my tie as I stroll into the staff quarters. "Something smells good, baby."

"Lasagna and garlic bread. Salad on the side."

Damn, I love this woman.

"You have ten minutes to take a shower."

I have a much better idea about how I can spend ten minutes. I wrap my arms around her waist and kiss the nape of her neck.

"Justin! Aren't you going to shower?"

"No, I've been thinking about you all day, *Mrs. Trainer*, and I think we should get in as much sinning as possible before you're legally mine."

She pushes away from me slightly.

"About that, Justin..."

I look at her warily.

"Second thoughts?"

She smooths my shirt over my chest and smiles.

"No, silly. I was just wondering when we're going to tell Mr. Anderson. And Maria."

I shrug.

"Is it any of their business?"

"I'm sure Mr. Anderson will want to know."

"Yeah? I'm sure he won't give a shit."

"Hmm, well, perhaps we'll leave it for now."

"Whatever you say, baby."

"Besides, I think Mr. Anderson and Maria are still in the honeymoon phase, so to speak."

"I know I'm going to regret asking, but what do you mean?"

"Well, I was checking the stock in Mr. Anderson's bar when I saw them coming out of the bedroom with his toy that..."

"Stop right there, baby. I really don't want to know."

"Justin Trainer! Are you a prude?"

I stare at her in disbelief.

"Hell no! I've worked for the King of Kink for more than a year. Kind of opens a man's eyes. I just don't want a blow by blow description."

I can't believe I just said that, and I cringe.

Rachel starts laughing.

"No blowing of any sort, I promise."

"Aw, baby."

Dinner is fantastic, but then again everything Rachel does is fantastic. I'm a lucky dog.

I settle down in front of the TV in her bedroom with a can of Coke and wait for Rachel to come and get some quality lovin'. We don't get as much time together as either of us would like. Frankly, I could spend 24/7 with this woman and never get enough.

"Justin, do you know what Mr. Anderson's plans are for the rest of the week?"

Rachel walks into the room with her schedule.

"We're in Chicago all day tomorrow and won't be back till early evening. Other than that, a regular week. I think Maria is planning a movie marathon evening tonight."

Rachel's eyebrows nearly hit the stratosphere.

"Really?"

"Yeah, the boss is totally pussy-whipped."

And the thought makes me feel all warm inside.

Rachel stares at me and I realize I've had another foot in mouth moment.

"Um, you know, without the actual whipping..."

She smirks. Damn woman's been playing me.

I launch myself at her and grapple her around the waist. I carry her into the bedroom and soon, we're a tangle of arms and legs, and I owe her another white blouse. Well, hell! They should make them of tougher stuff, those buttons fly off everywhere.

I'm heading for second base, when my damn cell rings.

It's my ex's ring tone.

Technically, it's 'O Fortuna' from *Carmina Burana*, but I always think of it as the music from *The Omen*. It brings back memories of our wedding night.

"Carla?"

"Justin, it's ... it's Lilly!"

Immediately, my heart rate triples.

"What's happened?"

I can see Rachel's concerned expression and I know it must mirror mine.

"We're in the Emergency Room now. They think it might be appendicitis." There's a stifled sob. *"They're talking about operating."*

Oh, God. Not Lilly. Not my Princess.

Carla's voice is strained.

"Jay, I'm so scared."

"I'll be right there, Carla. Whatever she needs. You understand? Whatever she needs. I'm leaving now. Call me on the way if anything ... if there's anything I need to know."

"I will."

And she hangs up.

I've been involved in lot of crazy shit in my life. I've been in firefights on three continents; I've driven tanks over land peppered with IEDs. When Rachel was held at gunpoint, I was shit scared, but at least it was a situation I was trained to deal with. But this ... hearing my baby is sick...

Rachel is standing at the door.

"I've got your coat," she says. "Drive carefully. I'll tell Lance and Mr. Anderson."

Unable to speak, I merely nod at her. She tries to smile reassuringly, but her lips freeze half way. She kisses me on the cheek and I'm out the door.

The elevator is so fucking slow, I want to scream.

When I screech out of the parking garage, the traffic is thinner now, but it's slow enough to have me grinding my teeth. I'm vaguely aware that I'm gripping the steering wheel so tightly, my hands are cramping. Once I'm on the expressway and hitting 100mph, it helps. Some. All I can think about is that my baby's sick; they want to slice up my baby.

It's after midnight by the time I reach the hospital. Some dick in a uniform tries to tell me I can't leave my car in the no-parking zone. The glare I give has him stepping back. I want to hit him really badly—not because of him, but because I want to feel something other than nauseating fear. Instead, I toss him my keys, ignoring his shout that the hospital doesn't do valet parking. They can tow it for all I care.

The ER receptionist gives me a professional smile. She's seen the look I have in my eyes before. I don't know how she does her job. How can she see that every fucking day and not make her want to stab out her own eyeballs? And suddenly I realize something: that's how Anderson feels every time he looks in the mirror. He only sees his own ugliness—and Maria shows him beauty.

But there'll be no beauty in the world if I can't see my baby.

"Lilly Trainer, she's eight. Her mother brought her in."

"Just a moment," she says, calmly.

I want to rip her eyes from her computer screen. I take a deep breath as she scrolls through her files.

She looks up.

"I'll have a nurse take you to her."

I manage to mumble thank you. I don't know if she heard me and I really don't fucking care.

A chunky guy in pale blue scrubs walks over to me.

"Mr. Trainer? I'm Grant Chambers. I'm the charge nurse that's been looking after your daughter. At the moment, the doctors are trying to decide whether it's severe gastroenteritis or appendicitis. We're running some blood work and we need a sonogram. For now, we're keeping her quiet and hydrated. Lilly's mom is here with a friend."

The nurse takes me into a curtained cubicle and I realize why the hospital employs a guy like a linebacker for Friday night ER, because Carla's *friend* is a guy with his arm around her, sitting next to *my* daughter.

Lilly's face is pale against the pillows, her dark curls fanned out. She's so still and quiet, my lungs struggle to pull in air.

"Justin."

I turn at the sound of the voice. The hippy-shit, limp-dicked, long-haired, Fritz-the-Cat reject is staring at me, his hand held out. *Keep standing like that, buddy, and I'll rip your fucking arm off.*

"I'm Steve."

He drops his hand.

Not as dumb as you look, Steeeeve.

I lean down and lightly brush the hair from Lilly's face. She doesn't move.

I straighten up slowly.

"What are they saying?"

My words are directed to my daughter's mother. I can't call her 'the bitch' right now, not when she's looking at our child like that, like half of her has been ripped away. Whatever our problems, she's always loved Lilly. I never knew what that meant until now.

"They haven't decided yet."

"What the fuck are they waiting for?"

I know my voice is too loud for a hospital, but I can't help it. I wonder if I've gone too far, but Carla just looks at me tiredly.

"They're doing everything they can, Jay. They don't want to operate if they don't have to. The doctor said he'd be back with the results from the blood work in twenty minutes."

I run my hands over my hair in sheer fucking frustration.

Carla leans back and I see for the first time that she's holding Lilly's hand in her own. It looks so small, like a tiny doll's hand. My baby is so young.

"I'll get us some coffee," says Steve.

I nod, but don't look at him.

A minute passes. It's so quiet. Shouldn't there be beeping monitors? Shouldn't there be some sign that these fuckers are looking after my baby?

I stand and start pacing up and down the small cubicle.

Carla stares at me but doesn't say anything.

After another minute of pacing, I'm about to go postal.

Steve returns with coffee, at least, that's what he says it is. It looks and smells like goat urine.

"Where's the fucking doctor?" I snarl.

I'm about to have a serious, Anderson-shaped tantrum, that may or may not involve a range of offensive weapons, when some stiff in green scrubs walks in.

"Miss Palmer?" he asks, calmly.

"Yes!" Carla replies, sounding desperate.

The doctor glances at me and the hippy.

"Um, I'm Steve Pollini, Carla's partner. This is Justin Trainer, Lilly's father."

What kind of name is 'Pollini'? Makes the fucker sound like an appetizer at a cheap Italian restaurant. "Have some garlic bread with your Pollini." Stupid fucking hippy.

"Ah. I'm Doctor Mathers. Well, I'm afraid the tests have been inconclusive."

"What the fuck does that mean?" I growl at him.

He replies with that infuriating hospital-voice that's supposed to be all low and soothing. Makes me want to rip his tongue out of his fucking patronizing skull and use if for fish food.

"Well, Ms. Palmer, Mr. Trainer, there's definitely inflammation in Lilly's gut. That will certainly result in the intense pain she's been suffering..."

I close my eyes. I don't want to think of my baby suffering, my baby in pain. *Make it me, not her!*

"...and this can mimic the symptoms of appendicitis. However, there's no abdominal rigidity and that's a good thing. We could well be dealing with a case of severe gastroenteritis. At this point, I want to keep Lilly for observation; she also needs to be hydrated because of the loss of fluids during the vomiting and diarrhea."

"That's it?"

"We're doing everything we can, Mr. Trainer, I can assure you.

Rest, fluids, and observation. Do you have any more questions for me?" I shake my head. "Ms. Palmer?"

Carla's eyes are wide and her lips tremble. She looks at me, then slowly shakes her head.

"No," she says, "I don't have any questions."

And then we wait.

Memories, so many memories. Waiting in a place like this when Lilly was born. All those ER trips in the early days because being parents is fucking scary and every time Lilly got so much as a cough, we were jumping in the car and racing to the hospital. When I wasn't deployed, that is.

When Lilly turned six, she asked me what my job was. I jokingly told her that I was the Invisible Man. She thought her daddy was a comic book hero, but with a better suit. Her mom thinks I'm a bad joke.

I'm not exactly five stars at waiting. I fucking hate it. Give me something to hit, give me something to shoot at. Don't make me sit here counting the ways I can scare the shit out of *Steeeeve*. Okay, that bit isn't so bad, but waiting for my baby to be better is fucking killing me.

And anyway, this is a different kind of waiting. When I'm on a job, I can be patient. I know that sounds unlikely, but it's true.

I'm not on a job now, and my gut is twisted in knots. I feel so fucking useless—helpless. And I don't like it.

A nurse bustles in. She takes Lilly's temperature and adjusts her IV. She smiles. It means nothing.

I get a text from Rachel.

How's Princess Lilly?

Too early to say. Could be appendicitis. Could be stomach flu. No fucker here knows.

Lilly is strong. Give her my love. Try not to shoot anyone.

I will. No promises on the shooting.

Love you, Justin Trainer.

Me 2

"Is that Rachel?"

I realize Carla is asking me a question.

"Yeah."

"She's good for you, Justin. You seem ... calmer."

What a fucking joke. I'm climbing the walls here.

"Oh, yeah?"

"Yes, really. I thought you'd charge in here, stomping all over everyone, waving your gun."

"I thought about it."

She smiles tiredly.

"That's what I mean, you're calmer."

My lips twitch in what might have been a smile if I wasn't so fucking worried.

And then we wait and wait some more.

Steve disappears to ... hell, I don't remember what he went to do and I don't give a shit. I prefer it when the hairy fucker isn't here. Christ knows what Carla sees in him. He's the polar opposite of me...

Oh, right.

Lilly's eyelids flutter and I think she's waking up.

"Hey, baby. Daddy's here."

She smiles in her sleep, but she doesn't open her eyes.

I sit back, sighing.

"So, how's it going with you and Rachel?"

I raise an eyebrow.

"You really want to know?"

Carla shakes her head and attempts a tired smile.

"Not really. I just need some distraction."

"And you thought talking about my love life would do that?"

"So, you do have a love life?"

I feel like telling her to take a job with sex and travel, but I don't.

"I've asked her to marry me, Car. She said yes."

Carla takes a deep breath.

"You're getting married?"

"Yep."

"Once wasn't enough? Sorry, Justin, that came out wrong. I'm really happy for you."

She sees my skeptical stare.

"No, really, I am. Lilly will love being the flower girl. Oh, sorry, I don't know what you have planned."

To be honest, I hadn't really thought that much about getting married. I'd just thought about *being* married. It could be a Vegas wedding with an Elvis impersonator for all I care. It'll be whatever Rachel wants. But now Carla's said it, I can just picture Princess Lilly all dolled up, carrying a basket of flowers.

"Yeah, maybe, I don't know. We haven't discussed it. It's kind of new."

"Well, congratulations."

"Thanks." I hesitate for a moment. "So what about you and the hi— Steve?"

She shrugs her shoulders.

"Maybe. We'll see. He loves Lilly. He makes a great father ... I mean, step-father."

I scowl at her.

And just like that, the peace pact is over.

"Oh, for goodness' sake, Justin! He sees her more than you do! You're always working. The number of times you've canceled on Lilly are unreal!"

"That is a fucking lie. I canceled one time, *one time* because I was stuck at work. I've made it up to her a thousand times over!"

"Don't be ridiculous, Justin! You can't *make it up* to an eight year-old child who has had to learn that adults make promises but don't always keep them. You can't *make that up* to her."

I shoot her a venomous look but say nothing.

"What the hell did I ever see in you? You're still a foul-mouthed jarhead!"

"Mommy?" says a soft voice. "Is Daddy here yet?"

"I'm here, Princess," I say softly.

"My tummy hurts."

"I know, sweetheart, but the doctors are going to give you medicine to make it better."

"Where's Steve?"

I look up to see Carla staring at me in triumph. Anger rushes through me, but I bite my tongue for Lilly's sake.

"He's running an errand, baby girl. He'll be here soon."

Her eyes close again, and she drifts back to sleep.

"Well, I hope you're happy now," hisses Carla.

"What?"

"You woke her up with your ranting!"

"Bullshit!"

The curtain is pulled back by an embarrassed Steve, and Dr. Mathers who looks tired and irritated. I know how he feels: Carla and I have been doing this for the better part of a decade.

"Um, everything okay in here?" asks Steve.

"Just peachy, Steeeeve," I reply, earning a scorching look from Cruella de Vil's uglier sister.

The doctor sighs. He's seen it all before.

"Well, Lilly is doing much better now. Her temperature is down, and she's responding to the fluids and pain medication. I'm fairly certain she's out of the woods."

"So, it's not appendicitis?"

"No, Mr. Trainer. Gastroenteritis can look very dramatic, but Lilly is going to be fine."

"Thank fuck for that."

He smiles.

"Indeed."

Carla smiles at Steve, and Steve smiles at Carla. It's a fucking smile-fest. It's so sweet, it makes my teeth ache.

By the following afternoon, Lilly is sitting up in bed, complaining about missing her favorite TV show. It's still *Dora, the Explorer*. My baby is still a baby.

"Hey, Princess. You want to come and stay with your old man soon? Rachel would love to see you."

"Can Mommy come, too?"

"Um, no. Mommy's busy that weekend."

"Okay."

"I love you, Buttercup."

"Me too, Daddy."

God, I love that kid. So much.

I'm tired, but relieved. I didn't kill Carla, and I didn't maim Steve. Who needs anger management classes?

"Are you staying, Justin?" she asks, between gritted teeth.

"Yeah, I'm going to check into a hotel, stay around for a couple of days."

I know Anderson will be cool with that. The twisted fucker has a heart: who knew?

"Oh, lovely," she says, under her breath.

But then my cell rings.

"Trainer, it's Mason. The blackmailer has struck again."

Fuck.

Carla sees the look on my face and turns away.

"Just go, Justin. Do your job. It's what you're good at."

Chapter Twenty-Four

THREE GO CAMPING

The blackmailer is getting tired of Howard blocking him at every turn. His latest tactic is to release videos on hundreds of sites at once. Yes, Howard can track them down and stop them, but even with a team of super-geeks helping him, it's becoming more and more likely that someone will start putting names to faces and asses.

Howard seems to take it in his stride. Maybe he imagines it's like one of those endless computer games he played in college; and maybe that's better than acknowledging that the footage would probably ruin the boss.

But after another month of cat and mouse, the blackmailer disappears into the ether of the internet and we're chasing ghosts again.

Thank fuck I have backup from Mason's team and can take a few precious days for a short vacation. If you keep pushing yourself, you're in danger of burning out, and then things can get missed or you become sloppy.

I need the break, but that's not as important as the fact that this is something I've been promising Lilly and Rachel for a while now.

Lilly wants to go camping, even though I'm not sure she realizes what it means. Rachel knows and is pretending that she loves camping, even though I can tell it's not really her thing. So, I'm calling it camping because that's what Lilly is excited about, and I'll take my old two-man tent to pitch under the stars, but in reality, we're borrowing Bill's cabin that's set in fifty-five acres of forest on the shores of Lake Towhee.

I can tell that Rachel is nervous because it's our first time away together, and her first time spending more than a few hours with Lilly. She's worried how Lilly will be overnight without her mom there, but when I took her to a sleepover for kids at the Natural History Museum last year, she was fine.

I understand her anxiety, because this is also the first time that Rachel will meet Carla.

Yeah, that's going to be interesting.

Anderson has let us take the Rover and seems bemused by the fact that two of his staff are spending a long weekend playing happy families. Mrs. Anderson waves us off with a genuine smile: "Have fun, you guys!"

Rachel climbs into the Rover, fiddling with the seatbelt.

"Babe, it's going to be fine."

She gives me a tight smile.

"I know."

We make good time on the drive out and I pull up outside the house. Rachel takes a deep breath and steps out of the car.

The front door flies open and Lilly charges at me, throwing her arms around my waist.

"Daddy!"

"Hey, Princess."

The she looks up at Rachel.

"Hello again, Lilly. Are you excited about going camping? I know I am."

Lilly nods, unusually shy, and at that moment Carla walks out.

"Justin."

"Carla."

Rachel steps forward.

"Hello, Carla. I'm Rachel. It's so nice to meet you at last."

They shake hands, and I can see Carla subtly sizing up Rachel. She seems surprised, but I'm not sure why.

"Good to meet you, too, Rachel."

"I was hoping to meet Steve, as well. Lilly has told us so much about him."

Carla's lips tip upwards briefly.

"He's at work. I'll tell him you said hi."

There's a short, somewhat awkward pause, then Carla launches into mom mode.

"I've packed spare clothes and Lilly's swimsuit, but don't forget to spray her with *Off* because bugs bite her all the time. I've packed her ball cap, sun lotion and some natural aloe vera gel because ordinary after-sun makes her itch."

There's a long list of does and don'ts and I can see Rachel is dying to take notes, because that woman is so organized, but we're camping—you need to have a certain amount of spontaneity.

"Bug spray, sun lotion, ball cap, aloe, no gluten, only one scoop of ice cream, brush teeth before bed: got it," I say, earning a scowl from Carla.

Rachel smiles reassuringly.

"My brother-in-law keeps the cabin well stocked for my nieces— I've seen how much girls need," she says kindly. "And there's a ton of outdoor games, too."

Carla looks slightly reassured, then turns to Lilly.

"And ask Daddy to make sure your cell phone is charged so I can call you, and if you need anything you can call me."

I press my lips together to keep from reminding Carla that I'm Lilly's father and if she needs anything during the four days we're away, I'll get it for her. But I don't, because I know that Carla loves Lilly and handing over to me and Rachel for a few days is not something she's comfortable with.

"There's a strong signal at the cabin," Rachel says, "and Bill always leaves a spare charger there."

They exchange a look, and on Carla's face there's acceptance, maybe even gratitude. Then she turns to our daughter.

"Bye, honey," she says softly, hugging and kissing Lilly. "Have fun. Call me, okay?"

Carla gives a brief smile then watches as Lilly climbs into the booster seat and checks that she's done the seatbelt right.

"Okay, Mom!"

As Rachel climbs into the front passenger seat, Carla walks around to my side of the car.

"She seems nice," she says quietly.

"She is."

"Older than I was expecting."

I give her a cold stare and she shrugs.

"Just ... take care of Lilly."

"Of course."

We all wave as I drive the hell out of there, ready to spend time with my two best girls.

By the time we get to Lake Towhee, we've sung every camping song that Rachel and I know, worked our way through the music from every Disney musical ever produced, and we're all ready to toast some marshmallows over an open fire.

There hasn't been a single cross word or complaint, and my cell phone hasn't rung once. Life is good.

The campsite is busy, full of families enjoying themselves, but large enough that you don't feel hemmed in. The wide lake is fringed by tall trees, and I'm happy to see that Bill's cabin is slightly set apart from the others, and at the end of a dirt track.

Lilly is bouncing in her seat, excited to start camping.

I unload the trunk, carrying three boxes of supplies into the cabin. Rachel has the windows open to air the place. It smells of pine and only a little stale.

But before I do anything else, I make sure that my Smith & Wesson is securely locked in a steel box in the Rover's trunk.

Rachel catches my eye as Lilly dances past.

"Did you have to bring that?" she says quietly, biting her lip.

"You know I do."

Lilly turns and looks at Rachel.

"Daddy always takes his weapon, Rachel. It's a tool, just like any other tool. As good or bad as the man using it. My daddy is good so it's okay."

She waltzes away and Rachel stares at me, a tiny smile on her face.

"She is definitely her father's daughter."

They walk away together, talking about what we'll have for supper. I follow them with my eyes, but honestly, I need a minute. Hearing Lilly say what she did, I feel so many emotions all at once: pride, fear, understanding, and most of all, an overwhelming rush of love for my daughter, for Rachel, for this second chance at life.

My eight year-old daughter never ceases to amaze me. Is that what being her father means? To be surprised, stunned, shocked, as I watch her grow, day by day, year by year.

Carla and I, we've done so many things wrong, we were so wrong for each other—but we've done one amazing thing right.

I'm going to keep on trying to do things right, and looking at Rachel, it's like seeing the light at the end of a very long, dark tunnel. She'll help me find the way.

But then I hear Lilly calling for me. Right now, more than anything, Lilly wants the tent, so I haul it out of the trunk and lay it out, showing her how to push the tent pegs into the dirt. She even tries hitting them with a mallet but that's a little hazardous to her toes, so I take over. Then I show her how to tighten the lines.

As soon as it's ready, she scoots inside, sitting criss-cross.

"I love camping, Daddy!" she says.

The smile on my face is ridiculously proud and happy.

"I love it, too, Buttercup."

In the time it took to put up the tent, Rachel has made us all sandwiches and hot chocolate, and lit a small fire in the fire pit, S'mores at the ready.

I place the sleeping bags around the fire and we eat our food, getting crumbs and chocolate everywhere. And when Lilly falls asleep without brushing her teeth, I shrug my shoulders and carry her into the cabin, placing her on the bottom bunk bed. As I take off her tiny shoes and ease her out of her child-size clothes, the pressure in my chest increases. I've had so few chances to do this in the last couple of years, I've missed so much. I'll do better. I promise myself I'll do better.

I watch my daughter sleep for a long time, watching her small chest rise and fall, watching her eyelashes flutter as she dreams, and I wrap the blankets around her, because that's all I can do to keep her safe in this big wide world. Watch over her and keep her safe.

By the time I leave Lilly's room, the door slightly ajar so I can hear her in the night, Rachel has put out the fire and cleaned up.

I pull her into my arms, just holding her, feeling her softness against my chest.

"Thank you," I say quietly.

She smiles up at me.

"I've had a lovely day. Lilly is so precious."

"Yeah, she's the best part of me."

Rachel shakes her head.

"No, this is the best part of you," and she lays her head over my heart.

At daybreak, I wake up suddenly, hearing a noise inside the cabin, and our bedroom door is pushed open.

"Daddy, I had to go to the bathroom and I'm cold. Can I get in the big bed?"

Rachel shifts sleepily.

"Of course, Princess," she answers for me.

Lilly climbs over me and snuggles down between us. She pats my stubbled cheek with her tiny hand.

"You have prickles, Daddy," and then she falls fast asleep.

I lay watching the two most important people in my world.

Life is good.

Chapter Twenty-Five

IT'S A WONDERFUL LIFE

I have a wedding to plan. Unfortunately, it's not *my* wedding.

Maria finally capitulated to everything the boss wanted: her brothers and grandfather will be moving in next door. Rachel helped Maria find a live-in couple, a husband and wife, who'll be housekeeper-cook/driver-caretaker for the condo. Frank gets to keep his job as doorman and has added security to his duties. I have to train him—that'll be an experience he won't forget.

The boys are excited about their new schools, slightly less excited about their new uniforms, and Joachim has transferred to NYU. Maria is happy to have her family so close, and the boss is happy to have Maria close to him.

Me, on the other hand, my baby girl is still too far away, and Ms. Smith is stubbornly refusing to set a date, stating only that she'll think about it once the happy couple are back from their honeymoon. Which means when *I'm* back from their honeymoon.

When I signed up for close protection duties, going on the boss's honeymoon wasn't what I had in mind. Fuck's sake.

The wedding is going to be low key, only fifty invited guests at the Anderson Seniors' mansion in Scarsdale. The main challenge, I hope, will be keeping out the paparazzi. Everything happened so fast the paps are assuming that Maria is pregnant. She's not. And from what we know of her medical history...

Anderson Senior isn't happy about some of the alterations we've had to make to his property. Who wants security fences in the wedding photos? But that's the reality now. Yes, you need all the serious infra-red shit to make sure trespassers are kept out, along with a good CCTV, but you also need a visual giant fuck-off sign. It lets people know that we're watching. So, a mix of obvious as well as unobtrusive and hidden surveillance equipment works best.

Mason coordinated the checks on all the caterers, along with the guys who put up the dining tent, string ensemble, and anyone else who is going to be on the property. Fifty guests and fifty staff. Seriously. And Anderson has pulled some strings with Air Traffic Control Center and gets a no-fly zone over Scarsdale for a few hours. The paps are pretty upset about that, citing the First Amendment, Freedom of the Press and all that shit. And what about the boss's right to have a quiet wedding with no goddamn cameras and no skuzzy bastards with long lenses who've rented a heli to hover over your parents' home while you're trying to promise the woman you love that you'll be with her forever?

That's a luxury you give up when you are mega rich or mega famous. People were paid to keep their traps shut about the big day, but an assistant florist blabbed.

Any outdoor event is a security nightmare. For a start, it's much harder to lock down an external site, and the margin of error and the ratio of possibilities is that much greater: Chaos Theory—also known as Shit Happens. But the outdoor setting at the Andersons seniors' home was what Maria wanted, and I was going to do my part to make sure they got it all. Hopefully, we'll be lucky with the weather, too, so from everyone else's perspective it will be a perfect day.

The guests are an interesting mix: Anderson's parents; Dolores and Abigail who are both bridesmaids; Pam and her wife, Sheila; Maria's family and Joachim's date; then assorted cousins and friends

—all on Maria's side—including two guys from the stand-up comedy club.

Landon is *not* invited, and I can't help wondering what the boss told his parents about why their *old family friend* wouldn't be attending the nuptials.

At least it's not a re-run of the Grand Slam Banquet Hall in the Bronx. Although that had a certain charm of its own, once you got used to the day-glo pink.

"Justin, darling, relax. There isn't one single thing more that you can do. Your blood pressure will be sky high if you carry on like this all day."

Rachel places a soft kiss on my cheek and steps away. She knows me too well.

"Ms. Smith, the only thing that gets my blood pressure going around here is you, but it ain't rushing to my head."

I stalk up behind her and push my hips into her fucking amazing silk-covered ass just to make my point. She looks so beautiful in the pale blue dress that matches her eyes, her hair loose and shining like gold. I get hard just looking at her. And silk—fuck —that does things to a man. Well, this man.

"Hmm, well, you'll have to hold that thought, probably for the next three weeks."

Three long, lonely weeks.

"I wish you could hold it for me, baby."

"Justin! We have to leave now and I don't want to be ... rumpled."

"I'm going to miss rumpling you, baby. I'm going to miss you, period."

My woman has a wedding to get to, and I can't help wishing it was ours. But that will have to come later.

Rachel was so happy that the boss invited us as his and Maria's guest. We'd gotten a printed invitation, one of the small handful that were sent out. And along with it, an appointment for Rachel to have an outfit made at one of those high-end couture shops.

I got a new tux, tailor-made to take account of my Smith &

Wesson. The boss knows I won't be leaving that behind just because he's getting married—especially because he's getting married.

Plus, Rachel was treated to a spa day, hair and makeup, all of which took place at home. Rich people have people who make that happen. I'll have to thank Ryan. She smells so good I want to take her here and now. Although getting arrested for public indecency probably isn't what you'd call a good career move. Especially at your boss's wedding.

All I know is that she looks fucking amazing.

"Just promise me one thing."

"What's that, Justin?"

"Don't make me wait too long to call you Mrs. Trainer."

Her eyes soften and those fuckable lips curve up in a smile.

Those lips.

I drive us to Scarsdale along with John Evans. He'll be driving Rachel home tonight while I'm on Anderson's private jet to Dublin, Ireland, on the first stage of the honeymoon.

I hate that she'll be going home without me, but Evans has promised, on pain of dismemberment, that he'll look after her.

I feel proud as fuck to take Rachel's arm and lead her to our seat in the third row, thinking that she looks more beautiful than the white roses and peach blossom flown in from hothouses along the East Coast for this wedding.

The string ensemble play Bach's *Air on a G-string* which makes me smirk, and Rachel smacks my arm lightly.

Maria's three brothers sit on the bride's side, all dressed in designer tuxes with matching bow ties and cummerbunds. Even the youngest, Juan, doesn't seem too bothered by having to sit still and wear a three-thousand dollar suit. Either that, or it's the glass of champagne I saw him covertly drinking earlier. Hey, who am I to stop the brother of the bride from imbibing on her wedding day? Besides, I figured the kid deserved it for putting up with the monkey suit.

If it wasn't for the fact that I'm kind of on duty, I'd be doing the same thing.

And even though part of me is somewhat cynical about a billionaire's wedding—and I know for a fact that Maria insisted on a pre-nup that protects Anderson's wealth—she's not marrying the boss for his money and has the paperwork to prove it. There's something so hopeful in the boss's eyes, like he can't quite believe Maria is promising to be his.

Personally, I think she should head for the hills while she still can, but for some reason, she's chosen the boss.

Women are funny like that.

You can imagine the questions the paps throw at her every time she leaves work:

"Hey, Maria! What first attracted you to billionaire Devon Anderson?"

That's when she insisted on the pre-nup.

As the music floats upward, we all shuffle to turn and look at the bride.

Her long hair is swept upward in a simple and elegant style, something classy that Rachel would know the name of but I don't; a deceptively plain dress with long sleeves in lace and skirt that sweeps the well-trimmed grass.

A full veil covers her face and she's holding her grandfather's arm.

The old man walks stiffly, and it looks as though Maria is holding him up rather than the other way around. I can see a manly tear glistening on his leathery cheek, his fierce eyes full of pride for his granddaughter.

"Oh, she's so beautiful," Rachel sighs, and I have to agree, but not as stunning as the woman by my side.

My opinion may be slightly biased.

Anderson looks like all his dreams have come true, and maybe they have, although before he met Maria, I doubt he dared to dream that he'd have someone like her to stand at his side through the great game of life.

I never pitied a filthy rich bastard more; and then he met her and I didn't have to pity him anymore.

The music changes and a woman starts to sing softly and sweetly, although I only recognize the opening words, *Ave Maria*.

I can see from the look on Maria's face that this is a surprise to her, and I think she might be crying because she swipes at tears under her veil, then beams at Anderson.

He's in the grip of some intense emotion that doesn't involve smiling: I think he feels too much to show the deep, heartfelt pleasure that this amazing woman is going to be his wife.

The music draws to a close and the Priest speaks.

"Dearly beloved, we are gathered here in the sight of God and in the face of this congregation, to join together this man and this woman in Holy Matrimony, into which holy estate these two persons present come now to be joined. Therefore if any man can show any just cause, why they may not lawfully be joined together, let him now speak, or else hereafter forever hold his peace."

I actually hold my breath, waiting for a cavern to open up at my feet or for Imperial Stormtroopers to scale the Scarsdale walls, but nothing happens, and I breathe out in relief. Rachel gives me a curious look, but I just shrug.

Maria speaks her vows first.

"Devon, you are my friend, my confidant, the person who makes me smile every day, and the one I can rely on to laugh at my jokes, especially the lame ones. You make me feel special every day, you make feel loved every day, and I see our future in your eyes as we grow old and gray together. I promise that I love you and cherish you, just as you are. Today, forever, always."

His eyes widen and I see his jaw working before he can speak.

"Maria, I didn't dare hope to meet you—my heart didn't believe that someone so perfect for me could exist in this world. I carry your heart with me, I carry it in my heart. I am never without it. Anywhere I go, you go."

"Oh, that's so romantic," Rachel whispers.

"I've heard that before! He copied it," I whisper back, slightly outraged.

Rachel elbows me in the ribs.

"It's e.e. Cummings, and it's *very* romantic."

I grumble to myself. I'll do better than using words of some dude named Eeyore! But the boss isn't finished yet.

"Your smile is the sun that warms my cold heart; when you open your eyes in the morning, dawn has arrived; the day begins and ends with my love for you—forever and always."

The happy couple exchange rings and walk back down the aisle with grins as big as Texas.

The boss is married and no firearms were discharged. I call that a win

Chapter Twenty-Six

JOHNNY ENGLISH

Coming Next! Trainer's adventures in Europe with people who don't speak American!

Warm beer. Doncha just love it? Maybe it's a law in England that says you can't serve beer under 50 degrees. Oh wait, they use Celsius here, which means, um, the beer is, what 10°C? Whatever: it's not cold.

What surprises me more is that I'm getting a taste for bitter, that suspiciously dark beer that looks like it's been made from chipmunk ass. I blame Jim Rayment, beer-swilling ex-Army (Hereford Regiment, also known as the SAS). I haven't seen him since the Crowne Plaza, Times Square last year, so we spend some time catching up.

He tells me he's a card-carrying member of the Campaign for Real Ale. Ale? Have I just wandered onto the set of *Game of Thrones*?

But I love, *love* London cabs. Specifically, Black Cabs: the drivers are awesome. They know their way around better than any GPS. Goddamn they can drive. Talk too much, but they know their business.

I haven't done any driving since we got here, so in theory I can have the occasional drink, not that I really care. I'm here to work.

Yep, Mr. and Mrs. Anderson are finally on their honeymoon.

That was a week ago. They spent five days driving across Ireland, drinking Guinness and dancing a tango on the Giant's Causeway.

Right now I'm sitting in a pub in London that you could generously call a dive, next to a hairy-assed Brit who is doing his best to teach me *English* English, as opposed to *American* English, which is an entirely different language, or so he says. It's an education in the local lingo.

I'm trying to write a postcard to Lilly. It's got a picture of Buckingham Palace, but Rayment keeps interrupting me, insisting that I need to be 'educated'.

So far we've done currency. I've learned that a *pony* is £25. A *monkey* is £500. A *ton* is £100, but if you *drive ton-up*, you're breaking the speed limit at 100 plus mph.

And £1 is a *pound, quid* or *knicker*. It would be legitimate for a *bloke* to say to a *mate*, "Here's the ten knicker what I owes you."

Okay, so I have to admit that my blood-alcohol level wouldn't bear very close investigation at this precise moment in time, but what the fuck? It's an evening off. And nothing against Mr. and Mrs. Anderson, but going with someone else on their honeymoon officially blows.

The boss is getting it left right and center—probably—and all I get is a couple of minutes Facetime with the lovely and very-far-away Rachel. My balls will be bluer than the Queen's carpet.

Anderson is totally in love, and Maria ... *Mrs. Anderson* ... is totally adoring. Which adds up to totally sickening for the poor sap —that'd be me—who has to follow their every loving, ever-loving steps. Except for tonight.

Rayment's beta team is on the case, escorting the happy couple to a performance of the *Merry Widow* at the Royal Opera House, Covent Garden, which seems to be tempting fate I'd say. But since no one asked for my opinion, I'm getting quietly wasted in a soccer-themed pub where the photographs are of some dude named Nobby Stiles. Not wanting to cause an international issue, but Nobby? Does that sound like a famous soccer player?

It kinda reminds me of when I was a kid and I wanted a really cool nickname. I got my friend Dylan to call me Hawkeye for a whole year. Fuck, I loved that nickname. I could see myself running wild through the woods, hunting with the Mohicans and all that. Until my teacher, Miss Van Hendon (known to us as Van Helsing), told me that Hawthorne's character Hawkeye had a White name, too—Natty Bumppo. I was only ten, but even then I didn't think it was possible to have a more uncool name. Seriously. No one called me Hawkeye after that.

It's been a long day. The intrepid honeymooners have visited Whitechapel, following the trail of Jack the Ripper. Maybe I'm old fashioned, but following the route taken by a serial killer 120 something years ago doesn't constitute my idea of honeymoon heaven. It seemed macabre to my way of thinking, but then again Mrs. A. has just married Mr. I-had-a-dungeon-in-my-penthouse. Go figure.

But when the tour guide started going into a considerable amount of grisly detail that made Maria look nauseous, I'd had enough. Anderson was scowling and about to throw an epic shit fit in the middle of the cobbled street. I decided to have a quiet word in the guide's ear, explaining that if he continued describing the murders in graphic anatomical detail, he'd soon be feeling said anatomical detail via the toe of my boot.

Discreet. That's me.

I hadn't expected to like London so much. A city is a city, right? But here history really is all around you. Something built a couple of hundred years ago is practically brand new. The Whitechapel tour included a run down to Wapping and Ratcliffe Lane which was originally 'red cliff' because of the color of the soil, another site of notorious murders and not far from a pub where pirates were hanged five hundred years ago. Five hundred goddamn years ago!

The pub's still there, although they don't stick heads on spikes anymore. But if Anderson catches anyone else staring at his new wife, it might come back in fashion.

We walked past part of an old Roman Wall when Maria wanted to visit the Tower of London. It felt weird. Two thousand years of history as we watched the Thames float past. It screws with your brain.

Anderson arranged for Maria to get an individual guided tour after the Tower had closed. I organized a boat to take them in via the river entrance named Traitors' Gate. Maria got a kick out of that, and I got a kick out of seeing her so happy. And as for the boss, it's kinda scary seeing him baring his teeth all the time.

So, yeah, the happy couple did all the touristy things, and Rayment had all the local knowledge to make it happen.

"So, you must like your gaffer, because you've been with him a while now, huh, JT?"

"Yep, nearly eighteen months."

Jeez.

"The wife seems nice."

I had the same thought when I first met Maria, but she's so much more than that. She's got the Scion of Sorrow singing a new tune and it's good to see. I know he still gets nightmares, but it's not nearly as often now. Maria is beating back his demons one by one.

I don't want to talk about the boss anymore, and Rayment knows when he's being shut down.

"So, what you been up to, Jimbo? Work gone quiet?"

"Is that a bleedin' joke, JT? Nah, it's been full on. I've just given up doing celebrities. Lost me fuckin' nerve, din' I."

"What do you mean?"

I can't imagine Rayment *losing his nerve*. What the fuck?

"I used to do a lot of red carpet work, but it's put more gray hairs on me head than Desert Storm. Seriously, mate, when you've got crowds like that and all that's keeping them back is a poxy rope and a couple of bollards, all it would take would be one tiny thing to set it off. Then you haven't got a crowd of fans, you've got a howling mob. You don't know if someone's got a gun, a knife, a hypodermic needle. It's a bleedin' nightmare waiting to happen. I know, I know. If the security have the surroundings controlled and there are good physical measures in place, fencing for a start, then it's a matter of managing expectation between me and my team, venue security and the principal. How much space do they need? Are they to be photographed without protection in shot? Are fans searched prior to entry? Who needs that kind of crap in their lives? Know what I mean?"

He shakes his head, and I can completely understand where he's coming from. It's the ultimate nightmare of close protection work —that you won't be able to control the situation. We spend our lives trying to control the uncontrollable, trying to outguess the unexpected. The boss likes to be low-key which makes my job a helluva lot easier. But I never forget that he's a potential target. He's a billionaire, and that makes him visible. Maria is a billionaire's wife—that makes her a target. I don't even know if she's realized that from now on her life will be lived in a gilded cage.

"What's keeping you off of the streets now then, Jim?"

"More your sort of work: security for high value-low profile peeps. There's no shortage of one-offs for people like me. Next month, I'll be out in Libya looking after some French geologists who are scoping out new oil wells. Then I've got two months in Nigeria. That'll be grim, but it pays well. This is a picnic by comparison."

He sees the expression on my face.

"Don't worry, JT. My team has your boss covered. There won't be any slip-ups, not on my watch. Wiltshire tomorrow, right? We've got two cars as well as the four-by-four that mister and missus will be riding in. More under the radar than a limo. I like the way Anderson thinks."

That is a scary thought.

"You want to ride upfront or with the happy couple, JT?"

"Yep. I'm with the Andersons. Who's driving?"

"Dead Ed."

"Okay."

'Dead Ed' is one of the best on Rayment's team. I don't ask how he got his nickname—some British humor just doesn't translate. Although the guy does remind me of a zombie. You know the kind, where the head has been bolted on backwards. He's freaky, but he's a damn good driver. Especially in a country where they all drive on the wrong side of the road. And so many damn roundabouts! Who the hell invented those and what were they on at the time? And mini roundabouts, or *double* mini roundabouts. Too fucking weird.

So our driver is 'Dead Ed'. I worry about Rayment's sense of humor. And fuck me, the jokes were bad.

"You'll like this one, JT. Last night there was a big fight in our local fish and chip shop—a lot of fish got battered."

Yeah. Like I said.

I was too tired to reply when I heard him mutter under his breath, "Bloody colonials."

But just to prove that we all carry our problems with us, when I get back to the hotel, Mason calls me.

"Trainer, Howard is closing in on the blackmailer. Plus, I've dug up some more dirt on Landon. It's looking ninety percent certain that he's the one pulling the strings."

Fuck. I knew this was going to be bad.

"What do you want me to tell Anderson?"

Million dollar question.

"Nothing right now. Not until we've got concrete information to give him. The poor bastard's on his honeymoon. I don't want to give him 'maybe' or 'could be'. When we know something for sure, yeah, then I'll tell him."

"He won't like you keeping information from him."

"Don't I fucking know it, but right now information is what we're short of. But just to be on the safe side, ramp up the security at all sites. And tell Howard."

"Okay, Trainer. Your call."

Yeah, my call.

I can see that Rayment is falling under Maria's spell, too. He's met Anderson before so he knows what a double-hard bastard he is, but now his assessment of Maria being a 'sweet kid' is being re-evaluated. Rayment's a smart guy and he can see the dynamics at work. Anderson might think he's calling the shots, but Maria is the one in charge.

After a full day of sightseeing at Stonehenge and Avebury stone circles (although we avoided any ritual sacrifice), Maria looks exhausted. That brings out Rayment's protective side, and I can't help raising an eyebrow as he grumbles about 'that little girl' being all worn out. He glares at Anderson. It's pretty fucking funny. If you're me.

The drive back to the hotel is quiet. We're still in a convoy of three cars with the SUV in the middle. Rayment calls it a four-by-four, which as it doesn't have sixteen wheels, makes no sense to me whatso-fucking-ever.

Rayment's team has been discreet during the trip. The last thing Anderson wanted was for Maria to feel like she was being watched all the time—which she is, of course. But I can do discreet, too. I wasn't born wearing a shit hot, made-to-measure suit. I can do casual. You're not going to catch me in Bermuda shorts and a Hawaiian shirt, because that shit just isn't cool, but my woman got me a couple of pairs of chinos and some polo shirts. The Smith & Wesson kinda stands out, even under a linen jacket, but I am not going anywhere without my weapon. Anderson hates it.

There are a few details to iron out for the next leg of the honeymoon to Italy. The security will consist of ex-Legionnaires who served in the first Gulf War and Sarajevo. That was a bad fucking business. It'll be interesting to meet them. Mason says they're the best. They mostly work out of Dubai these days, but Mason pulled some strings.

We're traveling to Italy by train, the Eurostar to Paris and then picking up another fast service to end up in Sorrento, then a short boat trip to the island of Capri. I don't know if the boss is trying to do trains, planes and automobiles, or if he just wants to fuck on other forms of transport. I don't give a shit. What I do care about is that this Eurostar goes *under* the English Channel—that's *under* the fucking ocean. I know, I'm a Marine—but we go *on* the ocean— *on* the fucking ocean. I am not a fucking submariner. That shit is just wrong on so many levels. I don't even like going in the Holland Tunnel, but at least that's only a mile and a half long. The Channel Tunnel is over twenty miles. Shit. That makes me nervous. If there's an accident or a fire, there's no way I can guarantee to get Maria and Anderson out.

I shake away the dark thoughts and keep my eyes open as we effect the handover at Waterloo Station. And just to really put me off my fucking stride, I've got those irritating fucking Abba lyrics going around in my head.

I'm having an out-of-body experience.

Fuck me. I need a vacation. With all the shit that went down during the summer, the only leave I could take was that fantastic, long weekend with Rachel and Lilly.

It was great having my two best girls getting to know each other, but not nearly long enough. Rachel taught Lilly to bake chocolate chip cookies. Lilly's mom can't bake anything. She burns water. Probably by staring at it.

At Waterloo train station, I head out first to meet the French security who will be taking over from Rayment's team.

"JT, this is Marcel and Yves Dupont."

God help me, it's the Thomson Twins. All I need now is Tintin and Snowy. Seriously? Did they use a cookie cutter to make these guys? Hardly the most discreet undercover security Mason and Rayment could find.

My eyes swivel towards him, and the bastard is about ready to burst at the expression on my face.

"Yeah I know, but don't sweat it, JT. They know what they're doing. Met up with them in Kuwait. Men, this is Justin Trainer, CPO for Mr. and Mrs. Anderson."

"M'sieur," says A.

"Bonjour," says B.

"Why me?" says C (which is me).

But I say it very, very quietly and determine to piss in Rayment's shoes next time we meet up, maybe rig up a boobytrap involving blackpowder and dog shit. Choices, choices.

We shake hands, and Rayment signals he's out of here. I see relief on his face. I know where he's coming from: any job where you or the client doesn't get killed is another that you've won. He gets paid, he goes home. Job done.

There's a certain satisfaction in being able to hand over the responsibility. I don't say anything to Rachel, but I think she gets what it's like for me. I'm never off duty, not really. Whether I'm with her, or with Lilly, I'm still working. Anderson is pretty fair about it, but things still happen at the last minute. That's what I'm paid for. But the weight gets heavy after a while.

No one can do it forever, but the alternatives are boring and bleak.

A few days ago, from her guidebook-of-really-weird-British-shit, Maria told us that they used to kill witches by laying them down and putting a large stone over them. Then they'd add another stone, and another, and another, until the weight of all the stones pressing down killed the alleged witch. Sometimes I feel like that—I feel the weight pressing down. I'm 33—can't stay the hard man forever. No one can.

Or maybe it's just because this fucking train takes me under the ocean and I can feel the pressure of tons of water waiting to squash me like a tiny little bug.

Maria and the boss have rented their own compartment which has a private bedroom. I wonder what the opposite of the mile high club is, because the 'down under' has connotations that I really don't want to think about. And that's not even taking into account Australians.

I can't blame Anderson—the bastard—but it leaves me fucking horny for Rachel. So when I call her that night, I'm really hoping for some phone sex.

"Hey, baby. How are you?"

"Oh! It's so good to hear from you. I'm fine. I'm at Allison's."

In the heart of the coven.

"Yeah? Say hi from me. On second thought, don't say anything, she'll put a hex on me."

"Justin! That's my sister you're talking about!"

"I know, baby, but it felt like she tried to rip out my entrails that time I ate her cooking."

She giggles. God, I love that sound.

"I miss you, baby. I miss that sound you make when I..."

"Is that so? I'll have to see what I can do about that, but I'm actually standing in the middle of the grocery store at the moment."

Oh.

"Allison says hi."

"Okay," I mutter. "Keep a silver bullet handy."

"Bye, Justin!"

"Bye, baby."

And she's gone.

Things go smoothly in Paris. We visit the Left Bank of the Seine which is opposite the Right Bank, and visit some art galleries. We visit the Tuileries Palace that doesn't have a palace and look at some flowers. What a shock. Notre Dame, the Eiffel Tower, the opera, the ballet. It all goes smoothly.

And then we get to the South of Italy and the beautiful island of Capri.

It's hot. It's sunny. The boss has rented a 120 foot yacht. It should be relaxing.

But then my cell phone rings.

"Hey, Pam. How are you?"

"Peachy with a slice of pie," she says dryly, and I wonder if the job has driven her to drink. "How's it going on the love boat?"

"Let's just say I'd rather chew off my foot up to my eyeballs than stay here with Anderson much longer, and I'm *really* looking forward to gray and rainy New York."

She sniggers.

"I thought honeymoons were supposed to be romantic?"

"I'm not on *my* honeymoon," I remind her. "I'm working."

She sighs.

"Yes, I know. About that. I need to speak to Devon. Is he available?"

"Sure, Pam. Give me a minute."

Later on that afternoon, we discreetly follow Maria and Anderson through the crowds of tourists in the local town. It's hard to stay focused when it feels like a damn vacation; too easy to relax and take your eye off the ball. Look at those amateurs who were guarding Kim Kardashian in Paris. There she is, flashing around the diamond bling, I mean ring, showing the world of social media that she has rocks in her head as well as on her hand, and her fucking security don't even bother to check out the inadequate locks on the door of the apartment that she's using. The place may as well have had a welcome mat for burglars.

The woman and her ass were both traumatized, and her man thinks rapping about how hard he is will get the job done. It should never have happened.

One guy I knew who was in this line of business used to put a small stone in his boot when he was working. Said the irritation kept him sharp. Mad fucker.

The happy couple wander around some more the island, and I'm getting bored. Anderson doesn't usually move this slowly and it's fucking irritating. I can feel a headache coming on and I've really had enough of being away from home. I miss the large, gray skies of New York; I've missed too many of Lilly's evening Facetime calls because of the time difference; I miss Rachel. Fuck, I miss her.

Finally, Maria indicates that she's ready to head back and we head off in the convoy of SUV's. I'm in the front of Anderson's, and Marcel (I think) is driving.

No lives were lost, no paps in sight. We're going home tomorrow.

Thank you!

Chapter Twenty-Seven

BACKDRAFT

Gray sky. *Check.*

Rain on the window. *Check.*

New York in the fall. *Check.*

Hot woman in my bed. *Checkmate.*

I'd really like to stay here and watch Rachel nap after our strenuous afternoon that turned into evening, but my stomach is rumbling loud enough to wake the dead, and then my cell phone rings—it's Lilly.

I called her the moment we touched down on US soil, but her phone was off so I left a message.

"Daddy! You're back!"

"Hey, Princess! How's my number one girl?"

There's a long pause.

"Am I your number one girl, Daddy?"

"Of course you are, pumpkin. Why would that change?"

"Mommy says you're marrying Rachel."

Carla and her fucking loose lips!

"Well, that's right, sweetheart, I am."

"So, *she'll* be your number one girl," Lilly says sadly.

"No way, honey. You'll *always* be my number one gal. Rachel is my..." I hunt for the right words. "Rachel is my number one woman."

"She's not my mom."

"I know that, baby. You have a mommy," *even if she's on my least-popular-person-this-lifetime list.* "Rachel will be ... like an auntie."

I can hear sniffing on the line, then Carla's strident vocals pollute the air.

"Well done, Justin. You've been back thirty seconds and you've already made my daughter cry."

"*Our* daughter, Carla, and what the fuck were you doing telling her I'm marrying Rachel?"

"Well, it's true, isn't it?"

"I was going to tell her in person. I told you that before I went away! Were you trying to fuck it up for me?"

"Don't put this on me, Justin, and stop swearing—you know how much I hate that."

Is she serious?

"I'm coming over."

"What? No. It's too late. It's after seven now. By the time you get here she'll be in bed."

"Then I'll come tomorrow."

"We have plans."

Rachel rubs my back and I take a deep breath, calming my voice.

"Carla, she's upset. I should have told her everything before I went away so you didn't have to. I fucked up, I know that, but you shouldn't have told her either."

She's silent.

"Let me come over tomorrow. Let me fix this with Lilly."

"Fine."

And then she hangs up.

Rachel strokes my shoulder soothingly.

I need to spend some time with my daughter.

It's late when the Andersons get home, but I'm not surprised that the boss goes to his office before turning in. I drag on sweats and a t-shirt and go to speak with him.

He's surprisingly okay about me asking for a day off to see Lilly. Maybe it's a new found appreciation for family life—or the fact that he's virtually comatose from a wide variety of Maria-tal bliss.

"Take the time you need, Trainer."

"Thank you, sir."

He nods and turns back to his computer. When he sees I'm still standing in front of him, he frowns.

"And?"

"And Rachel ... Ms. Smith ... I've asked her to marry me."

He looks bemused.

"And?"

"She said yes."

There's a long, pregnant pause.

"I hope that doesn't mean she's thinking about resigning?"

"No, sir. Not unless you..."

"Not at all. Mrs. Sm— Ms. Smith is a valued employee. I hope she will continue in her present position. And Mrs. Anderson likes her."

That's a relief. I thought he'd be cool about it, but the boss is predictably unpredictable.

"Congratulations, Trainer. I'm happy for you. Both of you. When do you plan on getting married?"

"We haven't discussed that. In the winter?"

He nods.

"Fine. When you've decided what you want to do for your honeymoon, take the jet."

What the fuck? 'Take the jet'?!

I manage to stammer out a thank you. Damn it, that guy pisses me the fuck off! When did he start being so *nice?*

I'm planning to arrive at my ex's house early in case she changes her mind and decides to take Lilly out for the day.

I wake up before dawn and slip out of bed quietly so I don't wake Rachel. I should probably be doing some romantic shit like leaving a note on the pillow or a rose; I don't know, maybe a bar of candy. Nah, it would probably be weird if I left a pack of Oreos—no one likes crumbs in the bed.

I'm not good with this parenting shit. It's hard to know the right things to say. I'm not a part of Lilly's everyday life, even though I call every day if I can, and text two or three times a day. It's not the same thing. How can it be? A few minutes Facetime doesn't compensate for not being there. And Carla lets me know it every time we communicate. I have so much guilt, the Pope wants to friend me on Facebook.

When I get there shortly before 8AM, I see a strange car parked in the driveway. It's probably Steeeeve's, but seeing it there sends a jolt through me. I don't care that he's with my ex— he's welcome to her, but jealousy burns through me at the thought of him spending time with Lilly.

I knock on the door and wait. I can hear a flurry of voices—it doesn't sound like anyone is pleased to see me.

But then Steeeeve opens the door. Gotta hand it to the guy, he has more balls than I gave him credit for. He's wearing pajamas, a robe and a thin smile that's half hidden by long wispy hair. But he holds out his hand, his eyes widening slightly as I shake it.

"Steve."

"Justin, this is a surprise."

"Is it? I told Carla last night that I'd be over for Lilly, but no worries. I hope I'm not too early."

I don't give two shits whether I'm early or not, but I promised Rachel that I'd *play nice.*

"Uh, no, not at all. Lilly is eating breakfast. Would you like to come in for a coffee while you wait?

"Thanks, Steve."

I walk into the kitchen, my stomach clenching at the sight of domestic bliss. It looks so homey, even if Carla is glaring at me.

"Daddy!"

Lilly bounces out of her seat, spilling milk over the table as she skips toward me. I pick her up, hugging her tightly.

"Surprise," I whisper laugh.

She giggles, then demands to be put down, a scowl on her little face.

"I'm not talking to you," she pouts, marching back to her chair and plopping herself down with her arms crossed.

"Why's that, Princess?"

I know, of course, but I need to let Lilly tell me herself.

She turns her head away, refusing to answer.

"I think I'll take that coffee now, Steve," I say.

Carla's head whips around, her glare transferred to Steve who seems to wilt under her hostile gaze. *I know what that's like, dude.* I consider offering the use of my body armor. But don't.

I sip my coffee, talking to Steve about the football season so far. Turns out he's from Spokane Valley which is only ninety miles from where I grew up. He's a Redskins fan. A lot of the kids at school used to follow them, since Idaho doesn't have an NFL team.

Not that he knows much about football, but we toss around a few topics before we find some common ground. He's trying, and I appreciate that. It must be weird for him, too.

I have a lot of memories in this kitchen. I installed the cabinets and the dish washer; I laid the wooden floor and went with Carla when she picked out curtains. Fuckin' boring day that was.

But I also remember Carla nursing Lilly in the chair that she's sitting in this morning, both of us dizzy with tiredness after being woken for the fourth or fifth time during the night.

Now another man is sitting at the table and taking my place as Lilly's dad. But he seems like a good guy, so I just have to suck it up and be grateful. Gotta say, it stings like a motherfucker.

Lilly is still pretending to ignore me, but like her mom, she loves to be the center of attention, so it's not long before she's squirming in her seat.

Eventually, I run out of small talk. It doesn't take long. Steve glances at Carla who hasn't said a word to me yet.

"So, I hear congratulations are in order," he says with a wary smile, glancing at Lilly.

I can't help grinning.

"Thanks, man. I thought I'd take Lilly to buy her official flower-girl dress today, but..."

Lilly squeals so loudly, I wince.

She throws herself into my lap, still shrieking at full volume.

Steve chuckles at the expression on my face, and even Carla cracks something that might be called a smile.

"So, um, I need some help here," I admit sheepishly. "Any suggestions for where a princess could buy a flower-girl's outfit?"

Carla gives an evil laugh.

"You're taking Lilly shopping for dresses?"

"Uh, one dress," I say nervously.

"You'll have so much fun," she smirks. "I have *lots* of suggestions —Lilly *loves* shopping. I'll make a list of dress shops, shoe shops and somewhere for accessories."

I am in so much trouble. I give her a wide grin.

"Can't wait."

While Lilly races to get ready, Carla gives me a list of six weddingy dress shops and three kids' shoe shops in Bridgeport. Holy shit, that's a lot of shopping. Good thing I joined the Marines —I'm trained to survive in all environments. Plus, I know somewhere we can have pizza. I'll need the energy.

Steve stands up and shuffles off, muttering something about putting on his pants. But it leaves me alone with Carla.

Immediately, she attacks.

"You can't just turn up here whenever it suits you."

I want to lobby that back, but I don't.

"That's not what I want either," I say evenly, "but Lilly was upset last night—upset with *me*. So I need to be here to fix it."

"We agreed on scheduled visits."

"Yeah, we did, and I'll do my best to keep to that, but it doesn't always work, you know that. You also knew that I wanted to be the one to tell Lilly about marrying Rachel."

Her cheeks redden.

"Lilly asked me a direct question! I couldn't lie to her."

I sigh.

"That's fair enough, but you could have given me the heads up."

"You were in Europe!"

"Yeah, and emails, texts and phone calls still work over there. Who knew?"

"Don't be sarcastic!"

"Then don't make excuses, Carla," I say, my carefully controlled temper starting to crack. "If you had to tell Lilly that I was getting married, I'll understand that. I *don't* understand why you didn't tell *me*."

There's a long silence as she continues to glare.

"Are you going to marry Steve?" I ask when it becomes clear that an apology isn't on the horizon.

"That's none of your business," she snaps.

"It matters to Lilly, so it matters to me," I say reasonably. "He seems like a nice guy."

"He is."

I finish drinking my coffee while Carla stabs at a piece of toast with the butter knife.

"We're talking about it," she says, looking up. "Marriage."

I watch her face, feeling the finality of her words. We were together a long time, me and Carla. We should never have gotten married, but a lot of guys wanted a ring on their girl's finger before deployment. It seemed like the smart thing to do at the time. But now, looking at Carla, that's all gone. We weren't great together, but we did one good thing.

"I hope it works out for you."

She blinks, surprised.

"Lilly means the world to me," I say quietly.

"I know she does."

We stare at each other, exchanging more with that one look than we ever did with words. It's an ending, but maybe it can be a beginning, too.

Then Lilly comes racing down the stairs, talking so fast she trips over her words, and I smile at her excitement.

I'm going dress shopping with my eight year-old daughter. It's going to be sheer hell. I can't wait.

"Steve seems like a nice guy," I offer cautiously while I eat a late lunch with Lilly.

It kind of sucks to admit that twice in one day, but if it completes the mission...

We're surrounded by bags, and we've got a lot more than a flower-girl's dress and shoes. I've survived four hours of being dragged all over town and endured being stared at like a pervert while I waited outside the ladies changing rooms.

In one store, there was a tense stand-off between me and the woman assistant who refused to let me in to help Lilly even though my daughter was yelling for me to go zip her up. Eventually, a mom who was with her kid went to help Lilly, but it pissed me the hell off. Being a dad is hard enough without this shit.

Lilly shrugs. "Steve's okay."

"Rachel is real happy that you're going to be our flower-girl."

Lilly shrugs again.

I clear my throat nervously. I really want this conversation to go well.

"Rachel says you guys can do some more baking next time you visit..."

"Okay."

Then she looks up sadly.

"I wish you and Mommy were getting married. I don't like being divorced."

She's killing me, literally stomping on my heart.

She stares down at her pizza, frowning.

"Mommy says she loves you like a friend, but she loves Steve like a boyfriend."

I half smile, half cringe at Carla's lie. Although since I met Rachel I don't hate Carla quite as much as I used to. Not sure I'd ever describe her as a friend, but if helps Lilly...

"Mom's right. She and I ... yeah, we're friends. And we both love you very much. You know that, right? You're the important one."

She looks away.

"But you're marrying Rachel. So I *won't* be important. My friend Mandy, her dad married someone else and now he's got a new baby and he never sees her anymore." Her lip trembles. "You'll forget about me."

I put my arm around her and hug her tightly.

"I could *never* forget about you! You're my baby, my Princess. Lilly, you'll *always* be important to me. I promise."

"Promise?"

"Promise."

"Cross your heart and hope to die?"

Solemnly, I cross myself.

"Cross my heart and hope to die, I will *never* forget you. You will always be important to me, Lilly. Always."

She gives a watery smile.

"Okay."

"I love you, Princess."

"I love you too, Daddy."

After that, the week goes downhill rapidly.

The boss is in a meeting with Pam, and I'm reading through some new employee records when a sharp, high-pitched wail fills the building.

"Fire alarm! Evac protocols—everyone out. No personal possessions. Do not use the elevator!"

I'm shouting these commands over my shoulder even as I bring up the fire alarm schemata on my phone. Smoke in the server room: it's the real thing.

Ryan swings into action, pulling Tessa up by her hand and dragging her to the fire escape.

I know that the alarm is linked to the New York City Fire Department, so the fire trucks will be on their way.

The boss has his laptop under one arm, breaking all the rules, but pushing Pam in front of him.

"Trainer, report!"

"We got fire in the server room, sir. Building evac protocol."

He nods, his face grim.

As we start to descend the thirty floors, at each exit, there's a security officer making sure that his or her floor is vacated. Rest rooms are checked, supply rooms are checked—no man or woman is left behind. We've practiced this: now it's the real thing.

On the stairs below, we hear screaming.

The boss's voice booms out.

"Keep calm, walk, don't run."

His voice has a slightly calming effect, but the panic is bubbling under—it won't take much to cause a stampede down the concrete stairs.

He spots Maria, waiting for him on the fifteenth floor and he doesn't know whether to kiss her or cane her for not following protocol and getting the hell out.

"Devon! Thank God!"

He pulls her into his arms, then hurries her down the stairs.

I know that standard building regulations enforce a thirty minute rule: all fire doors and walls have to hold for thirty minutes; we evacuate the entire building in seventeen. I want to shave four minutes off that time.

The fire trucks have already arrived, and officers are sprinting up the stairs to do another sweep of each floor.

I'm relieved when everyone is outside and my security officers are checking the names for their floors. Everyone is accounted for. *Thank fuck.* Only one injury: a sprained ankle that's being checked out by paramedics.

I pass the information to the Fire Captain and he nods then goes to talk to the boss. Howard is making his way through the crowd toward us.

"Anyone injured? Damage?" Anderson barks.

"One sprained ankle, sir. All personnel accounted for. The fire was in the server room."

The boss sees Howard.

"Likely damage?"

"Too early to say, boss, but the Halon was effective: suppressed the fire in under twenty seconds. Damage, probably minimal, but I'll need to do some checks first. I think at least two servers and a shit load of cable got nuked. The ambient oxygen level dropped so quickly, it stopped the fire from spreading."

I've never heard Howard so succinct.

"Data loss?"

"Negative, boss. All maintained by the back-up protocols. You have twenty-four-seven at the offsite data storage facility. I already called them—they're good. Mr. Mason is sending a bunch of guys to make sure their safety hasn't been compromised."

The boss takes a breath and Mrs. Anderson holds his hand tightly.

"Good. Thank you, Howard."

"Dev," Maria whispers. "Was it an accident?"

He hesitates, then forces a smile.

"Probably just a faulty wire."

Howard opens his mouth to argue, then catches the boss's eye, shoves his hands in his pockets and starts to whistle.

This is one lie I can forgive.

I text Rachel to tell her we're all okay—I don't have time to call right now.

Mason has a team on site, working with the fire investigation department. When they finally leave, I organize a clean-up crew. I'm bone weary with hours of work ahead of me, but I do the one thing that will soothe me.

The phone rings.

"Justin! Oh, it's so good to hear your voice!"

Her words wash over me, easing the tension. I have someone to go home to—that feels damn good. I'm supposed to be the one who keeps Rachel safe, but she saves me every day.

Back at Wolf Point later that evening, the boss calls an emergency security meeting. I'm waiting at the elevator for Mason to arrive.

"How was the honeymoon, Trainer?" he smirks.

If anyone else asks me that I might have to start taking meditation lessons, either that or just beat the crap out of them. Decisions, decisions.

"The *boss's* honeymoon."

Mason laughs.

Bastard.

"Fair enough. Was he happy with the safe room?"

I have to admit Mason's team did an A-1 job on the new safe room installed at Wolf Point: steel door with strike-plate screws to resist battering; reinforced ceiling; generator and separate ventilation system; comms with CB radio, separate landline and cellular phone; CCTV into the house; firearms; flashlights; blankets; blow-up mattress; gasmasks; chemical pisser. Bastard even programmed my computer to let me know when the supply of bottled water and dried foods should be replaced each month. It would take a crack team at least four hours to break inside.

I really hope Anderson doesn't lose the key. Kidding—I have the entry code, so does Mason.

"Yeah, he was happy with it, as happy as he gets."

Mason raises his eyebrows.

"I use the term loosely. Go on in. I already got rid of the last body."

"You're a funny guy, Trainer."

I know. I think I'm getting laugh lines.

Once we reach the boss's office, it's all business.

"Mason, thoughts?"

"It's arson."

"Fuck!" The boss speaks for all of us.

"Whoever did this was clever," Mason continues, "but my guess is that the aim was to let you know that there are vulnerabilities rather than do damage. Someone is sending you a message."

Anderson turns to me.

"Trainer? Do you concur?"

"Yes, sir. My recommendation is that we review your list of known enemies. But I think we can assume that our friendly local blackmailer is responsible."

And I'll be finding out who was sitting down on the job when said arsonist got in to the building and into the server room.

He sighs.

"I know."

"We'd have to include all the recent redundancies," Mason adds, dotting all the i's and crossing the t's.

Anderson nods at the computer screen.

"And Frederick Landon," I say quietly.

Anderson turns his cold eyes on me.

"Yes, add him to the list," he says finally. *Thank fuck.*

We agree to increase the security at DMA Tower and upgrade the remote server from 'always-invoked' to 'evaluatable' on the MILS system. Personal security for all the Andersons is increased. That isn't going to go down well. I hope Lance Banner has his Kevlar on hand because Abigail Anderson is going to kick the shit out of him when she finds out that being a college sophomore now comes with very fucking close personal security and that he's her new best friend.

I take a deep breath and bring up a tricky topic.

"Sir, are you going to alert Mrs. Anderson to the increased security she'll be subject to?"

I can see him wincing, but he's adamant.

"She doesn't need to have that additional concern."

I think he's wrong, but I've raised the matter and now I have to let it drop.

"Here's what we know," says Mason, flicking through his specialist team's preliminary investigation report. "A maintenance guy showed up two days ago. It was a new man, but from our regular contractor. He had the firm's van and valid ID. Security had no reason not to let him in. Turns out it he'd only recently joined the company but it was with false papers and ID. He was maneuvered into a position of trust. We're squeezing the head of HR now to find out how. This was planned. Calculated."

I'll add finding a new maintenance contractor to my to-do list.

"And?"

"What worries me is that he could have done a lot more damage with the access that he had. So the question is, what else does he have planned?"

"No, Mason. The question is, who is the fucker and where can I find him?"

"We're working on it."

At 2AM, the meeting draws to an end. We've got a lot of shit to shovel tomorrow.

Three days later...

I have a meeting with the boss and Mason to get an update on security issues and the ongoing investigation into the fire at DMA Tower.

When I get the heads up from Evans telling me that Mason is on the way up, I stick my head inside Anderson's study.

"Sir, Mason has arrived."

"Send him in."

He seems in a good mood—no twitching eyes, no drumming fingers, no ass tightly sealed like a walrus in winter. Yup, marriage seems to suit him. Well, Maria seems to suit him, but the fun hasn't started yet.

I meet Mason at the elevator and he looks like he's waiting for a salute. *Dream on, buddy. You're not my C.O. anymore.* The only person I salute these days is Rachel. Fuck, she looks hot when she wears my old dog tags and nothing else.

Mason updates us on the sit-rep. Security has been tightened again at DMA Tower and the off-site server location; extra units have been put on all the Alvarez men, and the Andersons, even Abigail—no matter how hard she squealed. Shit, she'll probably have Lance singing show tunes to 'cheer him up' or something.

The boss even has somebody watching Dolores. She's been seen with Maria several times, so could be a potential target.

That's the thing about knowing a billionaire, suddenly you're in the frame, under the sniper's sites. Doesn't matter how nice you are, or how good you are, or how innocent you are—all those dollar bills have a cost.

Mason doesn't have a whole lot to report. Howard is isolating the CCTV footage from DMA Tower in the two weeks prior to the arson event. He promised Mason he'd have the results later on this evening. Or, to be more exact, he said,

"Mason, dude! Stress less, man."

Sometimes it's hard to believe the guy's IQ is 191.

So Anderson pedaled across to his parents, and I have the afternoon off. Yeah, this afternoon I'm going to get off.

Rachel

I never thought I'd fall in love again.

Brian was my childhood sweetheart and although we weren't blessed with children, we had a wonderful marriage for 12 happy years. His death devastated me. I never thought I could even love another man. I didn't want anyone else. As time passed, I immersed myself in work and spent as much time with Allison's family as I could. Those girls mean the world to me.

But there were times when I had to step back because I'm not their mother, Allison is, and I was just their favorite (only) aunt. At times I was lonely, and there's only so much work you can do to fill the gap inside yourself.

When I met Justin, I would never have dreamed—not in a million years—that he'd be interested in me. I was surprised, shocked even, when I realized that he was. I was flattered. But then the terrible, gnawing guilt began. Moving on from Brian was painful. I felt like I was being unfaithful even *thinking* about being with another man.

But Justin was so patient with me. I think he understood—I *know* he understood how hard it was for me.

And he's everything any woman could want in a man. He's kind and good and sweet, a wonderful and thoughtful lover, a beautiful father to his daughter, loyal to a fault, and a hard worker.

And he loves me. He loves *me*. With all my insecurities, with all my baggage, with every wrinkle and fear and imperfection. Every day he surprises me. Every day he makes me feel loved.

I'd like to think that I've gotten over the fact that he wears a gun to work. But yes, it bothers me. I suppose that's my upbringing, but I see the good in him, too. And despite what he thinks about himself, he *is* good.

And did I mention *hot?* Even Allison has to admit that. I spent quite a lot of time with my sister while Justin was away. And even though she'll never see eye to eye with him, she agrees that he is a fine figure of a man.

And the conversation went something like this:

"So, you're really going to marry Justin, huh, sis?"

"Yes, I am. Now Mr. Anderson's wedding is over, we'll have more time to plan."

"Are you *sure* about this? After Brian ... you said yourself, you aren't happy that Justin's work can be dangerous. I know the sex is good, but..."

"Allison! I'm not discussing my love life with you!"

"No? Well, have another shot of tequila. God, this stuff is

disgusting. I think it's the bottle Justin gave to Bill. I found it in the garage. He thinks I don't know about it."

There's a brief silence. I really wish my sister liked Justin, but I've given up hoping for that.

"Look, Rachel, I'm your sister and I love you. I just want you to be happy, but..."

"Allison ... Justin is it for me. We love each other and we're going to get married. No, I'm not happy that he carries a sidearm as part of his employment, but I've decided that life is too short to wait for perfection. Because in *every* other way, Justin is wonderful."

"He swears too much."

"I know."

"He thinks I'm a bitch."

"I know."

"He does have a great ass."

I can't help laughing.

"I know."

She sighs.

"I loved Brian, we all did. He'd been part of the family pretty much our whole lives. We all lost someone we cared about, but you lost your husband and your best friend. I've seen how hard it's been for you. You're amazing, the strongest person I know, but you haven't been happy."

She holds my hand, squeezing tightly as tears glaze my eyes.

"But since you've met Justin, I've seen you smile again, laugh again. If he makes you happy, that's all I care about and I'll always support you. I love you, sis."

And that was how we left it.

When Mr. and Mrs. Anderson leave for their lunch, Justin prowls into the staff quarters.

"Miss me, baby?"

He undresses me with his eyes and a devilish smile crosses his face.

Chapter Twenty-Eight

THE BRIDE OF FRANKENSTEIN

Another day, another dollar—or a billion, depending on which end of the food chain you're at.

It's been busy since the fire with all of Mason's team working overtime. I'm halfway to DMA Tower to pick up Mr. and Mrs. Anderson when Mason calls me with an update.

"The perp has been identified. His name is Wyatt Kranz."

"Should that name mean something to me?"

"Yes and no. He's a paid up member of an S&M club right here in New York. His membership was paid for by Frederick Landon."

"Holy crap, the boss won't like that. Do you have an address on Kranz?"

"Yes, but he hasn't been there in over a month."

Fuck.

I have to sit on that intel until I can speak to the boss in private. Maybe there should be no secrets between a husband and wife, but that's not my call—if Anderson wants to tell Maria, that's up to him.

Unfortunately, he doesn't follow his usual habit of going straight to his home office. Instead, he shows every intention of having a quiet, work-free evening with Maria.

"Sir?"

"What is it, Trainer?"

"I have information ... from Mason."

Maria looks from me to Anderson, then frowns. For a moment, I think she'll insist on coming with us to hear the news, but she changes her mind.

Anderson isn't happy—the swearing clues me in on that. He's even less happy when I told him that Kranz is missing. He hasn't been seen at his apartment since a week before the fire at DMA Tower. You do the math.

The boss knows the club where Kranz was a member, but hasn't been there in seven years, which is way before Kranz joined. When I tell him about the connection to Landon, he grows silent and dismisses me immediately.

But Maria is waiting outside the office. I doubt she heard anything since the door was closed, but she knows that she's being excluded from something important.

"Hi, Trainer," mutters Maria, as she stalks past me.

She looks as happy as a pig at a barbecue.

"Mrs. Anderson," I reply, doing my best to blend into the scenery.

"Maria?" the boss calls out.

"Do you have something to tell me?" she asks, her voice deliberately sweet.

"No."

"What's going on, Dev?"

"Nothing you need to worry about," he answers.

I cringe at the look on Maria's face then skulk out of her eyeline.

Anderson follows, utterly bewildered. Guess he didn't study Women 101 at that private college of his, a course also known as *What to do, when you don't know what to do: clueless (for beginners)*.

Rachel is in their living room, so that should keep the carnage to a minimum, although Maria has a look in her eye that tells me

Anderson is about to get his ass handed to him. Could be interesting.

I take the long way around to my office, avoiding the warzone that is more usually called the living room. My office in the staff wing is far enough away so that I can't overhear them; near enough to get there quickly if weapons are involved.

Three seconds later, Rachel follows.

"I thought I'd come hide with you."

"I'm not hiding, I made a tactical withdrawal. There's a difference."

She raises an eyebrow and shakes her head.

"What on earth is all that about? The tension is so thick, you could cut it with a knife!"

I wince. *No weapons, please.*

But the boss's bellow from the main room lets us know he's still alive. The beast wants feeding.

I kiss Rachel's hair lightly, really wanting to do so much more, and my arms drop away, reluctance in every nerve ending.

As we're eating our supper, a shrimp salad that could make a man sell his soul—if I hadn't already given it to Rachel—I raise a thorny issue.

"So, I was thinking..."

"Did it tire you out, Justin?"

"Careful, or I might have to show you how *not* tired I am, just to prove a point."

"And that would be a problem because?"

This woman will be the death of me.

I can't help grinning.

"Nope, no problem. Looking forward to it, in fact."

She smiles.

"I'm sorry, I interrupted you ... you were claiming to have been thinking..."

And for a moment I've lost my train of thought.

"Um ... yeah! I was thinking about our wedding."

"Oh yes?"

"Well, we said we'd talk about it once the Andersons were back from their honeymoon."

Rachel looks flustered.

"Yes, we did."

"Okay, you're freaking me out, baby."

She sighs.

"Sorry, it's just ... I want to be married to you, Justin, I do. I just don't want to *get* married. All the fuss. As long as we do it quietly—just you and me at a Courthouse. Is that alright?"

"Whatever you want, baby. I just want it to happen. And soon."

"So you wouldn't mind if it was small? Just Allison and the family? Who would you invite?"

"Lilly."

Rachel smiles.

"Of course! Who did you have in mind for a Best Man?"

"That'd be me, baby."

She snorts with laughter.

"Modesty becomes you."

"You know it!"

"Seriously? One of your military friends?"

"That okay?"

"Of course not. But no firearms at the reception."

I think she's teasing but the only guys I'd invite love their weapons more than they love, um, their weapons.

"So, who do you have in mind? Who else do you want to invite?"

"Paul Malone, guy I did basic training with. And Cyclops, um, Jase Henbrey, guy from the Unit."

"Is that all?"

I'd ask Jim Rayment, but I'm pretty sure he's got a long-term contract in Kuwait.

"Yup. That's my guest list. And, ah, I kind of already told Lilly that she could be the flower girl."

Rachel beams.

"That sounds pefect!" She pauses. "What about Mr. and Mrs. Anderson?"

"Fuck, Rachel! They're our employers, not our friends."

"It would be a nice gesture."

"I don't know, Rachel. I'd feel like I was working if Anderson was there."

"Well, what if we invited Lance, Doug, John and Mr. Mason, too?"

"Ah, hell. I see those fuckers 24/7 as it is!"

"Well, just think about it. We could have a nice dinner somewhere in town. A private room. There would still only be seventeen or eighteen of us."

I do the math and realize she's already decided how it's going to be. Yeah well, the only job the groom has is to show up in a spiffy suit. I can do that. I'll give my woman whatever she wants.

"Where do you want to go for honeymoon, baby?"

I don't care where we go, as long as it's somewhere with a king size bed and room service. I have standards.

"What do you want, Justin?"

"You. Naked. With ice cream. Location is unimportant." *Maybe chocolate. Women like chocolate. Melted chocolate. Plus, it's dirrrrty.*

She laughs.

"I see! Well, I think we can do that. But it'll have to be somewhere warm..."

"Or somewhere cold with very good heating."

Rachel ignores that.

"What about Hawaii? I've always wanted to go there."

"Yeah, Hawaii would be good. You'd like it."

Rachel looks disappointed.

"Have you already been there?"

"I was stationed at Kaneohe Bay for six months, but I promise, you'll love it."

"Well, it was just a suggestion. I'll look into the cost of flights."

"No need. Anderson says we can use the jet."

"Excuse me?"

Oh, guess I forgot to mention that.

"Yeah, the boss said we could go by AndersonForce One."

Rachel gets this wistful, goofy look on her face.

"Oh, he's such a good man. I'm so glad we're inviting him to our wedding."

Yeah, I know I have no choice in this. Rachel is batting 400 and it's game over.

"Well, Ms. Smith, I'm looking forward to calling you Mrs. Trainer."

She hesitates, and suddenly I'm not so sure, and it's a real fucking kick in the gut. She cocks her head to one side.

"Do you want to? I mean, you want me to use your name?"

"Fuck, yes!"

"Then I will."

"You will?"

"I said so, Justin, and I meant it."

I'm a lucky sonofabitch. But now I have another question.

"How come you never went back to being Rachel Lucas? You don't have to tell me…"

She rarely talks about her late husband, and I don't like to ask. Which tends to a lead to a whole lot of questions neither of us want to address.

"I don't mind telling you," she says softly. "When Brian died, his name was the only thing I had to hold onto. If I changed my name back, well, it would be as if he'd never existed. I know that doesn't make much sense…"

I hate it when she's upset. *I'm such a fucking dumbass for bringing this up.*

"It makes perfect sense, baby."

I head back to my office and read through the background checks on five potential new employees at DMA Tower to distract me. I reject one, a woman with gambling debts. She can do the job, no doubt, but her history shows she's a weak link that the company doesn't need; she could be bribed. Even as I reject her, I know I'm crushing someone's hopes for the future.

My cell rings and Mason's ID is on the screen.

"Trainer, I have an update on Kranz."

My old C.O. gets right to the point.

"I'm thinking he's getting help from someone because we can't trace him through his credit cards."

Fuck, just what we don't need. It's Aston Van Sant all over again —we never did find out who'd been helping him, although I'm thinking the Manhattan de Sade is in the frame for both.

"I'll get Anderson. He'll want to know."

I find the boss and put the phone on speaker while Mason explains the situation.

"Fuck." Anderson swears softly. "What is Landon planning?"

There's silence, because none of us has an answer.

"Surveillance on my family? And the Alvarez's and Ms. Quinlan?"

"As agreed, Mr. Anderson. But it would be easier if they were aware not to communicate with Mr. Landon."

"I ... I'll tell them something..."

"And if they'd be prepared to restrict their movements further. Your parents have extended their vacation in Florida, and I have a team watching them 24/7."

"Thank you, Mason."

"Sir, should we inform the police?"

"No. No police."

He stalks out of the room.

"Will Abigail Anderson cooperate?" Mason asks me.

"Doubtful, because as far as she's concerned, Landon is an old family friend and completely trustworthy. Just make it harder for her to evade us. New faces, keep swapping the teams. Change the shift patterns, nothing regular."

"Okay, Trainer. Status update report will be emailed within the hour."

I hang up and am surprised to find that Anderson has returned to my office.

"There's something I wanted to ask you, Trainer."

"Sir?"

"You're aware that the remodeling at the Farm will be completed this month?"

"Yes, sir."

"Mrs. Anderson and I plan to spend more time there, although of course we'll keep Wolf Point. But I was hoping that you and Ms. Smith will make the move with us. You would have your own separate cottage, as well as keeping your suite here."

He pauses.

Of course, I'd considered what his marriage to Maria would mean for our working arrangement, and I was wondering how he'd want to play this.

"You would have space to bring your daughter, if you wanted to. I'm aware," he pauses again, a slight smile on his face, "I'm aware that you have reservations when it comes to Lilly staying here. That wouldn't apply at the new house."

We both know he's referring to his frequent and overt displays of let-it-all-hang-loose-fuckery that I've walked in on more times than I care to remember.

"I hope you'll think it over."

"Thank you, sir. I'll discuss it with Ra— with Ms. Smith."

He nods and leaves the room.

Ladies and gentlemen, meet the new improved, recently upgraded Devon Miguel Anderson.

A few minutes later, the Andersons disappear to their bedroom and I finish up in my office.

I pull open my desk drawer and stare for the thousandth time at what it contains.

I look up to see Rachel smiling at me.

"Time for you to turn off that darn computer, come to bed, Justin."

I stand up slowly, my face serious, and take her hands in mine.

"Rachel, I love you for so many reasons. Your smile, your kindness, the goodness that shines through you. You give me hope in a fucked up world and I want to spend the rest of my life bugging the hell out of you just to see the challenge flashing in your eyes. I want you to be my wife and wear my ring, because it's either that or a giant sign following you around telling every other bastard to fuck off."

And I open the small box and hold it out to her in the palm of my hand as I drop to one knee.

"Marry me."

She takes a long, shuddering breath and opens the ring box.

"Oh, Justin, it's beautiful!"

The ring is platinum with nine diamonds in a channel setting, and it looks fucking perfect as I slip it onto the fourth finger of her left hand.

She pulls on my arms to bring me nearer and she smiles. Her skin is warm under my fingers and I'm desperate to kiss her.

"Did you practice that speech?"

"I practiced *a* speech, but not that one. I'm more an in-the-moment kind of guy."

"I noticed."

And she kisses me sweetly, warmly, sensually. It's so much, but not enough. I press her into my body and feel her heat against me.

"Bedroom," she breathes into my skin. "One minute."

Thirty seconds later, I follow.

Chapter Twenty-Nine

REALITY BITES

Kranz is out there somewhere, and now Landon has disappeared.

Mason fired the two guys who were supposed to be following him. He's not saying it, but my guess is they were probably bribed to look the other way because Mason doesn't hire idiots. But that doesn't help with locating the old bastard since he's dumped his cell and car that we were tracking, and hasn't used any of the credit cards we have associated with him.

My guess is that he felt the hot breath of Devon Anderson on the back of his neck and decided to head for somewhere that doesn't have an extradition treaty with the US.

He must know that fucking with a billionaire comes with severe consequences: I figure he's crazy, not stupid, but who really knows?

So I can't really blame Anderson for acting like he has a broomstick up his ass. Doesn't mean to say I like it either. About Anderson. I've never had a broomstick up my ass, although the boss may have...

Evans is on duty along with Reynolds, while Banner continues to watch Abigail Anderson—poor bastard.

Mason had suggested that a female operative might make Mrs. Anderson might feel less *watched*. I don't want to work with anyone

I don't already know at this point. I've got nothing against female CPOs; it's not like we'd have to swap knitting recipes.

At least Maria understands that we have a job to do. Unlike Abigail *I-wish-her-brain-was-as-fast-as-her-mouth* Anderson. She's still trying to give her team the slip. Her game-playing is giving Mason more gray hairs than a badger at a fur convention.

Dolores is being watched, too, and spotted her tracker within ten minutes. That surprised me, but then I learned that her father was Army, so she's grown up understanding which rules need to be followed. I was intrigued to hear her view on guns was the complete opposite of Maria's. The right to bear arms is in the Constitution and I can't see that changing anytime soon. If the powers that be could make sure that only the good guys had guns, I'd be all for gun control. There is nothing more fucking scary than an untrained person with a weapon.

This evening, we're at another of Anderson's tedious dinners. I don't know how the guy can stand them. He looks at them as part of his job, and he certainly works the room well. He knows what to say, who to say it to, and when. It's like watching an actor at the top of his profession take the stage, enthralling the audience.

I'm the only one here who knows him well enough to see that he's more on edge than usual, the reason being obvious. Even though she has protection, it's the fear factor of having left Maria at home in a city where Landon is out for blood.

The first sign of trouble is when I get a text from Reynolds who's guarding Maria tonight. And Dolores.

> Situation controlled at Wolf Point. All clients safe. Suggest immediate return.

"News?" asks Anderson.

"A situation has occurred at Wolf Point. It's been contained but Reynolds wants us back."

He swears colorfully. I'm more a black-and-white guy myself.

He tries to call Maria. Either her phone is off or she's deliberately not answering.

He wanted her to have as normal a life as possible. But she's his wife and there immensely valuable in her own right. Neither of them wanted to acknowledge that. And now he's paying the price. He'll have a heart attack before he's thirty-two if he doesn't learn to chill the fuck out.

Not that I blame him. If it was Rachel ... well, I *do* know how it feels. I remember when Van Sant had her—the panic, the furious impotence of not being there. Thank God she's at Allison's.

I call Reynolds.

"We're on our way back. Report."

I don't put the phone on speaker since I'd rather hear the news first and concentrate on that before I have to relay it to Anderson and hear all his fucking bad language.

"T, we've had a situation at Wolf Point. Mrs. Anderson and Ms. Quinlan had gone for drinks after work, as you know. Evans told them to wait inside the bar while he brought was the car around, but it seems they'd stepped outside. Kranz approached them from behind, knocked Ms. Quinlan to the ground and grabbed Mrs. Anderson. But Evans took him down and he's in police custody. Mrs. Anderson is unharmed and Ms. Quinlan has a bruised cheek and a sprained wrist from falling, but no other injuries. They're both shocked and have been checked out by paramedics."

"Was Kranz armed?"

"No, but..."

I have a very bad feeling in my gut as I wait for him to finish.

"Evans reported seeing a black Audi driving fast from the area. He thinks it could have been an attempt to kidnap Mrs. Anderson."

"Did you get a number plate?"

"No."

"Was it Landon?"

"Couldn't say."

"From now on, we work in teams of two at all times. Tell Mason."

"On it, T."

Holy fucking shit. I don't need to be Sherlock Holmes to work out that Kranz and Landon are psychotic batshit bastards.

And now I have to volunteer this information to Anderson. I've always thought that a volunteer is a man who didn't understand the question. This isn't going to go well.

Anderson's fury fills his face. It's his second worst fear come true, that someone would try to take Maria from him.

His worst fear is that they would succeed.

Rachel is keeping Evans, Reynolds and five police officers supplied with coffee. Evans has a friend on the force, so he's managed to get a spot for Banner to go with the forensic team back to Kranz's apartment. No report has come in yet. The wait is making everyone tense.

I have a job to do, but I need to hold my woman in my arms.

"I'm fine," she says softly, for the millionth time, trying to reassure me. "I was never in any danger. It all happened a couple of miles away. I'm okay. Maria's okay."

But it was close. All the work, all the protocols I've put in place, the best security that money can buy, and a fucker with a right hook manages to get through it all.

"Hey," she says, quietly. "Whatever you're thinking, it didn't happen. We're all fine. John stopped him..."

"He shouldn't have had to, Rachel. All this security ... it wasn't enough. It's never going to be enough."

I feel her hand on my back, stroking me, soothing me.

We hear the boss's footsteps at the same time, and she pulls away.

"You have a job to do, Justin," she reminds me, her voice calm and quiet.

Anderson hesitates in the doorway, and I'm sure the look I given him is blacker than his dark heart.

"I'm glad to see you're well, Ms. Smith," he says, his voice subdued.

"I'm fine, thank you, Mr. Anderson. How is Mrs. Anderson?"

"Sleeping," he replies, the pain behind his words clear.

His voice is strained and his eyes are burning, with fear, with anger, with a deep, intense rage. *That* I understand.

"And Ms. Quinlan?"

"Escorted home to pick up some clothes, then she and her mother and sister were taken to a hotel. Mason has a team in place to watching them 24/7."

I nod at Rachel, and a small smile catches around the edges of her mouth. She tries again, then knots her fingers together as she walks away.

Anderson clears his throat.

"Trainer, I..."

As I stare at him, it's clear that he's lost for words. And I have nothing to say to him either.

Your fault. I fucked up, too.

Your fault. My fault.

He looks as shaken and lost as I feel, although I'm trying to keep it under control.

Anderson nods slowly. He sinks into a chair and his head drops into his hands.

I know what he's thinking, because I'm thinking it, too: *How do I keep her safe? It's never going to stop.*

"May I ask how Ms. Quinlan is doing?"

He grimaces.

"Poor Dolores: in the wrong place at the wrong time. But frankly, if she hadn't taken the punch..."

Yeah, Maria would be in the back of Kranz's SUV going God knows where.

"He must have been following them. He knew he wouldn't be able to get to her once they were at Wolf Point. Goddammnit!"

He thumps the table with his fist.

My brain is reeling from the clusterfuck of swirling thoughts. It's hard to catch any one of them and focus.

I dig my nails into the palm of my hands and the small bite of pain brings a brief moment of clarity. And it gives me an idea. The King of Pain should like this one.

"Sir, Banner will be reporting from the forensic team at Kranz's house in about ninety minutes. May I suggest we go and kick the shit out of the equipment in the gym?"

His head snaps up and a look of grim determination replaces the hopeless fury.

"Yes."

I change into my sweats and together we take the stairs to the gym, then spend twenty minutes beating the crap out of the punch bag until our arms are too heavy to move, then running on the treadmill for fifty minutes. We'd both prefer running outside, but until we know the status on Landon or any other possible accomplices, the great outdoors is off limits. How the hell did that sick psycho end up ruling our lives?

When my lungs feel like they're bursting and I'm starting to get black spots before my eyes, I power down to a loping jog. Anderson is still burning, but his rage has lost some of his heat, and he looks focused and in control again. Before he met Maria, he would have summoned one of his fuck buddies, then beat the breath out of himself.

Control is an illusion, of course, because if the last few hours has taught me anything, it's that life is a game of chance. Tonight the dice rolled against Kranz. But it could have been Anderson that lost.

Or me.

Chapter Thirty

RUNNING ON EMPTY

Rachel is in our kitchen when I head for the shower. Cooking is therapeutic for her. Pretty ironic considering she's marrying a guy who could make a fine meal from TV dinners and whose former best friend was the microwave. But the military has a saying: any fool can be uncomfortable.

"I've made you scrambled eggs and bacon, so don't take too long in the shower."

Instead of replying, I pull her into my arms, not caring that I smell like a goat, and kiss her hard, demanding.

Eventually, she pulls away, breathless.

"What was that for, Justin?"

"Because you're here. And because I can."

She smiles her understanding and shoos me into the shower. I wish she'd join me.

The next morning, I can hear Anderson on the phone for the early call scheduled with Mason.

Maria is just leaving his office, her face sad and a little hurt.

Anderson is still holding his emotions in tightly: he's afraid he'll explode, and he doesn't want Maria to be the target of his rage.

"Hello, Trainer," she says, her voice softened by sadness.

"Good morning, Mrs. Anderson," I reply, trying to express everything through those few words.

She tries to smile.

"May I ask how you're doing today?" *I'm sorry you were afraid. I'm sorry I failed you.*

"I'm okay." *I'm scared.*

I nod. *I know.*

"If you'll excuse me." *It'll be okay. I promise.*

Her eyes follow me into the office, and I hate myself for closing the door as she watches.

Anderson glances up, his face tight.

"You're on speakerphone, Mason. Trainer is here."

"The police caught Kranz trying to steal a car. They've taken him in for questioning. So far he's saying nothing and seems unconcerned. The police believe that he's expecting to receive bail and whoever is bankrolling him is paying for his silence. His apartment is still being processed."

Anderson looks like he's going to be sick, and he paces to the window, staring out at the crawling streets thirty floors below.

"Have they charged him yet?"

"Yes, second degree assault and attempted robbery—with up to seven years if he's found guilty, but..."

"But what?" snarls Anderson.

"But with no priors, he'll get bail."

"What the fuck?"

"Because he says that Evans threw a punch first and when Kranz tried to fight back, Ms. Quinlan got in the way. Even if he had priors, there would be a good chance he'd get bail."

I shake my head in disbelief.

"I want that possibility closed down," Anderson enunciates carefully.

"Sir, I don't think that will..."

"That's no longer your concern," says Anderson, his voice ice cold.

And I wonder which of his many connections he'll call to make that happen, which of the politicians or judges he's fucked will be happy to do a favor for Anderson.

"Yes, sir."

Mason's disembodied voice is emotionless.

"Report back in one hour."

The call ends abruptly and the room descends into tense silence. Then Anderson throws me an unreadable look and strides out.

I head back to my office. The security protocols need some more fucking revisions. I'm not even sure where to start anymore and I'm doubting my abilities.

Banner is waiting for me while Reynolds is keeping the media at bay outside. Of course the vultures have descended: police at reclusive billionaire's penthouse; beautiful young wife the target of a stalker—even if that wasn't exactly what happened. It still makes a juicy story. What's not to like?

"Last night was a complete clusterfuck," I announce unnecessarily. "Who wants to tell me why?"

"Mrs. Anderson should have waited inside as she was instructed..." Evans begins.

"You're telling me that *the client* is at fault?" I ask, my voice dangerously quiet as I eyeball him.

"If she'd understood the implications—the level of threat—Mrs. Anderson may have behaved differently," Evans replies, his tone calm.

He's right, of course. But that doesn't excuse it.

I move on to point number two in the security handbook of 'how not to get unemployed because you've let the client get killed'.

I'm interrupted when I hear Anderson calling me. Fuck, how can I concentrate when he keeps interfering? But like a good little pet, I respond to my master's call.

"Sir?"

"Tell Reynolds that Mrs. Anderson is going to work. Can you drive them, please?"

I bet that was a short and interesting conversation between two of the most stubborn, hard-headed people I've ever met. Who'd have thought Maria would have Anderson's balls in a clamp so soon into their marriage.

"Yes, sir."

It's not like I'm going to tell Anderson, 'Hell, no!' although sometimes it's really tempting. You know when you go to the same coffee shop every morning and order the same drink the same way? Some days you just want to say, 'Double vodka and Red Bull' just to see the look on their faces.

And while I'm not happy about Maria leaving the mansion before we locate Landon, at least Maria will be out of the building while security is tightened yet again. I want this whole fucking building—and next door—more waterproof than a duck's ass.

Her grandfather knows the score and the boys have been advised that they need to be careful: each of them has one of Mason's men with them 24/7. The two younger boys are enjoying the notoriety of having armed escorts at school—Joachim, not so much.

"Reynolds! You're up. You're on escort with Mrs. Anderson today. Try not to let her on the loose this time."

"Boss," he says, without rising to my fucking hilarious witticism.

After we dodge the media waiting for her outside, I drive Maria and Banner to DMA Tower, deliver her into Pam's tender care, then head back to Wolf Point.

I'm glad to see that Reynolds has already gone to work on reformatting the elevator and garage codes, even though Kranz didn't access the building, but the gloom doesn't exactly lift when Detective Cooper, the lead investigator, arrives shortly after.

He wants to interview the boss.

This is going to be interesting.

Despite Cooper's irritation, I wait at the back of the room, listening to the entire interview. I'm not going to leave a ticking time bomb of insanity alone with an officer of the law, even if he is armed.

Cooper: Can you tell me about your relationship with
    Wyatt Kranz.
Anderson: I don't have a relationship with him.
Cooper: Have you ever met him.
Anderson: No.
Cooper: Are you aware that Kranz is an associate of
    Frederick Landon, a friend of your father's?
Anderson: I became aware of that information
    recently.
Cooper: How recently.
Anderson: Last Thursday.
Cooper: Were you surprised?
Anderson: Yes.
Cooper: Why?
Anderson: I believed that Mr. Landon was a true
    family friend. His connection with Kranz has
    caused me to revise that belief.
Cooper: What is your relationship with Frederick
    Landon?
Anderson: I have invested in his chain of cigar bars.
    A silent partner, you might say.
Cooper: And he was your piano teacher as a child?
Anderson: Yes.
Cooper: For how long?
Anderson: Ten years.
Cooper: You must be a very good pianist.
Anderson: [*no reply*]
Cooper: How would you describe your relationship
    with Frederick Landon?

Anderson: Business partners.

Cooper: Nothing more?

Anderson: No.

Cooper: Nothing more, ever?

Anderson: Y our point?

Cooper: Mr. Trainer is your bodyguard, I understand.

Anderson: He's my driver.

Cooper: And formerly under the command of
    Lieutenant-Colonel Norman Mason, US Marines?

Anderson: Is there a point to this line of questioning?

Cooper: Do you know why Kranz might have
    targeted Mrs. Anderson?

Anderson: She's my wife.

Cooper: Anything more personal?

Anderson: There isn't anything *more* personal.

Cooper: I meant...

Anderson: I'm aware what you meant. No, but we
    have reason to believe that Kranz was involved
    with an arson attempt at DMA Tower. We can't
    prove it, but we can, however, prove that he was
    trespassing at DMA Tower the day before the
    fire.

Cooper: Arson? None of this has been reported!

Anderson: My security team has been handling it.

Cooper: Apparently not.

Me: [*I really don't like this guy. Scrawny motherfucker.*
    Ugly suit.]

Anderson: My wife is the most important thing in
    the world to me. Do you think I give a shit about
    anything else?

Cooper: I'd like to see the dossier your team has
    prepared.

Anderson: Trainer will see to that.

Cooper: Is there anything you'd like to add?

Anderson: No.

Cooper: I'll need to interview Mrs. Anderson.

Anderson: Why?

Cooper: [*impatiently*] Because, Mr. Anderson, she was
    at the scene. And she was the target. I can
    schedule an appointment at her office and...

Anderson: No. Here.

Cooper: That's not necessary.

Anderson: It's very fucking necessary.

Cooper: [*Sighs and nods*] Thank you for your time, Mr.
    Anderson. I'll see myself out.

Anderson: Tell that bastard Kranz that if he ever
    comes near my wife again, I'll fucking kill him.

Me: [*Shit.*]

[*Cooper exits.*]

Later that day, Anderson instructs me to collect Maria and
Banner, and then says I've got the evening off. Rachel, too.

I'm grateful for the alone time, but it makes me nervous for
Maria. Anderson's fuse is very short and Maria has a nasty habit of
tossing around lit matches. But hey, it's their marriage.

Banner is off duty now, and I tell Evans and Reynolds to stay out
of the staff quarters on pain of excommunication. I don't care if
they're hungry, thirsty, or geographically challenged. They stay. The.
Fuck. Out.

My thoughts return reluctantly to Maria. If I had to make a
guess, I'd say that Anderson is planning to teach Maria a lesson in
personal safety. I doubt it's in the approved Human Resources and
People Management Manual. It's none of my business, but I'm
worried nevertheless.

"She'll be fine," says Rachel, for the ninth or tenth time. Mr.
Anderson has learned his lesson. He won't do anything foolish."

"You think? Because when it comes to Maria, the man isn't
rational."

"Love isn't rational," she says patiently. "We've both learned *that*. But he does love her and right now he's scared. They'll work it out."

I wish that I had Rachel's faith in the miracle that is human nature, because in *my* experience while you're waiting for smiles, shit happens: the first time when you're not watching and the second time when you turn around to see where the stink is coming from.

"What can I do to distract you?" asks Rachel.

Now she has my full attention.

"Oh, Ms. Smith, that is a very leading question."

Evans and Reynolds are still in the staff living room which really pisses me the fuck off. They don't say anything as I march inside, they just pick up their coffee cups and plates of sandwiches and head for the CCTV room.

Yeah, and don't come back.

And then I take Rachel and won't let her go.

She's emotional and over-tired, and even in sleep she clings to me. And I want to sleep, I really do. I crave the empty vacuum of unconsciousness. I *need* to turn off my brain, but I can't. My thoughts are indistinct and hazy, and it's impossible to pick out one and chase it down, analyze it, dispose of it.

Why does love have to hurt so bad?

I ease myself out of Rachel's arms, afraid that my restlessness will wake her. I pull on sweatpants and head for the office. Odd how my place of work can be so calming. Shit, I really need to get another job or Anderson's therapist will be making time for a new patient. Although it may already be too late.

I try checking my emails then re-read Evans' report. When I hear footsteps in the corridor, I count down in my head...

Five...

Four...

Three...

Two...

"Trainer?"

One.

We have lift-off.

"Yes, sir?"

"Thank you."

He nods and leaves.

Now I *know* the world is going to end.

Chapter Thirty-One

BAD DAY AT BLACK ROCK

Evans calls shortly after I drive Anderson and Maria to work.

"Sit-rep?"

"Kranz is still singing the tune that it was Evans who started it."

"What?!"

"Yeah, Cooper wants to interview Mrs. Anderson with Dolores again."

"That won't go down well."

"No. But at least Kranz hasn't gotten bail."

Hmm, I wonder which strings Anderson pulled? Because you know what, we have due process in the good ole US of A; the right to a speedy trial. But Krantz has been waiting over two weeks to be arraigned.

"Everything in place for the ASA function tomorrow?"

"Yes. Extra security arranged and venue has been scoped. Report on your desk, T."

For nearly two weeks, things are quiet. I should be pleased, but it makes me nervous. It's like when Lilly was a toddler: if I could hear her, I didn't worry; but when I couldn't ... yeah, that's when it's time to worry.

Cooper has tried to schedule another meeting with Maria, but so far Anderson has refused to cooperate. He wants to keep Maria away from all the crazy. He doesn't seem to realize that he brought the crazy with him when he married her. Or maybe he does and feels guilty for it. Either way, he tries to block it out.

I was the same when my marriage was crumbling. I didn't want to believe I'd failed, but head-in-the-sand isn't the best solution.

Security is still tight. Not only is there no further information on Kranz, the blackmailer or Landon—and I'm certain that the fuckers are connected even more deeply than we know—but Anderson has meetings with lawyers about the Taiwanese shipyard. Pam has worked her balls off to set up this deal. It's not just worth billions of dollars, but thousands of West Coast jobs. Anderson wants it, but his Washington state businesses need it, or shipbuilding in the US will be on a new endangered list.

They're waiting for Anderson in the boardroom.

It's business as usual.

But just when it seems like everything is going to be okay...

It's Thursday evening when I hear the sounds of Maria screaming from the main room. I run from my office, Smith & Wesson in hand.

I skid to a halt, my heart thundering. Rachel puts her finger to her lips and shakes her head.

"What the fuck?"

She tugs me back toward the office.

"Don't," she says, softly.

"What the hell's going on? It sounded like World War Three in there!"

Rachel's eyes are serious but smiling and she clings to my arm.

"Maria just told him she's pregnant."

I look at her in amazement.

"But ... what ... isn't she ... isn't that..." my words tail off in stunned disbelief. "I didn't think it was possible—what she said about having had chemo..."

Rachel has this goofy smile on her face.

"I know! It's a miracle! Isn't it wonderful?!"

"Nice one, boss!"

Rachel shoots me a look that singes my eyebrows. Guess that was the wrong response.

"Um, I mean, isn't the boss happy?"

Rachel smiles and laughs and maybe cries a little.

"He's *so* happy! I think ... I think he was crying! Maria was screaming, well, you heard, it's just ... well, she never thought ... oh Justin! Isn't it wonderful? There'll be a child in the house—it's just what this place needs."

I think of Princess Lilly and how much I miss her, hearing her voice chattering away to herself, her amazing little girl smell, and her hugs—my baby gives the best hugs.

"Yeah, it'll be good for the boss—not sure how he'll handle it though."

"He did look shocked, scared, too."

I remember that feeling well. When Carla told me that I'd knocked her up, I panicked, wondering what kind of a father I'd make and how the hell I was going to protect this new life from a seriously fucked up world. Hell, if my own father was anything to go by, my gene pool should have been made extinct.

I'm not surprised Anderson is freaking out.

He's come a long way since he met Maria. It's a shame that he doesn't know it. He copes best when he's in control. Unlike now. *Yeah, well, dream on because you're married, buddy.* Throw a kid into the equation and we're at DEFCON1.

"They'll work it out," she says, soothingly. "They love each other," she says, confidently.

Love isn't the problem.

The next day, Maria is tired but glowing with happiness. Anderson seems dazed—he's in so much shit.

Not that I'm feeling smug. Much. Hardly at all.

"Banner," she sing-songs, "I'll be ready to leave in twenty minutes. Mr. Anderson will be making his own way to work."

"Would you like some breakfast, Mrs. Anderson?"

That's my Rachel—always the caregiver.

"I'm not hungry, thank you. I'm actually feeling a little sick…"

Anderson opens his mouth to speak but Maria silences him with a kiss.

He pulls back, a look of desire mixed with anger.

"We had a little argument about that," Maria says to Rachel. "Devon is learning how to lose an argument gracefully."

Rachel looks like she's trying not to smile. As she heads to the kitchen, I jerk my head at Banner, and we scatter before the hurricane hits, then sit in my office, as useful as dicks on a donut.

As ever, I let the job consume me. I knew a guy once who worked in bomb disposal: he could concentrate on disarming a complex IED even while bullets and shit were flying around him, because he knew that distraction was dangerous. He allowed himself to be utterly absorbed by his work.

I operate in a similar way. I can't prevent the ice storm from taking place in the living room after Maria's putdown, I just make sure I've got snowshoes and a shovel on hand. And the way Maria is cutting a swathe through Anderson's walls of anger and misery, I probably need my Kevlar vest, too.

I turn to my computer and start working through emails. Mason has sent details of the Taiwanese trip and Pam will be leaving soon. She delayed a day to see if Anderson would be going with her.

Seventeen minutes later, Banner stretches and stands.

"I'll go wait in the garage, T. Buzz me when Mrs. A. is on her way."

Three minutes later, Maria strides past my office. She doesn't look in my direction, although she has a huge smile on her face, so I simply let Banner know to bring the car around front. For a small woman, she looks like an Amazon this morning.

I feel real pity for the boss. In the almost two years I've known him, he's positioned himself so he doesn't have to deal with the emotions of others, let alone his own. Maria has torn down every wall, kicked open every door with her dainty, size six boots.

Five minutes later, Anderson appears in the main room and sits at the breakfast bar.

As always.

Egg white omelet.

As always.

Eating in silence.

Just like it was before Maria came into his life. But this time he's smiling to himself.

Weird. *Don't fuck this up, boss.*

As I leave to collect the car, Rachel places a soft kiss on my lips.

"Look after him," she whispers.

"He's a billionaire who's married the love of his life and knocked her up. I'd say life is pretty peachy for him right now."

"Exactly," she says, leaving me confused. Then she kisses me, leaving me confused but happy.

During the short drive to work, the boss hums. It's fucking irritating. He's never hummed before. He's sworn, yelled, and played tic tac toe on with the stock market on his phone, but he's never hummed.

If the world is ending, no one sent me the memo.

I have an urge to turn on the radio, but it would be just my luck to hear Simon and Garfunkel singing, *Hello, darkness, my old friend*, and then I'd have to redefine the meaning of irony.

My phone pings and a message from Reynolds is displayed on the center console: Maria has arrived at work.

I shrug. I'm a driver and a bodyguard. I'm not Anderson's friend and I'm not his therapist. Thank fuck.

It's a long day. Pam has flown to Taiwan. Ryan has been relegated to the outer office. No one goes into Anderson's domain.

He's taking phone calls and has a video conference with his international law team hashing out the last issues on the Taiwan contract.

I keep busy, working out a new security plan with Mason for Maria's family and at the Farm.

The highlight of my day is a text from Rachel; the lowlight is a conversation with Mason. He's heard a whisper that Kranz will get bail after all. I hope to hell he's wrong. The source of the intel is not the best, so we won't act on it yet. If he does get out, I want a heads up so I can have the fucker watched 24/7.

Finally, Anderson texts me to say he's ready to go home.

On the way, he tells me that we're flying to Vermont the next day. Leaving early.

But as he exits the car at Wolf Point, he turns to me.

"How do you do it, Trainer? How do you be a father?"

And isn't that the billion-dollar question.

"Well, sir, I guess you do it one day at a time, and by loving that little bundle of trouble more than anything else in the whole world."

He studies my face for several seconds, then nods and walks away.

I'm dog tired and fall into bed, Rachel wrapped around me as I lose myself inside her, feeling her love surround me. She clings to me and I want to promise her it's all going to be okay. But I say nothing, because I don't lie to my woman.

I wake in the night and hear a strange sound. Holy shit! I think it's the boss's piano. In the two years I've known him, I've never heard him play before, not that you can call this playing.

I slide out of bed, careful not to wake Rachel, then pull on a pair of sweats in case Maria is walking around anywhere.

When I approach the living room, I see the boss sitting on the piano stool, the only lighting from outside, and every second, he plays the same, solitary note on the piano, repeated over and over again. One note, struck continuously, marking the seconds throughout the night.

Then Maria enters the room. She doesn't turn on the light, but sits beside him on the piano bench. The boss pauses, his finger poised over the piano key, when Maria takes his hand.

"It's okay, Devon. It's okay. *We're okay.*" And then she lays her hand on her flat stomach. "All three of us, we'll be okay."

The boss's head slumps. When I see the tears on his cheeks, I leave as silently as I arrived, sliding back into my own bed. And then I concentrate on listening to the hopeful sounds of Rachel's soft breaths.

Seeing Anderson the next morning, you wouldn't know that you were looking at a man with half his soul ripped apart and taped back together. I can see in the glazed expression on the university receptionist's face that she's just as enthralled as ever.

It's an interesting day. The Agriculture Division has made some impressive progress in their GM research. But I know for a fact that Anderson wouldn't be here if he didn't need distraction from thinking about becoming a father. I'm guessing that he also wants reassurance that he's not a completely soulless bastard. What better way than to spend the day having his ego stroked by people grateful for his money, appreciative of his keen understanding and tenacious logic. I don't blame him for that. We all crave acceptance from somewhere. Those of us who are human.

"We're heading back now, Trainer."

Thank fuck for that.

I can feel a slight relaxation in the tense atmosphere when we land in Manhattan ninety minutes later. The nearer he gets to his wife, the safer he feels.

That Newton dude will have to write a new law of gravity for Anderson and Maria: they can't help being pulled toward each other. He's a cold planet to her sun.

The rotor blades are still turning when my cell rings.

"T, fuck, man! Mrs. Anderson got a call from her friend Dolores Quinlan and just skipped out on me!"

"What?"

He's not making sense.

"She took the Benz. Just fuckin' took off! She's not answering her cell and Ms. Quinlan isn't answering hers. I'm following Mrs. Anderson's car. She's heading north on ... no, she's taken the exit towards the New Jersey Turnpike."

Maria! What the hell are you doing?

Anderson's stare is intense.

"You're on speaker, Banner. Mr. Anderson is present. Where are you now?"

"I'm following Mrs. Anderson. She's speaking to someone on her cell. She seems agitated. Intercept or follow?"

"Follow. I'll tell Evans and Mason. We'll be there in..." I check my wristwatch and my eyes flick up to Anderson.

He nods.

"We'll be there in fifteen minutes."

Anderson closes his eyes.

I can tell that he wants to drive himself to release some of the painful tension that is swirling inside him, but it's safer if I take the wheel. He's too damn distracted and he knows it.

I update Mason, but there's more bad news.

"Trainer, Kranz has been released. For some reason *that really gives me a bad feeling*, my request to hear the status of his detention was 'lost'."

"Fuck! How long has been out?"

"At least three hours."

"How the fuck did he make bail."

"You're not going to like this," Mason bites out. "Landon paid his bail."

And there's the firm connection that we were looking for. Landon has finally played his hand—*but what's his endgame?*

The boss is restless, tugging at his tie, checking his cell phone for messages, drumming his fingers on his thighs. I've never seen him so agitated. His usual m.o. is to descend into stillness. It unnerves his opponents. But Maria isn't his opponent—she's his reason for living.

My cell rings again.

"This isn't a good time, Howard."

"T, the blackmailer made his move! He's spamming the internet with home videos. Warpath's face is blurred, but that encryption will last an hour..."

"And then?"

"The world will know Mr. A's kink."

"Fuck! Can you stop it?"

"Maybe."

I've never heard Howard say 'maybe' ever. That's not good.

"Don't tell me 'maybe', Howard. Give me something."

"I'm going to fianchetto his Bishop."

Is that a sex thing?

"Huh?"

"It's a Chess move, T. He'll underestimate my move, and then I'll checkmate him."

"Will that work?"

"99.43% of the time."

And he hangs up.

Anderson is staring at me, completely stricken. I don't need to explain. Everything has been timed to coincide: Dolores' phone call, Maria's disappearance, and the blackmailer.

"Trainer," he barks, "it has to be him! Forget the blackmailer, we have to find Maria! I'm going to kill him. If anything happens ... if..."

But he can't continue. He rubs his eyes so hard I'm afraid he'll gouge them out.

"Just find her!"

I keep driving toward Maria's last known location, waiting for Mason to patch through the GPS coordinates on the car's console.

My phone rings for a third time, and the sound fires acid through my veins.

"Banner, what's..."

"Mrs. Anderson just tossed her cell out of the car window. I think the asshole directing her realized it would be tracked."

"Can you keep eyes on?"

"Negative. Traffic is crazy."

"The Mercedes is lo-jacked."

"It's been disabled."

My blood pressure escalates.

"But Mason just ran all the Wolf Point cells and something strange popped up: Mrs. Smith's cell phone is showing at a location three miles away in a district that's scheduled for redevelopment—just a bunch of empty apartment buildings waiting for demolition, but she texted me an hour ago to say she was heading out to do some grocery shopping in the Village. It's too much of a coincidence, T."

"Fuck!"

"I tried calling her, but she's not answering."

I'm ice cold.

"I'm sorry, T," he says, his voice hoarse. "I'm keeping eyes on that location, but she ... the phone isn't moving. I'm sending the intel to the Rover now."

Anderson leans forward, his eyes fixed on the small screen. Finally, it pings to life. Neither of us speak as I violate every driving law ever made to close the distance between us and that small red dot on the screen.

We drive through the city, screaming around corners on two wheels and even catching air as I hit a speed bump. Soon, we're racing through the city and take the turn off into a desolate area full of weed-covered lots and 'keep out' signs.

There's still no sign of Maria or Banner and I estimate that we're less than five minutes behind him. Where the hell is he?

Then I see Maria's Mercedes parked at a crazy angle in front of a condemned building, the driver's door wide open as if it's just been abandoned, Banner's SUV beside it.

I brake hard and Anderson leaps out of the car as I draw my weapon. I'm right behind him as we both hear the sound of gunshots, so close together, it's hard to tell whether there were two or three. Unarmed, Anderson rushes forward, his wife's name on his lips.

Christ, no!

Chapter Thirty-Two

HEAT

The partially demolished building is a sniper's paradise and I run in a zigzag toward the boss, my Smith & Wesson in my hand.

Maria is down, blood trickling from a gunshot wound to her arm. Anderson kneels beside her, afraid to touch her, his eyes wide and full of fear.

Banner is lying with his eyes open and a red gaping hole in his throat and blood pooling around him. I check his pulse, but he's already gone.

"Dev! He killed Lance! Lance was trying to protect me! *Dios!*"

"Shh, don't talk. I'll call an ambulance."

"No, listen! It isn't him!"

And she points to Wyatt fucking Kranz who is turning white as he grips a flesh wound on his thigh.

"He made me do it!" he shrieks.

I pick up his weapon and stamp hard on the hand that was reaching for it. Kranz screams loudly, a very fucking pleasing sound.

I see a second gun on the ground: Banner's.

The boss is cradling Maria in his arms, his eyes screwed tightly shut and a low pitched cry like a wounded animal rips out of him.

"Dev, I'm okay," she says faintly. "But you've got it wrong. It's not him!"

I have just a few seconds to decide what to do.

I turn my gun on Kranz.

"You don't deserve to breathe the same air as them," I say, inclining my head toward Anderson and Maria.

The Smith & Wesson would take less than half a pound of pressure to send a bullet hurtling down the chamber. Just one small neural reflex and this fucker is out of the picture for good. He can't hurt anyone else.

I want to do it so badly. So fucking badly. But I hear Rachel's voice in my head. I know that she wouldn't want me to kill him in cold blood. But I wonder. Would any prosecutor charge me? Would any jury find me guilty? I don't think so. And what's more, I know the boss wouldn't let anyone convict me. But I hesitate: where are Rachel and Dolores? And where is Landon? Is he here or with the blackmailer? I need those answers because without them...

My decision is half a second too slow.

I never get to pull the trigger.

Someone else isn't hesitating.

A shot rings out and Kranz falls backward in a pool of blood, his fingers scrabbling weakly until he stops moving.

Maria screams and faints, and automatically I dive for cover, rolling until I'm hidden in the shadows behind an old oil drum. But Anderson is still kneeling on the cold concrete, cradling Maria.

And Frederick bitch-ball Landon is standing with a gun trained on them.

"How nice to see you again, Devon. I always liked you on your knees."

"Freddie."

The boss's voice is angry but resigned, as if he'd always known this day was coming.

Keeping to the shadows, I edge closer.

Landon has the pistol pointed at the boss's head. From four feet away, he won't miss. If I took him down, one twitch of his finger would send a bullet into Anderson's brain.

"I need to call an ambulance," the boss begs.

"Oh, I don't think poor Wyatt needs an ambulance now. Pity."

"An ambulance for Maria! Freddie, please! She's losing blood."

Landon ignores him.

"Wyatt was a useful assistant, although sorely disappointing in bed. He hated you," he says, smiling at Anderson. "He hated you as much as pathetic little Aston loved you. God, it was hard work keeping him in line."

"It doesn't make sense, Freddie. I never knew Wyatt Kranz!"

"That didn't stop him from loathing you. He was very much like you, you know. Let's just say ... he was at one of those *other* parties, the ones you tried so hard to suppress. But you can't stop people's basic needs, Devon. You of all people should know that. Pretending that you can be normal and have a normal life. Good grief, you even went so far as to fool yourself by getting married! But it was amusing to watch you have your little moment. It won't last, of course."

He's gloating, relishing the enjoyment of letting Anderson know how long he's been manipulating him, all the strands of Anderson's life that's he's been holding.

"But I didn't appreciate being left off the guest list, Devon. That was very, very wrong of you. Your parents asked questions, ones that I wasn't prepared to answer. I had to act very hurt. Well, that was fun. So amusing to be best friends with your poor, dear, clueless parents. If only they knew what a naughty boy you've been. But I think they're about to find out. In 37 minutes—then the Farm's tapes will be released. Unless..."

Anderson ignores his taunts.

"I need an ambulance for Maria. She's pregnant!"

Landon's lips curl in disgust.

"How utterly prosaic. You chose to breed like a common rutting bull with that little slut. You could have been extraordinary, Devon.

Instead you choose to be one of the common herd. It's pathetic. She will *never* be what you need."

"Please, Freddie. If you ever cared about me..."

He laughs, a cold, chilling sound.

"Care about you?" His eyes darken. "I cared that I had you under my control. I could see the potential—I simply wanted a fair return on my investment. You think those few million that you threw into my cigar bar business was enough? You owe me *everything! Everything! We should have been partners! Your business should be MINE! It should be ME that Presidents want to meet; ME who has every businessman on the East Coast pandering to his every whim—not you! NEVER YOU!"* He pauses, his mouth twisted. "And now you have 35 minutes."

His breathing is fast and I wonder if he's distracted enough for me to take him, but the gun is still pointed at the boss.

"But I could see the way you were going, so I set up a little blackmail scheme instead. Did you enjoy that, Devon? Did you enjoy knowing that I could take it all away with the press of a button? That's how much I control you. I can take it all! I *will* take it all!" He smiles smugly. "I want the assets of DMA Solutions transferred into my name. With immediate effect. Thirty-one minutes."

The boss stares at him blankly, keeping his emotions in check.

"You're too late, Freddie. The deal with Taiwan was signed this morning: five billion dollars, probably before you were awake. Your friends at Consolidated Iron aren't going to be very happy with you, are they?"

For the first time, Landon seems uncertain, and the boss presses home the slight advantage as I take half a step closer.

"That's why you used Dolores Quinlan to lure Maria out here."

"Not just her."

Anderson blinks.

"Then who?"

"Isn't that an interesting question," Landon laughs.

The boss plows on.

"I'll help you, Freddie. I'll protect you, pay off whatever you owe. Just ... please, call an ambulance for Maria right now."

Landon's eyes have a crazed light about them as he listens to the boss talking. His throat bobs, but the gun wavers only slightly.

"Do you really think I care about her or your little bastard? She shouldn't have been in the way. You and I were perfect together: perfect in bed and perfect in business."

Anderson cradles Maria in his arms, his eyes on her face.

"No, Freddie. We were imperfect in every possible way. But you didn't need to spy on me. Although Howard is taking apart your pet blackmailer right now. You didn't need to sell secrets to my competitors. You've lost, Freddie. But you know what? Even when I realized you'd betrayed me ... three-hundred and fifty million dollars, was that the last offer? I would have given you the money."

It's at this point that Landon realizes he's on the brink of losing everything. There are too many people here who know the truth about his crooked business dealings, including Anderson. From the look on his face, Landon hadn't counted on that. But if he kills Anderson, Maria and me, he still has a chance to get rid of the evidence. The police would be chasing Kranz's nameless, faceless accomplice, never guessing that Anderson's 'close family friend' was the killer. Landon could simply be a sucker who helped a friend with bail money. Mason's evidence was gained illegally—it could never be used in a court of law. And I doubt that Landon's mafia connections would be made known. Hell, up until this moment, I had no clue that he'd go this far.

Landon's eyes glitter as he licks his lips. He lowers the gun to point it at Maria.

"I think I'll take you up on that offer, Devon. And the price is five hundred million—I think that's fair. After all, I made you the man you are today. So take out your phone, and transfer the money to this account. It's untraceable, by the way."

He tosses a piece of paper at Anderson's feet.

If I can just work my way around behind him and...

"Trainer, stop skulking in the shadows."

His voice is strong, mocking, and full of murderous intent.

"Rachel would be so disappointed that her knight in rusty armor can't save her."

My lungs freeze as Landon laughs.

Oh God, this monster has Rachel?

"Did you really think I didn't know about the two of you? Panting after her like the bitch in heat she is? She'll be very upset that you've screwed up so badly."

"Where is she?"

I try to disguise my voice so it's harder for Landon to tell which direction it's coming from.

"She didn't seem very anxious to come with me, but when I told her that you were injured and needed her, she was much more compliant. I was very convincing, if I do say so myself. And as for Miss Quinlan, she was pathetically eager to 'save' her little spic friend."

I don't reply, pressing further into the dusty shadows of the abandoned building.

"I'm going to count to five, Trainer. And then I'm going to shoot Maria in the head, and this time I won't miss."

Anderson's face has lost all color.

"Do that and you'll never get a cent from me..."

"Shut up, Devon. You are a severe disappointment. I *trained* you. I *taught* you. I gave you the tools to be the businessman you are today: controlled, calculating, emotionless. You could have been great. But now look at you, reduced to a pathetic, sniveling mess."

One of the youngest billionaires in the US isn't successful enough for him? The thought is irrelevant and random. I need to focus.

"And you *will* give me the money. Even when your dear Maria is singing with the Angels, I'm sure you wouldn't want the blood of Miss Quinlan and Mrs. Smith on your hands, too." He turns his head an inch to the right. "I'm waiting, Trainer. Throw your gun out and walk towards me with your hands on your head, or I'll shoot the bitch, and I'll enjoy it."

I tighten my grip on the Smith & Wesson, watching for any sign of weakness or hesitation.

I see none.

"Five."

I inch closer, but he doesn't take his eyes off Maria.

I can see the boss's muscles tense, as if he's preparing to make his move.

"Four."

I creep closer, but the angle is all wrong. If I try to shoot Landon from here, I could kill Anderson.

"Three."

Where the fuck is backup?

"Two."

Shit!

"One..."

"Okay! I'm coming out."

I slide the Smith & Wesson toward Landon, hoping that I've judged the distance correctly.

It stops a few feet from him: too far for him to reach it.

I yank Kranz's gun from my waistband, aiming at Landon while I surge forward in a diving roll. Anderson's eyes widen with understanding and he explodes into action, throwing himself forward and across Maria's body. Landon pulls the trigger, but he's off balance and the bullet ricochets with an eerie shriek just inches from Maria and Anderson.

I roll and shoot in one smooth movement, then keep going. The bullet hits Landon in the center of his chest, throwing him backwards, a look of surprise on his face. His finger jerks on the trigger, and I feel a searing pain across my lower back.

I've been shot. I can tell that it's just a flesh wound as I stagger to my feet.

"Where's Rachel?"

I tower over Landon, watching the blood pool beneath his body. He's dying. The bullet has gone through a lung, and from the amount of blood I'm seeing, I'd guess it's severed a major artery.

"Where is she?"

Landon doesn't speak, he just laughs, coughing up blood that's so dark it's nearly black, his hand still holding the gun, even as his eyes close, the life draining out of him.

I put a second bullet into Landon's head. This time he stays down, and takes his secrets to Hell.

I can hear the sound of sirens coming closer and Anderson yelling into his cell phone. I have just a few seconds to cover my tracks. I clean my fingerprints from Kranz's gun, hoping like hell I've done a good enough job, then I press the pistol into Kranz's hand. I nearly have a heart attack when it twitches and I realize that the bastard isn't dead.

I leave my Smith & Wesson where it is.

I don't know how the boss will want to play this, about Landon, but I don't have a chance to ask him.

Four cruisers skid to a halt and police pour out, weapons drawn. I grab my ID and raise my hands in the air.

Thank Christ that Evans is with them.

"We need an ambulance," I order, pointing to Maria, ignoring the piece of shit at my feet. "She's been shot and she's pregnant—in the first trimester."

The police take over. It takes three of them to pry Anderson from Maria who's beginning to come around.

"Let them help her," I say urgently, grabbing his arm and pointing toward the paramedics. "They can help her."

He staggers back and nods.

"Oh, God! Maria."

I kneel down next to her, ignoring the slicing pain and the blood running down my leg.

"Maria, where's Rachel and Dolores?"

"I ... I'm not sure. He took them, I think."

"Where? Where did he take them?"

She shakes her head, then passes out.

"Sir, I need to find the women."

I think Anderson hasn't heard me, hasn't seen me, but then he looks up.

"Anything you need: money, men, just do it."

Maria is moved to the ambulance and Anderson sits beside her, holding her hand, his eyes fixed on her pale face, his mouth moving wordlessly.

The ambulance's red, flickering lights fade into the distance.

I want to follow, to try and get some answers from Maria, but the police are all over my ass, and I have to stay and deal.

I make an executive decision to lie my nuts off. The story I give is that Dolores was with Rachel when Kranz forced her to call Maria, and I have no clue why Landon was at the warehouse. But my main concern is Rachel, not the holes in my hastily patched together story.

I send Evans to guard the boss and Maria at the hospital. He tries to get me to go with him so that my wound can be seen to, but finding Rachel and Dolores is top priority.

Damn it, Maria! Why didn't she ask for our help? A heartbeat. In a heartbeat, we'd have done whatever she needed.

Now she's being rushed to the hospital and Rachel and Dolores are still missing. Evans promises to phone Maria's grandfather and get her brothers to the hospital.

The police are securing the area and a team of Crime Scene Investigators are on their way.

Paramedics work on Kranz, and to my surprise, it looks like the fucker will make it.

He's conscious but incoherent, crying and blubbing uselessly. I want to shake the truth out of him. He holds the key to this. If Landon trusted him—or blackmailed him into helping—he knows more than he's telling. Not that he's telling anyone anything at the moment. A woman officer is trying to calm him down as the paramedics work to stem the bleeding.

I interrupt Kranz's mindless, pathetic sniveling and get in his face, ignoring the police officer.

"Where's Rachel Smith and Dolores Quinlan?"

"W-w-what?"

He wipes an arm across his bloody, tear-stained face.

"Don't fuck with me, you sick bastard!"

"Hey!" yells the cop. "Back off, buddy!"

I ignore her and the paramedics and haul Kranz up by his jacket.

"WHERE IS RACHEL?"

He points a shaking finger to the crumbling stairs. The police officer yells a question, but I'm off and running, cops trailing behind, the woman cop flanking me, her weapon in her hand.

The stairwell is dark, the steps littered with rubbish and used syringes. I stumble as I race upward, thankful when the cop behind me switches on her flashlight.

On the next floor, we work like a team, entering the room low, checking the perimeter. I immediately see a door at the back that's locked with a shiny, new padlock on the front of a steel door. *This is it, I know it!*

"We'll need a crowbar to open this," says the woman cop.

I want to shoot the lock, but if Rachel is on the other side, I could end up hurting her. Plus, that's a steel door and ricochets are fucking dangerous.

I spot a pile of scaffolding poles and drag one out, using it as a lever. The door won't budge.

"Fuck!"

The woman cop adds her weight, trying to force the lock, then two more cops run over and finally, finally we manage to pry the door open.

I hope Landon hasn't booby-trapped this door, or I'll be going out in a fucking blaze of glory. My last thought before I yank open the door is that Rachel would be so pissed at me.

The padlock hangs in a mangled heap and I enter crouching down, keeping low, reducing my profile. The woman cop has my back.

The room is pitch black, but the rest of the cops are pouring in behind us with their flashlights.

I shout out, my voice ringing through the vast space.

"RACHEL!"

No answer.

I peer through the darkness, and one of the cops shines a beam of light and I see the bright halo of Rachel's blonde hair.

She's lying on the floor with Dolores next to her. Thin rope is looped around their wrists, ankles, and neck.

I sink to the floor next to her, so fucking afraid.

Rachel's shirt is ripped open and I can see the rose pink bra she's wearing. I bought that for her.

Bile burns my throat but I focus on the job.

I check her pulse.

"She's still breathing." *Thank you, God.*

Dolores' chest moves with shallow breaths, but her eyes are closed and her color sallow. She doesn't look good.

I hear one of the police officers calling for another ambulance.

Rachel's eyes flutter open.

"Justin?"

"I'm right here, baby. You're going to be fine. An ambulance is on its way. Does it hurt anywhere?"

Tears leak from her eyes.

"I've been so stupid, Justin," and her fingers scrabble for my hand.

"It's okay," I whisper. "You're safe now."

"I d-don't remember anything after that man ... I knew I shouldn't, but he said you were hurt ... I'm so sorry, I'm so sorry. And Dolores was there..."

"It's okay," I repeat. "You're fine."

"I ... I can't move my legs!" she gasps, starting to panic.

"Stay calm, sweetheart."

"Justin! I can't move my legs!"

She starts to thrash around but I grab her shoulders, forcing her to look at me.

"Rachel!"

She starts to sob, and I crouch down next to her and pull her into my chest.

She seems so shattered, so broken. I stroke her hair and promise everything will be fine. I hope I'm not lying.

Without speaking, I take out my Ka-bar combat knife and cut the thin cords that bind her. She curls into my body, her tears soaking the collar of my shirt.

We stay there until paramedics try to put her on a stretcher, but she starts to panic.

"Don't leave me!" she begs.

I scoop her up and stagger to my feet, wincing from the pain in my back and leg as I carry her down the narrow staircase to the waiting ambulance, while the paramedics take Dolores on a stretcher.

"I won't leave you," I reassure her urgently.

Tears still leak from her eyes.

"Are you angry with me, Justin?"

"So angry," I say, stroking her cheek.

Her eyes squeeze shut as she tries to fight back more tears.

I lift her into the ambulance and paramedics load Dolores into another.

Rachel holds tightly to my hand the entire journey. I ignore the paramedics and phone Mason, filling him in on the situation.

"We lost Banner—his family will need to be told. He has ... had ... a brother in Indiana."

Mason swears.

"We've punched out of the Marines—there aren't supposed to be casualties anymore!"

Mason tells me that Howard has outsmarted Saruman for the last time, and Mason's team have gone to pick him up. A news channel found one of the home videos featuring a 'top businessman and senior senator' and are sensing a story, but with the images still blurred, it's unlikely that they'll ever figure out that the senator and Anderson were in the starring roles.

Mason does his job and when we arrive at the hospital, we're met by security, and a team of two doctors and three nurses.

"They're going to take good care of you, baby," I say, my voice breaking.

"Don't leave me," Rachel begs again.

"Never, baby. Never."

One of the nurses tries to stop me from following them. I think I'm annoying her by dripping blood all over her nice floor, but I don't give a shiny shit.

"How's she doing, T?" asks Evans

"She's going to be fine," I say gruffly. "My girl is tough."

"Fuck, man. I'm so sorry."

Rachel dips in and out of consciousness. There's no sign of trauma, so their best guess is that she's been drugged. Dolores hasn't woken up yet.

"We'll draw some blood to do tests, but I'd say they've both been given benzodiazepine, probably a large dose of Valium. We'll keep an eye on Mrs. Smith's breathing, but in all likelihood, she'll be able to sleep it off."

Hearing those words makes my knees buckle.

"And if you want to be of any use to her whatsoever when she wakes up, you'll let me take a look at that bullet wound. You must have lost a pint of blood by now."

I nod and let him lead me to the next bed to patch me up.

Evans sits with Rachel while they work on me. I want someone with her every second. Evans understands what this means to me, and I trust him.

Eventually, I'm stitched up, and have been given a couple of shots: one for the pain and one an antibiotic. My pants are ruined and my clothes are covered in blood and filth from the condemned building.

A nurse finds me some scrubs to wear, and I limp back to sit by Rachel.

Evans stands up when he sees me and shakes my hand. We exchange a look that says more than words.

"Any change?"

"She's sleeping. The doc says she'll be okay. How are you holding up, T?

"Vertical. Breathing. How's Dolores?"

"Out of danger."

"And Mrs. Anderson? Maria?"

"Her brothers are here and the grandfather. But when they told him the news, they had to put the old guy on oxygen. He'll be okay —just the shock, you know?" He smiles. "But Mrs. A. is fine, just a flesh wound, but they're keeping her in to monitor her overnight."

I feel intense relief at the news and let myself relax one level.

"I'm staying with Rachel, but find out all you can. And I want to know where they've taken Kranz. I want to know *exactly* which room he's in. The police will be guarding him—make sure he's secure. And I want it fucking yesterday!"

Evans nods.

"Done."

He turns on his heel and leaves.

I know he's feeling pretty fucking pissed about the way the whole situation went down. And Lance Banner: we lost one of our own.

Security is *my* call.

No more civilians calling the shots. This is *my* gig, and I'm so fucking tired of being treated like a dog without a dick.

Next, I call Ryan with an update.

He's shocked but gets right to work. He'd make a good Marine. Without the hair gel and eyeliner, although there was this one guy ... long story.

He promises to get Anderson's PR team to handle the media too, because this is going to be big news.

"I'll inform senior management," he says. "They need to know what they can say and what they can't say, and I'll get a message to Pam. She'll want to be here. I'll have the company jet fueled and on standby for her within two hours. That should give her time to wrap things up with the Taiwanese."

I don't give a fuck about that, but I know a lot of jobs are riding it, so I let it go.

Waiting for Rachel to wake up is one of the worst nights of my life. I drift in and out of an uneasy sleep, more alert when the pain meds wear off about five in the morning.

And then her blue eyes open and she stares right at me.

"I knew you'd come."

My eyes begin to water and I lean forward, almost afraid to touch her.

"I thought I was going to lose you, baby."

I can hear the break in my voice.

Her hand rests on my neck and I can feel her fingers stroking my hair.

"I never gave up. I knew you'd find me."

And then I can't stop the tears anymore, because I nearly didn't find her, I nearly lost her. And if I had, I wouldn't have wanted to go on living.

She doesn't say anything, leaving me a little dignity as she continues to stroke my hair.

When I've finished acting like a pussy, I sit up and wipe my eyes.

"I love you, Justin Trainer. I love you so much."

I'm too burned to talk, so I just lift her hands to my mouth and kiss them gently.

She smiles and runs a gentle finger over my lips.

"My poor, sweet soldier."

"Marine, baby. No need to go insulting me."

She laughs gently, then her smile fades.

"You're wincing!"

"Nah, that was me smiling. You're confused."

The joke falls flat.

"Justin?"

"It's just a flesh wound, baby. I'm fine."

"You ... you were shot?!"

"Baby, it's just a scratch, I promise."

"But you're sitting so awkwardly..."

Her voice trails off, worried and distressed. Now is definitely *not* the time to discuss this. For one thing, it's fucking embarrassing.

She fusses some more, until I threaten to strip off all of my clothes to prove that I'm okay.

Finally, she changes the subject.

"How's Maria? And Dolores. How are they?"

"They're both doing okay."

Her eyes close, and she drifts back to sleep.

Later the next day, they send her home.

No lasting effects.

I could have kissed the doc who told me that, except for the fact that he looked like a Sumo wrestler with the breath of a buffalo.

Allison tried to persuade Rachel to go stay with her, but she was determined to be at the house when the boss and Maria come home.

Several reporters are hanging around the garage entrance at Wolf Point. They yell questions at the Rover's blacked-out windows, but we're through them in a few seconds.

The next day Maria comes home.

And I realize something: Wolf Point is the longest I've lived in any one place since I was a kid. I've found a place where I fit.

Fuck me sideways now, because I've just said I fit with Devon *I-don't-have-all-my-dogs-barking* Anderson. Yeah, he's not as fucked or fucked up as he was, but that's not what you'd call a ringing endorsement either. Yeah. Well, call me Kathy Bates and give me a typewriter because I just don't care.

I'm relieved to drive the happy couple home and drop them at the lobby where Evans escorts them inside. Packages safely delivered. Job done.

I park the Rover in the underground garage and lean against the side of the elevator as it surges upward, weary to my bones, letting the peacefulness of Wolf Point wash over me. Another few minutes and I'll be with my woman, holding her in my arms, then eating her fine cooking. What more does a man need?

But as I walk into the building, I hear music playing. It's familiar, but ... *holy fucking shit!* That's not from a playlist, that's someone actually playing the piano.

I sneak a look and I'm surprised as hell to see the boss sitting at the piano playing real music, and it ain't *Chopsticks.*

Damn, he's good. Really good.

And I realize, with Landon's death, he's finally exorcised the old ghost of the abuse he received from his piano teacher. Music can finally mean something other than pain.

And sitting next to him on the piano stool is Maria, her eyes closed and a huge smile on her face.

I back away, because this moment is perfect and private. Yep, today is a good day.

I take a moment to head to the CCTV room, remove my Smith & Wesson, locking it into the safe and putting the holster in my desk.

Since Landon died, we've all breathed easier and finally, finally, I can relax when I walk into our home.

I'm surprised to get a text from the boss—is the recital over already? So I jog up the stairs to his office and find that he's already sitting at his desk. He sees me and looks up.

"Trainer, a moment."

"Sir."

I step into his office, alert for any emergency that might have occurred in the last twenty minutes.

"Take a seat. Please."

Please? Am I getting canned? I try to remember if I accidentally shot any employees today or discharged my firearm in the DMA Tower. Nope, don't think so.

I sit in the chair opposite his desk, wary now.

"I thought you'd like to know that I've been in touch with Lance Banner's brother."

I nod, because Mason already told me this. He also told me that the boss sent a large check so that Lance's brother will never have to work again, and set up a trust fund for a new gymnasium at Banner's old high school.

"He wishes to have a private memorial service: family only. I have sent my condolences."

We all have. All of the men who worked with Banner.

"Thank you, sir."

"I never thanked *you*, Trainer," he begins. "For saving the lives of Maria and ... and of our child."

His voice began strongly, but now it's cracking with emotion.

"You risked your own life for them, for me—and the words 'thank you' don't seem enough. They *aren't* enough. There's no amount of money that will ever, *ever* make up for that, no price I could put on ... on their safety. But ... I want you to know, to understand how truly grateful I am. You saved my family. Thank you."

His little speech has left me stunned and damned uncomfortable. I clear my throat.

"Just doing my job, sir."

He gives a wry smile.

"I thought you might say that. But still, I am indebted to you. And I'd like you to have this."

He hands me an envelope.

"Sir?"

"Open it later."

He stands up and holds out his hand, so I shove the envelope in my pocket and we shake hands.

I leave his office bemused. I was doing my job, what I'm paid to do. I was guarding the billionaire and his wife. If anything, I fucked up and got myself shot while I was doing it. But Maria and the boss made it out of there and the little spawn is safe, too. Yeah, I guess that's a win for the home team.

I walk into our apartment and see Rachel standing by the kitchen counter.

She turns around and smiles.

"Justin, you're home." She leans her head on one side and stares at me quizzically. "Is everything okay?"

I scratch my ear.

"Yeah, the boss just thanked me for saving ... you know."

Her smile is soft and pleased.

"Good," she says simply, then walks over and kisses my cheek. "Dinner will be ready in fifteen minutes."

I nod and head to our bedroom, shedding my jacket and tie as I walk through the apartment. Then I turn around and pick them up —I guess Rachel's training is beginning to sink in.

When I grab my jacket, I hear the crinkle of paper and remember the envelope that Anderson gave me. I sit on Rachel's side of the bed and open it. Inside, there's a check.

It's a good thing I'm sitting down because I count the number of zeroes in disbelief. And then twice more. But the number doesn't change.

Twenty. Million. Dollars.

I stare at it, counting those zeroes again, just to be sure.

There's a note with it, written in Anderson's precise handwriting.

There is no price I can put on my family's safety, or what it means to me, but I hope that this money will help secure the future for you and your family.
Sincerely,
Devon Anderson

I stare at the note and the check, my brain spinning. Part of me wants to give the money back because I was just doing my job. But another part knows what this money will mean for Lilly: no college tuition to worry about; no scrimping to save for a down-payment on a tiny apartment; no worrying about paying the rent or the mortgage or putting food on the table for the family—all things I've worried about at one time or another.

And I realize something else. Anderson is giving me my freedom. I don't need to work for him or any other fucker out there. I never have to work again. I can't imagine what that would be like. Anderson has more money than God and I've never seen anyone work harder. I can't imagine not doing *something* with my time.

I wonder how this will change everything, and then I start to worry that Rachel won't marry me. The woman is so damn honorable that she'd say all sorts of dumb shit about not marrying for my money.

Fuck me, I'm rich!

But Anderson is right. You can't put a price on your family; you can't put a price on happiness. And I already have everything I want.

I decide not to tell Rachel about the money until she marries me. Then she'll have no choice but to accept it.

I stuff the check and note back in the envelope, and then hide it in my old sea bag at the back of the closet.

I lay on the bed, my hands behind my head as a slow smile spreads across my face.

I'm a freakin' millionaire!

Chapter Thirty-Three

THE OMEN

Gradually, life returns to normal. Or as near normal as it ever gets working for the boss. He treats Maria like she's made of glass and it's pissing her off. It's pretty funny really. I would have said he's whipped, but bearing in mind some of the shit I've seen go down in this house, that's probably not the best analogy.

As for me, life is good.

And I've got a wedding to plan.

Scratch that. Rachel is planning a wedding. I'll just shit, shower and shave, then show up when she tells me.

Well, it's not quite that simple, not when your future wife invites a billionaire to your wedding.

Yep, it's official: my twisted, fucked up bastard of a boss is going to be at my wedding—and I'm going to smile. Either that, or Rachel has promised I won't get laid for a month. Woman fights dirty.

"You know that you want him there really, Justin," she laughs. "Admit it! You like him. You care about him."

"Pays the bills."

She rolls her eyes.

"Fine. Be a *guy* about it. But you and I both know that you like working for Mr. Anderson." She raises her eyebrows. "'Keeps life interesting'—that's what you said."

Crap. I did say that.

"And you admire him," she says quietly.

She's not going to make me say it out loud, but she's right. And she knows it.

Anderson tries more than anyone I've ever met to be a good man. He works hard and enjoys a level of wealth that is impossible to comprehend, but he's selective about how he spends his money. He's not ostentatious. He doesn't shove five grand of coke up his nose everyday like some people I've worked for. He doesn't use hookers and he doesn't cheat on his wife. I can't say I'm sorry that he's given up his orgies. I'm relieved it's all over.

So, yeah. It's true. I admire the boss. But those words are *never* passing my lips. Although, if Rachel grabs me by the balls again like she did last night, all bets are off. Just sayin'.

As for Landon, the police aren't pursuing me for his death. That's been pinned on Kranz. He's denying it, of course, but as Landon was killed with his gun, it's his word against all of ours.

Turns out that Landon really had been funded by some of Anderson's competition who had ties to the Mob, but he hadn't been able to steal the info on the Taiwan deal, so he owed a lot of bad people a lot of money. Van Sant was manipulated or blackmailed into filming the orgies, we'll never know which, but I think in his own twisted way, he really did love the boss. As for Landon, it's a helluva lot more complicated. I don't know if the boss will ever come clean about the guy. His parents know something is up because Anderson refused to go to his funeral, the *old family friend*.

The cops think Kranz is looney tunes. He told them that he knew Landon from the same S&M clubs, and that Landon knew the boss from the scene. But as there is no record anywhere of the boss's involvement, that particular scandal went away. I don't know whether to credit Howard for the disappearing trick, or the amount of money that Anderson had to lay out to make it all vanish. A combination of both seems likely.

My thoughts are a little different: I think that Landon saw Kranz as a potential scapegoat rather than a true partner; I definitely don't think Landon hired him for his brains. Either way, the boss has made sure that Landon's memory is whiter than white.

He let the police and his parents believe that Landon was in the wrong place at the wrong time, like Rachel and Dolores, and had simply been posting bail for an old friend, without understanding the consequences.

I don't know if it was out of some sort of fucked up sense of loyalty or because he didn't want to upset his parents. Maybe he just wants to forget about him.

Saruman, a.k.a. Oscar Black/Rufus Lovell/Maryann Summers was quietly disappeared by the CIA. My belief is that his skills have been recruited, so maybe the guy will end up saving the world after trying to end Anderson's.

Howard is back to quietly working away on his terra-farming projects or what the hell else goes on in that mind of his. I'll say one thing: he's loyal to the boss through and through.

I heard a whisper that when Kranz was arraigned while he was still in hospital recovering from the gunshot wounds that I wish had ended him, he'd pleaded not guilty. I don't know what happened after that, but it doesn't look as if he'll stand trial, due to the fact that the shrinks are saying he's two cans short of a six-pack —his attorney advised him to plead not guilty by reason of insanity. That surprised a lot of people, and I can't help wondering if the boss pulled in some favors so that Maria doesn't have to be cross-examined on the stand. I wonder what it takes to get a sane but sadistic fucker like Kranz declared unfit to stand trial? How much cash would you have to lay down to grease the wheels? How many important people would you need to have in your pocket?

Yeah, well, I said the boss is a good man—I didn't say he's a saint.

I wanted to get married at Christmas, a quiet wedding. Small.

Simple. Rachel said she was too busy for that, what with moving over to the Farm with the Andersons.

It feels strange not living in the city even though I drive the boss to DMA Tower two or three times a week, but Rachel loves our new cottage with its own backyard, and for the first time ever, I was able to have Lilly stay over. Carla bitched about it—of course—but she didn't try to stop me.

A March wedding has been nixed, too. I think Rachel wants to wait until after Maria's baby is born. Yeah, because things get so much less busy with a newborn in the house. There's going to be a nanny, because Maria is adamant about going back to work, so it looks like the staff numbers will be increasing exponentially.

Life has settled into a pattern, more or less. Until that night...

"Justin, why did you set your alarm so early? Did you forget to tell me about a flight?"

Rachel's voice is groggy.

Then I suddenly realize that it's not the alarm, but my cell phone.

Howard Hughes calling.

"Shit!" I sit up suddenly.

I answer the phone and hear Anderson's voice on the other end. He's trying to sound calm, but I can hear the underlying panic.

"I need to get Maria to the hospital."

"Yes, sir."

I don't even get to finish the second syllable before he's hung up.

"Is it the baby?"

"Yep."

"Oh no! Her C-Section was scheduled for next Tuesday!"

"Yeah, well Anderson Junior is already on the way." *I can hear 'Ave Satani' playing in my mind.* Kidding.

"Give my love to Maria. Let me know when there's news. Don't forget her maternity bag—it's..."

"In the boss's home office where it's been for the last month."

She smiles and kisses me, totally distracting me from pulling on my pants.

"Go!" she laughs, shoving me out of bed.

"You're cold, woman," I grumble.

"Come back with good news and I'll show you how *not* true that is."

Yeah, like that's really going to help me leave.

Five minutes later, I've got the car in front of the main house.

Anderson looks tense. Maria is calm, but clearly uncomfortable, both hands wrapped around her enormous belly. She looks like a piece of string with a knot tied in the middle.

We've had a pregnancy plan in place since the day Anderson officially told his employees. We've had plans for every prenatal appointment, every potential problem from Maria feeling unwell, to some sort of apocalyptic future where New York is plunged into darkness, hospitals are without power, and flesh-eating zombies stalk the streets. Okay, maybe not the last bit, but every detail, every possible angle has been worked out in advance.

Obviously, we've had a plan for the baby coming early, but given Maria's history, they'd planned a C-Section for next week.

I hope this all goes smoothly.

I drive to the hospital as smoothly and carefully as possible—while trying to break a few land-speed records as I do it. The boss holds Maria's hand the entire time.

I know how he's feeling—I remember it too fucking well. When Carla was pregnant with Lilly, I felt guilty every time she had heartburn or reflux. I winced as her ankles swelled and her tits became tender. I massaged her back, her feet, her neck—everything that she let me get close to without her yelling at me for knocking her up in the first place.

Women's bodies are made for babies and we're just the tools who considerately act as sperm donors. Other than buying copious amounts of chocolate and providing aforementioned massages, we're out of the equation.

But it totally sucks ass to see the woman you love in pain.

As I race along the darkened country roads, I think about the last two years—the Anderson years. I think back to that twenty-nine year old that I first met: the one who had the world at his feet, but who was so broken inside, he believed himself rotten. The man who would only allow a minimum of connection with the human race, keeping everyone and everything at a distance; who contracted men and women to fuck, because he believed that he was unworthy and undeserving of love. That man is almost gone.

I see a shadow of him sometimes, and perhaps he'll never be entirely absent, but the man sitting in the backseat holding his wife's hand as they prepare to bring new life into the world, he's a man who is full of love. And finally, after all this time, he's full of hope, too.

All I need now is a fucking orchestra to play me a love song. It's so sweet, I'm in danger of going into diabetic shock.

The dark streets give way to the neon glow of the hospital and white, clinical lights.

Anderson waves away the nurse who is waiting with a wheelchair. He carries Maria into the hospital. She rolls her eyes at me and smiles.

"Good luck, Mrs. Anderson," I call after her.

I park the car then make all the necessary phone calls: Mason and Pam Russo. Those are the priority calls. Level two calls can wait until daylight. Yep, it's all in the plan.

I feel like a real spare part waiting in the maternity area. For a start, everyone assumes that I'm a father-to-be, but just too chicken shit to be with my woman. Every nurse and female within a quarter mile radius throw me dirty looks. I wish I'd worn a button that says, 'Don't hate the help'.

I can't see Anderson, but I sense his presence when a young nurse leaves the birthing suite in tears. Yup, the boss hasn't lost his touch. It does mean, however, that the obstetrics consultant is on her way.

At 6AM, Evans arrives with breakfast, courtesy of Rachel: freshly-baked cinnamon rolls and four thermoses of good coffee.

"How's it going, T?"

"Nothing to report—the boss is yelling his head off: situation nearly normal. Kick back, John, nothing will happen till the top doc gets here."

He pulls a face.

"Not my area of expertise. I'll take your word for it. So how soon before she downloads the boss's kid?"

"John, buddy, there's a reason you're still single."

A male nurses passes us, a huge grin on his face. "Good luck, daddies!" he calls out.

John jumps, then puts an empty chair between us.

He stays a while to shoot the shit, then heads off to make the level 2 calls: the Andersons, Dolores and Javier Alvarez. The old man insisted he wanted to be called day or night; Maria insisted that he was only to be called during daylight hours on pain of death or decapitation—possibly both, but she didn't say in which order.

A kid who looks about nineteen is pacing up and down. His girlfriend has kicked him out of the hospital room—I heard the yells down the hall. Something about wishing she'd stuck to sucking his cock instead of ... yeah, we get the picture. I give him a cinnamon roll. He inhales it then begs me for a cigarette. I can't help with that.

I save the rest of the rolls and coffee for the Andersons. Maria loves Rachel's cinnamon rolls. If she marketed them, I reckon they could bring world peace, they're that good. But I must be off my game, because I realize that Maria isn't allowed to eat at this stage and would probably choke her husband for eating in front of her. Hmm, I may have not thought that one through. I hope they give her enough drugs not to remember. I blame Rachel—her cinnamon rolls can make a man forget his own name.

When the Alvarez and Anderson families arrive with Dolores close behind, I leave Evans to deal, then head home for a few hours and take a nap.

By 10PM, Anderson Junior still hasn't made an appearance. I

swap over with Evans while he takes Maria's grandfather and brothers back to the Farm to rest.

The waiting room is empty now, but I can hear Anderson's voice echoing down the corridor. He's yelling, although he's trying not to. I can hear Dr. Ziegler's voice trying to calm him down. *Good luck with that, doc.*

"Mr. Anderson, this isn't helping! As soon as her blood pressure is stabilized, we'll perform the C-section. She's getting the best care, I can assure you," the doc continues, placating him.

Don't you just hate it when doctors say that sort of thing?

She leaves him in the corridor, pacing up and down.

If the boss doesn't stop panicking, I might have to shoot him to put him out of his misery.

Rachel has been sending food parcels throughout the day, but Evans says he hasn't seen Anderson eat anything yet.

He's summoned back into the birthing suite and almost falls through the door to get there more quickly. I can hear Maria's soft voice soothing him.

I think that happens a lot: the woman giving birth ends up comforting the poor sucker who can only watch as the woman he loves is ripped in half. Fate is one sick fucker.

Twenty minutes later, Evans stands beside me, shocked into silence as Maria is wheeled away for surgery. Anderson is beside her, dressed in blue scrubs, his eyes burning with fear.

All his money, the best medical attention he can buy, and it doesn't meant shit. Not at this moment.

We wait.

My eyes start to desiccate as I stare at the clock on the wall, each slow tick mocking me. Evans chews a thumbnail absentmindedly. The Smith & Wesson digs into my side and I can't take off my jacket—seeing a man with a weapon probably isn't appropriate in a hospital. I'm sensitive like that.

So I wait.

And finally, finally comes the news that's been a long time wanting.

Anderson appears, stunned but smiling, with blood staining the blue scrubs.

"She's fine," he whispers. "They're both fine. I have a daughter."

"Congratulations, sir," I say, offering him my hand.

"Thank you, Justin," he says, a grin spreading across his face. "I'm a father!"

"Welcome to the club, sir."

He laughs delightedly, shakes hands with Evans, then disappears back to Maria.

"Did he just smile?" asks Evans.

"Yup."

"Did he just call you 'Justin'?"

"Yup."

"Fuck me!"

"You're not my type, John."

EPILOGUE

Three months later...

Fucking weddings.

What's wrong with just standing in front of the judge, swapping rings, signing a piece of paper and heading to the local sports bar to see the Yankees' game? Simple. Everyone enjoys it. No stress. Is it that hard to imagine?

Apparently, if you're female, the answer to that is yes.

Besides, I'm out-maneuvered and out-gunned. Rachel has hit me with the lethal shot:

"Lilly is so looking forward to being our flower-girl, Justin! You've already bought her dress! You can't disappoint her like that."

No I fucking can't. She knows it. I know it. The whole freakin' world knows it—and I'm so whipped.

"Allison has agreed to give me away..."

The sister who makes Morticia Addams look like a cheerleader? The sister who'd like to use my guts to make suspenders? Oh the joy.

"Have you decided who you're going to have for a Best Man, Justin?"

"I told you: I'm the best man, baby. There's no one else."

"Very funny. Seriously, who do you have in mind? John Evans? Someone from your Unit, perhaps?"

"Evans! Best Man? Are you kidding me? He'd probably shoot me in the leg trying to get the ring out of his pocket!"

"You do talk nonsense sometimes, Justin. What's wrong with John?"

"Nothing. I don't *need* a Best Man!"

"Fine. If you don't find someone within twenty-four hours, I'll ask Mr. Anderson to stand up with you."

She stalks out of the room, and I roll my tongue back up and shove it in my mouth. *She did* NOT *just threaten to make Devon I-still-keep-handcuffs-in-my-briefcase Anderson my Best Man!*

Desperate times call for desperate measures. I try a few of the guys in my old Unit, but it's not looking good. Paul Malone, a.k.a., Troll, is in Libya providing security for a team of men defusing mines and destroying small arms ammo—dufus even posts the burns he does on Youtube. Jase Henbrey, Cyclops, is on a sweet deal at a Sultan's palace in Dubai, getting fat on good food and too much standing around with his thumb up his ass (probably a safety precaution); Cliff Moreton is running a training seminar at Parris Island so can't get leave to come mix with the great, the good, and the Andersons.

Bastard.

Rachel is unsympathetic, probably due to the fact that I've had months to get with the program, but have left it until two weeks before the wedding to find a Best Man.

Mason, Evans and Reynolds are already guests. I get so desperate that I even consider asking Howard. Hell, maybe Pam would do it—she's got bigger balls than most men I know.

"No way, Justin," Pam laughs in my face. "You're on your own with this one. Besides, Howard has a date, and I don't really think you'd want him making a funny speech. I mean it would be funny, but probably in Klingon."

"What do you mean Howard has a date?"

"Just that. He's got a date for your wedding."

"Animal, mineral or vegetable?"

Pam smirks at me.

"Species, human, as far as I know. Gender, female."

"Howard has a date with a woman?"

"Yes."

"And it's not his mother?"

"Nope. A real live woman. Rumor has it, his girlfriend."

"Holy shit! We've just proved the existence of God!"

I'm happy for Howard, really. But now what the fuck am I going to do?

I scroll through the contacts list on my cell phone. There is one possibility...

Jim Rayment. Ex-SAS. *Who dares wins*, and all that. He might be back from Kuwait by now. At least I know he's trained to cope with high stress situations—even a wedding.

It takes some arm-twisting and the bastard insists on season tickets to see his soccer team Arsenal as payment. I agree to the bribe, but nearly pull the plug when he asks for a dance with Rachel, as well. He's an expert at winding me up and I'm fucking clockwork.

I didn't want a bachelor party and Rachel knew that. So it was with some sense of surprise that I found myself on Anderson's private jet on my way to Vegas, along with Reynolds, Evans, Rayment and Allison's long suffering husband, Bill—my soon-to-be brother-in-law.

"Heard you got shot in the line of duty, you wanker," says Rayment.

Bill's eyes widen and he looks impressed. I really wish Rayment hadn't said anything. I glare at him and he just grins back. It's a scary sight: he got his front teeth knocked out during a training op with wanna-be bodyguards and he hasn't gotten around to replacing them yet.

"It was a flesh wound," I answer, uncomfortable with Bill's eyes on me, Reynolds and Evans sniggering like a couple of school kids.

"Did it hurt?" asks Bill.

"Just his pride," Evans chuckles.

Bastard.

"Where were you shot?"

"Right in in his ego," Reynolds laughs, cackling like a hen at an egg-laying competition.

I change the subject amid all the knowing smirks and innuendos, Bill is the only one not in on the joke.

We drop a few hundred at Mirage's casino, take in a floorshow at the Flamingo, and end up at a strip club run by the Mafia. Bill begs me not to say a word to Allison, and proceeds to stuff ten dollar bills in the thong of a brunette like it's 1999 and the world is about to end. Nope, not a stereotype in sight. Except when Evans pukes his guts over Al Capone's uglier twin and ruins his crocodile boots, splattering them with diced carrot. Me, I don't touch any drink anyone else has bought for me and remain a functioning professional at all times (yeah, I'm lying). I don't even look when $20,000 worth of surgically enhanced tits are just begging to be motorboated right in front of me. Okay, I may have glanced.

And then, after consuming copious amounts of alcohol, I finally agree to show Bill my scar from getting shot. So in the middle of the strip club, I drop my pants and boxers, and point to the vivid red scar across my left butt cheek.

After which, we were escorted to our limo by four security guards.

None of which is necessary for Rachel to hear about. And if Evans says he has photographic evidence, I'll politely remind him that I'm armed and dangerous, and I know where he lives.

What happens in Vegas, stays in Vegas.

Rachel was a helluva lot more sympathetic when she learned the truth.

"Nine deployments, two fucking wars, and I get shot in New Jersey by an amateur. In my ass. It's fucking embarrassing."

"Poor, baby. Want me to kiss it better?"

And finally, finally, after what feels like a lifetime of wanting and wishing and hoping, today is the day when Rachel Rebecca Smith becomes my wife—Mrs. Trainer.

Lilly is dressed like the princess I've always said she is, and is currently being looked after by Maria, and giggling as if she's on helium. She sounds so happy and it cuts me to the core. In a good way. Because despite all the odds and all the crap that I've seen, I'm here and alive and about to become sickeningly happy for the rest of my life.

Except for my Best Man who looks like he'd rather eat dung. Whose idea was it to invite the ex-SAS hard-as-brass-balls bastard to our wedding? Oh wait, that would be me—in a weak moment.

"You ever thought about getting married again, Jimbo?"

He fixes me with an unblinking, thousand yard stare.

"Turkeys don't vote for Christmas, mate."

Yeah, I really need a Best Man to cheer me up. Asshole.

I throw back four fingers of whisky and follow it with a Mentos mint chaser.

"I've got the car parked out back," he mutters out of one side of his mouth. "Still time to make a run for it."

"I'm marrying Rachel not Glenn Close."

He stares at me, his face unmoving. Kinda reminds me of me—except uglier.

I pull on my vest, straighten the bow tie and pick up my jacket.

"Oi, JT," Rayment coughs. "Do you want to leave your piece?"

He gestures towards my shoulder holster.

Fuck. I don't think the Smith & Wesson matches the tux.

"Mind you," he smirks, "as you're getting married, perhaps you'd better keep the gun handy."

Bastard.

The wedding is taking place at the Langham Hotel in downtown

New York. Anderson has rented a private dining room for the day with stunning views of the New York skyline. It's the boss's gift to us because he knows anything that involves the newly newsworthy Andersons invites unwanted media interest. His gift is to give us privacy so I don't have to be on duty. I appreciate it, I do. But I'm still yearning for a quiet drink in a sports bar.

I stand at the head of the room with Rayment at my side. I'm not nervous, I'm eager. I *want* this. I *want* to be married to Rachel. I want it now before she realizes that she can do so much better. God, I love that she has low standards.

Bill is sitting with his daughters looking relaxed. Megan is now sixteen years old with the same taste in makeup as your average drag queen, and Kimmi is thirteen going on thirty with lime green nail polish and matching eyeshadow. Classy. Celia, my soon-to-be brother-in-law's mother, glares at me from a seat near the front. I think it's just her glass eye glinting in the candlelight—hard to tell.

Mason is looking smug, sitting at the back with Reynolds and Evans. Pam is sitting with Sheila, and Ryan is sitting with Gene. Howard is indeed with a woman, and she looks normal, attractive even.

Shit, I'm getting married on the day before the Apocalypse.

Maria and the boss are on the other side of the room. Maria looks alternatively happy and tearful, but I put that down to her post-baby hormones dancing a fandango, and the fact that she's left baby Amelia Teresa with Dolores for the first time; Anderson looks impassive, and ignoring the lascivious glances thrown by Megan, and somewhat more discreetly, by Allison. Maria looks amused, but fastens her hand around Anderson's arm a little more tightly. I see him glance down at her and smile. A genuine, happy smile. I want to say it looks unnatural on him, but he smiles so much these days, I've taken to wearing sunglasses indoors.

The music starts and Rayment whispers, "Heads up: officer on deck."

Then 'Kiss from a Rose' echoes through the hidden speakers.

It's one of Rachel's favorite songs. Today, the words mean everything. I know she picked it for me—for us.

You became the light on the dark side of me.

God, this woman. She knows ... she knows *me*. She understands. My woman. My world. My everything.

Rayment sniggers.

"If she's the rose, you must be the thorn."

"Yeah, well you're the prick."

"At least I didn't get shot in the arse," he mutters.

Bastard.

Almost afraid, I turn and look. My woman has her hair swept back elegantly and she's wearing a pale blue, floor length dress. It's simple and natural and beautiful—just like her.

I meet her eyes and emotion threatens to un-man me. I feel ... I don't know what I feel—proud, happy, destroyed, fulfilled, adrift, repaired, saved. And love, so much love, it's overwhelming.

If I fucking cry now, I'll have to shoot myself to find a way to explain the tears. I'm regretting not wearing the Smith & Wesson.

Princess Lilly is walking in front, her little face solemn, clutching a basket of white and pink rose petals. But then she looks up and sees me, and gives a little wave before she remembers to be serious. My face splits with a smile and Rachel winks at me.

And I realize I'm a lucky bastard. I have everything I want in the world right here. Everyone that I love is in this room. And the friends that I've lost, I feel they're somewhere near, cheering me on.

Then Rachel is standing by my side and promising to be mine forever. Forever.

"Justin, I love you because ... because there aren't enough hours in the day when I want to tease a smile from you. Because you dare to love, because you take a chance on life, because you never stop showing me your love, because you care, because you're a good man. Because if you weren't in my life, it would be a dry and tired and without joy. You are the sun on my face, and the stars in my sky, and hearing your voice brightens each and every day. I love you so much. I will love you through this world and beyond. Always yours."

And I can't speak. The words won't come.

I stand, breathless and voiceless, watching the tears gather in Rachel's eyes as she looks at me, our fingers entwined.

Rayment prods me in my left kidney, causing me to squeal like a girl.

"You're supposed to say your sodding vows, you muppet," he whispers loud enough for everyone to hear.

"Fuck off, I know!"

Everyone is trying not to laugh, except Princess Lilly, who looks stern.

"Daddy said a bad word!" she sing-songs.

I pull myself together and take a deep breath. I'm about to blow my reputation as a man of few words.

"I fell in love with you the day I met you, and I've been in love with you every day since. You've seen my highs and my lows, and you've never stopped supporting me, helping me, loving me. It took me a long time to get you agree to marry me, but I knew you'd see reason in the end..." [*Muffled laughter*] "...and I will do everything in my power—everything—to make you as happy as you deserve to be. I don't know why you picked me to love, but I'm so fuc— very happy that you did. I will never take you for granted and I will love you every day while there is breath in my body, Rachel Rebecca Smith Trainer. Thank you for being mine."

There's muted applause and sighing from the womenfolk—and from Rayment—who is fucking soft for an ex-SAS staff sergeant.

Gently, as if she's made of gossamer, I push a plain, platinum band onto the fourth finger of Rachel's left hand, where, God willing, it will stay until the end of time.

The cool metal of a matching ring slips onto my hand and I stare down at it. I've never worn a wedding band before, not even when I was locked in unholy matrimony with Carla. This is new, this is for me and for Rachel. And no fucker is *ever* separating me from my jewelry. Okay, that sounded weirder than I intended, but it's the truth. My wedding band is now part of me: blood, body and bone.

"You may now kiss the bride."

I throw the officiant a look that says, *Damn straight!*

And I take my woman in my arms and kiss her until there's no air in my lungs. Lilly's giggle brings me back to the real world, and Rachel's cheeks are a delicate shade of pink.

"That's how you do it, JT! Thought I was going to have to show you, you lily-livered bastard!" roars Rayment.

Lilly slaps his wrist.

"Stop swearing! You're a naughty man."

"You tell him, sweetheart," I say. "That's my girl."

Maria stands up and starts taking photographs on her cell phone while Lilly tosses more rose petals into the air, frowning at Rayment who looks abashed.

Too fucking funny! Nine year old Lilly staring down an ex-SAS flathead. Yeah well, she is her father's daughter and I couldn't be prouder. I just hope she doesn't kick him in the kneecaps, as well.

Suddenly, the doors spring open and seven men pour in. I'm about to reach for my missing Smith & Wesson, when I realize that four of them are in Marine uniform and forming an arch with sabers, along with:

"Troll! You bastard! I can't believe you came!"

"Course I did, T! Not about to miss you getting your own monogrammed ball and chain!"

He's followed by Cyclops and Cliff, looking ridiculous, stuffed into too-tight suits.

"I can't believe you bastards pulled this stunt!"

"Language, Justin!" hisses Rachel, trying not laugh.

"Did you know about this, Mrs. Trainer?"

"Why yes I did, Mr. Trainer. What are you going to do about it?"

Her eyes are challenging.

"I'm going to kiss you soundly, Mrs. Trainer!" and I do.

A ragged cheer goes up and we walk beneath the arch, smiling hugely. Fuck. My face hurts.

Married life is a blast.

The meal is something else, or so Rayment tells me later. I don't remember much about it, just that Rachel looked beautiful and happy and smiled the whole time. I don't remember smiling quite so much, but looking at the photographs later, I realize that I did. I'll have to get a job as a crossing guard if I don't get my face back in order at some point. Who heard of a close protection officer who doubled as a toothpaste model? Credibility, that's all I'm saying.

Rayment's speech was short and loud, and Rachel had to put her hands over Lilly's ears. Allison pretended to be shocked but I saw her talking to Jimbo later, and giggling as he flexed his biceps for her. I thought I was going to vomit $600 champagne over her bunion-pinching shoes. Celia just squawked like a goose at a feather-duster convention and drank half a bottle of brandy before passing out, um, retiring to her room.

The party is winding down and I'm itching to get Mrs. Trainer alone in the honeymoon suite, when I feel a twitching in my right eye which can only mean that the boss is close by.

"Congratulations, Trainer. I think you'll be a very happy man."

"Thank you, sir. I think so, too."

"There's every chance that you'll be as happy in your marriage as I am in mine," and he glances at Maria, who is glowing with happiness and one glass of champagne too many.

He clears his throat.

"And I wanted to thank you, Trainer, for everything you've done for me and for Mrs. Anderson. Without you ... I ... Maria ... it's not been an easy adjustment for her—all of this—but she trusts you and you've made it better for her. I thank you for that. We both do. Anyway ... Mrs. Anderson thought that you'd both enjoy a three-week honeymoon in the Caribbean. You'll find the jet waiting at Teterboro for you tomorrow afternoon."

He throws me a sly glance.

"I didn't want to make the flight too early."

"That's ... three weeks? Have you got security cover for that?"

He laughs.

"Enjoy your vacation, Trainer. And please cash that check sometime—it's giving my accountant a headache."

Then he strolls away smiling.

Bastard. Now I have to be grateful to him. Twice over.

Rachel walks up and takes my arm.

"Everything okay?"

"Did you know about the Caribbean?"

She smiles enigmatically.

"Mrs. Trainer, have you been trained in covert ops?"

"I think you're about to find out Mr. Trainer," she says, kissing my lips and rubbing my back suggestively. "But there's something I've been meaning to ask you..." She flushes slightly. "We haven't really talked about it..."

"What is it, baby?"

"How do you feel about being a father again?"

Rachel's voice stops me in my tracks.

"You mean...? Are you...?"

She raises an eyebrow and smiles at me.

"No, not yet. But I'm hoping after the honeymoon..."

Shit! I think time just stopped!

But why the hell not? Janet Jackson got knocked up at fifty and seemed pretty damn happy about it.

"Right! That's it!" I yell, much to the guests' surprise. "Party's over—everyone out. Mrs. Trainer and I have some business to take care of."

And to the sounds of laughter and jeers, I whisk her off her feet and carry her out of the room. The sound of happiness follows us down the hallway.

"Honestly, Justin! Couldn't you have waited another half an hour?"

"Nope."

And in all honesty, I couldn't have waited another second. I want my life with her to start now. Right now.

And forever.

THE END

THE VERY END

THE COMPLETE AND UTTER END.

REVIEWS

Reviews are love! Honestly, they are! But it also helps other people to make an informed decision before buying my book.

So I'd really appreciate if you took a few seconds to do that.

Thank you!

MORE BOOKS BY JHB

Series Titles
The Education Series
An epic love story spanning the years, through war zones and more...
*The Education of Sebastian (Education series #1)
*The Education of Caroline (Education series #2)
*The Education of Sebastian & Caroline (combined edition, books 1 & 2)
Semper Fi: The Education of Caroline (Education series #3)

The Traveling Series
All the fun of the fair ... and two worlds collide
*The Traveling Man (Traveling series #1)
*The Traveling Woman (Traveling series #2)
*Roustabout (Traveling series #3)
*Carnival (Traveling series #4)
*Gypsy (Traveling series #5)

The Justin Trainer Series
The bodyguard and the billionaire

Guarding the Billionaire (Justin Trainer series #1)
Saving the Billionaire (Justin Trainer series #2)

The EOD Series
Blood, bombs and heartbreak
*Tick Tock (EOD series #1)
* Bombshell (EOD series #2)

The Rhythm Series
Blood, sweat, tears and dance
*Slave to the Rhythm (Rhythm series #1)
*Luka (Rhythm series #2)

Standalone Titles
Contemporary Romance
The Lilac Cadillac
Battle Scars
One Careful Owner
*Lifers
At Your Beck & Call
The New Samurai
Exposure

New Adult
*Dangerous to Know & Love
Dazzled
Summer of Seventeen

Paranormal
*The Dark Detective: Venator (Book #1)
*The Dark Detective: Paukúnnum (Book #2)

Novellas
Playing in the Rain
*Behind the Walls

Anthologies of Short Stories
*The Year Book Volume 1
*The Year Book Volume 2
*The Year Book Volume 3

Audio Books
One Careful Owner
(*narrated by Seth Clayton*)

On the Stage
Later, After: Playscript
Trailer

With Alana Albertson
Father Figure

* These titles are published in languages other than English.
Please check Jane's website for details—and receive **a free short
story every month** when you sign up for her newsletter :)

QR code for Jane's website

ROMANCE WITH STUART REARDON

Books written with my lovely co-author

Two book series - contemporary romance

*Undefeated

*Model Boyfriend

Three book series - romcom

*Gym Or Chocolate?

*The World According to Vince

*The Baby Game

Standalone

Survivor Love Island *(romcom)*

*Touch My Soul *(novella)*

WRITING AS BERRICK FORD

Police Thrillers, UK

Dead Water
Dead Man's Dive
Dead Reckoning
Dead Shore

www.berrickford.com